The Warning

A J WILLS

Cherry Tree Publishing

The Warning

Copyright © A J Wills 2023

All rights reserved. No part of this publication may be reproduced, stored in a retrieval system, or transmitted, in any form or by any other means, without the prior written permission of the author, nor be otherwise circulated in any form of binding or cover other than that in which it is published and without a similar condition being imposed on the purchaser.

This book is a work of fiction. Any resemblance to actual persons, living or dead is purely coincidental.

Chapter 1

I'm trying to stay positive, but the house is nothing like I imagined. It's grey and gloomy, grovelling under a shadowy canopy of trees like something out of a Victorian Gothic novel. Its thick stone walls are mottled with centuries-old grime, the paint around the windows faded and flaking and what passes for a garden is under siege from a legion of thistles and nettles.

'So?' Justin asks, bubbling with excitement. 'What do you think?'

He cranks on the handbrake and releases his seatbelt, swivelling around so his knees angle towards me.

'It's the old gatehouse lodge.' His eyes are black and unblinking. 'Isn't it amazing?'

I bite my bottom lip as I stare out of the passenger window, trying to summon up some enthusiasm and imagine a life here. It's supposed to be a new beginning. A fresh start for us, but my gaze is drawn to the missing roof tiles, a section of guttering that needs replacing and the dirt on the windows. It's not the vision of Cornish country living I'd pictured for us when he first announced he wanted us to move here.

But I don't want to burst my husband's bubble. The last time I saw him this excited I was in labour with Sebastian.

'It's incredible,' I say, forcing a smile. 'It has so much character.'

I'd imagined some quaint stone cottage on the coast, in a chocolate-box village with fishing boats bobbing in the harbour and wide, sandy, vanilla-coloured beaches and views over big skies and dark seas. Not this, a haunting and foreboding relic surrounded by nothing more than woodland and open countryside. It's in the back end of nowhere, down a network of narrow lanes at least half an hour's drive from Falmouth and more than two miles away from the nearest village. But I daren't tell him I think it's too remote.

Justin snatches my hand out of my lap and squeezes it tightly. 'I knew you'd love it,' he says. 'Isn't it funny how your memory plays tricks on you, though? I could have sworn there were at least two chimney stacks. And I'm sure there used to be a big oak tree over there that we used to climb.' He points through the windscreen. 'The house looks smaller, too. It seemed enormous when I was a kid.'

'Maybe you're just bigger,' I suggest.

'I loved the summers here.' A wistful mist glazes his eyes. 'They seemed to last forever.'

I glance up at leaden skies and the thick black clouds chasing over the tops of the trees. The only family holiday we ever had in Cornwall had been marred by lashing rain which left us shivering in thick jumpers on the beach.

Justin used to come here every year with his family and couldn't believe his luck when he found the house was no longer a holiday home, but was being advertised for rent on a long-term tenancy. He thought it was fate drawing him back.

He'd called the agents without even talking to me, worried that any delay might mean we would lose out. He told them we'd take it without a viewing, and this is the first time I've seen it in person, and the first time Justin's been back since he was a teenager.

He's not told me much about Treloar, other than that the lodge forms part of a large country estate that's been owned for years by the Carlyon family, who still live in the big manor house further along the sweeping drive. I guess I'll have plenty of time to find out more about them now we're here.

'How old were you when you last came?' I ask.

He shrugs and pushes out his bottom lip. 'Sixteen? Seventeen? I can't remember exactly. A long time ago, but the memories are as clear as if they happened yesterday.'

'We'll build new memories,' I tell him. It's what he wants to hear.

'We will.' He squeezes my hand tighter. 'Come on, let's take a look around.' He dangles the keys we picked up earlier in front of my face. 'I can't wait to see what it's like inside. Leave the stuff in the boot,' he says, hauling himself out of the car. 'I'll bring it in later.'

We don't have much. Only a couple of cases of clothing. Pitiful for twelve years of marriage. But the fire robbed us of everything.

I follow Justin through a picket gate and along an overgrown path to a heavy wooden front door, trotting to keep up with him and his long, enthusiastic strides.

'Welcome to your new home,' he beams, slotting the key into the lock. It's one of those big cast iron keys with an ornate shamrock bow. He struggles to turn it, shifting it back and forth in its housing until it eventually catches and the door falls open.

I resist the urge to wrinkle my nose as we're assaulted by a waft of musty, damp air. The house has clearly been left shut up and empty for a long time. The first thing I'm going to do is throw open all the windows and give it a good airing.

An old coir mat lies askew in the gloomy hallway, disintegrating with age and shedding brown, wiry fibres across a cracked, terracotta tiled floor patterned with a floral mosaic. The tiles need a good sweep, but they're a beautiful original feature.

I'm about to step inside when Justin bends down and scoops me up like I'm a virginal bride. I squeal and giggle nervously as his arms shake with the effort of holding me up. It's been a long time since I've laughed at anything.

'What are you doing?' I scream.

'Carrying you over the threshold.'

He staggers through the door, my head narrowly missing the frame. He dumps me unceremoniously back on my feet, huffing and puffing.

'Silly bugger.' I punch him playfully on the arm.

He grabs his lower back and winces. 'I thought you were lighter than that.'

I cast my eyes at the floor, stung by what I'm sure he thinks is a harmless joke. I'm painfully aware that I've put on a few extra pounds in the last year. But who could blame me? For a while I had no appetite at all, but then food became a comfort. And I've not exercised for almost a year. There has seemed little point. Maybe he's right. This move can be the beginning of something new. For both of us.

'Oh, Megan, I'm so sorry. I didn't mean — '

'It's okay,' I mumble. 'It's fine.'

'I know it all feels weird at the moment, but this house is going to help us heal and find ourselves again. It's going to take time, I know that, but just look outside. There's nothing and no one for miles around, apart from trees and fields. I can't think of anywhere better we could be.'

I reach up on the tips of my toes and plant a kiss on his lips. 'I know,' I say, raking my fingers down his chest.

I hadn't quite appreciated how much this house means to Justin. The memories it holds and the place it occupies in his heart. But I can see it written across his face. I was worried when he first proposed coming here, especially as it meant moving away from the city to somewhere so quiet, but he's done it with the best intentions. For me. And for the sake of our marriage, which has been creaking under such intolerable strain. If that means embracing a new life here in Cornwall, in a strange house, removed from the familiarity of our old lives, then that's what I'm going to do. I owe Justin that.

He reaches for a light switch and flicks it on. But nothing happens. He tuts and rolls his eyes. Not a great start.

'Listen, why don't you look around while I check the fuse box. I expect they've switched off the electrics while the house was empty,' he says.

He stalks off, heading for the cupboard under the stairs with the torch on his phone creating long shadows.

I leave him to it and poke my head into the kitchen, the first room off the hall. It's plenty big enough and there are loads of cupboards and a wide expanse of worktops, but it's in desperate need of modernisation. Not a patch on the kitchen in our old house with its sleek lines, crisp white surfaces, integrated appliances and eye-wateringly expensive boiling water filter tap Justin insisted we had installed when the kitchen was refitted. I loved that kitchen, but it was only wood, plastic and metal. If the last ten months have taught me anything, it's how pointless it is to be emotionally attached to stuff that has no real sentimental value.

The lounge is another room that feels stuck in the nineteen eighties, but with a large fireplace and a wood-burning stove, it's actually pretty cosy. I can imagine us curling up on the sofa with a glass of wine and the fire blazing on a cold autumnal evening.

It's a far cry from the life we used to have, but we'll get used to it. It's an opportunity to reboot. We can't remain stuck in the past forever, no matter how painful it is to move on.

A series of thuds and bangs come from the cupboard under the stairs, and Justin swears loudly.

'Everything okay?' I call out.

'Yeah, yeah, it's fine,' he shouts back.

I've learnt it's best if I don't interfere with these things. I doubt there's anything I can do to help anyway. Electrics aren't my area of expertise.

I trudge up the stairs, keen to check out the state of the bedrooms. It's supposed to be a three-bedroomed property. Too big for the two of us really, but at least we'll have the choice of rooms. I only hope the beds are half decent. I draw the line at a lumpy mattress, although beggars can't be choosers. We lost everything in the fire, so we needed a fully furnished rental until the loss adjustors approve our insurance claim. In the meantime, it means we have to put up with someone else's furnishings.

The treads creak and moan under my feet as I ascend, my heart pattering in my chest, not from the exertion of climbing, but from the niggle of anxiety that tightens in my gut. I'm not sure why.

I hesitate, listening.

Another loud thud comes from the cupboard below and Justin whelps in pain. I filter it out, cocking my head to one side.

Why do I have this unnerving feeling we're not alone?

I'm being stupid. There's no one else here. It's obvious from the dust and the smell of damp the house has been empty for months . It's just my mind's silly reaction to moving into a strange old house. I don't believe in all that nonsense about ghosts and ghouls and bumps in the night.

I climb the rest of the stairs slowly.

Come on, Megan. Get a grip.

The banister on the landing wobbles unnervingly when I grab it, and for a second I fear it's going to come away in my hand. I'll need to get Justin to look at that later. It's downright dangerous.

There are five doors off the landing. The first one I peel open reveals a small airing cupboard housing an ancient-looking hot water tank shrouded in solidified foam. The door alongside it is open and inside is a bathroom with ugly green tiles and a mould-speckled shower curtain hanging limply over a wood-panelled bath.

I assume that means the door at the far end of the landing leads to a bedroom at the front of the house, one that by rights should have the best views across the valley. It's the one I want.

The handle is stiff and creaks noisily. The door opens a crack and I'm struck by a new smell. Not the damp and mildew I detected earlier, but something more human. Sweat. The sour stench of body odour, the kind that lingers and makes you gag. And stale cigarette smoke.

I cover my nose and mouth with my hand and hold my breath as the door swings inwards achingly slowly. I swallow hard, but my throat is dry. Adrenaline races through my veins. My heart pumps faster, the tips of my fingers as cold as icicles.

I stare into the room and gasp.

'Justin!' I scream, paralysed, my feet rooted to the spot. 'You'd better get up here. You need to see this.'

Chapter 2

Justin comes bounding up the stairs like a herd of wild horses, eyes wide and face sombre with concern.

'Megan?'

I lower the hand covering my nose and mouth, and point silently into the room.

'What the hell is it?' he asks, his brow furrowed.

I press my back to the wall so he can see for himself.

His Adam's apple bobs up and down. He gasps, then runs a hand through his hair, staring open-mouthed at the grubby blue sleeping bag laid out on top of the bare mattress on the double bed and the mess littering the floor. The bottles of water. The fizzy drinks cans. An empty carton of milk that's fallen on its side. A pouch of tobacco. An old mug filled with ash and cigarette butts. There's even a pair of jeans, screwed up in a heap in the corner.

'Someone's been living here.' I wrap my arms around my body and glance towards the stairs, as if whoever's been here might reappear at any moment.

Justin steps cautiously into the room and squats to inspect the litter. He pokes at an empty can with his finger like a cat pawing at a mouse to see if it's still alive. 'It stinks in here,' he says, putting the back of his hand up to his nose.

Then he stands, his eyes roving, as if he's searching for something. 'I'll call the agency and get them to sort this out. It's unacceptable.'

'Someone's been living here, Justin,' I repeat. This isn't like finding a fuse has blown or that a curtain rail's fallen down, problems you can easily fix. Didn't the agency check the house before they gave us the keys?

'I know,' he says. He puts his hands on my arms and looks at me earnestly. 'And I said we'll get someone to sort it out.'

'How did they even get in here?'

He shakes his head. 'I don't know, but they won't be coming back. I promise.'

'You don't know that.'

I shrug his hands off and storm back down the stairs. This was a mistake. This isn't the right house for us. When Justin's gone back to work, I'm going to be left here all alone and vulnerable. And there's no one around for miles I can call on for help.

What the hell have we done?

Forty minutes later, we hear a car approaching, followed by a loud knock at the door that echoes through the house.

'Harriet Quinlivan, A1 Property Services,' the woman standing in the porch announces, thrusting out her hand. 'I'm so, so sorry. I came as quickly as I could. A bit of a problem, I hear?' Her bright red nails are immaculate. They must be acrylic. Nobody can grow nails that perfectly manicured.

Justin tentatively shakes her hand. Then she offers it to me.

Her skin is soft, her grip firm and businesslike. She smiles at me so warmly, it's annoyingly disarming. I want to hate this woman for ruining our new start, but there's something instantly appealing about her. It's not just the smile, it's her calm confidence, and the fact she's come in person, apologising profusely. It's hard to stay mad with her.

'You said on the phone that you think someone's been in the house? You found something in the bedroom?' She raises a neatly trimmed eyebrow.

'Squatters,' Justin growls. 'Don't you people check your properties before you lease them out?'

I don't like the tone he takes with her, all officious and patronising. There's no need to talk to people like that. She's come to help.

To her credit, Harriet's smile doesn't slip an inch.

'It's unforgivable,' she says. 'I really can't apologise enough. May I take a look?'

Justin grunts and steps aside to let her in.

She's a little older than me. You can see it in the creases around her eyes and the lost elasticity in the skin around her neck, but she conceals it well with her perfect make-up and highlighted honey-coloured hair that hangs fashionably just above her shoulders. In her smart business suit and high heels, she makes me feel positively dowdy.

'We've checked all the doors and windows,' I explain, 'but there are no obvious signs of how they got in.'

'Right,' Harriet says, nodding. 'I'm sure we can get to the bottom of it and make this right for you. Not the start you imagined, is it?'

Justin shows her upstairs while I wait in the kitchen. I have no desire to see that bedroom again until it's been tidied up and thoroughly cleaned.

They're not up there for long.

When they come back down, Harriet's amiable smile has faded. She fishes in her bag and pulls out a mobile.

'Leave it with me and I'll get this straightened out. I just need to make a call,' she says, wandering into the lounge, out of earshot.

'Are you okay?' Justin asks.

I nod, but I'm far from okay. The thought of spending the night in the house fills me with dread. How am I going to sleep? Even with Justin here, I don't feel safe knowing someone's been living here and that they could return at any time.

Justin pulls me into a hug and I bury my head into his shoulder, savouring the firmness of his body, his chest pressing against mine. I know he was only trying to do the right thing by moving us out here, but I wish he'd talked to me first. I know why he was so keen to return. It's a place where he remembers being happy. And he thinks it's somewhere we can be happy together again after everything we've been through, but I'm not sure this is going to work.

'I don't think I can stay here tonight,' I mumble.

'What do you mean? Why not?'

'Why do you think?'

'Because of some idiot squatter?' he says.

'I don't think I can feel comfortable until I know for sure they've gone and won't be coming back.'

'You heard Harriet. She's sorting it. Besides, we don't have anywhere else to go.'

'We could book into a B&B for the night. Please, Justin. One night, that's all I'm asking.' I really have tried to be positive about the move, but I never expected to find squatters camped in the house. In our bedroom. It's too much. 'Would it really be such a big deal? And that way, Harriet would have the time to have the place properly cleaned. Then we could start with a fresh slate tomorrow.'

Justin sighs. 'I wanted today to be perfect. A new beginning for us.'

'I know,' I soothe, 'and it will be. We can come back tomorrow and pretend today never happened.'

'This isn't how I imagined it would be. I want you to be happy again, Megs. I thought this move, this house, would make everything right,' he says.

The way his whole body seems to deflate, like a balloon pricked by a thorn, tears at my heart.

'It will do,' I assure him, 'in time. But right now I'd be happier if we didn't have to spend the night here. You understand, don't you?' I clamp my palm tenderly on his cheek.

'I'm sorry,' he says.

'There's nothing to apologise for. You're a good man, Justin Pike, and I love you.' Frankly, I'm amazed he's stayed with me. I doubt many men in his shoes would have done.

Harriet's high heels tip-tap across the tiled hallway. As she strides into the kitchen, Justin lets me go, looking a little sheepish.

'Right, Colin's on his way over,' she says, all white teeth and smiles. 'He'll be here shortly.'

'Colin?' I ask.

'He looks after all the maintenance around the estate,' Harriet explains. 'He'll clear the room out and give it a good clean. You won't even know anyone's been here. I've also asked him to check all the doors and windows. We don't want any more surprise visitors, do we?' she grins.

I'm glad she can see the funny side. She's not the one who has to live here.

'Was there anything else while I'm here?' Harriet asks. 'All the instructions for the kitchen appliances should be in the drawer by the microwave. The code for the wifi is on the back of the router under the stairs, and details about bin collections are in a folder in the lounge.'

'Actually, there was no electricity when we arrived,' Justin moans. 'It was switched off at the meter.'

'The downside of living in the country, I'm afraid. The fuse box is quite sensitive and tends to trip at the slightest thing. As you've probably guessed, the house has been empty for a while. You've fixed it now?'

'Eventually.'

'Fantastic. Well done you,' she says, rather patronisingly. Justin bristles. An awkward silence simmers between us.

I clear my throat, my cheeks flushing with embarrassment, my mind blank. I don't usually struggle for conversation, but I can't think of a single thing to say.

'Just the two of you, is it?' Harriet finally says, breaking the tension. 'It's a big house for two. No children?'

I wish the floor would rip open and swallow me whole. Is this what it's always going to be like? People asking if we have kids and neither of us knowing quite how to answer politely.

'No,' Justin says, his jaw tight. 'It's just me and Megan.'

We're saved from further awkward questions by another loud bang at the door.

'That'll be Colin,' Harriet says, marching out of the kitchen and into the hall. She answers the door like she owns the place, which I suppose in a roundabout way she does.

The man she invites in is dressed in a set of dirty blue overalls, his face lined with age. What's left of his grey hair stands up in wisps on the top of his head, revealing a thumbnail-sized scab just above his forehead.

'Colin, thanks for coming over so quickly. This is Justin Pike and his wife, Megan. They've just moved in — '

'I know who Justin is,' he grunts, staring at my husband with a surprising sourness. In one hand he's carrying a toolbox. The other is clenched into a fist at his side. He's dour-faced and appears to be totally humourless.

'Hello, Colin,' Justin says cheerily. 'Good to see you again. You haven't changed a bit.'

Colin's lip curls. 'Didn't expect to see you back,' he huffs.

I grab Justin's hand tightly and tuck myself behind his shoulder. The atmosphere between the two men is decidedly icy, but I have no idea why. They must know each other from when Justin stayed at the house with his parents, but that was over twenty-five years ago.

'How are things?' Justin continues lightly, as if he's catching up with an old friend. Can he not sense the tension? 'Still keeping busy? How are the Carlyons these days?'

Colin looks at Harriet. 'Upstairs, is it?'

'The master bedroom at the front,' she tells him.

'Right-o.' He stamps his muddy boots on the mat and we watch mutely as he clambers up the stairs on stiff joints.

'It shouldn't take him too long, I'm sure.' Harriet clasps her hands together. 'But, listen, as a gesture of goodwill, we'd like to put you up in a hotel tonight, just until we can get things straightened out here.'

I could hug her.

'Really, there's no need,' Justin says. 'We'll be fine.'

I elbow him in the ribs.

'No, I insist. It's not good enough. You're right, we should have checked the property before you arrived. Why don't we meet here again tomorrow morning and we can start afresh?'

'That would be wonderful. Thank you,' I say, before Justin can protest again. There's no way I'm turning down a free night in a hotel, let alone staying in the lodge tonight.

Justin sighs. I know he's disappointed but it's not his fault. Tomorrow's a new day and, as Harriet says, we can all start anew as if today never happened.

'Wonderful,' she beams. 'I'll get the office to make the reservation and why don't we say I'll see you back here tomorrow at ten.'

Chapter 3

The hotel overlooks the beach and has its own gym, spa and pool. Our room is in a cosy attic space with incredible views across the bay. It can't have been cheap, even for one night. Not that I'm complaining. It's been so long since we've stayed in a hotel, especially one this fancy. Tomorrow, we'll be back at the house and our new reality, so I'm determined to enjoy it.

'This is something else,' I say, running a hand over the luxurious Egyptian cotton bedsheets as Justin dumps our cases in the corner.

'Yeah,' he admits, grudgingly. 'It is nice.'

'I'm sorry we're not staying in the house tonight. I know how much it means to you, but you understand why I was so freaked out, don't you?'

'Of course, but I'm the one who should say sorry. You've been through so much, finding squatters in the bedroom is the last thing you needed,' he says. Remorse glistens in his eyes. 'I just want you to be happy, Megs.'

But I'm not sure I even know what the word means any more. The heavy weight of sorrow has clung to my heart for so long, it's become a friend. I savour it. Relish it. Because how can I reject it? It's the daily reminder of the loss of my dear, sweet boys.

Justin keeps saying we need to start living our lives again, but how can ever move on and forget? Or forgive myself?

I slump on the bed with my head in my hands. Tears spring from nowhere, hot and thick, the surge of emotion wracking my body.

I've done little else but cry in the last ten months. Justin's become so used to my sudden outpourings that they no longer come as a surprise to him. He kneels on the floor in front of me and kisses the top of my head.

'Come on, Megan, it's okay.' He strokes my arms and rocks me soothingly.

I attempt to picture my sons' faces in my mind, but the harder I try, the more indistinct they become, their features morphing and dissolving into a jumble of memories just out of reach. Like a feather on the wind, every time I reach to grab them, they spin and tumble from my grasp.

What the hell is wrong with me? What kind of mother am I? I should be able to recall my sons' faces with perfect clarity. Instead, I have to focus on the smaller details rather than their constituent wholes. Sebastian's flyaway sandy hair. The rash of freckles across the bridge of his nose and that gappy smile we'd have had to get fixed when he was older. The scar on his knee, a jagged, pink reminder of the afternoon he tripped and fell on the patio, and the way he always liked to bump down the stairs on his bottom, even after he turned seven and should have grown out of it.

Felix's infectious laughter, his perfect button nose, inquisitive hazel eyes and permanently sticky, stubby little fingers. The peculiar way he had of holding a pencil like he was a handling a chopstick, unconsciously sniffing his way through the day, driving me to distraction, and how he still self-soothed himself to sleep, sucking on an upturned finger wedged in his mouth, even though he'd started school that September.

These memories are all I have now, and I'm terrified of losing them. If only I could package them up, roll them in bubble wrap and store them in a sealed, padlocked box because what if my mind won't retain them? What if they deteriorate with age and, like the memories of Sebastian and Felix's beautiful faces, become lost forever?

Justin's in pain, too, but he hides it well. He's able to put on a brave face and internalises his anguish in a way I've never been able to do, although I'm sure it isn't good for him. He doted on the boys, loved spending time with them, building train tracks in their bedrooms, chasing them around the house like a fool, and kicking a ball around in the park. How he'll ever forgive me for their deaths, I don't know. By rights, he should have walked out and never looked back. But he didn't. He stayed and comforted me, insisting I wasn't to blame, even though it was a blatant lie. And for that small and undeserved mercy, I'll always be grateful.

Eventually, my tears dry up, my body comes back under control, and I'm left feeling hollow and wrung out. I press my head against Justin's chest and listen to the steady beat of his heart.

'Why don't we get some fresh air?' he suggests. 'It would be a pity not to take advantage of the beach, as it's right on our doorstep.'

I sniff and dry my eyes with a tissue. The sea air probably will do me good. The alternative is locking myself away in this room for the rest of the day and I've spent too long shut behind closed doors, wallowing in my self-pity.

'Okay,' I mumble.

It's a beautiful afternoon. The sun is finally breaking through the cloud and the drizzle that had been falling earlier is clearing away. We walk hand in hand along the entire length of the beach, watching the waves roll onto the shore and dogs of all shapes and sizes chasing balls for their owners, who smile and nod as we pass.

The exercise makes me feel much better. A little more human again.

'Let's eat in the restaurant tonight,' Justin says when we finally make it back to the room. My hair's thick with sea salt and my lips are chapped.

'The restaurant?' My heart freezes. 'Can't we order room service?' I can't bear the thought of all those people staring, raising their eyebrows, watching the woman who killed her own children enjoying herself. They'll think it's obscene. It *is* obscene.

'It'll be good for us.'

'I - I don't know, Justin. It feels... weird.'

'Please,' he says. 'We haven't been out since... '

'The fire,' I finish for him. 'I know, but what will people think?'

'Nobody knows us here, Meg. We're just another couple enjoying a night at the hotel and a meal in the restaurant. And anyway, I don't care what other people think.'

'But what if someone recognises us?'

'They won't.'

There was extensive coverage of the fire in the media for a few days. Some tabloids used a family photo of the four of us taken on a holiday to Rhodes the previous year that they stole from my Facebook page. It's entirely possible someone could recognise us, although it probably is unlikely. The fire was almost a year ago now, although it still seems like yesterday to me.

But what's the point of arguing? I ought to be grateful Justin's still wearing his wedding ring. And if he wants to eat in the restaurant with me, who am I to deny him?

'Okay, fine,' I say. 'We'll try the restaurant, but perhaps they can find us a quiet corner, out of the way.'

His face breaks into a wide grin. 'We might as well make the most of it while we're not paying,' he says, although I'm not sure Harriet said anything about picking up our food bill.

With a weary reluctance, I shower and wash my hair. But then I have to decide what to wear. I can't go to a restaurant in jeans and a T-shirt, which is my attire most days, when I can be bothered to get dressed at all.

I root around in my case and find a white blouse and a pair of navy quarter-length trousers. I throw them on and check my appearance in a full-length mirror by the door.

I wince. This doesn't feel right. I'm really not in the mood. I'm tired and there are big, black bags under my eyes.

'Why don't you wear that dress?' Justin says, buttoning up his shirt.

'What dress?'

'That red one, you know, with the flowers.' He dives into my case, rummaging through my things, screwing everything up, until he finds the flimsy summer dress I'd forgotten I'd bought.

'This one.' He holds it up at arm's length.

'What's wrong with what I'm wearing?'

'I just think the dress would be better,' he says. 'And why don't you wear your hair up?'

'Fine.' Anything to keep him happy. He'll only sulk if I protest, and I don't want to sour his mood. I suppose I should be pleased he cares. Most husbands don't show any interest in how their wives dress or do their hair. I'm lucky like that.

I strip off my blouse and trousers and pull on the dress, but it's tight around the hips and shows off more cleavage than I'm comfortable with. Looking at my reflection in the mirror, I'm not sure it's that flattering. I probably should have tried it on before I bought it, but after the fire we had to replace everything in such a hurry that I just grabbed anything in a daze.

'I don't know,' I say, turning side on, sucking in my stomach.

'You look great.' Justin admires me from across the room with a lascivious twinkle in his eye, although I don't want him getting any ideas just because I'm not in jeans for a change.

The dress doesn't suit me at all. It's a bit tarty, although with a wrap-over cardigan perhaps I can make it work.

'Do you really like it?'

'You look a million dollars,' Justin says, planting a kiss on my lips. 'I'm going to be the envy of every man tonight.'

Fortunately, the restaurant is quiet even though it's a Saturday night. There are only a few other couples dotted around and despite my concern, nobody pays us the slightest attention.

A waiter shows us to a table by the window with views across the water and as I sit down and pull my chair in, I finally allow myself to relax.

'Can you bring us a bottle of champagne,' Justin asks the waiter.

'Justin,' I hiss, 'I don't think we should be celebrating.' What would people think?

The waiter hesitates, uncertain.

'And two glasses,' Justin adds. The waiter trots off with a bow and an appreciative nod. 'What?' Justin raises his eyebrows with an air of innocence.

The waiter returns with a bottle, glasses and an ice bucket. 'Special occasion?' he asks.

'We're celebrating our new life in the country,' Justin says. 'We move into our new home tomorrow.'

'Congratulations.' The waiter shoots us a smile as he pops the cork and expertly pours the champagne.

I could die. I can just picture the headlines now if the papers find out.

Killer mother's champagne celebration to mark new life in the country

I don't know what Justin's thinking.

But what can I say? I'm pleased he's happy. After the boys' deaths, he spent weeks in a depressed stupor. He didn't work for two months and would disappear off in his car on his own for hours at a time. I've no idea where he went and I didn't ask. I guess he needed space to think and to process.

I busy myself studying the menu. It's all in French, although thankfully there is a translation in tiny italics below each item and anyway, Justin orders for both of us, so I don't have to worry.

'What do you think about the house?' he asks when our starters arrive.

'You mean apart from the squatters? Yeah, it's nice.'

'Nice?'

I don't know what he wants me to say. It's old and draughty and none of the decor or furnishings look as though they've been updated in thirty years. 'I like it. Honestly, I do, but you know, it's going to take a little while until it feels like a home.'

'I was worried you'd hate it,' he says, reaching across the table to take my hand. His palm is hot and clammy.

'Not at all, although… ' I glance down at my plate.

'What?'

'Maybe we could add some new locks to the doors and windows?'

'Locks?'

'It would make me feel safer,' I say. 'The house is in the middle of nowhere. What if that squatter comes back when you're not there?'

'You're letting your imagination run away with you, but if it makes you feel better, I'll get someone to fit some additional locks, okay?'

'I know you think I'm being silly.'

'You're not getting cold feet, are you?' he asks.

'Of course not.'

'It's not like we're going to be there forever. It's only until we know what's going on with our place.' Justin sits back and sips his champagne, glancing out of the enormous picture window at the setting sun shimmering across the surface of the sea.

'I'm never going back there,' I whisper in horror. The mere thought of returning to our house makes me sick to the stomach. I've been having nightmares about the fire as it is.

Until today, we've been living in a temporary rented flat in Plymouth, but Justin said it was too small and that he wanted to get out of the city. I didn't even know he was looking at other places, until he told me about the lodge at Treloar.

'I'm not talking about moving back in,' he says. 'I told you, once we've sold it, we can move wherever we like.'

'And how much longer's that going to take?'

'I don't know. Six months? A year?'

The loss adjustors haven't even approved our insurance claim yet. It doesn't seem to matter that we've lost our home. They operate at a snail's pace. And even when they've settled, I've no idea how long the rebuild's going to take.

I certainly hadn't anticipated it could be another year. I don't know if I can survive at the lodge for that long. When Justin's away working, I'm going to be left there alone. Maybe it's time I thought about going back to work. It would at least give me something to take my mind off everything else.

'Give the lodge a chance, Megan,' Justin says, as if he's reading my mind. 'I know you'll get to love it.'

'Of course I will,' I say. 'It's just another big change, isn't it?'

'You'll feel better about it when Colin's cleaned out the bedroom and we can make it our own.'

I hope he doesn't just bag up all the mess and that he actually makes the effort to clean the room and get rid of that awful smell. I might give the carpets a clean myself when we get back anyway, just for peace of mind.

'Was it my imagination or was there a weird atmosphere between you and Colin?' I ask, toying with the stem of my glass.

'What do you mean?' Justin's face is the picture of innocence.

'You must have noticed it, surely? He was quite prickly with you.'

'Was he?' Justin pokes out his bottom lip and shakes his head as if he has no idea what I'm talking about.

'Yes, he was really off with us, bearing in mind he can't have seen you in twenty years. Did something happen between you in the past?'

'Of course not,' Justin says. 'I never really had anything to do with him. He was just the odd-job man around the estate. I barely even spoke to him.'

'But there must be something,' I press. 'He was so cold.'

'I don't think so.' Justin shakes his head again. 'Not that I can think of, anyway.'

He says it with utter conviction, but I'm not sure I believe him.

'That's weird. He definitely wasn't happy to see you. I'm not making it up.'

Justin shrugs. 'I don't know,' he says, and smiles thinly.

I can't imagine he has any reason to lie to me, so why can't I shake the feeling he's hiding something from me?

Chapter 4

Harriet is already waiting for us at the lodge the next morning, perched on the bonnet of a gleaming white sports car, clutching a bottle of red wine with a bow tied around its neck. Even though it's a Sunday, she's dressed in a smart coral pink jacket and trendy black trousers that flare over a pair of high heels.

'How was the hotel?' she asks, jumping up with a pearly white smile as I climb out of Justin's car.

'Lovely,' I say. 'Thank you.'

'I hope it goes some way to making amends for yesterday. Anyway, today's a new day and a new start.' She thrusts the bottle of wine at me. 'A little housewarming gift. Welcome to your new home.'

Yesterday's gloomy skies have lifted and with the sun rising in a steel blue sky, the lodge doesn't look nearly as foreboding as I remember. The walls a little less crooked. The windows not as dark. The trees surrounding it less dense.

'Shall we get you settled in?' Harriet says, sashaying off down the garden path while Justin grabs our cases from the boot. 'Colin's done a good job, actually. You'd never know anyone has ever been here.'

Except I do know.

Harriet opens the door with a set of keys she pulls from an expensive-looking Mulberry bag in the crook of her arm and I'm hit again by the musty odour of the old house. Of dampness and decay. Mould and dust.

Behind us, Justin grunts and huffs with our luggage.

Harriet pulls me inside, still grinning. 'Why don't you run up and take a look?'

'Oh, I'm sure it's fine, thank you.'

'Come on, I'm not leaving until I'm happy that you're happy. This is your home now.'

And before I can protest, she's trotting up the stairs, encouraging me to follow.

Justin staggers into the hall and dumps the cases, sweat beading on his forehead. We exchange a glance and he shrugs.

'Humour her,' he says.

I suppose there's no harm in checking. And if it's not been cleaned to my standards, she'll have to have it done again.

Harriet's standing by the bedroom door with her hand on the handle, waiting for me like she's a presenter on one of those TV home improvement programmes on the cusp of the big reveal.

'Ready?' she asks.

I nod.

She throws the door open and the first thing I notice is that the smell of body odour and stale cigarette smoke has gone, replaced by a slightly sickly citrus scent that reminds me of one of those air fresheners some people hang in their cars.

I peer inside. The room's been transformed. There's absolutely no trace anyone has been squatting here. The duvet has been folded neatly on the end of the mattress, the floor cleared of empty bottles and cans and the carpet spotless. Even a framed picture, a reproduction of a famous Constable that had been hanging askew on the wall, has been straightened.

I'm pleasantly surprised, not sure Colin was going to be as thorough. I hug the bottle of wine to my chest.

'What do you think?' Harriet asks. 'Happy?'

'Yes, thank you. That's a big improvement.'

A hand on my shoulder makes me jump. My heart jolts in my chest. I didn't hear Justin creeping up behind me.

'How's it look?' he asks, peeping over the top of my head.

'Much better.'

'So, can we unpack now?'

He makes it sound as though we have piles of cardboard packing boxes stacked in the back of a removal lorry outside instead of the pitiful few items of luggage we fit in the boot of the car. But there's no point replacing the things we lost in the fire, not until we're back in a house of our own.

'I guess so.' I force a smile.

'Great, well, why don't you get started while I pop to the supermarket and get some food in. I'll only be half an hour.'

And then he's gone again, thudding down the stairs. The front door slams and the engine of his car starts up. It's silly but thank god Harriet's still here. I'm still not ready to be alone in the house.

'Did Colin work out how they got in?' I ask.

'He's checked all the doors and windows,' she says. 'Everything's secure. You won't be troubled again.' She says it with conviction, but she didn't answer my question. 'Honestly, I think you're going to be really happy here, Megan. And look, I'm sorry if I put my foot in it yesterday. I didn't mean to speak out of turn. It was clumsy of me.'

I stare at her blankly.

'When I asked if you had children,' she adds. 'I don't know what I was thinking.'

'Oh,' I say. 'It's fine.' A fleeting snatch of Sebastian and Felix's smiling faces flashes across my mind, but for once I push it away. I don't linger on them, trying to focus on the details and fix them in my memory. I don't want to get emotional in front of Harriet. What would she think if I suddenly burst into tears?

'Even so,' she says. 'I feel awful. I need to learn not to open my mouth before engaging my brain.'

I don't want to have this conversation.

'I'd offer you a cup of tea, but I'm afraid until Justin gets back from the supermarket, we have nothing in. And it's a bit early to start on the wine.' I hold up the bottle and laugh nervously.

Harriet checks her watch. 'I ought to be getting going anyway.'

'No, stay,' I blurt out, the words exploding from my mouth before I can stop them. I glance at the floor, embarrassed. What am I doing? It's a sunny Sunday morning. Justin's only going to be gone for less than an hour. I'll be fine here on my own. And I'm going to have to get used to it soon enough. 'Sorry, you probably have things to do.'

'Actually, no. I'm not really supposed to be working today, but I wanted to be sure someone was here to meet you,' she says. 'There's a flowerbed at home that desperately needs weeding, but honestly, it can wait.' She smiles kindly.

With those impressive red painted fingernails, I can't imagine Harriet pulling on a pair of gardening gloves and tugging up weeds.

'Do you live around here?' I ask.

'I have a cottage just outside Falmouth.' She follows me back down the stairs and into the kitchen where I place the wine on the counter by the kettle. I'm grateful she doesn't seem in any hurry to leave.

'Well,' I say. 'I'm glad you're here.'

She frowns. 'What do you mean?'

'You probably think I'm totally overreacting, but it really unsettled me finding all that stuff in the bedroom, knowing that someone had been living here.'

'Oh, Megan, I'm so sorry.' She reaches out and rests a warm hand on my forearm. 'It must have been quite a shock.'

I swallow a rising lump in my throat. 'I've always lived in the city. This house is so remote and the thought of being here on my own... '

'You were in Plymouth before, weren't you?'

I nod, bracing myself for the inevitable next question about why we've chosen to move.

Instead, she says, 'You'll get used to it.'

'It's just so quiet.'

'I think it's peaceful. I love it here, but that's just me. I couldn't bear the thought of being in a big city with all that noise and light and people,' Harriet says.

I like the noise and light and people. It makes me feel safe.

'I'm worried about being here on my own when Justin's back at work. There's no one around for miles, is there?'

Without a car, I'm going to be totally cut off and if something happens, I don't even have any friends or family nearby for support.

Harriet bites her lip. 'The big house is just at the end of the drive. The Carlyons are away at the moment, but Colin's usually around somewhere. He has a cottage on the estate, up behind the back of the main house. I'll ask him if he wouldn't mind you having his number, just in case. And you can always call me if you're worried about anything.'

'I know I'm being silly.'

'No, you're not. It's a big deal making a fresh start somewhere new. I mean, if you like, I could show you around the area. That might help?' she offers.

'I wouldn't want to impose.'

'It's no trouble. I'd like to help.'

'Tell me about the Carlyons,' I say. 'I know they own the estate, but other than that, I know little about them.'

'They're pretty reclusive. You probably won't see much of them. Sir Roger used to be the sitting MP until he lost his seat about fifteen years ago. And then there's Lady Grace who keeps herself to herself, although I don't have much to do with either of them. Their daughter, Arabella, runs the estate, so that's who we're supposed to deal with.'

'Arabella? Justin mentioned her name, I think. He used to come here on holiday with his family. He told me he was friendly with the Carlyon kids. There was a boy as well, wasn't there?'

Harriet nods. 'Finn. He's a bit of a dropout. He fell out with his father years ago over a business deal that went south. You're more likely to find him on the beach surfing than hanging around on the estate. Not that you'll find any of them up at the house. Sir Roger owns a property in the south of France. He and Lady Grace spend half the year there. And Arabella lives in London with her husband.'

'So the house is empty?' I have a vision of a sweeping manor house with turrets, dramatic gables and ivy-clad walls, locked up and abandoned.

'Colin keeps an eye on things while they're away, but yes, no one's there at the moment,' Harriet confirms.

'That's a shame.'

'This is a beautiful part of the world, but we don't get the Mediterranean temperatures. I don't really blame them.'

'I suppose not.'

'Feel free to take a look around the gardens while they're away. In fact, you're welcome to roam around the whole of the estate. You'll find some lovely walks through the woods.'

'I might do that. Thank you.'

'And I'm serious. Let me give you the guided tour soon. I can show you some great beaches and some lovely pubs,' she says.

'Sure,' I say, not wishing to be rude. She's only trying to be friendly.

'Let me take your mobile number. I think I only have Justin's.'

'My number?'

She's already pulled her phone from her bag and is tapping at the screen with her long talons. 'Yes, let me put it straight into my phone.'

'Okay,' I say, not really sure if this is a good idea. I hardly know her, but how can I refuse? And besides, it might be useful to have someone close by I can call. I reel off my number as she types it into her phone.

My mobile buzzes in my pocket.

'There, you have my number as well now. So if there's anything else, just call me, okay?'

She slides her phone back into her bag and stares into my eyes so intensely I have to look away.

'Megan,' she says quietly.

My heart races in my chest, my pulse thrumming.

'Yes?'

'There's something else I need to tell you. Something you ought to know,' she says.

She bites her lower lip and takes a deep breath. Her mouth opens to speak but at the same moment, I hear a car pulling up outside. Wheels rumbling. Engine purring. A car door opening and closing.

'Justin,' I say. 'He's back.'

Harriet glances out of the window. Justin's struggling down the garden path carrying half a dozen bulging shopping bags.

'What was it you wanted to tell me?' I ask.

Harriet shakes her head. 'It's not important,' she says. 'It doesn't matter.'

Chapter 5

Our first night in the house wasn't as bad as I was worried it would be. Justin cooked a wild mushroom risotto, which we washed down with the bottle of wine Harriet gave us. And despite the strange, heavy silence that echoes around the house, or maybe because of it, I slept like a baby, waking only briefly in the night when I was startled by the screech of an owl, so loud I momentarily thought it must be in the room.

Sunlight is already filtering through the thin curtains when I'm finally roused by the sound of the shower running in the bathroom next door. I allow myself a moment to come around, savouring the warmth of my duvet cocoon, focusing on the wind sighing in the trees and the chorus of birdsong outside the window.

There's no traffic hum. No planes droning overhead. No small children screaming and shouting in the street. We're a long way from our old life in the city here, but is it really such a bad thing? The boys would have loved it. All this outside space to explore and trees to climb. It would have been a welcome distraction from the corrupting and insidious lure of video games and electronic devices.

God, I miss them so much.

A day doesn't go by when they're not at the forefront of my thoughts.

What kind of adults would they have grown up to become? How would their faces and personalities have developed? What adventures might they have experienced? I think about the lovers they'll never meet and the children they'll never have, and it breaks my heart over and over.

The first Christmas without them was the worst. We didn't even bother celebrating. How could we? It was too painful to even contemplate. Choosing and decorating a tree had become a family tradition we all looked forward to, but without Sebastian and Felix in our lives, what was the point? What was the point of anything? I don't think we'll ever celebrate Christmas again. It brings back too many agonising memories.

Just as I'm spiralling dangerously back into the depths of despair and regret, a shuddering clank of pipes signals the shower being shut off and a moment later, Justin strides into the room wearing only a small towel wrapped around his waist.

'Morning, gorgeous. How did you sleep?' He plants a warm, wet kiss on my cheek.

'Fine,' I mumble, pulling myself together. I don't want him to think I've been wallowing in self-pity again.

'It's so dark at night here, isn't it?' he says.

'And quiet.'

He grins broadly. 'I thought we could go exploring around the estate today.' He sits on the end of the bed and rubs my leg affectionately.

It sounds like a lovely idea, but before I can tell him, his phone rings.

He snatches it up from his bedside cabinet, running a hand through his damp hair.

'Yes? What?' He jumps off the bed and paces up and down, frowning. 'It's really not ideal, Angie. I'm supposed to be on leave this week. No, I'm sorry, I can't. You'll have to cope without me.'

My soul sinks. They want him back in the office.

Justin hangs up and stares pensively at his phone as if he's torn by an impossible decision. He promised faithfully he wouldn't need to work this week while we settled into the new house.

'Who was that?' I ask, sitting up with the pillows shoved behind my back.

'Jeremy's supposed to be running a course in Bristol this afternoon, but he's called in sick. They've asked if I can cover for him, but I told them no. I'm not leaving you here when we've only just moved in. It's not fair.'

'Can they reschedule?' I ask, pleased he's chosen me over the company for a change. He's already taken so much compassionate leave this year, but as a co-director, he can do as he pleases.

'Not really. It's one of our biggest clients.' He chews a fingernail, his shoulders hunched and tense. 'It won't look good if we have to cancel.'

'Can't you explain to them that Jeremy's ill?'

Justin sighs heavily. 'Maybe. Look, I'm sorry, Meg. I think I'm going to have to pop into the office for a few hours to sort this out after all.'

'You're joking?' He promised he wouldn't do this, that plague and pestilence wouldn't drag him away this week and now, at the first sign of trouble, he's running back to the office.

But I'm not going to cause a scene. Arguing with him won't change his mind.

'I'll only be a few hours. You know I wouldn't leave you unless it was important. Take a walk or something. Explore the estate.'

'I don't want to explore the estate without you,' I moan.

'I know. Trust me, I don't want to go either. But I'll be back before you know it.'

'Fine,' I mumble, folding my arms across my chest. 'Go.'

'Don't be like that.'

'I said it's fine. But you'll be back early, won't you?'

'I'll do my best,' he says, leaning over me and kissing the top of my head.

He gets dressed in a whirlwind, grabbing a clean shirt and a suit from the hideous mahogany wardrobe we inherited with the house.

'I'll call you later.' He kisses me on the lips, smelling of mint and shaving foam, and then he's gone. The front door slams, his car rumbles off into the distance, and I'm left alone, dazed and numb.

I'd thought we'd be spending the day together. Instead, I'm going to be here all by myself. It's my worst nightmare. Maybe I will go for that walk. If I stay cooped up in the house all day, it'll drive me mad.

I take my time in the shower, cursing the water pressure, which is so low it barely flows at a trickle. I dress, dry my hair and make the bed before venturing down wearily for a coffee. As I reach the kitchen, my phone buzzes in my back pocket.

It's probably Justin messaging on his way to Plymouth to apologise for abandoning me, but I'm surprised to find it's a text from Harriet.

How was your first night in the house? X

That's so sweet of her to check in with me. My thumbs fly across the screen as I type a reply.

Fine, thanks. We enjoyed your bottle of wine last night.

I watch as my message is delivered and read, and then Harriet types a reply.

Are you two going to look around the estate today?

It's a reminder I'm here on my own all day.

Probably, although Justin's been called into the office today, so I'm on my own now.

I add an emoji of a woman slapping her forehead in despair.

Harriet replies with a sad face emoji.

I'm over your way later. If I get a chance, I'll pop in and say hello.

Great. Maybe she'll elaborate on what it was she was about to ask before she left yesterday. It was all a bit cryptic.

There's something else I need to tell you. Something you ought to know.

Well, it couldn't have been that important, although I hate it when people say things like that and then clam up. Was it because Justin had come back and she didn't want to say anything in front of him? Something about the house? Maybe she's found out who was squatting in our bedroom.

I type a quick reply and put my phone back in my pocket.

I'm here all day. Hopefully see you later.

I only met Harriet a couple of days ago, and I still know hardly anything about her, but her promise to visit puts a smile on my face.

I flick the kettle on and take the empty bottle of wine out to the recycling bin at the back of the house, before wandering into the lounge to open the curtains.

Through the window, I watch a flock of sparrows flap noisily out of a dense hedge and a pigeon grazing on the lawn take flight with a lazy beat of its wings. Watery sunshine drizzles through the clouds, highlighting the first budding shoots on the trees that encircle the house. There's no denying it's an idyllic spot. But it's not home. Not yet anyway. Everything about it feels alien, from the way it smells, still dusty and damp, to its peculiar sounds. The popping and gurgle of the pipes. The creak of old timbers. The rattle of the glass in the windows.

And another sound.

Something more familiar and yet completely unexpected.

In the kitchen, the kettle hisses to a noisy climax and clicks off with a sigh.

And in the silence, the strange sound becomes louder.

If I didn't know better, I'd say it was a phone ringing. An electronic trill like something from the early days of the first mobiles.

I cock my head, standing motionless, convinced I must have imagined it.

But no, there it is again.

Where the hell is it coming from?

It's only faint, but I'm sure it's coming from somewhere inside the house. I tiptoe into the hall.

Now it's stopped and all I can hear is the fizz of silence in my ears and the low hum of the refrigerator in the kitchen.

I release the breath I was holding and lick my lips. This house is playing tricks on my mind. Or rather my mind is playing tricks on me. But it sounded so real. Is this what it's like to descend into madness? Hearing things that aren't really there?

No! There it is again. Quiet but unmistakable. It's definitely a phone, but it's not mine and unless Justin has hidden an old mobile in the house, it's not his either.

I think it's coming from upstairs.

I climb on weak legs, my thighs trembling.

The ringing stops when I reach the landing, just as I was getting close. It was louder up here, but still muffled, as if it might be hidden in a drawer or a cupboard.

I count in my head, ticking off the seconds.

One. Two. Three. Four. Five...

And then it starts over.

Thirrup - thirrup. Thirrup - thirrup.

I dive into the bedroom. I'm close now. It's louder still in here. And yet I can't quite locate it.

I throw open the drawers of the dark wood antique dresser, rifling through piles of my underwear, tights and T-shirts, Justin's socks, ties and boxer shorts. But it's futile. And anyway, if there was a phone in here, we'd have spotted it when we were unpacking, surely.

I work frantically, my heart racing. If the phone stops now, it might not ring again and I may never find it.

I skid across the carpet and pull open the wardrobe doors where a dozen of Justin's near-identical blue work shirts are hanging alongside a couple of my dresses and some pairs of jeans.

But there's no phone.

I force myself to slow down, to really listen.

It has to be in this room somewhere. I spiral around on a spot at the end of the bed with my eyes drifting upwards to the ceiling.

I'd not noticed the small loft hatch yesterday, but now I'm convinced that's where the ringing is coming from.

I try standing on the bed, but as the mattress sags under my weight, my fingers brush the ceiling and the hatch remains stubbornly out of reach. I need something else to stand on, so I rush downstairs and grab a chair from the dining room.

When I return to the bedroom, the phone's fallen silent again.

I place the chair under the loft hatch and climb onto it. A chill waft of air hits my face as I push the hatch open, scratchy dust particles catching at the back of my throat.

The loft is in complete darkness, and I'm still too low to see what's up there.

All I can do is reach up and feel around with my hand. My fingers rake through silky fibres which I realise with disgust must be cobwebs and I retract my arm with a squeal.

Come on, Megan. Grow a pair, will you?

With a shudder, I tentatively reach into the loft space again. A coarse layer of insulating fibreglass grazes my skin and a thin splinter from a roughly sawn rafter stabs my finger.

At first, I don't find anything.

But then, as I'm about to give up, I touch something round and hard and cold. Some kind of ball? It has a patterned edge and some sort of wire hook attached to one end.

It's not a phone. It's an old Christmas bauble made of shiny gold plastic and adorned with silver glitter.

I toss it back and try again, standing on the tips of my toes and reaching into the hatch up to my armpit.

And then I find it. A heavy block of plastic with what feels like a keypad of numbers.

It's an old Nokia, like the first phone I ever owned. A grey plastic brick with a row of tiny silver buttons. I shiver with excitement, my heart tapping out a quickening rhythm. Its screen is alight with a message.

Four missed calls.

What on earth is a mobile phone doing in the loft? I guess the previous tenants must have left it. But how can that be? The battery indicator shows it's still three quarters charged. No phone I've ever owned has held its charge for more than a few days, let alone for several months. It doesn't make any sense.

Carefully, I lower myself down and sit on the chair, staring at the phone in my palm.

When it rings again, I jump so violently I almost throw it across the room.

What do I do now? Answer it?

What if it belongs to the squatter who was living in our bedroom? What if he was dealing drugs and this is his burner phone his supplier used to contact him? I don't want to get caught up in something like that.

I gawp open-mouthed at the screen, not sure what to do. It could be anyone on the other end of the line.

Caller Unknown.

What the hell? They won't know who I am.

'Hello?' My voice cracks as I answer.

There's a brief hesitation on the line. I strain to hear if there's someone there. I catch the whisper of a breath. And then a click. And the line goes dead.

That's odd.

I check the screen to confirm we're no longer connected.

I'm curious now. Why would someone call and then hang up immediately it's answered?

Without thinking, I hit the redial button and put the phone to my ear.

But instead of ringing, all I hear is dead air, and then an automated voicemail asking me to leave a message.

I hang up, more confused than ever.

This is weird. First there was the squatter and now this phone.

I glance around, my heart drumming a furious beat, wishing I could be anywhere but in this room. In this house.

When the phone unexpectedly chirrups and buzzes in my hand, a frightened yelp escapes from my lips.

There's a new notification on the screen.

1 new message

Part of me doesn't want to look, but the other part, the more dominant, curious part, can't help it.

I click the text open and stare at it in horror, not believing what I'm seeing.

What the fuck?

WHATEVER YOU DO, DON'T TRUST YOUR HUSBAND

Chapter 6

With trembling hands, I read the words over and over until my eyes are swimming.

Don't trust my husband?

What the hell is that supposed to mean? Why wouldn't I trust Justin? It's insane. Obviously someone's idea of a joke. A cruel prank. But who would do such a thing? I don't even know anyone here in Cornwall. Unless it was Justin himself, thinking he's being funny. He could have hidden the phone in the attic while I was sleeping last night.

But I don't know, it doesn't feel like the kind of thing he would do. He's not like that. And he knows how fragile I've been feeling, that I'm in no mood for jokes.

But of course, I'm being stupid.

I've assumed the message was meant for me. That I was supposed to find the phone. But that's crazy. It's obviously intended for someone else.

I let out a sigh of relief. Justin's never given me any reason not to trust him. At least not for a long time. I trust him implicitly. After all, he's stuck by me when any other man would have run a mile.

My shoulders slump and I smile at my stupidity. I need to get my act together. I'm still so jumpy, not thinking straight. After I came off those pills my GP gave me for the depression, I thought things would get better, but I guess my head's still foggy.

I turn the phone over, examining it thoroughly, looking for a clue that could lead me to who it belongs to or who left it here. It can't have been here long because the battery's nearly full. I suppose someone might have been clearing out the loft before we arrived and it fell out of their pocket. A previous tenant, maybe. Or someone from the rental agency. But if it was someone from the agency, why didn't they do anything about the squatter living in the bedroom? Which brings me back to the only reasonable conclusion, that it must belong to whoever was camped out here when we arrived.

I should tell Harriet. She'll know what to do with it. Regardless, I don't want it in the house.

Although I am curious now. Who wouldn't be? It's such a strange message.

Don't trust your husband.

My mind goes into overdrive imagining who this man might be and all the things he's done or is capable of doing.

Infidelity?

Fraud?

Theft?

Murder?

An icy chill runs through my bones and a hard ball lumps in my throat. I should switch the phone off and put it somewhere safe until I can hand it over. I don't want to be bothered by it constantly ringing and buzzing. And besides, these messages have nothing to do with me. I shouldn't be reading them.

My thumb caresses the casing as I search for the power button, but before I find it, the phone pings with another message.

The notification taunts me, the screen lit up, illuminating my hand and wrist.

I shouldn't read it. I've already established the messages are for someone else.

But what if it helps to identify who the phone belongs to? Then I could do the right thing and return it. And anyway, a quick peek isn't going to do any harm, is it?

And in an instant I'm opening the text. The screen goes blank for a nanosecond before the message appears.

DON'T IGNORE THIS MESSAGE. YOUR HUSBAND IS A DANGEROUS MAN.

Dangerous?

The hairs on my arms stand to attention and a shiver rolls down my spine. That sounds a bit more serious than someone having an affair. And what is it with the capital letters? Nobody texts in capitals unless they're deranged...

God, it sounds important.

I don't know what to do. Really, I should ignore it. Switch the phone off and forget about it. At least it's confirmation I'm not the intended recipient, because nobody could ever describe Justin as dangerous.

He can be loud and a little brash sometimes, especially when he's had a drink. Arrogant, maybe, to some people who don't understand him. He can even be vain and impetuous. An acquired taste, some have said. But dangerous? I don't think so. He's kind and loving, sensitive and supportive. Who else would have stood by me after discovering I started the fire that killed our children? That takes a special kind of man.

And I do trust him. I really do. There was only that one time he let me down, but we were both young and we all make mistakes. I probably wouldn't even have found out about it if it hadn't been for one of his loud-mouthed mates who let it slip one night over dinner.

I was furious but I'm totally over it now. It's buried in our past. I realised quickly it wasn't worth breaking up over, and we even gave it a name. *The Amsterdam Indiscretion*. I think it helped to make a joke of it, and actually, the whole thing strengthened our relationship rather than weakened it, with us both promising we'd never keep secrets from each other again.

It was a moment of weakness, that's all, fuelled by alcohol and the pressure of all the lads together on a stag party in Holland, three years into our relationship.

Twelve of them went, all egging each other on, drinking too much. Showing off. Acting up. Her name was Scarlet, he eventually confessed, and she cost him a hundred euros.

At first I was disgusted. And embarrassed. And confused. I couldn't understand why he'd do that to me until I understood it wasn't about me. And it wasn't even about the sex. It was just one of those crazy stag party things. He didn't even enjoy it.

It was a stupid mistake. And if I'd let it destroy the best thing that had ever happened to me, well then, more fool me.

Justin had been my first serious boyfriend. There had been other boys at university, but nothing that lasted more than a few months, or on some occasions, the odd night.

Justin was different. Captivating, kind and attentive. When he talked to you, he made you feel like you were the only person in the room and the most beautiful girl he'd ever laid eyes on.

We met at a wedding, of all places. It sounds like a cliché , but I wasn't even on the guest list. I was waitressing, a job I'd taken to pay the bills after I'd left university and was still trying to figure out what to do with my life, but it gave me the freedom to stay in Plymouth and saved me from having to return to living with my parents in the hell of suburban Hertfordshire.

When Justin caught my eye as I was juggling an armful of empty plates, my cheeks flushed and I didn't know where to look. I almost tripped over my own feet as I noticed him watching, his steely green eyes pinpointing me like a laser. He seemed well out of my league with his model-like high cheekbones and sculpted jaw, and yet he was definitely staring at me, interested.

I loved how he was holding the attention of his table, like he was an actor on a stage, everyone hanging on his words, laughing at his jokes and waiting wide-eyed for his punchlines.

And yet when I approached with a bottle of champagne to fill their glasses ahead of the speeches, he gave me his undivided attention and made me feel like the most important person in the room, even though I wasn't supposed to engage with the guests. It was utterly intoxicating. And when he asked if he could take my number, I didn't think twice about scribbling it down on the back of his name card and sliding it under his glass.

I never really expected him to ring, but two days later he called to ask me out on a date, and for the next few months we embarked on a passionate affair. When we weren't in bed, wrapped up in each other's bodies, he took me to restaurants and the theatre. Romantic walks along the coast and Sunday breakfasts in what became our favourite café, coiled around each other with lattes and cinnamon pastries on 'our' sofa in the window.

It was Justin who encouraged me to give up waitressing and apply for teacher training, and after a year back at college, I was offered a job in a busy secondary school in a tough part of the city. Meanwhile, Justin's own career as a business consultant flourished. We couldn't have been happier.

Until Amsterdam.

I didn't say anything the night his friend let slip that something had happened with this woman, Scarlet, but I bided my time, waiting for the right opportunity to confront him. Somewhere public where he couldn't make a scene. I had so many questions. Who the hell was she? Were they still in touch? Was he in love with her? Was he planning to leave me for her?

We met after work at a wine bar in town. I arrived early and ordered a bottle of Merlot and was already on my second glass when Justin swaggered in, the top three buttons of his shirt undone and looking as devilishly handsome as when we'd first met.

I told him about my day. He told me about his. And then I took a deep breath, smoothed down my dress over my thighs and asked the question that had been eating me inside for the past two weeks.

'Who's Scarlet?' I couldn't look him in the eye.

Justin cleared his throat and stared into his glass. 'What?'

'Come on, Justin, don't play games with me. What really happened in Amsterdam?'

He shuffled uncomfortably in his chair and his cheeks flushed pink. We sat in silence for what felt like an eternity before he finally croaked, 'I'm sorry. I was drunk.'

So it was true. 'Are you still seeing her?'

'No.' He put his glass down and took a deep breath. His shoulders rose and sunk and then he spoke the words I never expected to hear. 'I paid for her. I'm so sorry. It was stupid. I don't know why I did it.'

'A prostitute?' The room fell away like I was spinning off into outer space.

'Everyone else was doing it and I know it's weak, but I didn't want to be the odd one out.'

'How many others have there been? I want the truth,' I cried, my world falling apart.

'None. That was the only time, I swear. I love you.'

'You have a funny way of showing it.'

'I mean it, Megan. You mean the world to me and I could never live with myself if you didn't forgive me. Please,' he begged, taking my hand as a swell of nausea bloomed in my stomach. The thought of my boyfriend in some filthy room in the seedy underbelly of Amsterdam's red-light district was enough to make me sick.

'How can I ever trust you again?'

'I'll make it up to you.'

And before I knew what was happening, he was down on one knee, still gripping my hand.

'Megan Waite, this might not be my best ever timing, but would you do me the enormous honour of marrying me?'

A hush descended on our side of the bar as people turned to watch. Was he for real? Was he actually proposing?

'I love you more than the world. I want to spend the rest of my life with you and have lots of little Megans and Justins. Please say yes. I'm begging you.'

In an instant, I melted. It was one little indiscretion, after all. A sordid, dirty little liaison. Sex, that's it. He didn't love her like he loved me. And he would never see her again. What he was offering me was a future. Marriage. Kids. Security. Happiness. It's what I'd been dreaming of since I was a little girl.

I bit my lip as he stared up at me from the floor, imploring me.

'I don't have a ring,' he said. 'But we'll get one. We can go shopping tomorrow and you can pick out the biggest diamond you can find.'

'Get up,' I said. 'You're making a fool of yourself.'

'Is that a yes?'

'Of course it's a yes, you idiot.'

'You'll marry me?'

'Who else is going to have you?'

It seems like a dim and distant memory now, but true to his word, he's never let me down again. Far from it, Justin's been a wonderful husband and father. He's not dangerous. Or threatening.

But the messages aren't about Justin. They're about someone else. Someone who could be out there right now posing a serious threat to his wife.

I can't just ignore them. It could be the difference between life and death. The responsible thing to do would be to tell whoever has been sending these texts that they haven't got through.

My thumbs fly across the keypad, composing a reply.

I'm not sure who you're trying to contact, but I think this phone has been lost.

I hit send and after a second or two, the message vanishes off into the ether. As I wait for a reply, palms sweaty, I worry I might not have been explicit enough.

I type another message, just to be sure there's no misunderstanding.

Let me know who you're trying to reach and I'll do my best to get the phone returned to them ASAP.

It's all I can do, although I can't tell if my messages have been read, let alone received. I'd forgotten how rudimentary these old phones are. It's not like my smartphone. I'll just have to hope it's not too late.

I stand and wander across to the window while I wait for a response. If I don't get one, that's not my problem. I've done my best. I can't be held accountable, can I?

A light breeze rustles through the leaves of the trees and in the distance a line of fluffy white sheep meanders through a field in single file.

The phone pings in my hand.

I snatch it up to read the message, hopeful of finally solving this ridiculous mystery.

But it doesn't.

It only deepens it and sends a shuddering spike of fear through my whole body.

This has to be a joke.

But there's no ambiguity. It's there in black and white. Taunting me. It isn't my imagination going wild. This is really happening.

But it can't be right. It's someone trying to frighten me. But who? And why?

My mind whirrs at hypersonic speed, but no matter which way I look at it, I can't make any sense of it.

GET OUT WHILE YOU CAN. WHATEVER YOU DO, DON'T TRUST JUSTIN.

Chapter 7

I hurl the phone across the room. It strikes the headboard of the bed and comes to rest on my pillow. I edge away from it as if it's an angry cobra, my back pressed up against the dresser with the handles digging into my spine.

I can't breathe. I can't move. I can't think.

What the hell is this?

If this is someone's idea of a joke, it's in poor taste. It's not in the slightest bit amusing. In fact, it's terrifying. Who would do this?

It must be someone who has had access to the house and could have planted the phone. Someone who knows me. Who knows us. Someone who could be watching the house right now.

I scuttle across the room and yank the curtains closed, almost pulling them off the rail in my haste, and then back away from the window, confusion and fear mixing in a heady cocktail that leaves my brain spinning. My lungs feel like they're being crushed inside my ribs.

Oh god, the back door.

Did I lock it after I took the wine bottle out to the recycling first thing?

I race out of the bedroom, across the landing and throw myself down the stairs, my socks slipping on the treads as I almost lose my balance. I skid across the tiled hall floor and gasp with relief when I see the back door is shut. I snatch the key and twist it, confirming it was locked after all. But it's a small comfort.

I scurry to the front door and check that's locked too, rattling it in its frame to make sure it's secure. Then I double back into the lounge with its wide patio doors that open onto the back garden and provide lush picture views through the trees and across the valley. Hurriedly, I tug the curtains closed, plunging the room into a hazy gloom, panting like I've just run a marathon. And then into the dining room where I do the same. And finally into the kitchen where I struggle with a dusty roller blind that squeaks as I tug on the chain to lower it.

I stagger out of the room, into the hall, eyes wide, all my senses alert, trying to control my breathing. Listening. Waiting.

But the house is quiet with a throbbing, weighty, reassuring silence.

I'm alone. And safe. For the time being, at least. Nobody can see in and no one can get inside.

What *am* I doing?

These aren't the actions of a sane woman, but I can't shake the words in that message from my head.

WHATEVER YOU DO, DON'T TRUST JUSTIN.

I should call him and let him know what's going on. I want him here with me. I need him here. I don't have anybody else.

I pull my phone from the back pocket of my jeans and unlock it, my finger poised over his name in the contacts list.

But what am I going to say?

That I've found an old mobile in the house that I suspect a stranger has planted and that they're using it to warn me I should leave him? That he's dangerous?

He'll think I'm losing my mind.

Perhaps I am.

No, that message was very real.

Someone thinks I'm in danger from my own husband, which is the most ludicrous thing I've ever heard. But Justin's hardly going to drop everything in the middle of a crisis at work and drive back here just because I received a weird message on a phone that doesn't even belong to me.

I lower my mobile and slide it back into my pocket. There's nothing he can do anyway. I could call the police, I suppose. And say what exactly? I haven't been threatened and I'm not sure three unexplained text messages exactly count as harassment. They could trace the number and find out who's been sending them, but why would they? I'm sure they have far more important things to deal with.

Get a grip, Megan.

So much for going out exploring the estate. There's no way I'm leaving the house on my own now. For all I know, it could be a plot by someone who knows I'm here alone to lure me out of the house and kill me.

Megan, stop it. You're blowing this totally out of proportion. This is Cornwall, not the Bronx.

Slowly, I clamber back up the stairs and poke my head around the bedroom door. The old Nokia is still lying on the pillow where I threw it, taunting me like a bad memory. I don't want to see it, and I certainly don't want to hear it ring again. I could destroy it, of course. A couple of substantial whacks with a rolling pin or the iron should do the trick. But that won't erase the memory of those words from my head.

Instead, I cross the room cautiously, pick it up and, after checking there are no new messages, power it off and shove it into the drawer of my bedside cabinet. Out of sight and out of mind.

Then I climb into bed, curling into a ball, burying my head under the duvet and screwing my eyes tightly closed, shutting out the world.

After a while, my heart rate slows and the tightness in my chest eases. I still can't think of anybody who'd be spiteful enough to send hoax messages about Justin. Or why. Are they getting a thrill out of scaring me? Or is there an ulterior motive I can't see? Someone trying to drive a wedge between us? Another woman, perhaps, hoping to get me out of the way?

I don't know how long I stay there like that in my bed, but it's warm and safe. A reminder of being a child. And it feels like the only place I want to be.

It's some time later when the sound of a car pulling up outside causes my adrenaline levels to spike again. I freeze, listening hard. It's the first sign of life I've heard all day. I check my phone, surprised to see it's already mid-afternoon. My stomach rumbles with hunger. I've been hiding for hours and not even bothered to grab any lunch.

Could it be Justin home already? He said he'd try to get away early.

I toss the duvet aside and brush my hair out of my eyes.

An intrusive banging at the front door makes me jump. I swallow hard, but my throat is dry.

When I don't answer, three more loud thuds at the door echo through the house.

Curious, I step out of bed and creep down the stairs with my arms wrapped protectively around my body.

I pad silently across the hall and press my ear to the door.

Nothing.

Perhaps they've gone.

'Hello,' I whimper. 'Who is it?'

'Megan? It's Harriet. Open the door.'

'Harriet?' I fly at the lock, fumbling with the key and eventually haul the door open a crack wide enough for her to squeeze through.

'What are you doing — ' I begin, but the words dry up as I see what she's carrying in her arms.

'Isn't he gorgeous?' she says, stepping inside.

I shove the door shut and lock it behind her.

The puppy cocks his head to one side, one ear flopping over his face, the other bent backwards comedically. He stares at me with big, black eyes that make my heart swell. He whimpers nervously.

'Is he yours?' I ask, reaching out to scratch his head. He nips playfully at my fingers with needle-like teeth and then tries to lick the back of my hand with his warm, rough tongue.

'He's a gift,' Harriet says, her eyes glistening with pleasure. 'For you. A housewarming present.'

She puts him on the floor and tries to pass me the end of his lead as he sniffs the tiles curiously, his back legs trembling.

'What?'

'Don't you just love him? He's adorable, isn't he?'

'Yes, but — '

'I thought you'd be more of a dog person than a cat person,' Harriet continues.

I've never owned a pet in my life, unless you count the gerbil my father bought me when I was five and which escaped from its cage overnight and was never seen again.

My jaw drops open. I don't know what to say.

'He's a rescue pup. The animal sanctuary called me about him last night. He'd been dumped and was found sniffing around the bins outside a supermarket in Penryn,' she explains.

As I look closer, I can see his ribs sticking out painfully and he has a missing patch of fur on his neck. He looks badly undernourished.

'They know I'm a sucker for all the waifs and strays and this little one badly needed a new home.' Harriet crouches down to chuck the puppy under his chin with her long, painted nails.

I've not known Harriet for long but I didn't peg her as an animal lover. She doesn't seem the type with all her fancy clothes and the fact she's always so impeccably turned out.

'You should see my house.' She rolls her eyes. 'Overrun with cats. The problem is, I can't say no. One look at their sad little eyes and I'm a complete pushover. I'm sure the sanctuary has me on speed dial these days.' She laughs.

'It's very kind — '

'I thought he'd be just what you needed to keep you company and to help you settle in,' she says.

'I can't keep him,' I blurt out.

'Oh, why not?' The excited smile drops from Harriet's face.

'Justin would go spare. He hates dogs. He's allergic. I'm really sorry, you'll have to take him back.'

'Maybe give it a couple of days? See how you get on. I know it's not a replacement for children, but — '

'Harriet, I can't!' I burst into tears, all my pent-up frustration and anger boiling over.

'Oh, Megan, what is it? Don't cry.' She puts a comforting arm around my shoulder and I bury my face in her neck.

'I'm sorry,' I mumble.

'I didn't mean to upset you. It was supposed to cheer you up, especially after everything you've been through.'

Everything I've been through?

'No, it's fine,' I say. 'It's me being silly. You weren't to know. It's very thoughtful of you.'

Harriet pulls away and unclips the dog's lead from his collar. He wanders into the kitchen to explore as I wipe my face dry with a tissue.

'No, I should have known better.'

'Honestly, it's fine. What will you do with him?' I ask. I can just imagine Justin's face if he came home to find I'd taken in a rescue dog.

Harriet shrugs. 'I don't know. Maybe I'll take him home and introduce him to the cats.'

She glances into the kitchen, notices the blind is pulled down, and then spots the curtains in the lounge behind me are closed. She frowns. 'Megan, what's going on? Is everything okay?'

I let out a long sigh. For a minute, in all the excitement of Harriet turning up with a puppy, I'd completely forgotten about the phone and those stupid messages. But now it comes flooding back to me.

I want to tell Harriet all about it. To offload. But I don't want her thinking I'm crazy, especially as I've barely known her five minutes, although I could really use a friend to chat to right now and I have no one else to confide in.

'The thing is, and I know this is going to sound weird, but I found an old phone in the loft earlier,' I explain.

She looks at me blankly. And I tell her everything.

'That's extraordinary,' she says when I've finished. 'Are you sure the messages were for you? It's not even your phone.'

'They mentioned Justin by name.'

'Could be a coincidence.'

I raise an eyebrow. 'Come on, Harriet.'

'Okay,' she says, holding up her hands. 'That is a bit far-fetched. But who would do something like that?'

'That's the whole point, I don't know. I guess someone's trying to frighten me.'

'And succeeding, from the look of the place. Have you told Justin?'

'Of course not,' I say. 'How can I?'

'What about the police?'

'I'm not sure they'd take me seriously,' I say.

'So what are you going to do?'

I throw up my arms in despair. 'What can I do? Nothing. I've switched the phone off and put it in a drawer for now. I thought it might have been left behind by a previous tenant. Maybe you should take it and see if the last people who lived here know anything about it?'

But Harriet shakes her head. 'The house has been empty for months. I'm not even sure we have any forwarding details for the last tenants.'

'Oh,' I say, disappointed.

'I suppose the question is, *why* would someone send messages like that? Don't bite my head off, but could there be any truth in them? Could Justin be a threat to you?'

'What? No! Of course he's not. He wouldn't harm a fly, let alone lay a finger on me,' I say, shocked she could even think it. It goes to show how little she knows about us.

'No, of course. You know Justin better than anyone. So someone trying to cause mischief, then?'

'I can't think what else it could be.'

'That's awful, Megan. Some people are just sick in the head.'

'I guess.'

'Are you going to be alright here on your own?' She runs her hand up and down my upper arm in comforting strokes.

'I'll be fine. Justin should be back at any time and, to be honest, it's helped to talk about it. I shouldn't have let it get to me, should I?'

'Don't be silly. I'd have been exactly the same. I'm glad I popped in now. You know you can call me any time if you need to chat, don't you?'

I can't believe how kind she's being to me. She's an absolute lifesaver and it makes me feel marginally better knowing I have someone I can call on.

'Thanks, Harriet, but you'd better take that dog away. If Justin gets back and finds it here, he won't be happy.' It's a shame, a dog would be good company for me when Justin's at work.

'I mean it, Megan. Call me any time, day or night, and let me know if you get any more messages.'

'I will. Thank you.'

'Right, come on, mutt. Let's get you out of here,' she says, disappearing into the kitchen to rescue the puppy from whatever mischief he's found.

She re-emerges, dragging him by the lead on his backside across the tiles.

'Actually, before you go, there was something else I wanted to ask you,' I say.

Harriet lifts her chin and frowns. 'Oh, yes?'

'Yesterday, you were about to tell me something important just before Justin came back from the supermarket. What was it?'

'Oh,' Harriet says, letting her gaze fall to the floor. 'That.'

'Please, it's been really bugging me. What was it you wanted to say?'

Chapter 8

'It's nothing really.' Harriet casually plucks a stray puppy hair from her jacket.

'If there's something you want to say, please, just tell me.'

'It's nothing sinister, honestly,' she says, which makes me think maybe it is. 'It's just that I know what happened, okay?'

She glances up at me through long, thick lashes, but she's talking in riddles. I've no idea what she's trying to say. I shake my head, waiting for her to elaborate.

She sighs heavily and flicks her eyes to the ceiling. 'I mean, I know about the fire. I know about Sebastian and Felix.'

Hearing my sons' names trip off her tongue so lightly is like a thunderbolt striking me square in the chest. A dizzying lightness floods my head.

She knows.

I've never been recognised in public before, although I shouldn't be surprised. The story was all over the news, but no one has ever said anything to my face before.

'How?' I gasp.

'I thought you looked familiar, so I looked you up.'

A veil of shame and humiliation envelopes me, what little self-respect I'd rediscovered in the last few months shrivelling up like a weather-beaten tomato rotting on the vine.

'It wasn't difficult,' Harriet continues. 'Your names and photos are all over the internet. I shouldn't have been snooping, but the way Justin was behaving made me curious.'

I peek out from behind my hands. 'What about the way Justin was behaving?'

She shrugs. 'He was so snappy when I mentioned kids I thought it was odd. And I had this niggle that I recognised you both from somewhere.'

'Oh god.' My legs tremble under the weight of my body. 'You must think... '

'I can't imagine how awful it must have been for you, Megan, you poor thing.'

'What?'

'Losing your children in a fire. I can't think of anything worse. How on earth did you cope?'

The way she looks at me, her eyes filled with sadness and sympathy, churns my emotions. Tears bubble up in my eyes again, her pity and concern opening the floodgates.

'You don't think I'm... evil?'

'Evil? No!' she gasps. 'Of course not.' She wraps me in her arms, smothering me in kindness and expensive perfume, and all I can think about is my tears staining her smart jacket. 'You're not evil. How could you say that? You lost the two most precious things in the world. No mother should have to go through that.'

'But it was my fault,' I cry. 'It's my fault they're dead.'

She pulls away from me, grabs my shoulders firmly, and fixes me with an unyielding gaze. 'Don't say that. You didn't mean to kill them. It was an accident. The investigation cleared you of any wrongdoing. I read all about it.'

'I left a heater on in the room under the boys' bedrooms,' I sob. 'I knew it was faulty and yet I still plugged it in and left it on when I went to bed.'

'It could have happened to anyone.'

'But it didn't. It happened to me, and I'll have to live with that for the rest of my life.'

She hugs me again, pulling me so tightly against her body, it forces the breath from my lungs.

'I think you're braver than anyone I've ever known,' she says.

I shake my head. 'I'm not brave. That's ridiculous.'

'I don't think many people could have survived what happened to you, Megan.'

Survived? She makes it sound as though *I'm* the victim. Nonetheless, it gives me a warm glow inside, knowing there's someone other than Justin on my side.

The puppy yaps noisily. When I look down, he has one of Justin's shoes clamped between his jaws. He cocks his head at us and we both laugh at the absurdity of it. The shoe's almost as big as him, but he's clearly pleased at claiming such a worthy prize.

I'm grateful for the distraction and dislodge myself from Harriet's embrace, feeling a little foolish at how easily I've opened up and revealed myself to her.

'Why don't I make some tea,' she says.

'Justin's likely to be home at any minute. I don't want him to find a dog in the house.'

Harriet's eyes narrow. 'It's only a dog, Megan. I'll tell him he's mine. I don't know what you're so worried about. You make him sound like a monster.'

'No, it's just that... '

But she's already walking away, heading for the kitchen.

I follow her, pull out a chair at the table and sit with a tissue, damp with my tears, crushed between my palms.

Harriet brews two mugs of tea and takes the seat opposite.

'Do you want to talk about it?'

'The fire?'

She nods, holding her mug to her mouth in both hands while blowing on the tea to cool it. 'Only if you want to.'

I've never talked to anyone about the fire, other than Justin and the fire investigators. But then, I don't really have many close friends. In fact, there's no one. Like Justin says, so many people are just users. They're only interested in talking about their own problems, sapping your energy with their negativity, or taking advantage of cheap child-care, while bitching about you behind your back. He's right, I don't need that kind of toxicity in my life.

Harriet's different. Genuine. Caring. It's probably because she's a little older than me. I warmed to her the first moment we met.

But do I want to talk to her about the fire? Does she really want to know? If she hears the truth, maybe she won't be so sympathetic.

I take a deep breath and exhale slowly.

'A lot of it's still a blur,' I say. Probably because of the sleeping pills I took after a couple of glasses of wine that night, but I decide to omit that detail. 'Justin was at a charity fundraising dinner.'

He looked so handsome that night in his dinner jacket, all groomed and freshly shaven. As usual, I had to fix his bow tie for him. He was hopeless. All fingers and thumbs. I don't know why he didn't buy one of those ready-tied ones, but he insisted on doing things properly. And wearing a ready-tied bow tie was not doing it by the book.

'The boys and I ate pizza in front of the TV and I let them stay up later than normal, as a treat,' I continue. 'After they'd gone to bed, I think I must have gone into the snug to finish my wine. I put the heater on but forgot about it when I went up.

'The next thing I remember, Justin was yelling at me to wake up. I hadn't even heard him come home. He was frantic, shouting about a fire and not being able to get to the boys. That's when I first smelt the smoke. He tried to get to their rooms, but the flames were too fierce. The whole landing was alight. It was terrifying.

'I screamed at him to do something. He had to save them. And he tried. He really tried. But he couldn't. There was nothing either of us could do.'

I stare at my hands, the memories of that awful night washing over me in a deluge. The clawing stench of thick, black smoke, like plastic and wet leaves on a bonfire. The roar of the flames engulfing everything in their path. The heat so intense it peeled the paint off the walls.

'He dragged me to the bedroom window, kicking and screaming, and made me jump while he stayed inside, trying to reach the boys. He wouldn't give up. I should have stayed with him, but he was so insistent. He said he didn't want me to die.

'When the fire crews finally arrived, it was already too late. We found out later that they'd probably died in their sleep because of the smoke, not the fire, which I suppose is a small comfort, at least.'

The words dry up in my throat, the memories still painful. I'll never forget the sight of those two firefighters in thick overalls and full-face respirators, like something out of a sci-fi movie, carrying Felix and Sebastian's lifeless bodies out of the house and laying them in the back of an ambulance. It's a memory that still haunts me in my nightmares.

I didn't stop crying for forty-eight hours.

My world had been destroyed. Almost everything I loved and cherished had been snatched from me in an instant. And there was no one to blame but me.

'The investigation concluded the fire was caused by the electrical heater I'd left on overnight in the snug, which was directly below the boys' rooms,' I explain, forcing the words out of my mouth. I want Harriet to know who I am and what I've done. I want to be judged. 'It had a faulty thermostat and I'd left it too close to the curtains. They said once the fire had taken hold, my babies stood no chance of surviving.'

'A tragic accident,' Harriet whispers. Her eyes are bloodshot and damp.

'No,' I say, shaking my head. 'It was reckless. How could I have done that? My job was to protect my children, and I let them down in the worst possible way.'

'You can't beat yourself up like this, Megan. It's not healthy. It's not what your boys would have wanted either, I'm sure.'

Funny, that's exactly what Justin had said. He was absolutely devastated. Bereft. And yet he was still looking out for me, thinking about my feelings. He even tried to blame himself.

'I knew the heater was faulty,' he'd said in the awful aftermath when we clung to each other, physically and emotionally, because we didn't know what else to do. 'I should have thrown it out. I don't know why we kept it.'

But he was only trying to make me feel better.

I've replayed that evening over and over in my mind so many times, but much of it remains a blank. I remember opening a bottle of wine and taking a pill before bed, worried because I hadn't been sleeping well. I can remember cooking the boys pizza and nagging Felix because he wouldn't eat his crusts. I remember we watched one of those early evening talent shows they loved. I can even recall tripping up the stairs as I chased them both to bed, stumbling on a toy truck one of them had left on a lower tread. But not much else. I guess that's what shock does to you. Your brain hides the worst parts of your behaviour from your memory as a kind of self-protection mechanism.

'And how are you coping now?' Harriet asks. 'If that's not a stupid question.'

How *am* I coping? I still feel numb. Hollow. Guilty. Regretful. Empty. At one point, soon after the boys' funerals, I contemplated ending it all. I could have done it. It would have been easy. I couldn't see the point of going on, but that would have been the coward's way out. I realised my penance wasn't death, but the one thing that was worse than death. Living in the knowledge that I'd killed my own children.

I shrug. 'I'm okay. I think.'

'It must have put an enormous strain on your marriage.'

I'm not sure many marriages could have survived what Justin and I have been through, but we're rock solid. United in our grief. Tentatively feeling our way forwards together.

'We're doing alright,' I say, sipping my tea.

'You're lucky he's such a good man.'

'I am.' And I know it. I'm grateful every single day that we're together. That he had the compassion and understanding in his heart to forgive me. Which is why it's so odd that someone out there is trying to drive us apart and make me believe he's somehow dangerous.

Harriet must be able to read in my expression what I'm thinking. 'You shouldn't take any notice of those messages,' she says. 'It sounds like someone just trying to mess with your head. Is there anyone you can think of who might have a reason to do that? Maybe it has something to do with the fire.'

'Oh god, do you really think so?'

'Unless you can think of anything else?'

I received some nasty, vindictive, hate-fuelled messages through social media in the aftermath of the fire. People, anonymous mostly, who thought it was perfectly acceptable to tell me I should have been the one to die in the fire, that I was an evil bitch, an unworthy mother, that I was going to rot in hell. One particularly unpleasant man had threatened to send razor blades in the post and described in bloodthirsty detail exactly what he'd do to me if he saw me in the street. Justin called them petty-minded trolls, and although it upset me, I simply deleted all my social media accounts and thought no more of it.

Could it be one of those people? Someone who's become obsessed by the case and found out where we were moving? It seems implausible, but not impossible.

'Do you think I'm in danger?' I ask.

'From Justin?'

'No! Of course not from Justin. From whoever left that phone here for me to find.'

'Hard to say, but I wouldn't have thought so. I think someone's trying to scare you, that's all.'

The rumble of a car pulling up outside drags me back to the present. It's so quiet here that any vehicle noise immediately grabs my attention. Instinctively, I glance at the window, forgetting I've pulled down the blind.

'Bloody hell, that'll be Justin.' I jump up and snatch Harriet's empty mug from her hand. 'You've got to go and take that dog with you before he sees you.'

The puppy has curled up in a ball by her feet, his head resting on his over-sized paws.

Harriet blinks at me like I'm insane.

'Please, Harriet. He'll go mad if sees a dog in the house. Hurry.'

Reluctantly, she rises and scoops up the puppy in her arms.

'Honestly, Megan, don't you think you're overreacting a bit? It's only a puppy. How could you not fall in love with his little face?' She says it in a sing-song baby voice that makes me cringe.

'I know. He's very sweet, but you don't know Justin. He'll hate him.'

'Fine,' Harriet says, letting me usher her towards the back door as I hear Justin's keys in the lock. I shove her out into the garden with an apologetic smile.

'Sorry, Harriet, but thanks for listening to me ramble on.'

'Anytime. Remember, you have my number.'

The front door crashes open as I press the back door shut. I hear the thud of Justin's briefcase as he drops it on the floor and the brush of material as he shrugs off his suit jacket.

I wipe my eyes, trying to erase any evidence of my tears, and pull my hair into a loose ponytail over my shoulder. Then I step into the hall to welcome my husband home.

'Do you have visitors?' he asks suspiciously.

'What? No, I've been on my own all day.'

'Well, whose is that car outside?'

Shit. I forgot about Harriet's car.

'I mean, Harriet popped in briefly. Didn't you see her on your way in?' I bluster.

He's about to say something, but hesitates with his mouth wide open. He throws his head back, squeezes his eyes shut, and sneezes loudly.

Three more sneezes follow in quick succession.

That bloody puppy. What was Harriet thinking, bringing him here without checking with me first?

'Has there been a dog in here?' Justin asks, blowing his nose in a handkerchief he pulls from his trouser pocket.

'A dog?' I ask, trying to look innocent. 'No, I don't think so.'

I hate lying to my husband. But it's only a little white lie. And those don't really count, do they?

Chapter 9

I suppose Harriet wasn't to know Justin's allergic to dog hair. And cat hair. It's why we never allowed the boys to have pets even when Felix came home from a sleepover at a friend's house begging us to buy him one of those silly crossbreeds that look more like big teddy bears than dogs, because Noah had one and they'd spent the afternoon throwing balls for him in the park and he'd slept on Felix's feet all night.

But now I've been forced into lying to Justin. I could see from the bags under his eyes and the scowl he was wearing when he walked in the door that he'd had a bad day and I didn't want to make his mood worse. I'll put the vacuum cleaner around later and I'm sure he'll be fine.

'What did Harriet want?' Justin snaps, sneezing again. His eyes are rimmed red and tears are streaming down his cheeks.

'She didn't want anything. She just popped in to see how we're getting on.'

'She seems to be around here an awful lot. You don't need someone like that hooking their claws into you, especially in your fragile state,' he sniffs.

'Don't be like that. She was concerned about me, that's all. Anyway, it was nice to have a girly chat for a change.'

Justin raises an eyebrow. 'Oh, yeah, about what?'

'Girls' things. You wouldn't understand.'

'Is that right? Is there any wine open?' he asks.

I head into the kitchen and find a bottle of Pinot Grigio in the fridge. It's a bit early, but he's obviously had a tough day and if it helps him to unwind, it's not such a bad thing.

I pour two glasses. Justin knocks his back in one and helps himself to another.

'I just don't want you getting sucked into a one-sided friendship, Megs. You know what these women are like. They're all take, take, take. You need to look after your mental health.'

'She knows about the fire,' I say.

Justin's glass freezes halfway to his mouth. He stares at me with watery eyes as he lowers it. 'How?'

'How do you think? It's all over the internet. It's hardly a state secret.'

'Well, there you go then. Exactly what I was saying. She's probably only trying to make friends with you to get the gossip. You want to be careful,' he says.

'She's not like that.'

'How do you know? You've only known her five minutes. She's the rental agent, for pity's sake.'

I think he's wrong. Harriet's seen how lonely I am and is trying to be friendly. That's all. Justin has such a suspicious mind sometimes, although he'd say it was because he doesn't want me getting hurt. He thinks I've been damaged enough.

'How was your day, anyway? Did you sort out that problem with the course?' I ask.

He waves a dismissive hand. 'I don't want to talk about work.'

I know better than to press him. If I push it, he'll only get snappy with me and we'll spend the rest of the evening sulking with each other.

'But you won't have to go in for the rest of the week? They're going to honour your leave?' I press.

'Tell me about your day. That's far more interesting.'

I breathe out heavily through my nose. He promised he'd take the week off when we moved, that he wouldn't abandon me here until we were settled. It's not fair, especially with this creepy business with the phone.

'Actually, something odd happened,' I say, running my tongue over my front teeth.

'What kind of odd?'

'I found an old mobile phone in the loft.'

'What were you doing in the loft?' He frowns. I watch his expression carefully. I've still not entirely ruled out the possibility Justin planted the phone as a wind up. But if he knows anything about it, he's hiding it well.

'I was looking for somewhere to store our cases and I noticed there was a loft hatch in our bedroom,' I lie, not sure why I don't tell him the phone was ringing.

'Oh,' he says, his interest waning. 'The last tenants probably left it.'

'That's what I thought.'

I should tell him about the messages and how upset I've been. What's the point of keeping it from him? We promised after the *Amsterdam Indiscretion* that they'd be no secrets between us. But this is different. I know he'll get upset and he'll only worry that someone's trying to cause trouble, but what he doesn't know can't hurt him.

'Listen, why don't I cook tonight?' he says. 'My way of apologising for leaving you today.' He puts his empty wine glass on the kitchen counter and folds his arms around my waist, pulling me close. He kisses me on the lips and I inhale his scent, musky aftershave and an odd mix of dirt, citrus and dust. The smell of his office and the air freshener in his car. 'And while I'm cooking, why don't you take your wine and finish it while you're having a long soak in the bath.'

'Sounds idyllic,' I murmur into his neck.

The old pipework in the house rattles as I fill the tub up to its brim. Water sluices out of the overflow outlet and soon the bathroom is foggy with steam and the mirror over the sink frosted over. At least the water is hot, even if the house is old and the plumbing creakingly ancient.

I slip out of my clothes, tie my hair up and slide my body under the water, savouring the heat as my muscles relax and my worries momentarily melt away. The bath has always been my refuge, especially when the boys were young. It was the one place I could enjoy some time alone, unencumbered by the demands of small children.

I take a breath and sink my mouth and chin under the water until my eyes line up with the surface, the ripples and whorls disappearing around the twin peaks of my knees into a near perfectly reflective skin. I try to clear my mind and relax, but I can't stop thinking about that stupid phone in the loft. The messages. The warning. The implication that I'm somehow in danger while I remain in the house with Justin. Maybe I should have told him.

Downstairs, I hear the clatter of pans. Justin whistling to himself. The rattle of cutlery. The oven door banging shut.

I let my gaze drift, floating up towards the ceiling and the wonky rail attached to the wall, supporting a limp shower curtain speckled with mildew. A plastic power-shower and the ugly crinkled hose that snakes up to the shower head that's dripping beads into my bath water. And in the corner, a thick rash of black spores that coat the painted wall I'd not noticed before, hidden behind the shower curtain when you're standing in the room but clearly visible from the bath. As I look closer, I can see parts of the plaster are coming away too. Water's obviously seeped in behind and blown it.

I sigh to myself. It's something else I'll need to get Harriet to sort out. All those mould spores in the air are unhealthy, and we're paying enough every month that we shouldn't have to put up with it.

As the water grows tepid and the skin on my fingers puckers and wrinkles like soggy walnuts, I haul myself out of the bath, pull out the plug and wrap myself in a towel.

In the bedroom, I perch on the edge of the bed and call Harriet's number. It's after normal working hours, but she said I could phone any time and I'd rather speak to her while Justin's preoccupied. I don't want another lecture on Harriet's suitability, or not, as a friend.

She answers on the second ring.

'Megan,' she says, sounding equally surprised and delighted.

'Sorry to call so late, but I was taking a bath and I noticed there's an awful mould problem in the bathroom I hadn't noticed before. Any chance you could get someone to look at it?'

'Oh, right,' she says. 'Sure, no problem. I'll get Colin to investigate.'

'Thanks. I appreciate it. It looks like the plaster may have blown.'

'There's always something in old houses, isn't there?' She laughs. 'How was Justin tonight?'

'Yeah, fine. Well, apart from all the sneezing.'

'Oh,' she says, confused.

'The dog. I told you, he's allergic.'

'Did you blame it on me?'

I hesitate. 'No,' I say. And leave it at that. She doesn't need to know I lied to my husband. Even if it was only a little white lie.

'Any more messages?'

'I haven't checked,' I say, turning my head towards the bedside cabinet where I've hidden the phone.

'That's probably for the best. Forget about them and carry on, that's what I say.'

Except now she's put the idea in my head, it's like an itch I can't ignore.

'I'm sure you're right,' I say, already on my feet and shuffling around the end of the bed.

'Okay, well, I'll speak to Colin first thing and ask him to look at the bathroom.'

'Thanks.' My hand's on the drawer handle, easing it open. I hang up on Harriet with a muttered goodnight, and reach inside, my fingers wrapping around the heavy plastic casing of the old Nokia.

I stare at it for a second or two. Do I want to do this?

But my thumb's already on the power button, sparking the old mobile into life.

I shiver as I wait for what feels like an eternity, not sure whether it's because I'm cold or because of the anticipation of what I'll find.

Downstairs, Justin's whistling, although he has a terrible ear and it's impossible to recognise the song.

A blue logo animates on the screen before it goes blank.

A few long seconds later, the phone pings and a notification appears. There's another new message.

With my heart in my throat and my hands damp with nervous sweat, I open it, holding my breath.

Capital letters.

No ambiguity.

Another warning.

I'M DEADLY SERIOUS. LEAVE HIM BEFORE IT'S TOO LATE.

This is beyond a joke. Do they really think I'm going to pack my bags and walk out on Justin just because of some stupid text message from some anonymous benevolent guardian angel?

I'm not standing for this.

Using two thumbs, I type out a hurried reply. I don't know why I didn't do it before.

This isn't funny. I don't know who you are, but this stops right now.

I hit send.

But it's not sated my anger. I type another message.

Don't make me call the police.

It's the only threat I can wield. I doubt the police would do anything, but hopefully it's enough to get whoever's sending these stupid texts to stop.

I send it and power the phone off before hurling it into the back of the drawer and slamming it shut.

I'm not going to look again. I won't give them the satisfaction. I've got far more important things to worry about than crank calls and hoax messages. What a pathetic, tiny-minded individual to get off on doing something like this. It's like the trolls who targeted me after the fire. Keyboard warriors with pathetic lives who had nothing better to do than to make my life more of a misery than it already was.

'Megan, are you nearly done? Dinner's ready. I'm about to serve up,' Justin hollers up.

'Just coming.'

I dress hurriedly and stomp down the stairs. Justin's carrying two plates through to the lounge. It smells amazing. Some kind of beef stew from the look of it.

'What's eating you?' he asks as I follow him through and slump onto the sofa.

'What do you mean?'

'You've got a face on you like thunder.'

'Sorry.' I shake my head and bury my face in my hands, massaging away the tension.

'What's up?'

'Nothing. I'm fine.' I throw him a forced smile. 'This looks delicious.' I take a plate and balance it on my knees while Justin returns to the kitchen for the wine and our glasses.

'Are you sure you're okay?'

Now would be the time to tell him about the messages. But that would mean admitting I lied to him earlier. Or at least that I hadn't told him the whole truth.

'Yes, I'm fine, although I've found mould in the bathroom and the plaster's peeling away.'

'You're kidding?' His face crumples in disappointment. He wanted this house to be perfect for us.

'Harriet's going to send Colin to look.'

'Good old Colin.' There's a hint of sarcasm in his voice, but I let it go. He tops up my glass and hands it to me.

'What do you fancy doing tomorrow?' I ask, trying to put the phone to the back of my mind. 'I never got the chance to explore the estate today, so I was thinking maybe we could take a walk up to the house in the morning. I'd love to look around the gardens while the Carlyons are away.'

Justin falls silent, poking at his food with his fork.

'Justin?'

He puts his fork down and sighs. 'I'm sorry, Meg. I should have told you earlier. I need to work tomorrow.'

I knew it. Despite all his promises, the office is taking precedence again.

'Really?' I make no attempt to hide my disappointment.

'I need to get up to Bristol to run Jeremy's course. We weren't able to reschedule. I'm afraid it means I'm going to be away for a few days.'

Chapter 10

Justin leaves early the next morning, before I'm properly awake. We went to bed on a sour note, barely speaking after he confessed he had to go away for work, so I suspect he's grateful to disappear without having to face me.

I'll get over it. It's just disappointing I don't get to spend the day with my husband. I'd love to have gone exploring with him. Instead, it's another day alone in this odd house with its strange smells and noises, knowing someone's trying to freak me out.

I should have thrown the phone away or insisted Harriet took it. I certainly shouldn't have sent those messages while I was angry. Now they'll know they've got under my skin and that's only likely to encourage them to keep going.

With a weak sun shining a soft light through the curtains, I sit up in bed and reach into the bedside cabinet drawer. I wasn't going to look again, but curiosity is a powerful drug. I need to know at least if my messages have provoked a response. They might even give me a clue about who's been sending them.

I power the old Nokia on and wait for it to come to life.

Seconds tick past slowly.

The familiar logo animates, accompanied by a short tune.

I wait. I watch.

But this time there's nothing.

A small part of me is disappointed there's no new message. Have they even seen the texts I sent last night? Of course, there's no way to tell with these old phones.

But there might be other clues hidden on the phone. I never thought to look before.

I scroll quickly through the menus, hunting through the contacts lists, sent and received messages and the call log. But there's nothing, only the texts I've received and the two I sent last night. The only useful piece of information is the number that's been used to call and message. But it's just a string of numbers. Useless on its own without a name. It could belong to anyone. It could even be one of those pre-paid burner mobiles.

I toss it back in the drawer, partly relieved, partly frustrated. I don't believe for a second that Justin's a threat to me, but it's made me ask the question, and I hate myself for that.

I'm not going to sit around all day dwelling on it. It looks as though the weather's decent, so I'm going to get out. I *will* look around the estate, even if Justin's not here. It's about time I found my bearings and started appreciating the countryside. In fact, without Justin here, I might as well go for a run. I need to clear my head and get a sense of perspective. Hiding inside won't help. It's just going to drive me crazy.

It's been so long since I've exercised, I've almost forgotten how much I love running. The feeling of freedom. The rush of endorphins. The space to think. Your mind focused on nothing but your breathing and the strength in your legs.

I've mentioned to Justin a few times that I've been thinking about getting back to my job as a personal trainer, but he's not convinced I'm ready. He wants me to take my time to heal fully. But there's nothing to stop me from getting back into shape. And that's got to help with my mental health.

I pull on a stretchy pair of blue leggings I picked up a few months ago, and pair them with a thin vest and a long-sleeved top. Then I rummage in the bottom of the wardrobe where I've thrown the boxes of shoes I've bought and never worn in the aftermath of the fire, and find the pair of brand new running shoes.

Outside, I warm my calves and hamstrings with a few springy jumps and set off at a leisurely pace, heading towards the big house at the top of the drive. My feet crunch along the gravel and before long I'm breathing heavily, my legs leaden and my lungs screaming at me to stop. At least the pain and discomfort keeps my thoughts from that phone and the messages. It's a welcome relief.

I push on, easing into a steady rhythm, and as my muscles warm up, it all feels easier, my body remembering what it's supposed to do.

There's nothing like the magic of running to snap you almost instantly out of the darkest mood. Why I didn't keep it up after the boys died, I don't know. I'm sure it would have helped.

Running on the drive is harder going than I'd expected, with uneven patches of gravel threatening to turn my ankle. I've always had weak ankles and don't want to risk an injury, so when I see a path leading into the woods, my instinct is to follow it.

The ground under the trees is much softer and soon I find a spring in my step, dancing lightly between thick trunks and sprawling bushes, skipping to avoid perilous roots and crashing through vines and brambles whose long-reaching tentacles sprawl across the path.

Eventually, I spot the big manor house through the trees and slow to a quick walk with my hands on my hips, catching my breath. It's nowhere near as grand as I'd imagined, although it's much bigger than the lodge we're renting, of course.

It's handsome rather than stately, designed simply in granite block work, overlooking an immaculate, lush green lawn. A curl of wisteria coils up the front wall and extends along the frontage under the first-floor windows, but in common with the lodge, it has a neglected, forlorn air about it.

I bet inside it's all high corniced ceilings, wood panelling and marble open fireplaces. I can only imagine the raucous parties it's witnessed over the years.

With a quick glance over my shoulder, I steal across the verdant lawn, curiosity drawing me closer. I step gingerly into one of the flowerbeds below a ground-floor window and press my nose up to the glass.

It's dark inside but I can see a long mahogany table in the centre of the room, antique oil paintings of sombre-looking dead people hanging from lipstick-red walls and a sideboard laden with cut-glass decanters. It's as splendid as I'd expected, although everything appears a little frayed around the edges, as you often find with these old houses.

I'd love to take a proper snoop around inside and see how the other half lives. Maybe when the Carlyons are back from their French retreat, I can bag myself an invite.

Now I've stopped running, a chill seeps into my bones. I need to keep moving and as I'm still feeling fresh, I want to go further. To push myself and see how my fitness levels really are faring after being inactive for such a long time.

A quick check on a mapping app on my phone shows there's another marked footpath that takes a wide loop around the woods, through some fields and back close to the lodge.

I set off at a slow jog and push myself to go faster until my breathing is laboured and my legs burn. The wind grazes my face and brushes through my hair as my feet pound relentlessly over the soft ground that rises and falls through some stunning scenery.

Inevitably, my thoughts return to the phone and those vile messages making Justin out to be something he's not.

He's never given me any reason to be concerned. All couples argue from time to time, and we're no different, although I do my best to avoid it. I hate conflict. I saw what it did to my own parents' marriage, how my mother's continual nagging and nit-picking eventually drove my poor father away. I vowed I would never be that woman. Justin means too much to me. Even more so now. He's all I have left.

I suppose he can be a little overprotective at times, but it's only because he cares. He likes to look out for me. It would be worse if he showed no interest, like some husbands. I'd hate to be in a loveless marriage like that.

The woodland opens up into a wide, green valley dotted with sheep and cattle. I climb stiles and splash through muddy puddles until eventually I arrive back at the lodge, tired but invigorated.

Sweat drips from my brow into my eyes and I let my hair fall loose over my shoulders. It takes a minute or two for my breath to come back under control and as I stand up straight with my hands on my hips, shaking out the lactic acid in my calves, I'm buzzing. I feel so much better than I did yesterday, stuck in the house all day brooding over those messages, worried someone was watching me.

It seems ridiculous now. Whatever those texts are all about, they're just words. They can't hurt me if I don't let them.

I pull the house keys from the zipped pocket in the back of my leggings and amble to the front door, still breathing hard.

I slip the key into the door and attempt to unlock it.

But the key won't turn.

Odd.

I jiggle it back and forth. These old locks can be temperamental sometimes and require a bit of a knack. I'm sure if I just...

I put my other hand on the handle for balance and the door swings open.

That's strange. I'm sure I locked it when I left. In fact, I'm certain I did. I remember, the key was stiff and it took me two or three attempts. I know my mind was preoccupied, but I didn't imagine it.

Maybe Justin's home. Did he forget something and have to pop back? But there's no sign of his car.

Tentatively, I push the door fully open and peer into the hall.

The house is silent.

My pulse quickens.

The image of a silhouetted stranger creeping around the house, reaching into the loft with a mobile phone, flashes through my mind. Has someone been watching the house, seen me leave and let themselves in?

I plant my feet noiselessly on the tiled floor in the hall, grateful I'm wearing rubber-soled running shoes, all my senses alert.

Do I need a weapon? After all, I'm here on my own and no one's going to come running if I scream. I dart into the kitchen and snatch a kitchen knife from the block.

A loud, dull thud comes from upstairs.

Shit.

My limbs turn to stone. Heavy and immovable. There *is* someone in the house.

Another thud. Louder. It sounds as though it's coming from one of the bedrooms.

What do I do?

There's someone up there.

There's someone in our house.

Chapter 11

I take the stairs one step at a time with my thighs trembling. I grip the knife tightly, aiming it ahead of me, wincing at the creaks and grunts of the old treads with my eyes trained on the landing above, half expecting someone to come rushing at me at any moment.

'Hello?' I call out weakly, my voice a hoarse whisper. 'Who's there?'

Another thud, like someone dropping a sack of potatoes. And the rustle of material. The shuffle of feet.

My heart patters like a thousand tiny pistons. What if it's a burglar? Or the squatter back again? What do I do?

I'm shaking so hard, I can barely hold the knife steady. My vest top sticks to my back with sweat and my fingers feel icy cold.

Maybe I should call the police.

I reach around to the small of my back and yank open the zip in my leggings. My phone's a tight fit in the pocket. I have to tease it out with stiff fingers, and as I finally free it, it slips from my hand. I cringe as it lands noisily on the stairs, bouncing to the bottom where it hits the tiled floor with a crunch that I'm sure is the sound of the screen cracking.

With a snatched breath, I freeze as still as a statue.

But there's only a deathly silence, as thick as tar, from above.

I try to swallow, but my tongue's swollen in my mouth.

Do I go back for my phone? Or keep going?

A shadow flickers across the open bathroom door.

I take another step, flexing my hands around the handle of the knife, as a different emotion pushes its way to the forefront of my mind.

Outrage displacing my initial fear.

How dare someone break into our house, invade our home, touch our things, violate our privacy. Do they have no respect?

A few more steps and I'm on the landing, my eyes glued to the bathroom door, my shoulders and upper arms locked with the knife at arm's length in front of my chest.

'I know you're in there,' I shout, with more confidence than I feel. 'Come out slowly. The police are on their way.'

When a head emerges from the bathroom, I almost stumble back down the stairs in shock. Wisps of grey hair poking out at careless angles from an almost bald head. A scowl of confusion. A drinker's strawberry nose.

'Colin? What are you doing here?' I gasp, lowering the knife.

He raises a hammer and points with it over his shoulder. 'I've come to look at your mould problem, like I was asked,' he grumbles. His eyes widen when he spots the knife I'm clutching between white knuckles.

'I thought you were a burglar.'

'You were out. I let myself in.' He grunts and disappears back into the room.

My body slumps with relief.

Of course, Harriet mentioned she would send Colin over, but I didn't think he'd let himself in without warning us he was coming. It's not very professional.

I move to the door. Colin's standing in the bath with a chisel in one hand and the hammer in the other, poised over the hideous old tiles.

'You have a key?'

He glances up at me. 'I got keys for all the properties.'

'Well, it would have been nice if you'd let me know you were coming first,' I moan.

'I was told it was urgent.' He lifts the hammer and swipes at the chisel. It connects with one of the tiles, and with a loud crack, the tile splits in two. With another blow, it splinters off the wall and crashes into the bath in a puff of dust.

'How many other people have keys to the house?'

He shrugs. 'I don't know.'

'What do you know about a phone that was left in the attic in the front bedroom?'

He's about to tackle another tile, but lowers the hammer and chisel and sighs. 'I don't know nothing about a phone,' he says. 'I'm just here to fix your mould problem.'

'Right. It's just that someone's been sending me weird messages through an old phone I found.' I watch Colin's reaction carefully. If he has a key, he would have had the perfect opportunity to plant the phone in the loft. And he's already made it clear he's no fan of Justin's. Maybe he's being spiteful and thinks he can get at Justin by breaking us up.

He looks at me blankly.

'Colin, have you been sending me messages? Because if you have, it's not funny. I don't know what's happened between you and Justin in the past, but he's my husband and I love him. If you've got some kind of grudge against him, I suggest you take it up with him directly. You're not going to split us up with a couple of stupid texts.'

He stares at me like I've lost my mind.

'Like I said, I'm just here to sort out the mould.' He turns back to the tiles and cracks another one off the wall.

Maybe I'm wrong. Perhaps Colin has nothing to do with it, but at least I've said my piece and if it is him, he knows I'm onto him.

'What's the verdict then?' I ask eventually, after watching him knock four more tiles off the wall. 'Is it bad?'

'Leaking pipe behind the plaster. Probably been like it for years. All these tiles need to come off.'

'Oh.' It sounds like a big job. 'How long's that going to take?'

'Three or four days, at least. Maybe more.'

'Three or four days? But we'll be able to use the bathroom in the meantime?'

'Nope. I'm gonna have to turn the water off for a few hours later, too.'

Terrific. That's all I need on top of everything else. I'm still caked in mud and sweat from my run and I won't be able to take a shower. I'll have to wash in the kitchen sink. The day gets better and better, but at least we don't have burglars. Or our squatter back.

'I'll leave you to it then,' I say.

'Right-o.'

'Actually, before I go, I meant to ask, did you find out how that squatter got into the house?'

'Nope.'

'Right, it's just that I'm concerned they might come back and it would be good to know how they got in.'

'Probably the last tenants. They must have left a window open or summat.'

'Yes, I suppose you must be right.'

Or someone else has a key to the house, and they were able to let themselves in and out at will. If that's true, they could be back at any time. But then, there must have been so many tenants and holidaymakers who've had access to the keys over the years, anyone could have made a copy.

Of course, the other people who must hold keys are the owners. The Carlyons. What did Harriet say their names were? Sir Roger and Lady Grace, I think. Posh sounding. Justin used to be friendly with their children and they all used to play together when he came here on holiday, but I don't know where they are now.

'You've worked on the estate for a long time, haven't you, Colin?' I ask, sensing this might be my opportunity to find out more about them.

'I've worked for Sir Roger's family since I was a lad,' he says.

'What are they like?'

'They're alright.' He answers so dispassionately I might as well have just asked him if he prefers his coffee black or white.

'They're in the France at the moment, aren't they?'

'That's it. They always spend the winter in the villa.'

'What about their children? They've grown up and left home now, have they?'

'Yup.'

He's not exactly forthcoming, but I press on regardless while I have his attention.

'You must have known Justin when he was a teenager then?'

'I remember him alright.'

'What was he like? You didn't seem too pleased to see him again the other day.'

Colin finally stops working and sits on the edge of the bath to wipe sweat off his brow.

'I mean, it was almost thirty years ago. He was probably all skinny and spotty back then,' I laugh. 'He's not told me much about his childhood. I've seen a few old photographs, but I'd love to know what he was like as a kid.'

'You really want to know?' Colin growls.

The brusqueness of his reply catches me by surprise. 'Yes, absolutely,' I say, although now I'm wondering if I do.

'If you really want to know, he was trouble.'

'Trouble?'

'That's right. We all dreaded the summer knowing he was coming back.'

He says it with such venom and loathing that for a moment I'm speechless. I appreciate Justin isn't to everyone's taste. His self-confidence, bordering on arrogance, can sometimes rub people up the wrong way, but to talk that way about a teenage boy is odd. He couldn't have been that bad.

'And to be honest, I'm surprised he had the nerve to come back,' Colin adds, spitting the words out like they're traces of grit in his mouth.

'What do you mean? Is there something I should know?'

Colin stares at me, his eyes twitching as they roam across my face, working his jaw with a disturbing sucking sound.

The message I received on the old Nokia comes back to me.

DON'T IGNORE THIS WARNING. YOUR HUSBAND IS A DANGEROUS MAN.

No, that's something different. That's just someone trying to cause trouble. The two things aren't connected. They can't be. I mean, all teenagers can be a handful, can't they?

'Colin,' I press. 'What do you mean by that? What did he do?'

Colin scratches the back of his neck, but as he opens his mouth to speak, a phone rings somewhere in the house. My phone. I recognise the ringtone. At the bottom of the stairs, probably smashed and dented.

'You going to get that?' Colin asks.

I think about ignoring it, but it might be Justin and he'll panic if I don't answer.

'Hang on. I'll be right back.'

I dash down the stairs, almost tripping over my own feet. My phone's buzzing and jigging across the tiled floor and, sure enough, its screen is a crazy paving of cracks and smashed glass.

'Hello?'

'Megan, it's Harriet. Are you okay?'

I put my hand to my forehead. 'Um, yes, I'm fine.'

'You sound like you've just run a marathon.'

'I was upstairs. It's not a great time, Harriet. Can I call you back?'

'It's only a quick one,' she says. 'I meant to let you know I spoke to Colin first thing and he's going to pop in later to look at the bathroom for you.'

I groan. 'Yeah, you're a bit late. He's already here. Thanks.'

'Oh, great. Well, hopefully it's nothing too serious.'

'A leaking pipe behind the plaster, apparently,' I tell her.

I sense she's in the mood to chat, but I'm itching to finish the conversation with Colin. I need to know what he was about to tell me.

'No wonder you had mould.' She laughs, although there's nothing funny about it.

'Listen, Harriet, I'm just in the middle of something. Can I call you back later?'

'Oh, yeah, no worries. Sorry. I'll speak to you soon. Bye.'

I hang up and race back up the stairs.

Colin's returned to the tiles, noisily hammering away.

'That was Harriet,' I shout to get his attention. 'She was calling to let me know you were on the way.'

'Bit late.'

'That's what I said. Anyway, you were telling me about Justin,' I prompt.

'Was I?'

'You said he was trouble and that you were surprised he'd come back. What did you mean? What did he do?'

Colin rubs his nose with the back of a dusty hand. 'Nothing,' he says. 'It don't matter.'

'Come on, Colin, please. Tell me. I need to know.'

'I spoke out of turn. I shouldn't have said nothing.'

'But you did and now you've got me all worried, what with these silly phone messages.'

'It was a long time ago,' he says. 'It's probably all best forgotten.'

He picks up his hammer and smashes another tile into smithereens.

Chapter 12

While Colin continues to bang noisily in the bathroom, I shut myself in the dining room with a sheet of paper and a pen. Someone's gone to an awful lot of trouble to get my attention with this phone and the messages. This isn't a hastily written invective posted on social media by a dim-witted troll with nothing better to do. This is someone who's put time and effort into a plan to spook me out and get me questioning Justin's character. It's taken thought and preparation by someone who had, or still has, access to the house. Someone who must have a key.

I smooth out the piece of paper on the table and scribble in capital letters along the top: KEYS TO THE HOUSE. Then I underline it for good measure.

Underneath, each on a new line, I add:

1. Colin
2. Rental agency
3. The Carlyons - Sir Roger and Lady Grace
4. Previous tenants

I tap my pen against my teeth as I think about who else might have had access to the house and the opportunity to conceal a phone.

5. Squatter???

Colin said there was no sign of a break-in, so maybe it's a former tenant, although why would they target me and Justin? But then, what reason do any of them have?

So far, Colin's the only one with a motive, although it's a pretty weak one. He doesn't like Justin for some reason. Something to do with what happened here in the past. But I've looked him in the eye and I can't believe he's responsible.

However, something happened here, when Justin was at Treloar with his parents. I just need to get him to open up to me and tell me the truth.

I scan the list again. The rental agency must keep spare keys. Are they securely locked away? What about other staff members? Could one of them be holding a grudge against Justin? Or both of us?

Harriet said she'd found the news stories about the fire online after recognising us. What if she'd shared what she'd found out with her colleagues and someone's taken exception to the fact I caused the death of my own children? What if this is their misguided way of getting back at me? There have certainly been plenty of trolls queuing up online to tell me what they'd like to do to me.

I draw a circle around 'Rental agency' on my sheet of paper. The more I think about it, the more it seems worth investigating.

I need to talk to Harriet. She answers my call almost immediately.

'Who has access to keys to the lodge?' I demand.

'Why? What's wrong?' She sounds surprised by my abrupt tone, but this is important.

'I've been thinking about the phone. Someone must have had keys to the house to have been able to leave it in the loft.' My words rattle out of my mouth like bullets from a machine gun.

'Slow down, Megan. Have there been more messages?'

'Just the one.'

I'M DEADLY SERIOUS. LEAVE HIM BEFORE IT'S TOO LATE.

I have to remind myself it's just someone trying to mess with my mind.

'I thought you were going to call me if there'd been anything else,' Harriet reminds me.

'It has to be someone with a key to the lodge. The agency holds spares, doesn't it?'

'Yes, but — '

'So who has access to them?'

'Everyone. They're kept in a safe, but we all have the code.'

I clamp my hand to my forehead and prop my head on my elbow. Everyone? 'Did you tell anyone else what you'd found out about us? About me and the fire?'

'No, of course not. Megan, I wouldn't do that.'

'But what if someone else in your office knows? People don't like child killers, especially women who've killed their own children.'

'Megan, stop it. Don't say that.'

'It's true, Harriet. There's no point denying it. This could be someone in your office.'

There's silence on the line and for a moment I wonder if the call's dropped out.

'Harriet?'

'I'm here,' she says quietly. 'I'm just stepping outside. Hang on.'

I hear her footsteps tap-tap-tapping along a hard surface. A door squeaks open. The background hum of an office fades.

'Sorry, I'm here,' she says.

'Do you keep a record of who's taken keys from the safe?' I ask. 'Do you have to sign them in and out?'

Harriet's sigh whistles in my ear. 'No. We probably ought to, but not at the moment. Sorry.'

'Then maybe you could ask around, subtly? Find out if anyone's been snooping into our background. That would be a start,' I suggest hopefully.

'Sure. Of course. Nobody's said anything, but I'll do my best.'

'Thanks, Harriet. I appreciate it.'

'What are friends for?'

I laugh bitterly. If only she knew how long it's been since I had a friend I could trust.

'How's Colin getting on, by the way?' she asks.

I tune into the persistent banging and crashing going on above my head. 'He's cracking on, but I think he's going to be here for a few days, which means we're going to be without a bathroom for the time being.'

'I'm sorry.'

'Yeah, especially as today was the day I went for my first run in like forever.'

'I didn't know you ran,' Harriet says.

'There's lots you don't know about me,' I tease. 'I used to be a personal trainer, you know, before... '

'No! Seriously? That's amazing.'

'A long time ago. It seems like a different life now. I used to teach, but after the boys were born, I couldn't face going back to it, so I retrained. As Justin said, it made perfect sense as I've always loved sport and keeping fit, and working for myself I could dictate my own hours to fit around childcare.'

'You should get back into it,' Harriet says.

'I'd like to, but Justin doesn't think I'm ready to go back to work yet.'

'Nonsense. It would do you good.'

'You think so?' I lean back in my chair. It would certainly give me something to fill my days and maybe even help me meet some new people.

'One hundred per cent. We could do with someone like you around here to put us all through our paces. The area's been crying out for it. I'll be your first client.'

I laugh, but I'm not sure she's not joking.

'I mean it,' she continues. 'I'd sign up on the spot if you agreed to take me on.'

'I - I'm not sure,' I stammer. What would Justin say? It's not as if we need the money.

'Do it for my sake, if not your own,' Harriet says.

'You think I should?'

'I'm begging you.'

It would be good for me. I know my state of mind better than Justin, and if I start with Harriet as a client, it's only going to be a few hours a week. It's hardly going to be stressful.

'Alright,' I say. 'Why not?' Justin will understand when I explain how much this means to me and how it's exactly what I need to help me adjust to our new life in Cornwall. He won't object to that, surely? 'We'll need to do an assessment session first, to see what level of fitness you're at, and then I can come up with a dedicated plan for you.'

'Perfect. Shall we say tomorrow night? I can pop over after work.'

'Okay. I'll see you then. Here's to my first new client in Cornwall,' I say with a smile.

I'll just have to deal with Justin later.

Chapter 13

The decision to return to work feels like a turning point. It's not only an excuse to get out of the house but it'll give me a new focus and less time to spend dwelling on the past. That's what Justin wanted, wasn't it? For us to heal and reboot. Well, that's exactly what I'm doing.

The house was supposed to be a new start for us, but returning to personal training, a job I've always loved, feels like a bigger step. The thing I've been craving, without realising it. For the first time in a long time, I feel energised and even a little excited.

I refuse to let this nonsense with that phone and those stupid messages consume me. I know sometimes I can be a little obsessive about things, but not this time. I'm taking back control. In fact, there's something else I can do that I should have done before.

I scrape back my chair, pushing the sheet of paper and my pen to one side, and march up the stairs. Past the bathroom where I glimpse Colin, covered in white dust, standing in a pile of rubble that used to be the tiles on the wall, and head determinedly into our bedroom.

As I throw open the door, a fleeting flashback flickers across my mind's eye. Cans and bottles strewn across the floor. A grubby old blue sleeping bag laid out across our bed. The old man smell of sweat and stale tobacco smoke.

I falter for a second but push the memory away. The squatter's gone now. And they're not coming back. I refuse to be cowed by fear and I won't be intimidated, especially by anonymous text messages spouting nonsense.

The drawer to my bedside cabinet jams as I yank it open too forcefully, pulling it out of alignment. I have to jiggle it back and forth to free it, hearing the phone rattling around inside. Eventually, it slides open as if it was just teasing me. And there it is, lying there all innocently. The old Nokia with its tiny scratched screen and worn silver keypad.

I'm not even going to check it for any new messages. I've had enough. I snatch it up and hurl it across the room with a scream of frustration and all the strength I can muster. It strikes the wall with a loud crack and bounces onto the floor. As if to taunt me, the phone remains perfectly intact. There's not so much as a crack in the plastic casing. Bloody typical. I dropped my expensive smartphone down the stairs and now it's barely working. This old phone, by comparison, looks like it would survive a nuclear holocaust.

'Everything okay?' Colin's head pokes around the door. I clutch my breast in surprise. 'I thought I heard a scream.'

'Sorry,' I gasp. 'Yes, I'm fine. Thanks.'

He stares at me for a second or two, as if trying to assess whether I really am fine. 'Right you are, then. I'll get back to it.'

'Actually, Colin,' I say as he's about to leave, 'I don't suppose you have a hammer I could borrow?'

'A hammer?' He frowns.

'Yes.'

'Sure.' He withdraws from the room and reappears a moment later with a heavy-duty tradesman's claw hammer with a thick rubber handle and a meaty head. 'Will this do?'

'Perfect.'

He stands and watches, bemused, as I swing it and catch it in my palm a couple of times, testing its weight. This should do the job.

With Colin still watching, I cross the room, get down on one knee and strike the phone hard. It makes a satisfying crunching sound, the force of the blow causing it to jump off the carpet, like a heart attack victim on the end of a lifesaving electric shock.

I hit it again. And again. And again. Until there's not much left of it other than shards of splintered plastic and shattered circuit boards.

I stop to catch my breath, my shoulder aching, and push sweaty strands of hair out of my eyes.

'Thanks,' I say, handing the hammer back to Colin, who's standing in the door with eyes wide in shock and puzzlement.

'You're welcome,' he mumbles.

'Can I make you a cup of tea?' I ask casually, still panting from the exertion.

Colin's gaze doesn't shift from the remnants of the phone. He must think I've completely lost the plot. 'Milk, two sugars,' he mutters.

I'm dying to tell Justin about my decision to go back to personal training, but I know better than to call him when he's working, especially when he's running a course. He thinks it's unprofessional for me to call when he has clients, so I have to wait until the evening, when he has the time to ring me.

At least it gives me the chance to think about how I'm going to explain why it's such a good idea. I don't want him to think I'm acting on a whim or worse, undermining him. But this is what I need. It's going to help me get back on my feet, and that has to be a good thing for both of us.

When Justin does finally call, I've just nodded off in front of the TV. I jerk awake and snatch the phone off the arm of the sofa.

'Hey, babe, how's it going?' I say with a smile. He's only been gone for a day but I'm already missing him, especially being stuck in this old house on my own.

'Megan?' he shouts over the background noise of what sounds like a busy bar.

'How's it going?'

'Good. I can't talk for long,' he yells, slurring his words. He's obviously been drinking, but he often takes clients out in the evening when he's running courses. He says it helps to break down barriers. 'We're just having a few beers. Everything okay?'

'Yeah, it's fine,' I say, struggling to keep the disappointment from my voice. I'd hoped we'd have the chance for a long chat tonight. Now is clearly not the time to tell him about my decision to return to work. It'll have to wait.

'Did you get out of the house today?' I hear someone calling his name and the line muffles, as if he's holding his hand over the receiver.

'I went for a run.' I yell unnecessarily as I turn down the volume on the television.

There's a pause before the muffled line clears. 'What's that, Megs?'

'I went for a run,' I shout.

'Oh, that's good.'

'And Colin's been here working on the bathroom. He's found a leaking pipe in the wall.'

'What's that? I can't really hear you.'

'Colin's fixing the bathroom.' This is hopeless. What's the point phoning from a bar that's so noisy he can't hear me? He could have at least stepped outside.

'I've got to go. I'll call you tomorrow. Love you,' he says.

'Love you too,' I reply, but the pips in my ear tell me he's already hung up.

I lower the phone, gaze at the cracked screen and sigh. I admire how Justin's been able to bounce back so easily. It's not that he isn't hurting, but he's able to pull this mask down on his feelings and keep them hidden. It's allowed him to get back to doing what he does best, running his business.

Sometimes it would be nice to talk about what's going through his mind, but he doesn't like to be reminded about Felix and Sebastian and that they're gone. It's his way of coping, I suppose. I'd rather keep their memories alive by talking about all the funny things they did and the great times we had together, even if it is painful. The last thing I want is to put them out of my mind and forget about them.

Before dragging myself to bed, I go around the house checking all the doors are locked and the windows secured. I know I'm being overcautious, but I'm stuck here in the middle of nowhere and the house still gives me the creeps. I'd have been like this even if we hadn't discovered someone had been squatting in our bedroom. In time, I'm sure I'll get used to being so isolated, but for now, with Justin away, it's hard to relax.

Finally, I check all the electrical appliances are unplugged. I don't take any chances these days, knowing how quickly and easily fire can spread, and then I haul myself up to the bedroom. The smashed up old Nokia is in bits on the floor. I brush them towards the skirting board with my foot, promising myself I'll clean it up in the morning, and climb into bed.

I switch off the light and close my eyes, but I can't sleep. I'm tired but wired, all my senses on high alert. The noises in the house seem louder tonight without Justin here. The creak of timbers like small explosions. The scratching in the roof space above like fingernails down a chalkboard. The wind in the trees like the rush of a tempestuous sea. My mind's in turmoil, imagining every pop and tap is someone inside, creeping up the stairs in the dark, heading for my room.

When I do eventually slip into a troubled slumber, my dreams are plagued by terrifying dreams of men in dark clothing armed with keys, letting themselves into the house and stealing up the stairs, coming for me. Several times I jar awake, my body damp with sweat. It leaves me tense and exhausted, but grateful when the sun finally rises and chases the night away.

Colin arrives just after eight to continue on the bathroom. I never thought I'd be so pleased to see him, and at least this time he knocks, although he doesn't waste much time on small talk, preferring to get on with the job. That's fine. I don't have much to say, and when the crashing and banging begins again, I take it as a prompt to get out of the house.

With Harriet's fitness assessment due, I really need to work on my own condition. It would be pretty embarrassing if she was fitter than me. My legs are a little stiff and sore from yesterday's run, but I figure a slow, easy-paced recovery jog will do me good. Just a couple of miles at a low intensity to get the blood flowing again.

I pull on my leggings, find a clean T-shirt and long-sleeved top and, grabbing my running shoes, head out, leaving Colin to it. I set off at a steady pace, through the woods, following a narrow path that I now know heads deeper into the estate.

It must have rained last night as the ground is damp and springy beneath my feet, the leaves on the trees glistening with water droplets and the air heady with the peaty scent of damp earth. I splash through puddles and soon my feet and legs are soaked and mud-splattered.

At a fork in the path, I try a different route to the one I ran yesterday, but it quickly becomes difficult to navigate with thick nettles clumping in bushy patches and tangles of prickly vines that scratch my legs. It slows me down, but doesn't put me off. It's nice to be out again, filling my lungs with fresh air.

It doesn't take long before the path dumps me out close to the big house at the top of the drive once more, although this time I seem to be at the rear of the property.

I slow to a walk to reorientate myself. The back of the house is less grand than the front. It's where all the pipework and air ducting is hidden, together with some ugly brickwork extensions. There are all sorts of stone outbuildings tucked away around here too, stables and sheds and what looks like an old milking parlour.

It all looks sadly deserted, and with no one around I find myself drawn closer, the urge to take another quick peek inside and imagine what it would be like to live in somewhere so fabulous, irresistible.

It's such a shame the house is left empty for so many months of the year when you think of all the people who struggle to find a roof over their heads. There must be a dozen bedrooms or more in a place like this, all locked up and unused.

Even though there's an eerie quiet about the place, punctuated only by the caw-caws of crows flapping in the tops of the surrounding trees, I can clearly picture the house bubbling with life, the Carlyons' young family filling it with energy and laughter. It's sad now that the children, Arabella and Finn, I think Justin said they're called, have grown up and fled the nest and their elderly parents spend most of their time warming their ageing joints in the hotter climes of the Med.

At least they had their time together. The family fracturing slowly with time and age. The Carlyons had the opportunity to watch their children grow and flourish and eventually fly away. I envy them. That's something we'll never have. Our family was shattered, our children snatched from us, never destined to grow old, make their own way in the world or have families of their own.

I push away a threatening cloud of depression as I creep around the house and emerge onto the damp lawn where a blackbird hops across the grass, head bowed, hunting for worms. When it sees me, it takes flight, calling out in alarm and vanishing into the depths of a rhododendron bush.

One more quick look inside, that's all. A glimpse of a life I can only imagine, fuel for a fantasy of living in a house like this, the rooms and corridors flooded with the sound of children playing. Lazy family lunches at a grand table groaning with food. Christmases together under an enormous tree heaving with baubles and lights above piles of beautifully wrapped gifts.

I shouldn't torture myself, but who doesn't love to dream?

I aim for a bay window that bows out into the garden. I know it's wrong. I shouldn't be here, snooping around, but I'm not doing any harm.

The window is higher than I first thought and I have to step onto an ornamental rock positioned in a flowerbed to see inside. I clutch the stone sill, gripping it for balance with the tips of my fingers, and crane my neck.

My reflection stares back at me, a ghoulish silhouette against a background of trees and bushes. I lift one hand off the sill to shade my eyes and squint into the darkness.

Was that movement? A flicker of something shifting inside the house?

Or just the shimmer of a reflection in the glass?

I snatch a breath and hold it, not daring to move.

The house is supposed to be empty, the Carlyons away in France. Unless it's a cleaner or a housekeeper here to maintain the property while they're away. I hadn't considered that.

Shit.

Moving slowly, carefully, I step down from the rock, my feet tangling in a knot of vegetation, my eyes fixed on the glass.

I back away, one step at a time.

I can't be caught prying. How would I explain that? I'd die from embarrassment.

Maybe if I can make it to the shade of one of the enormous oak trees on the edge of the lawn, I can get away without being spotted. Run back to the lodge and no one will ever know I was here.

I almost trip on a raised edge around the flower bed, my arms wheeling to catch my balance. I bite my lip to silence a squeal.

And then I see it.

Right there in the window. Just behind the glass. A face. Two flat eyes. Staring right back at me.

Chapter 14

My hand flies to my mouth to silence a scream. I stumble backwards, my feet catching on my legs, and with limbs flailing, I land on the wet grass, my gaze never leaving the window.

But whatever it was, whoever it was, has disappeared as quickly as they'd come into view.

Did I imagine it?

I don't think so.

It was definitely a face. A man with deep-set eyes, a thin nose and was that a beard? It was all such a shock, I couldn't take it in.

It must have been one of the Carlyon's staff. Who else would be in the house? And I'm pretty sure they must have seen me. How could they not? I virtually had my nose pressed up to the glass.

Oh god, how embarrassing.

I scramble to my feet, brushing moisture and grass off my leggings as I slink away, head down, shoulders hunched.

What if they call the police? What am I supposed to tell them? They'll think I'm some kind of deranged stalker.

I'm halfway across the lawn, creeping on tip-toes towards the cover of the trees, when another thought creeps into my mind.

What if it was someone who isn't supposed to be in the house? An old, historic property like this, heaving with antiques and valuable paintings left empty for months on end, is a criminal's dream. What if

I've inadvertently disturbed an intruder? I can't walk away and pretend I've not seen anything. What if the house is being ransacked right now and I did nothing?

My heart is telling me to run, to get as far away as possible, but my conscience roots my feet to the spot in the middle of the lawn. I should call the police. I could say I was jogging and thought I'd heard a noise coming from the house. Better to be safe than sorry.

I reach for the zipped pocket in the back of my leggings where I usually carry my phone, but it's empty. Now I think of it, I'm not sure I picked it up before I left the lodge. I put it down by the side of my bed while I was getting dressed. Damn. Should I run back for it? It would probably only take me five minutes at a quick pace. But what if I'm wrong? What if I only imagined seeing someone?

I draw in a deep breath and, with baby steps, edge back towards the house and the big bay window, keeping low.

Adrenaline surges through my body and, as I step back into the flowerbed under the window, I shiver. Slowly, I stand upright, grab the stone sill and climb up onto the rock, every muscle wound tight.

I'm half expecting to be confronted by a scene of carnage. Chairs knocked over. Drawers pulled open and their contents spilled across the floor. Dark rectangles on the walls revealing where paintings have been removed.

But what I see shocks me even more deeply.

There's an eclectic collection of Louis XV-style chairs dotted around an elegantly carved marble fireplace and a freaky bearskin rug spread across a threadbare carpet, but it's what's covering the rest of the floor by the window that catches my eye and snatches my breath away.

Crushed beer cans. Empty bottles. Dirty ashtrays. And a grubby old blue sleeping bag, which I'm sure is the same one I found in our bedroom at the lodge, draped across a chaise longue. Whoever was squatting in our house clearly hasn't moved far.

'What are you doing here?'

I stumble off the rock, grazing my hand on the windowsill as I attempt to catch my balance, the voice taking me by surprise.

I whirl around, raising my hands in defence, instinctively looking for somewhere to run.

'I - I... ' I stammer.

But rather than coming face to face with the stocky, masked burglar I was expecting, a scrawny man with straggly, flyaway hair, unkempt beard and a faded yellow T-shirt that hangs limply on his skinny body is standing with his hands at his sides, fists clenched.

He looks more like a homeless drifter or a beach bum than a burglar.

'Who are you?' he snaps, looking me up and down with narrowing eyes.

'No one,' I say. 'I live here.' I aim my arm down the drive, towards the lodge. 'Who are you?'

'This is private property.'

I'm confused. He speaks as he if owns the place, or at least has the right to be here, which I don't.

'I was looking for Colin,' I lie, seizing on the first thought that comes to mind. 'We're renting the lodge. There's a problem with the bathroom.'

The man frowns. 'He's not here.'

'Right, okay,' I say, trying to sound nonchalant. 'I hadn't realised the house was occupied while the Carlyons are away. The rental agency didn't say anything about it.'

He stares at me for an uncomfortably long period. Eventually, he says, '*You're* renting the lodge?' He spits the words like an accusation.

'Yes, my husband and I moved in at the weekend.' He doesn't need to know Justin's away on business. 'Are you looking after the house while the Carlyons are in France?'

'It's my parents' house,' he says, 'and you shouldn't be here. This part of the estate is out of bounds.'

The penny slowly drops. But surely this scruffy, bearded man can't be Sir Roger Carlyon's son. Justin's childhood friend. 'Finn?'

He glares at me. 'Do I know you?'

'No, but you know my husband, Justin. Justin Pike.'

A wiry eyebrow shoots up, and his jaw falls slack. 'Justin? He's back *here*? In the lodge? Is this some kind of wind up?'

I shake my head. 'No, we were looking for somewhere to rent and when he saw the house was available, he couldn't wait to return,' I say. 'He's going to be thrilled you're still around. I think he assumed you must have moved away.'

'Why would he want to come back?' he says with such naked aggression, I'm momentarily thrown. 'He's not welcome here. He knows that.'

Why is everyone around here so hostile to Justin's return?

'Why? Did you two fall out or something?'

He glowers at me, silently. Finally, he says, 'You shouldn't be up here poking your nose around.'

I'm about to point out the irony of being lectured on trespass by a squatter, but think better of it. Didn't Harriet say that Sir Roger had washed his hands of Finn after some failed business arrangement?

'I wasn't poking my nose in anywhere. Like I said, I thought I heard a noise coming from the house and I was concerned there might an intruder.'

'You should go.'

'What happened between you and Justin? Did you two fall out?'

'He hasn't told you?' He glances down at his bare feet, black with dirt.

'Told me what?'

'Why don't you ask him? I'm sure he'll fill you in on all the gory details.'

'I have, but he says there wasn't anything. He said — '

But my words are cut short by the sound of an approaching car. A shiny black Range Rover slips into view from behind a broad oak tree, moving at a funereal pace up the drive.

'Fuck!' Finn yelps, his face tightening in horror.

'What is it?'

'My parents. They're not supposed to be back for weeks,' he says.

Then he turns and sprints away, vanishing around the side of the house.

His panic is infectious. I follow him, conscious I have no excuse to be loitering around the house. And I don't want to be caught by Sir Roger and his wife.

As I turn the corner, I spot Finn disappearing into the house through a side entrance. I run straight past, back by the old milking parlour and into the woods without a backwards glance.

I have nothing to hide, but I can't face the Carlyons today, not when I'm covered in sweat and still in my running gear. That's hardly going to make a favourable impression on them. But I do want to talk to them. And soon. Maybe they'll be able to tell me what happened with Justin and why everybody seems to have an objection to him coming back. But for now, it's best if I leave it and let them get settled in.

I pick up a trail through the trees, out of sight of the house and the drive and break into a gentle jog.

And now, at least, I have another suspect to consider. Someone who had access to the lodge and could have planted that phone, and who has a grudge against Justin, even if I have no idea why.

Chapter 15

Harriet arrives at the lodge on the stroke of six in her fancy sports car with its roof down, and dressed in a flattering pair of maroon leggings which she's paired with a loose cotton top over a black sports bra. Even in her gym wear, with her hair tied back in a tight ponytail, she looks elegant and sophisticated. How does she make it look so effortless?

She perches a pair of fashionably large sunglasses on the top of her head and greets me with kisses on both cheeks. It's so good to see a friendly face after my run-in with Finn and having Colin in the house all day.

'So tell me what you're hoping to achieve with these sessions. What are your fitness goals?' I ask, slotting back into the role of personal trainer. It's like riding a bike. Once mastered, never forgotten.

'I don't know really,' Harriet says, hands on her hips. 'I guess I just want to maintain my weight and be a bit healthier.'

'Sure, I can help with that. We'll build a programme for you that incorporates some cardio, but we'll also look at your muscle strength,' I tell her, before putting her through a series of flexibility tests to see what I've got to work with.

Finally, I take her on a short run up to the main house and back to assess her cardiovascular levels.

'So, what do you think?' Harriet asks, wiping the back of her hand across her brow as we return hot and breathless to the lodge. 'Am I a dead loss?'

I laugh. 'Not quite. Actually, you're in pretty good shape.'

'For a woman of my age?'

'I didn't say that! But you have some tightness in your hips and hamstrings. Plus, there's some reduced mobility in your right shoulder, but there's plenty we can work with,' I say.

'Brilliant. I can't wait to get cracking.'

'I'll draw up a fitness programme and we can take it from there.' I check my watch. We've been going for almost an hour but the time's flown.

'I'd better be getting off then,' Harriet says.

'Or stay,' I say. We've not had the chance to chat and I really want to tell her about my encounter with Finn, and the Carlyons' unexpected return. And with Justin away, I'm facing another lonely evening in the house on my own. 'I could make us something to eat.'

Am I being pushy? Over-friendly? I'm practically begging her to stay for dinner.

'Only if you want to,' I add hurriedly. 'I was going to throw together a quick stir-fry, but there's more than enough for two with Justin away. But you've probably got plans. A family to get back to.'

'I'd love to,' Harriet beams.

'Yeah?'

'Sounds wonderful. As long as you don't mind me in my gym gear, all hot and sweaty,' she adds with a grin.

'You and me both. I still can't use the bathroom, so I've been having to wash in the kitchen sink.'

Harriet pulls a face. 'Uh, really? Poor you.'

'Justin's picked a good week to be staying in a hotel.'

'When's he back?'

'Hopefully tomorrow night.' I can't wait. I'm used to him going away but I've never liked it, and it's been particularly tough this time around in the new house.

Harriet follows me into the kitchen and leans against a worktop as I dice peppers and slice carrots, shred cabbage and chop up baby corn before tossing it all in a frying pan with some noodles and prawns.

'I think I've worked out who our squatter was,' I announce over the hiss of the steaming pan.

Harriet raises an eyebrow.

'Finn Carlyon. I caught him at the main house. He tried to make out he was looking after the place while his parents were away.' I spare her the details of what I was doing there in the first place and how Finn spotted me prying through the window.

'I doubt his parents know anything about it. He and his father don't speak. Sir Roger's as good as washed his hands of him,' Harriet says.

I nod as I reach into a cupboard for two plates. 'And another thing, the Carlyons are back. They turned up earlier today when Finn was accusing *me* of trespassing.'

'He did what?' Harriet's eyes grow wide with surprise.

'I know. Crazy, isn't it?'

'Did you speak to them?'

'The Carlyons? No, I didn't want to bother them if they'd had a long journey home. I'll catch up with them later. Anyway, it put the wind up Finn.'

'I bet it did,' Harriet smirks.

I hesitate for a beat. 'What do you know about him?' I ask.

'Finn? Not much. He's a bit of a free spirit. Sir Roger spent a fortune putting him and Arabella through private school hoping he'd get a job in the City or follow in his father's footsteps into law. I'm sure he had ideas for Finn to go into politics too, but he wasn't interested in any of that.'

I serve up the food and we take our plates into the lounge to eat on our laps. It's only a casual supper. Sitting at the table in the dining room feels stuffy and formal.

'All Finn was interested in,' Harriet continues as she sits, 'was hanging out on the beach, surfing. He was a total dropout. A real embarrassment to his parents.'

'So what was this business venture?' I ask.

'Finn came up with the idea for a surf shack, near Newquay. It was only a small business, but it was something, and when he went to his father, cap in hand for a loan, Sir Roger agreed to lend him some start-up capital.'

'But it didn't work out?'

Harriet takes a mouthful of food, makes some appreciative noises, and shakes her head. 'Finn's heart was never in it. The business lasted less than a year before it folded and Sir Roger never saw a penny of his investment back. By all accounts, there was a big row and Finn was as good as cast out of the family. The last I heard, he was couch-surfing with friends.'

'You're well informed,' I say, impressed by her knowledge. 'How do you know all this stuff?'

She taps the side of her nose. 'Local gossip. I keep my ear to the ground and people tell me things. Everyone around here knows what Finn Carlyon's like.'

'Do you think he's got a key to the lodge?' I ask.

'I wouldn't have thought so, but it's possible, I suppose. Why, do you think Finn might have something to do with that phone?'

'It's just that Colin said he checked all the doors and windows and there was no sign of a forced entry. So how did he get in?'

'You're not worried he'll be back, are you?'

'I was, but I don't think he'll bother us,' I say. 'Especially since he knows Justin's back.'

'They were friends when they were kids, weren't they?' Harriet's eyes narrow.

'I thought so, but Finn said Justin wasn't welcome back here and couldn't understand why he'd returned.'

Harriet frowns. 'Did he say why?'

'Only that I should ask Justin. But did you notice Colin was really off with Justin as well? I've tried asking him about it, but he just clams up. Something happened, but I don't know what. Justin did something to upset everyone, but I can't get to the bottom of it.'

Harriet listens to me patiently. It feels good to offload. 'And you think the phone and the messages are connected to what happened?'

'Maybe. Until I can get some sense out of someone here about what Justin is supposed to have done, I don't know for sure. For all I know, it could equally have something to do with the fire.'

'No more messages?'

'No, and there won't be. I destroyed the phone with Colin's hammer. I'd had enough. All the while it was in the house, it was preying on my mind.'

'I'm sure you've done the right thing.'

'I know I have,' I say. Like removing myself from social media when the trolls started targeting me after the boys' death. 'Did you have time to ask around in the office, by the way?'

'Nothing yet. I'll keep my ear to the ground,' she says.

'I don't want to be constantly looking over my shoulder, worrying someone's out to make me pay for what I've done. It's not like I haven't suffered enough.'

'I know,' Harriet soothes. 'You've been through so much already.'

'The guilt and the pain are my penance, but it has nothing to do with anyone else, other than Justin. And he's forgiven me, even though he has every reason to hate me. That's why these messages are so surreal, trying to make me think he's dangerous. Whoever's sending them really doesn't know him at all.'

'I admire you. So many couples would have fallen apart in your situation.' Harriet finishes her meal and puts her plate on the floor. 'It must have put a strain on your marriage though?'

'Of course it did, but what choice did we have? Either we let the cracks develop into fissures that would eventually tear us apart, or we plaster over them and come out the other side stronger.'

'It can't have been easy though.'

'It hasn't. And we're still working at it. We're not perfect, but we'll get through this together.'

Harriet gives me a tight-lipped smile and reaches across the sofa to rub my arm affectionately. 'And if you ever need someone to talk to about it, you know I'm here for you, right?'

'I know. That means a lot. I don't have many friends, if I'm honest.'

'Not even in Plymouth?'

I shake my head. 'A lot of people pretend to be your friend, but they're totally toxic and in it for themselves, you know, people you meet at antenatal classes and parents of other kids at nursery and school, and I didn't really have anything in common with them. Justin made me see I was better off without them,' I explain.

So many of my friendships were taking a toll on my mental health and I didn't need it in my life. People who used me. Dumped their emotional baggage on me. I'd never really seen it until Justin pointed it out, but he was right. I had enough stresses and worries of my own, without burdening myself with theirs.

'Justin said that?' Harriet asks.

'Not many men would have been that perceptive, but he really understands me. I'm lucky to have him.'

Harriet sits up straighter and tucks her feet under her legs. 'Justin told you to cut the ties with your friends?'

'No, it's not like that. You're making it sound like something it's not. Anyway, what about you? You know everything about me and I know next to nothing about you.'

'What do you want to know?'

'Is there a Mr Harriet?'

She laughs and picks at the material of the sofa. 'No, I'm single.'

'Really, you surprise me.' I would have thought a good-looking woman like Harriet would have men flocking around her.

'I've just come out of a long-term relationship. My partner, Ollie, walked out on me a few months ago and I'm still trying to readjust to being on my own.'

'Oh, Harriet, I'm so sorry. I didn't mean to put my foot in it.'

'It's okay. You weren't to know. Anyway I have the cats to keep me company.'

'How many do you have?'

'At the last count, six.'

'Six?'

'I know. I can't help myself. I see these little bundles of fluff, all alone in the world, helpless, and I have to take them in. The house is in chaos.' She laughs, but there's a glimmer of sadness and regret in her eyes. 'It doesn't matter what it is. If it's abandoned or hurt, I've got to give it a home. I've had birds with broken wings, three-legged dogs, even a blind rabbit once.'

'It must cost you a small fortune feeding them.'

She shrugs. 'I don't mind. It's worth every penny.'

My phone rings. I glance at the screen and grimace at Harriet. 'Sorry, it's Justin. I'd better take it or he'll worry something's happened.'

'Of course. I'll clear up.' She jumps up and collects our dirty plates as I answer.

'Hey, Megs, how's it going?'

'All good. Missing you though.'

'Awww, I'll be home soon,' he says, bringing a smile to my face.

'Where are you?' I'm glad to hear there's no pub noise in the background tonight.

'In my hotel room. We're just about to pop out for something to eat. Thought I'd give you a quick bell.'

We? Another night out. I shouldn't be jealous. It's his job to schmooze with clients, but even so.

'Good day?' I ask.

'Not bad. What about you? Have you done anything fun?'

'I went for another run. Oh, and the Carlyons are back.' I decide not to tell him I ran into Finn until I've had the chance to find out a bit more about their history.

'I thought they were in France until the summer?'

'So did I. I guess they were missing Cornwall.'

Harriet sweeps back into the room and settles on the sofa, scrolling through her phone.

'Have you seen anyone else?' he asks.

I glance at Harriet guiltily. 'No, I've been on my own all day.'

He's already made it clear he doesn't think Harriet's a suitable friend. I don't want to antagonise him by telling him I've invited her for dinner. He'd only start asking questions and then I'd have to explain why she's here.

'Hope you've not been too lonely without me,' he says.

'When are you back?'

'Hopefully, tomorrow evening. I'll let you know when I'm on the road.'

'Okay,' I say, mentally making a note to prepare a nice meal. Something to make him appreciate what he's been missing. 'Drive safely.'

'I always do.'

'Love you.'

'I'll see you tomorrow.'

He hangs up and I shove the phone down the side of the cushions, conscious that Harriet was listening to every word.

'Why didn't you tell him I was here?' she asks.

I sigh. 'It's complicated. I told you, he doesn't think I'm ready to go back to work yet, so I didn't want to tell him over the phone.'

'Jesus, Megan, it's not the nineteen seventies. A woman can get a job without needing the permission of her husband,' she says.

'I know, I know. I will tell him. Of course I will, but it's not fair to do it over the phone.'

'You shouldn't let him boss you around.'

'I don't!' Is that what she thinks, that I'm some kind of doormat?

'Sorry, I didn't mean to speak out of turn. I just know you've been through a lot this last year. I'd hate to think Justin was taking advantage of that.'

I don't know what to say. 'He loves me,' is all I can manage, but as the words slip from my lips, I hear the defensiveness in my tone.

Justin isn't taking advantage of me. He's looking out for me. Protecting me. Harriet doesn't know what she's talking about.

She stands suddenly. 'It's getting late. I'd better get back,' she says. 'Thanks for dinner.'

'Won't you stay for a bit?'

'No, I have an early start. Thanks again for the assessment. Let me know how much I owe you,' she says, heading for the door.

I wave a hand. 'Don't worry about it. I don't charge for initial assessments.'

'I'm happy to pay.'

I shake my head.

'Fine. I'll speak to you soon then.'

And then she's gone, the front door thudding shut behind her, and I'm all on my own again.

Chapter 16

I haven't been able to stop thinking about Finn and what he said about Justin, nor the way he reacted when I told him he was back at Treloar.

Why would he want to come back? He's not welcome here. He knows that.

Why would Finn say that? Are those text messages his clumsy way of trying to tell me something? Not that I believe for one minute Justin would ever hurt me. But someone's gone to so much effort, I have to know who's behind it and why.

So the next morning, I decide to introduce myself to Sir Roger and Lady Grace. If anyone knows what happened here at Treloar between Justin and Finn, it's them.

It's a bright, warm day for the time of year and I stride briskly up the drive, watching crows dive and soar from the tops of the trees and bushy-tailed squirrels scampering through the undergrowth.

As I approach the house, a willowy woman with white hair and spindly arms is in the garden, pruning a rose bush with a pair of secateurs. I watch from a distance, slowing my pace. She has the poise and refinement of someone of nobility and influence. It has to be Lady Grace. She's almost exactly as I'd pictured her.

My limbs feel heavy, my mouth parched and my mind scrambled with nerves. Now I'm here, I'm not sure what to say. She's a lady, after all. A proper one. With a title and a manor house. I'm just a stranger who's renting a property on the estate. I'll just have to lay on the charm and hope for the best.

'You have a lovely garden,' I say, as I approach. 'It's going to look beautiful in a few weeks when the flowers bloom.'

Lady Grace snips off a dead stalk and with a stiff neck and arthritic joints, slowly turns to face me. She's physically frail, her skin papery thin, but her watery blue eyes reveal a spirited soul. Her penetrating gaze forces me to stare at my feet as she studies me from head to toe.

'I'm Megan.' I smile, but Lady Grace's demeanour doesn't change a fraction. She might be frail but she's as hard as stone. I've overstepped the mark. I've no right turning up and trying to start a conversation as if we're two old friends. How presumptuous of me.

I feel incredibly small. I'm half-minded to turn and run.

Instead, I continue to talk, filling the awkward silence.

'I moved into the lodge at the weekend,' I say. 'With my husband, Justin. I heard you'd returned from France, so I thought I'd come and introduce myself. I see you've brought some of the lovely weather back with you.' I glance up at the clear blue sky, laughing nervously.

Oh god, I want to die.

'I've been admiring your house,' I continue to ramble on, unable to stop now I've started. 'It's no wonder you were keen to get back. Did you have a good journey?'

I finally stop talking when I run out of breath. Lady Grace nods silently.

'So *you're* Justin's wife,' she says, her cut-glass accent straight out of Downton Abbey. 'Colin mentioned he was back.'

'That's right.' I shoot her my friendliest, most disarming smile.

She continues to stare at me as if she's trying to work me out. Judging me. I wish now I'd put on some make-up. Tied my hair back. Instead, here I am in jeans and a T-shirt, having washed in the kitchen sink again this morning. I really wanted to make a good impression, but I hadn't expected she'd be this cold.

A long, pregnant pause builds between us.

I chew my lip and shuffle my feet, my palms clammy.

Eventually, she draws in a long breath through her nose, as if she's finally come to a conclusion about me, and says, 'Would you like tea?'

My chin shoots up. 'Tea would be lovely. Thank you,' I say, sounding as desperately grateful as if she's a traffic cop letting me off a speeding ticket.

She peels off a pair of cream leather gardening gloves and places them on the ground next to her secateurs, then brushes a speck of invisible dirt off her plaid skirt.

I follow her into a delightful orangery where the air is warm and the early morning sun is streaming through floor to ceiling windows. We sit on chairs at a white painted wrought-iron table. A maid appears out of nowhere in a dark uniform, thick black tights and sensible flat shoes.

I didn't know people still employed maids. It all feels outdated. I presume they've been drafted back on the Carlyons' return. They couldn't have been here while Finn was squatting in the house. Does Lady Grace even know about that? Probably not, but it's not my place to say anything.

'Tea for two, please, Victoria,' Lady Grace asks the maid, who dips her head and withdraws so serenely it's as though she's floating on air. 'So tell me, how are you settling into your new home?'

A cute white terrier comes bounding into the room and sniffs my legs curiously. I let him sniff the back of my hand and stroke his flanks as he settles on my foot, rolling his eyes contentedly.

'It's very nice, thank you,' I lie. She doesn't want to hear that I think it's in urgent need of modernisation, that I found a large patch of mould in the bathroom caused by a leaking pipe and that every room smells of damp.

'No, it isn't, is it?' Lady Grace sighs. 'You hate it. It's obvious.'

I'm stunned. I was only trying to be polite but she's seen straight through me.

'No, no, the lodge is beautiful,' I bluster, my cheeks flushing.

'You don't need to sugarcoat it, dear. I can see you're not happy.'

I stare at her for a moment, fighting the surge of emotion she's unwittingly triggered, trying hard to hold it back. But out of nowhere, hot tears bubble up from my chest, balling in my throat and wetting my cheeks. No, I'm not happy, but I've been trying so hard to hide it. That this woman I've just met can see it so clearly is like someone cranking open the floodgates, destroying the carefully constructed dam I'd built to hold my sadness in check.

'I'm sorry,' I sniff. 'I didn't mean to cry.'

Lady Grace pulls a white lace handkerchief from her sleeve and hands it to me.

She allows me a few moments to compose myself, offering no actual words of comfort, I note. And then she asks, 'Where have you come from?'

'Plymouth,' I mumble, embarrassed. 'We had a fire. We lost our house. We lost everything.'

'I'm so sorry.'

'Our two young boys were killed.'

A bony, liver-spotted hand flies to her chest. 'How awful.'

'Felix and Sebastian. We came here to start over. Justin has such fond memories of Treloar, he thought he could find happiness here again. He used to come here with his parents on holiday. I think he was friendly with your own children?'

The maid returns with a tray and a pot of tea. She places two china cups and saucers on the table and pours from the pot before withdrawing silently.

The terrier is still on my foot, lying with his front paws stretched out and his chin on the ground. I like the comfort of his weight and avoid moving so as not to disturb him.

'Yes,' Lady Grace says. 'He was.'

'You remember him, then?' I ask, hopefully.

'Of course.'

'What was he like?'

She ponders for a moment, glancing up at the swaying branch of a horse chestnut tree in full bud. I scan her face, trying to read her thoughts. Is that the outline of a grimace? A slight narrowing of her eyes? A tightening of her jaw?

'He was... an exuberant young man,' she says with the care of a diplomat.

That certainly sounds like Justin. 'I don't think he's changed much,' I say with a rueful smile.

Lady Grace's face hardens. 'I don't mean it as a compliment. He was a terrible influence on my two.'

My smile falls. 'He's a partner in a business consultancy now. He's done really well for himself,' I say, compelled to defend my husband. 'The business is a great success.'

'I'm glad to hear it, although I have to say I'm surprised. I didn't think he'd ever amount to much.'

I can't believe what I'm hearing. To most people, Justin's success is an inevitable byproduct of his confidence and charm. So why does everyone around here have such a low opinion of him? It's almost as though they're talking about a different man.

'Well, he has,' I snort, rolling back my shoulders and sitting ramrod straight. I don't care if she's the Queen of Sheba. I'm not having her bad-mouthing Justin. 'What makes you say that? Did something happen here with him?'

'Perhaps you should ask Justin. He is your husband.' Lady Grace watches me over the rim of her cup as she takes a sip of tea.

'I was hoping you'd tell me.'

As she places the cup back on its saucer, her hand shakes and the china rattles. 'Ask him about the fire and how he almost killed my daughter.'

Fire? What the hell? The word is like a spear to my heart.

'Wh - what fire?' I stammer.

I see a flash of flames. Burning heat. The stench of smoke. Thick and black, clawing at my throat. The panic. The fear. The sound of my own screams drowned out by the roar of the blaze as it consumes everything in its path.

'Arabella was lucky she wasn't seriously hurt, or worse,' Lady Grace continues, her face darkening.

'I didn't know anything about a fire.'

'The children were playing in one of the outbuildings and thought it would be tremendous fun to start a fire while my poor Arabella was locked inside. Can you imagine anything more foolhardy? She was barely conscious when they got to her. She could have died.'

'Died?' Beads of sweat form on my brow and damp patches spread under my arms. It's hot in here. So hot. I can hardly breathe.

'She'd inhaled a lot of smoke.'

'And - and are you suggesting Justin might have started it?'

'He blamed Finn, but I'm sure it was all Justin's idea. That was what he was like. A bad influence,' Lady Grace says.

YOUR HUSBAND IS A DANGEROUS MAN.

No, not Justin. She must be mistaken. She's old and her memory probably isn't what it was. How can she sit there and so brazenly accuse him of something so awful.

'That can't be right,' I gasp.

'She was only fifteen. Not much more than a child. To think she could have been killed. It would have been such a tragedy.'

My head spins.

There's no way Justin could have done what she's suggesting, but why lie about it? She's painting him as some sort of thug. Probably because she disapproved of the friendship he'd struck up with her kids. Stuck up cow. I bet she thought Justin was beneath them, that they were too good for him. So she concocted this ridiculous story about trying to kill Arabella to discredit him. That must be it.

'You're wrong,' I shout, making her eyes widen in surprise. 'Justin isn't like that. You're lying.' I jump out of my chair, startling the terrier on my foot.

I don't think anyone's ever yelled in Lady Grace's face before and for a moment I think she might keel over with the shock.

'He's not a bad man,' I scream, tears pricking my eyes. 'You're making it up. You shouldn't say that about him.'

Her mouth falls open.

'My dear — '

I hold up my hand to stop her. She's said more than enough. 'I don't want to hear it.'

I push my chair back and it topples over, clattering to the floor.

'Thank you for the tea,' I mutter, hurrying away, my head down and my blood boiling.

'You wanted to know what he was like,' she calls after me.

But it's not what I was expecting to hear. I don't want a stranger telling me my husband tried to kill someone.

And yet, at the back of my mind, there's a niggling voice playing the same words over and over.

GET OUT WHILE YOU CAN. WHATEVER YOU DO, DON'T TRUST JUSTIN.

Chapter 17

Justin never mentioned anything about a fire. Maybe he was trying to protect me. He knows how sensitive I am. He probably thought he couldn't tell me because it would be too upsetting. But he must have known there was a danger I'd find out. And if what Lady Grace told me is true, that Arabella nearly died, why would he want to come back here anyway? Wouldn't he have been traumatised? And yet all I've heard from him is how happy he was here. Something doesn't add up. Someone is lying. But why?

If Lady Grace is to be believed, her teenage daughter almost died. It's not something you inadvertently forget to mention. And if she's telling the truth and Justin's kept it from me, what else has he lied about?

With my head whirling, I stomp back to the lodge. I'm going to get to the truth if it kills me.

The front door's locked when I get back, even though Colin's supposed to be here re-tiling the bathroom this morning after finally fixing the leaking pipe.

'Hello? Colin?'

Silence.

I trudge up the stairs and stick my head around the bathroom door. All the new tiles are up and the bath is spotless. I'm impressed. He's done a good job and worked quickly. There's some fresh plaster that needs painting but at least I can have a shower which is some consolation. All the time I've had to use the kitchen sink, I've felt grubby, and my hair desperately needs washing.

In the kitchen, Colin's left a handwritten note asking me to avoid getting the tiles wet for at least twenty-four hours. So much for my shower. I screw the note up, toss it in the bin and pull out my phone.

With one arm crossed over my stomach, I dial Justin's number. I don't care if I'm interrupting. This is important.

There's a long pause before his voice finally comes on the line.

I take a breath, ready to give him hell, before I realise it's his voicemail. He must be in the middle of a training session with his mobile off. I grunt in frustration, slamming the phone down on the counter. I just want to hear his side of the story, but I'm going to have to wait.

Maybe it's not such a bad thing. If I leave it until he gets home, I can look him in the eye. We promised each other we wouldn't keep any more secrets after what happened in Amsterdam. I hope Lady Grace has got it wrong, but it's a hell of a story to make up. And why would she?

The only other person who might shed some light on the mystery in the meantime is Colin. He was here at the time and must know the truth. He definitely knows something. He said as much when I asked him the other day. I don't care if he's not keen on talking to me. This time I'm not going to give him any choice.

I hurry out of the lodge and back up the drive, giving the main house a wide berth. I don't want to bump into Lady Grace again after I was so rude to her earlier.

I remember Harriet told me Colin lives in a cottage in the grounds somewhere behind the house, and it's easy to find, down a muddy track through the trees. It's a functional stone building but in a pretty spot, shaded by oak and horse chestnut trees and overlooking fields shimmering green with the early shoots of a summer crop. A pair of muddy wellington boots have been left on the doorstep and a bird feeder filled with peanuts hangs from a bracket on the wall.

I march determinedly up to the front door and bang on a brass knocker.

After a few moments, the door creaks open and Colin pokes his balding head out, studying me suspiciously.

'Summat wrong with the bathroom?' he asks.

'Tell me about the fire,' I demand. He's not going fob me off this time.

'Don't know what you're talking about.'

'I think you do. The fire here that supposedly almost killed Arabella. What did Justin have to do with it?'

Colin's eyes grow wide, shifting left and right nervously.

'Who told you 'bout that?'

'I had a chat with Lady Carlyon earlier. She didn't exactly have a good word to say about Justin. You told me you were surprised Justin had come back. Was that because of the fire?' I ask.

'I s'pose. Partly.' He opens the door fully and crosses his arms defensively across his chest.

'Partly?' I raise an eyebrow. Even now he's being evasive. 'Come on, Colin. I want the truth. I think I deserve that, don't you? Why were you so surprised that Justin's back? It's more than just the fire, isn't it?'

He chews a callus on the side of his finger, his gaze darting around like a pinball.

'Please, Colin. Tell me. Is there something I ought to know about my husband?'

He sighs, like a man defeated. 'You really want the truth?' he says.

'Yes,' I gasp. 'That's all I've ever wanted.'

He looks me up and down one more time before stepping back into the house. 'You'd best come in then.'

Chapter 18

We sit in a cosy snug with a low ceiling and an open fire overflowing with grey ash, in high-backed armchairs that look as old as Colin himself. There's a fug in the room of old sweat and overboiled veg. It takes all my willpower not to jump up and throw open a window to let in some fresh air.

'You said the other day that Justin was trouble. What did you mean?' I ask.

Colin folds his leathery hands over his stomach. 'He was always a cocky little bugger, always one with an answer for everything. I never liked him much. He was a bad influence on the Carlyon kids, but of course, 'cos he was older, they looked up to him. He encouraged them to do stupid things. Making them do dares and stuff. And kids got no sense, most of 'em.'

I shake my head. Is that all? It sounds harmless enough.

'One year they stole a bottle of vodka from the house and I found Arabella so drunk, she couldn't stand straight,' he says.

'So? Don't all kids dabble with alcohol?'

'She was only twelve.'

'Oh.'

'Another time, one of them caught an adder and let it loose in the house. Then there was the year they all went skinny dipping in the lake. And so it went on,' Colin continues.

'Sounds like they were all just having a bit of fun.' High jinks, my mother would have called it. Maybe I've overreacted. Nothing Colin's said is remotely a cause for concern. It's those bloody text messages, messing with my head.

Colin snorts. 'That was just the start of it, but every year it got worse and worse. They wound each other up to do more and more reckless things the older they got. Once, I caught Finn about to jump from an upstairs window. He'd have broken his blimmin' neck if I hadn't stopped him. Then I caught your Justin joyriding in my Land Rover around the estate.'

The sound of a wood pigeon cooing echoes down the chimney and I notice one of Colin's ugly crooked toes poking through a hole in his sock, the nail all cracked and yellowing. I swallow down my disgust.

'At least he wasn't on the roads,' I say.

'He was blindfolded. I was always worried one of them was going to wind up killed or summat. Every year, their pranks was getting more and more dangerous.'

There's that word again.

Dangerous.

I shuffle in my seat, the lumpy cushion doing little to protect my backside from the springs that are threatening to burst through the frame.

'And the fire?' I press. 'When was that?'

Colin sniffs and clears his throat of loose phlegm. 'It was the last year Justin's family was here, so I'd say around ninety-seven.'

'And this was another of their pranks?' I ask. I lean forwards, my elbows on my knees, sensing we're finally getting somewhere.

'It was some kind of idiotic challenge to see who could stay for the longest in one of the old storage sheds that they'd filled with smoke. God knows why. They found an old brazier, filled it with newspaper and bits of wood and leaves, and set it alight. I mean, what were they thinking?'

'And Arabella was trapped inside?'

'Justin had to drag her out unconscious. 'Course, none of them would own up to starting the fire, although Finn took the blame. His father was furious. And rightly so,' Colin says, scratching at a dark stain on his trousers.

'Hang on a minute,' I say. 'Justin dragged Arabella unconscious from a burning building?'

'That's right.'

Oh my god. Lady Grace has it all wrong. Justin wasn't to blame after all. He didn't nearly kill Arabella. He was a hero. He saved her life.

I flush with pride. Justin's not dangerous. He's the opposite. If anyone's to blame, it sounds as if it was Finn. It was probably lucky Justin was there. Maybe if he hadn't have been, Arabella *would* have died. I bet none of them have considered that.

'She said she couldn't open the door,' Colin continues. 'Although the strange thing is, there was no lock on it.'

'You mean in her panic, she couldn't work out how to open the door?' I know how disorientating it can be confronted with fire, heat and thick choking smoke.

I picture a teenage Justin, muscling Finn out of the way and bundling into the shed to rescue a helpless Arabella, with no fear for his own life or safety. That's so typical of him, like how he tried to save Felix and Sebastian, but was ultimately forced back by the flames. Maybe he never mentioned it because he was too modest. He didn't want to sound like he was bragging.

'Or maybe someone held the door closed so she couldn't get out.' Colin locks his eyes on mine with a challenging stare.

'What are you trying to say?'

'You tell me.'

'Justin? No, I don't believe it. He wouldn't do that. Why would he?' I struggle to keep the panic from my voice. Why would Colin say something like that?

'Like I said, Justin was a troublemaker.' Colin crosses his ankles, causing his toe to poke further out of the hole in his sock, like a deformed mouse peeking out of its burrow. 'He was the instigator. Always trying to push the limits.'

'But he saved her. He risked his own life to pull Arabella out of the building. That's what you said.'

'Only because he knew he'd gone too far this time. And if she'd been able to get out, she wouldn't have needed rescuing, would she?' Colin adds.

'You don't know that. That's just your opinion because you hate Justin.' I dig my fingernails into the arm of the chair.

'You asked what I thought had happened.'

'I wanted the truth,' I yell.

'Can't help you if you won't hear the truth.'

I breathe hot air through my nose, angry with Colin. Angry with Justin. Angry with everyone. 'You said Sir Roger blamed Finn. Why would he blame him if Justin was responsible?'

'Because Justin told him Finn was to blame and Finn was too weak to stand up to his father.'

'So he's a bully now, as well?' I huff.

'Your words, not mine.'

This is insane. The picture he's painting isn't of the man I know. Sure, Justin was only a teenager, but people's fundamental personalities don't change, do they? Colin's making out like he was some kind of psychopath. But I know my husband. We've been through more than most couples will endure in a lifetime. He isn't dangerous to me or anyone else.

'It *was* you, wasn't it?' My eyes narrow as a cloud of uncertainty lifts from my mind. For the first time, I have a sense of what's really going on.

Colin stares at me blankly.

'Come on, no need to act the innocent with me,' I continue. '*You* left that phone in the lodge for me to find. It's *you* who's been sending me those messages.'

'I didn't leave any phone in the lodge,' he protests.

'Don't play games with me, Colin. It's obvious. I know it was you. You could have let yourself in at any time and hidden it in the loft, knowing I'd be curious to look for it when I heard it ringing.'

His eyes grow increasingly wide as I speak. He has a decent poker face, but he's not fooling me anymore.

'I get it. You don't like Justin. It must have been a shock when you heard he was moving into the lodge, but you're not going to drive us apart. We've been through more together than you can imagine, and we're stronger than ever. So if that's your little plan to get back at him, I'll tell you now, it's not going to work, so back off.' I jab my finger angrily in his direction.

Colin stares at me like I'm a woman possessed.

'We're here to stay,' I add, 'so you might as well get used to it.'

Chapter 19

My head's a complete mess. I can't think straight. Everything's all tangled up and knotted like a ball of string shoved in the back of a kitchen drawer. It feels like the harder I tug at the knots to free them, the tighter they become. I know more now about what happened here at Treloar when Justin was a teenager, but instead of making things clearer, I have more questions than answers.

They run around and around in my mind like a hamster on a wheel as I trudge slowly back to the lodge with my head down, watching my feet kick through the gravel.

Did Justin really start that fire? Or was it Finn?

And the story about Arabella being locked in a store shed and almost dying is muddled with inconsistencies. Colin says she was trapped inside by Justin. But he also says Justin saved her life. He dragged her out of the building unconscious when she was presumably overcome by smoke. So either he's a hero. Or a villain. He can't be both. So which is it?

And why is Colin so hostile to Justin after all these years? There's more to this story, I'm sure of it, but how am I going to find the truth? Everyone seems to have an agenda, their own versions of what happened, skewed through the prism of time.

I'm convinced now Colin must have planted that phone in the house and sent those ridiculous texts. As if I was going to take the word of a stranger and leave my husband. Seriously? He really has no idea of the bond that binds us together. The fire and losing Felix and Sebastian were the worst things that could ever have happened to us, but it's also what's cemented our relationship. We're inseparable because we've been through that trauma together.

The only way to find out for sure what went on here is to speak to Justin. I'm sure he doesn't want to talk about it, but I need to hear it. I want to know every detail. No secrets. No lies. At least he's home tonight. I'll cook a nice meal and open a bottle of wine and when he's relaxed, I'll raise the subject.

In the meantime, I need to clear my head. It's spinning so fast, I'm almost dizzy with it. It's another bright, dry day. Perfect for another run, and since I've started going out again, I've realised just how much I've missed it in my life.

I toss my phone on a shelf by the front door and chase up the stairs to change.

But as I'm tugging off my jeans and stumbling onto the bed, hooking them off over my ankles, my mobile rings. I hastily pull on my leggings but by the time I've made it back downstairs, it's stopped.

Through the glaze of the cracked screen, there's a notification that I've missed a call from Justin. I try to call him back, but it diverts immediately to his voicemail.

I should have taken the phone up with me, although I'm not sure I'm ready to speak to him yet. I'd like to get my thoughts straightened out first. I don't want him to think I'm accusing him of anything. He was probably just calling to say he's on his way home.

A message pings onto the screen notifying me I have a new voicemail.

'Hey Megs, sorry, you're probably busy. Just a quick one to say I'm not going to make it home tonight. The course has run over and we've decided to knock it into another day rather than cut it short. I'll definitely be back tomorrow. Can't wait to see you. So, there, yeah, that's it really. Sorry. See you tomorrow.'

I slump to the floor, my back sliding down the wall. Another night away? He was supposed to be on leave this week and yet I've hardly seen him. It's not fair. He promised he'd be here. My whole body feels heavy with disappointment. So much for cooking a nice meal and enjoying a bottle of wine together.

I hate it here. Why did we have to come? The house is old and tired, everyone despises us, and I've never felt so alone in my life. Even after the boys died, I wasn't this lonely. Justin was there for me. We had neighbours and friends looking out for us. Justin's parents helping us through the worst times. Here, I have nobody, other than Harriet. It comes to something when my only friend is the bloody rental agent.

I thought Cornwall would be good for us. The peace, the solitude, the space to think and get well again. A new start, Justin said. Somewhere we'd find comfort and tranquillity. But it has been none of those things. I should have seen the warning signs the moment we stepped into the house. Finding Finn camped in our bedroom was a bad omen, but Justin had been so set on moving to Treloar, caught up in all the happy memories he said he had here, I didn't like to object.

But he hasn't bloody been here!

I really need to get out of the house. The walls are closing in on me and a strong solvent smell from the new tiles in the bathroom is giving me a headache.

I pull on my running shoes and hit the trails, easing into my run even as my tight thighs and calves protest. They're not used to it anymore but I don't care. I push through it. I need to clear my mind.

Running usually boosts my mood, no matter if I'm stressed or anxious or depressed, but today it's not working.

No matter how fast I run, no matter how much effort I expend, I can't stop my brain going over and over the same ground.

Did Justin start that fire?

Did he trap Arabella in a burning building?

And did he deliberately keep it all a secret from me?

Eventually, I give up, exhausted, and head back to the lodge.

I need to talk to somebody who'll understand. Someone who can sympathise and listen to me rant and rave for half an hour.

The only person I have is Harriet. She's said I can phone at any time if there's something on my mind.

'Hey, Megan, what's up?' she says, sounding remarkably spritely when she answers her phone. It's just what I need to shake me out of my mood.

'Did I catch you at work? Are you busy?'

'Never too busy for you.'

'Sorry, I just needed a sympathetic ear,' I say.

'Why? What's happened?'

'I spoke to Lady Grace this morning. She told me there'd been a fire here at Treloar years ago, and that Arabella nearly died.'

'Oh, yeah, that,' she says with a sigh.

'You knew?'

'I heard something about it. I told you, people gossip.'

'I also talked to Colin again. They both made it sound like Justin was to blame.'

The background office hum fades as a door opens and closes. It sounds as though she's stepped out of the office to somewhere quieter to talk.

'And? What do you think?' she asks.

'That's the problem. I don't know what to think. I'm pretty certain it was Colin who left the phone in the house for me to find though. The way he was talking about Justin, he obviously hates him.'

'Seriously?'

'He has the means, motive and opportunity. It has to be him.'

Harriet draws in a deep breath. 'Have you talked to Justin about it?'

'Not yet. I was going to speak to him when he came home later, but he's having to stay another night. He won't be back until tomorrow now.'

'Another night alone?' Harriet says.

'I'm afraid so.'

'No, I'm not having that,' she laughs. 'I'm taking you out.'

'What? No, Harriet, I don't want — '

'No arguments,' she says, dismissing my protests.

But I'm really not in the mood for going out. It was bad enough when Justin insisted we ate in the hotel restaurant last week. I can't be seen out enjoying myself. It wouldn't be right.

'We're going to the pub,' she adds.

'I can't,' I sigh.

'Of course you can. A girls' night out. No excuses, unless you have something else planned?'

'No, but — '

'Great, I'll pick you up at seven. We can talk then.'

Chapter 20

Harriet arrives just before seven in a car I've not seen before. A dark-coloured SUV. It's practical and anonymous, like the cars I used to see the mothers driving when they dropped their kids off at school. It's a far cry from her sporty little two-seater.

'Company car,' she says, noticing my sideways glances at the vehicle when she turns up at the door in a smart jacket, powder pink chiffon blouse and slim-fit beige trousers which show off her enviable figure. It's the sort of consciously effortless look I used to try to pull off.

I'm still in my jeans, but I have risked taking a shower, despite Colin's warnings about the tiles needing time to set, and put a brush through my hair.

'I feel a bit funny about going out,' I say. 'Why don't you come in for a glass of wine instead?'

'Come on, when's the last time you went out for a drink with a friend?' she says, dismissing my offer with a wag of her finger. 'I said I'd take you out and show you around. Consider this the first outing of many.'

'I'm just not sure it's appropriate,' I mumble. I don't want to be a killjoy or seem ungrateful, but the idea of going out to a pub where other people might see me makes me uncomfortable.

Harriet throws her arms up in exasperation. 'I'm not asking you to go out clubbing, for pity's sake. A couple of drinks in the local pub, that's all.'

She's not going to take no for an answer.

Ten minutes later, we're in The Crown, an attractive, white-washed pub with a picket fence around a deserted beer garden, a short drive from Treloar. It's a typical English pub, glowing with lively chatter and fuggy with the smell of hops and spilt beer.

We sit at a table fashioned out of an upturned barrel and Harriet orders two glasses of rosé wine from the bar.

'How did you find Lady Grace?' she asks, folding her jacket neatly on a chair.

'I may have upset her a little.' I wince as I recall standing up and shouting at the poor woman.

'Oh, well, nothing like making a lasting impression.' She laughs. 'What did you do?'

'It's what I said.' I tell her how the old lady had accused Justin of being responsible for the fire that supposedly almost killed Arabella and how I'd screamed at her she was wrong and didn't know my husband at all.

Harriet seems to find it amusing and smirks as I sheepishly recount the conversation.

'I'm not sure anyone's spoken to her like that before in her life,' I say.

'At least she won't forget you in a hurry.'

Then I tell her about my chat with Colin and his version of events.

'The thing is, everyone has a slightly different take on what happened, but they all point the finger at Justin,' I explain. 'But Colin also said that Justin saved Arabella's life when he pulled her out of the building. It's all so confusing, especially as Justin never mentioned any of this before we moved here. You'd think he'd have said something, wouldn't you?'

'He obviously has fond memories of Treloar. And look at it from his perspective. You'd just lost two children to a fire in your home. He was hardly going to bring up that there'd been a fire at Treloar, was he?'

I take a large mouthful of wine. It's cold and refreshingly tart. 'I suppose so, but I thought he would have said something after I confronted him about Colin. You remember how Colin was when he came to the lodge to clean up the bedroom? I can understand now why he was so off with Justin, but when I asked Justin about it, he was adamant he didn't know what was eating him.'

'I guess you need to talk to Justin,' Harriet says.

'I know, but he's busy swanning off god knows where, schmoozing clients. He was supposed to come home this evening, but now I have to wait until tomorrow. He promised he'd take this week as leave. It's so unfair.'

Harriet watches me over the top of her glass, legs crossed, sitting slightly sideways on her chair so that she's almost looking at me over her shoulder.

'What?' I say as she continues to gaze at me saying nothing.

'Nothing. It just seems a little selfish, that's all. He should have been around for you.'

'I'm sure he'll make it up to me. Anyway, tell me what you know about Arabella. You said she looks after the estate properties?'

'She's a right pain in the arse. She's on my case all the time about the lodge. I don't know why she can't just leave me to get on with my job,' Harriet says. 'She drives me mad.'

'Does she live locally then? Perhaps I could speak to her about the fire,' I say, finishing my wine and fishing in my bag for my purse.

'No, she lives in London. Married to some rich banker. They're out in Primrose Hill or somewhere posh like that. I don't think money's any object.'

'Do you want another?' I ask, pointing at Harriet's empty glass.

But she won't hear of me paying, insisting the drinks are on her as a thank you for taking her on as my first new client. I try to argue, but she won't hear of it and I don't want to make a scene.

Harriet slips to the bar and a smile of happiness creeps unexpectedly across my face, catching me unawares. This is lovely. Just what I needed. What I've missed. A friendly ear and a chat over a glass of wine with a girlfriend. I shouldn't feel guilty. Justin's certainly been out enjoying himself, and like he keeps telling me, we need to learn to live again.

Felix and Sebastian aren't coming back, no matter what we do or how much I wish we could turn back the clock. I can't change what's happened, but I can choose whether to let it define my life forever or to move on with their memory close to my heart.

'Does she ever visit Treloar?' I ask when Harriet returns to the table with two more glasses of wine. The first one's already gone to my head and I'm enjoying the alcohol buzz.

'Arabella? Not unless she's after something from Daddy.'

'Do you think she'd talk to me?'

'I wouldn't hold your breath,' Harriet says. 'She's a right haughty cow. Must be all those years of entitlement and privilege.'

'I could try though.'

Harriet nods, but she's frowning into her wine glass, running a finger slowly around its rim as if she's lost in thought.

'What is it? You look like you're miles away.'

She glances up and forces an uncomfortable smile. 'I was just thinking it's a bit odd, that's all.'

'What's a bit odd?'

'I shouldn't say anything. It's not my place.'

'No, go on. We're friends, remember? You can tell me anything,' I say.

'It's just, you know, two fires, thirty years apart. One girl almost died in the first... ' She lets the rest of the sentence hang, allowing me to fill in the blanks.

I shake my head vigorously. 'No, you're way off the mark.'

'You're right. It's a coincidence, that's all.'

A coincidence. Of course it is. Justin was out on the night I started the fire at our house. If he hadn't woken up when he did, I'd have probably died as well. Sometimes I wish I had. But that would have been too easy. My punishment is to live with the consequences of my actions.

'I'm sorry, I shouldn't have said anything. I've brought the mood right down, haven't I?' Harriet says, giving me sad eyes.

'It's fine.' I force a smile.

'Let's talk about something else.' She embarks on a ridiculous story about one woman in her office who binned a bouquet she'd been sent by her boyfriend because the card had fallen off and she thought the flowers had come from one of her clients who'd developed a thing for her and she didn't want her boyfriend getting upset.

She tells the story with passion and enthusiasm, dropping in funny accents and elaborating with exaggerated actions and mimicry, but I'm only half listening.

My mind's back on the fire at Treloar. The fire that almost killed Arabella.

If there was nothing untoward about it, if Justin had nothing to hide, why hadn't he mentioned it before?

We agreed no more secrets.

And yet I can't shake the terrible feeling that my husband has been lying to me.

Chapter 21

I should know my limits by now but Harriet's such a bad influence. She kept buying drinks, and I stupidly kept drinking them until I'd lost track of how many I'd had and didn't care anymore. This morning my head is thick and stomach rolling. My lips are dry and cracked, there's a nasty film on my teeth and I'm being hit by waves of nausea which have had me scuttling to the bathroom and dry retching over the toilet bowl several times already.

I sit at the kitchen table feeling like death, cradling a mug of black coffee hoping it will revive my energy levels. I don't even remember how I made it home, although I have a vague recollection of Harriet calling for a taxi and struggling not to be sick as we hurtled around the twisty lanes. The rest is a blank.

I remember having fun though. It's been a long time since I'd laughed like that. Since I'd laughed at all. Harriet is brilliant company. She has so many stories and anecdotes. At one stage, I was begging her to stop. My jaw was aching so much.

It was like lifting the lid on a pressure cooker, relieving all the tension and pain I'd been holding inside since the fire. She didn't judge me. She didn't care that I'd killed my children or want to talk about it incessantly, probing me about how I was coping and how I felt, like some well-intentioned "friends" have done in the past. We just talked and laughed like old mates.

I take my coffee into the living room, still in my pyjamas and dressing gown, and curl up on the sofa. I attempt to read the news on my phone, but between the cracked screen and my swimming head, it's impossible. I don't envy Harriet if she's supposed to be working today and her hangover is anything like mine.

Luckily, I don't have any plans. I never have any plans. I can take it easy. Maybe I'll watch a movie or read a book. As long as I'm dressed by the time Justin gets home. He wouldn't appreciate me lounging around in my dressing gown all day. Even in the darkest depths of depression after we lost Felix and Sebastian, he'd always insisted I made an effort to get dressed. It's the little things that make all the difference, he said.

Hopefully I'll be feeling brighter by the time he gets back. I have so many questions for him. So much I need to get straight in my head. All I want is the truth. I don't want to believe he was keeping secrets from me when he didn't mention the fire here at Treloar, but you don't forget something like that, do you?

Not that I'm in any position to judge. At least no one actually died at Treloar. So why hide it from me? We've always been honest with each other. Well, at least I've always been honest with him. But if there's no trust between us, how can there be a future? I forgave him once. I'm not sure I could forgive him again, although after everything I've already lost, I can't risk losing Justin as well.

I snatch up the remote from the coffee table, flick on the TV and channel hop from one trashy programme to the next. Who the hell watches this crap? So many home renovation series and American TV dramas, most of it total drivel. I'm about to give up and try the radio when I hear what sounds like a key scraping in the lock.

I sit up too quickly, making my head spin and my stomach plummet. Surely it can't be Justin home already? Unless it's Colin come to check on the bathroom, but it's rude not to knock before letting himself in, knowing I'm here alone.

My momentary panicked paralysis loosens its grip. I jump up and march into the hall, wrapping my dressing gown tightly around my waist, as the front door flies open.

But it's not Justin. Or Colin. It's a woman I've never seen before in my life. Stoic. Beautiful. Immaculate make-up, like it's been applied by a professional. Strong cheekbones. Dusky eyes.

'Yes?' I say, wrong-footed by her boldness. She stands in the door looking totally unfazed, like she belongs here.

'I want to see Justin,' she demands, lifting her chin and looking down her nose at me. 'Is he here?'

'He's not in right now,' I grumble, folding my arms across my chest. 'Who are you?'

It's hard not to jump to conclusions but when a young, attractive woman comes to the house demanding to see your husband, it's natural to be suspicious.

She looks me up and down with a sneer of contempt and I wish now I'd had a shower and thrown on some clothes, although I doubt it would matter what I was wearing, I'd always be eclipsed by this woman. She's tall and leggy like a model and carries it with a natural assuredness, bordering on arrogance.

'Well, when he's back?' she huffs, screwing up her nose. 'And who are you?'

'Megan. Justin's wife,' I say, drawing on as much confidence as I can muster, reminding myself this is my house and she's the intruder.

Her sneer fades and a look of incredulity and amusement crosses her face. 'You married him?' she scoffs. 'Oh my god, you poor thing. What did you want to go and do that for?'

I feel my jaw tighten as my hackles rise. Who does she think she is, talking to me like that? And then all the pieces of the jigsaw slot into place. She has her mother's eyes and the same nose, delicate and ladylike with a slight upturn at its tip, as if she's pressing it against a pane of glass.

'Arabella?'

'It's just Bella these days, thank you,' she replies, wafting an affected, limp-wristed hand in the air. 'He told you about me then?'

'I thought you were in London,' I splutter. She's nothing like I imagined. Far posher. Much more trendy and intimidating. But she's here and maybe I can finally ask her about the fire.

'I popped back to see Mummy and Daddy,' she says, as if the distance between London and Cornwall is nothing at all. 'And because I heard *he* was back. Now, here's the thing. I want you out.'

'What?'

'You heard. I want you out of the house. Preferably by the end of the day. I don't want you living here anymore.'

A nervous laugh tumbles from my mouth. 'That's ridiculous. You can't throw us out.'

'It's my house. I can do what I bloody well like. And I don't want you here.'

My jaw almost hits the floor. She can't evict us, can she? Not without giving us notice. I'm sure there are laws against that sort of thing.

'Look, whatever the problem is, I'm sure we can come to an arrangement,' I say, my panic rising. If she throws us out, we'll be homeless.

'Didn't you hear?' She leans closer and raises her voice as if she's speaking to a disobedient child. 'I want you gone. And the sooner the better.'

A light breeze blows through the open door where Arabella is standing perfectly framed, and I have a sudden urge to shove her in the chest, back out into the garden.

'Please,' I beg, 'don't do this. We have nowhere else to go.'

'That's not my problem. Just pack your bags and get out.'

'But why?' I'm shaking now. I don't know what to do. Where's Justin when I need him?

'Because he had no right coming back here after all these years, upsetting Mummy and Daddy like that,' she says.

But they haven't even seen him. He's been away working longer than he's spent at Treloar so far. 'But where will we go?'

'I don't know and I don't care.' She's getting increasingly agitated but I'm not going anywhere. Not until I've spoken to Justin. He'll have to come back and sort this out. It's not fair that I've been left to deal with this mess. I never wanted to come here in the first place.

'Look, can't we just sit down and talk about this for a minute?' I plead. 'We've had an extremely difficult and upsetting few months.'

'I'm not arguing with you. I'm telling you.'

'Yes, I understand, but this is our home now.' If only she would listen to reason.

'No, it's not. Don't you understand? I'm evicting you. Giving you notice.'

'It's not much notice, is it?'

Harriet wasn't wrong when she told me Arabella could be difficult. But we have rights. She can't do this.

'I'm sorry, Bella, I can see you're upset,' I say, trying hard to moderate my tone. There's no point escalating the situation. 'But we signed a contract. You can't just throw us out. If you have a problem, you need to take it up with the rental agency. I suggest you speak to Harriet Quinlivan.'

But she's not listening. 'You're not welcome here,' Arabella says, slowly and loudly. 'Why can't you get that into your thick head? Leave or I'll call the police.'

Now she really is being ridiculous.

'I'd better speak to Harriet myself,' I say, stepping forward with as much confidence as I can summon.

It works. Arabella takes an involuntary step back out under the overhanging porch.

'You don't need to call Harriet. This is my house and you'll do as I tell you.'

'Even so, I'll only be a minute.' And before she can protest, I slam the door in her face and bolt it so she can't get in.

I turn and fall against the door, with my back pressed against it as she bangs and shouts, every thud rattling my throbbing head.

I can't stand it. So I hurry into the living room, trembling like a baby chick. I know I should grow a thicker skin but I can't bear people shouting at me. Why can't everyone just be nice to each other?

I grab my phone out of my dressing gown pocket and call Harriet.

'How's your head?' she asks as she answers, sounding far chirpier than she has any right to be after the amount of wine we drank last night.

'Arabella's turned up at the house and is trying to kick us out. I don't know what to do. She can't evict us, can she? I mean not without giving us notice. But she's threatening all sorts and we don't have anywhere else to go. We'll be homeless. Oh god, Harriet, what am I going to do?'

Harriet takes a deep breath. 'Okay,' she says, with a calm authority that immediately eases my anxiety. She's on my side. She's going to deal with this. 'I'll be over as soon as I can. Don't worry, I'll handle it.'

Chapter 22

I sit on the stairs while I wait for Harriet, my head in my hands and my palms clamped over my ears. Arabella's not given up and is now going around the house hammering on all the windows. I've pulled the curtains closed so I can't see her, but it doesn't drown out the sound. It's insane. *She's* insane. If she keeps this up, I'll gladly move out.

Does she really hate Justin that much that she's prepared to drive down from London to evict us? But then, maybe everything Lady Grace and Colin have told me is true. If Justin did nearly kill her, it's no wonder she doesn't want him back at Treloar. So much for him saving her life. If she doesn't think he's a hero, there's definitely something I'm missing.

I really need to find out what Justin has to say about it all. I need to look him in the eye and hear in his words exactly what happened.

Eventually, Arabella stops banging and shouting, but only when Harriet arrives. Thank god. I hope she can talk some sense into the woman, even if I wasn't able to.

Outside, I hear the muffled sound of voices. Harriet and Arabella discussing me. Discussing us. I'm sure Arabella doesn't have the right to throw us out without notice. At least, I hope she doesn't. But Justin dealt with all the admin and paperwork. No, she can't. I'm sure Harriet's explaining it to her right now. She doesn't have the authority, never mind whether she owns the house or not. We're protected by the law.

It's not a long conversation. A car door slams. An engine roars into life. Tyres kick up gravel.

And then there's a gentle knock at the door, almost apologetic after Arabella's incessant hammering.

'Megan, it's me,' Harriet calls out.

I let her in and fall into her arms with relief. I could cry.

'It's okay,' Harriet soothes. She rubs my back and holds me tight. 'I'm here now. She's gone.'

'She can't throw us out, can she?' I sob into her shoulder. 'We have rights. We have a contract.'

'Absolutely,' Harriet says. 'She shouldn't have come here like that. I told her. She has to give you reasonable notice, no matter how strongly she feels about you living here. However, in the long term, if she wants you gone, there's not much we can do to stop her evicting you, I'm afraid.'

'I still don't understand why. She was ranting at me but wasn't making much sense. Does she still blame Justin for the fire? Did you tell her we have nowhere else to go?'

'I think she's just angry that Justin came back. Don't take it personally.'

'Of course I'm going to take it personally. She was here in the house yelling in my face.' I pull away from Harriet to dry my eyes with a tissue, composing myself. 'I suppose her mother let on Justin was back?'

'No,' Harriet says. 'Apparently Finn called her.'

'Can you talk to her again?' I grab Harriet by the arms, imploring her. She's not only the rental agent, but she's my friend. Maybe my only friend. I need her to do this for me, to make Arabella come to her senses. 'Explain our situation. Make sure she knows we'd be homeless.'

Harriet smooths the back of my hand and shoots me a tight smile of reassurance. 'I'll try,' she says, 'but it might make more sense if Justin spoke to her when he's back. Perhaps they can resolve some of their differences.'

'But she hates him. I'm not even sure she would speak to him. This is a nightmare.'

'Listen, you're not going to be homeless, okay? I'll help you find somewhere else to live,' Harriet says. 'Somewhere more suitable. I'll have a look through the books when I get back to the office and see if there's anything available. You never really liked this house anyway, did you?'

'That's not the point.'

It would be the easiest thing in the world to simply pack up and move. We don't have much. I could be gone with all our belongings within the hour and no one would ever know we'd been here. But we signed a contract. And paid a deposit. Why should we move? We're not doing anyone any harm. Sure, I'm not in love with the house, but it's the principle. Why should we leave just because Arabella is upset about something that happened a lifetime ago?

'You really want to take on Arabella Carlyon over this house?' Harriet asks, eyebrows raised.

'Not really,' I sigh. I think Justin might have a different view. I probably ought to call him. But he'll only get cross with me for interrupting his training, and there's nothing he can do from Bristol.

'Good. So I'll start looking at other properties and see if we can arrange some viewings over the next few days.'

I shake my head and lower my gaze. Justin won't stand for that. He'll blame me. He'll think I've rolled over too easily. 'At least talk to her again. Please? Make her understand she's being unreasonable. We're good for the rent and we're hardly going to trash the place.'

'I can try,' Harriet says, but there's a look of defeat about her. She doesn't think we have a chance in hell of changing Arabella's mind which means she won't make much of an effort.

'Tell her our house was destroyed in a fire. Tell her I lost my children and that I'm still in mourning. I don't care. Do whatever it takes.'

A frown creases Harriet's brow. She scratches her arm furiously. 'I'm not really sure it's my place to go to Arabella begging,' she says.

I knew it. She thinks it's a lost cause and it would be easier all round if we gave in to Arabella and moved out without a fuss.

And I thought Harriet was a friend.

'Fine.' I draw my shoulders back and cross my arms defiantly. 'I'll do it. I'll speak to Arabella. I'll tell her everything and I'll make her see sense.'

Chapter 23

After Harriet leaves, heading back to her office still promising to check out some alternative rentals for us, I shower and dress. I even put on a little make-up. Just a dab of foundation, some lipstick and a lick of mascara. Not exactly war paint, but a self-esteem booster before I confront Arabella. It's better than turning up looking pasty and gaunt. If nothing else, it should hide the bags under my eyes.

On the long walk up the drive to the house, I rehearse what I'm going to say. She caught me by surprise earlier, but this time I'm going to be prepared. If Arabella won't listen to reason, perhaps I can appeal to her maternal instincts. She'd have to have a heart of stone if she still wants to evict us after I've told her about the fire that snatched Felix and Sebastian from us.

My throat is dry, and my hands tremble as I approach the grand front entrance of Treloar House.

A maid, whose long black hair is tied up in a bun, answers the door.

'Yes?' she asks stiffly.

'I was hoping to speak with Arabella,' I say, forcing a smile to reach my eyes. 'Is she in?'

I'm certain she is. An expensive car with a private number plate with what appears to be Arabella's initials is parked outside, alongside the Carlyons' Range Rover.

The maid looks me up and down like I'm something the cat's caught. 'Is she expecting you?'

'No,' I say, picking nervously at the cuticle on my thumb. 'I'm Megan. We recently moved into the lodge. It's about the rental.'

The maid considers this for a moment, and then nods. She steps to one side, inviting me in. 'I'll see if she's available,' she says.

And then I'm inside the house that only a few days ago I was dreaming about, imagining myself here as the lady of the manor. The maid leads me down a long dark hallway where I catch the faint odour of boiled vegetables, and into a drawing room crammed with antiques and dark wood furniture at the rear of the house. A dusty crystal chandelier hangs from the ceiling and heavy red velvet curtains trail from rails above the windows. I sit on the edge of a sofa next to a fireplace, set with half a dozen roughly cut logs.

I cross my hands in my lap, a little disappointed. The room is cold and unwelcoming and lacks the grandeur I'd expected of such an imposing house. The rug under my feet is threadbare in places. A bouquet of plastic flowers on the windowsill is faded and drooping. And the paint on the walls has bubbled and is peeling in places.

A grandfather clock tick-tocks monotonously in the corner and time seems to slow as I wait.

And wait.

Five minutes pass.

Tick-tock.

And then ten.

After fifteen minutes, I'm becoming restless. Have they forgotten I'm here? Or is it some kind of power play to unsettle me?

When the door finally flies open and Arabella storms in, her face thunderous, I jump to my feet.

'Arabella, I - '

'I assume you're here to tell me you've come to your senses?' she says, arching a perfectly shaped eyebrow.

She's spoiling for a fight, but I'm not here to argue.

'I know things have happened in the past that I'm sure everyone regrets, but I was hoping we could have a chat, woman to woman.'

'What's there to talk about?' she snaps. 'I want you gone. I don't want you or Justin in the house a day longer.'

'Yes, I understand — '

'So?'

I never thought this was going to be easy, but she's not even listening to me.

'It's not that straightforward.' I sit down again, hoping she'll follow my lead and take a seat opposite. But she insists on standing with her arms folded across her chest, her foot tapping impatiently on the floor. 'If you kick us out, we have nowhere to go.'

'Justin must have known he wouldn't be welcome back at Treloar, so I assume his return was intended solely to taunt my family,' she says.

'Maybe if you understood our situation, it might put a different perspective on matters.' My forced smile probably looks more like a grimace. 'The thing is, ten months ago we lost everything in a fire at our house. And I mean *everything*. Felix and Sebastian, our two beautiful little boys, were killed.' I cough to clear the tightness in my throat. Now is not the time for tears. I need to hold it together. 'I don't know if you have children, Bella, but it's without doubt the worst thing that could happen to anyone. I wouldn't wish it on my worst enemy.'

Finally, Arabella slides onto the sofa opposite and sits rigidly. The first hint of a crack in her stern expression appears. 'I'm sorry. I didn't know.'

'We've been living in temporary accommodation ever since, but we thought it was time to get back on our feet, no matter how bleak that seemed,' I say. 'Justin wanted us to move somewhere where we could heal, away from all the terrible memories. At first, I couldn't see any future without our boys, but as much as it pains me to say it, he's right. We can't wallow in the past. We need to move on. We have the rest of our lives to live.

'He told me about all the wonderful times he had here at Treloar and was so excited when he discovered the lodge was available to rent. He thought it was fate. The one place we could be happy again.'

'I see,' she says, looking visibly moved. She sniffs and composes herself, drawing her shoulders back. 'That is all terribly sad, but I'm afraid it doesn't change anything. I can't have you living here.'

'I'm sorry?' Is her heart made of stone? How can anyone with a shred of compassion and humanity fail to be swayed by what I've just said?

'You heard me. I want you out. Justin isn't welcome here, and while you're married to him, I'm afraid neither are you.'

'But didn't you hear a word I've just said? About the fire? My boys?' I gasp. 'Please.' My voice rises an octave. 'What did Justin do that was so terrible you can't bear the thought of him here again?'

'You really don't know?'

'I know about the fire. How you nearly died and that Justin saved your life. But that was all years ago.'

'Saved my life?' She stares at me as if she can't believe what she's hearing. 'Is that what he told you?'

'Not exactly. We've not had a chance to speak about what happened. Colin explained it to me.'

'He did, did he?'

'Isn't it true?'

'Justin tried to kill me,' she says, her eyes wet with tears. 'He locked me in that building and wouldn't let me out, even when I screamed for help until I was hoarse. He held the door closed until I was unconscious. I thought I was going to die.'

'But he didn't let you die. Justin pulled you out.'

Arabella shrugs, her lips turning into a cruel snarl. 'I wouldn't have needed to be pulled out if he hadn't trapped me in there. The man is a psychopath, and he got away with it by blaming Finn.'

That can't be right. Justin isn't violent or aggressive. 'Are you sure?' I ask. 'Isn't it possible you were confused with all the smoke, and it was just that the door was stuck?'

She licks her lips and smooths an eyebrow with her finger. 'No,' she says coolly. 'I wasn't confused. Justin held the door shut. Finn saw it all.'

'But why? I don't understand why he would do that. It makes no sense.'

Arabella lowers her voice, speaking in barely a whisper. 'Because I humiliated him and he wanted to punish me.' Her head droops, her gaze falling into her lap.

Now I really am confused. 'What do you mean?'

'He tried it on with me when I was fourteen and he was old enough to know better.'

A flush of jealousy rises within me like the heat of a fever, leaving me in a cold sweat. But it was years ago. They were only teenagers. Long before Justin and I met. I have nothing to be jealous about.

'That doesn't sound like much of a reason to almost kill you,' I say.

'Really?' Her head jolts up, flames of anger behind her eyes. 'I told him no, but he wouldn't listen. I tried to push him away, but he was stronger than me. I was helpless. It was like he was possessed and there was nothing I could do to stop him.' She swallows, takes a moment and then says, 'The reason he tried to kill me was because I told him no, but he wouldn't listen. And then he tried to rape me.'

Chapter 24

Rape?

It's such an ugly, brutal word. It can't be true. Justin's not like that. Okay, he's no angel, but he wouldn't have... He couldn't have... I'm his wife. We've been married for more than ten years and he's never been in the least bit aggressive towards me, or any other woman. He's always been a gentleman. Loving and caring, always putting my needs over and above his own.

YOUR HUSBAND IS A DANGEROUS MAN.

WHATEVER YOU DO, DON'T TRUST JUSTIN.

Is this what those messages were trying to warn me?

'I don't believe it,' I gasp, rising on weak legs. I need air.

'Believe what you like. You weren't there,' Arabella says. For the first time since I've met her, she looks vulnerable. Her hard exterior melting.

'I'm sorry,' I murmur, although I don't know what I'm apologising for. 'I have to go.' I need to get out of this house.

I stumble down the hall, grasping the wall for support, my feet shuffling along the tiled floor like I'm dragging two lumps of lead.

And then I'm outside. The air is cool and fresh but my chest is tight, like someone's sitting on it.

Is she lying? It's not something you make up, but it was a long time ago. Neither of them were much more than kids and memories can morph and evolve over time.

I once read that our memories of events are only recollections of the last time we remembered them, and that they can change and skew. Is Arabella misremembering something from her adolescence that isn't exactly true? Maybe there was something briefly between them that went too far and she was embarrassed. It happens, doesn't it?

I simply cannot believe my husband is capable of anything so heinous, because if I did, then I'd have to question what else between us is a lie.

Have there been others?

How many?

No, stop this.

I can't go down that path. If I allow myself to believe it's true in the way Arabella remembers it, then my marriage is dead and I've lost my husband. And after losing my children, he's all I have left. Without him, I have nothing.

I don't know how I get back to the lodge, but before I know it, I'm standing at the door with the key in my hand. Inside, the hollow emptiness of the strange house hits me hard.

Why am I fighting Arabella so hard to stay here? The lodge means nothing to me. I know it's only been a week, but I can't ever see how I could call it home. I'm only fighting for Justin's benefit. But no one wants him here, especially Arabella, and it's obvious now she's going to make sure we leave. There's no fighting this. And even if we persuaded her to change her mind, how could we possibly stay?

Cornwall was supposed to be a place of renewal where we could rebuild our lives, but it feels like the moment we stepped foot into this property, we've been moving in the opposite direction, Justin and I pushed further apart. All I wanted was to save our marriage, to cling on to the one thing I had left. But now, even that's slipping through my fingers.

What the hell am I going to do?

Justin's due home any time. I'm going to have to sit him down and make him tell me everything. No more secrets. I don't care how uncomfortable or painful it is, I need him to tell me exactly what happened here, because without trust and honesty, there's no marriage at all.

I trudge wearily to the sofa and flop down. I'm tired. So, so tired. I rest my head against a cushion and close my eyes, but my mind won't switch off.

Arabella's words keep echoing through my head.

The reason he tried to kill me was because I told him no, but he wouldn't listen. And then he tried to rape me.

Rape?

God, please, no.

Don't let it be true.

YOUR HUSBAND IS A DANGEROUS MAN.

I grab handfuls of hair and tug at them so hard the pain is like a thousand needles in my scalp. Anything to stop the noise in my head.

And then my phone pings.

I don't want it to be Justin. I can't face talking to him right now, even if it is just a text.

Thankfully, it's a message from Harriet.

Did you speak to Arabella? How did it go?

I start to type a reply, but it's too complicated. How do I explain that my husband's been accused of rape? Nobody's going to understand there are nuances. Grey areas. Nobody knows Justin like I know him. All they're going to hear is that one awful word.

Rape.

But I need to speak to someone. And apart from Justin, Harriet is all I have.

I tentatively call her number, sitting up and holding my head in my hand.

'So? What happened? Did you talk her around?' she asks breathlessly.

'Not exactly, but I finally understand why she wants Justin gone so badly.' I swallow the hard ball in my throat but it stubbornly refuses to shift. 'I practically begged her to change her mind. I told her about Felix and Sebastian and how I'd lost everything in the fire, but she didn't care.'

'Oh, Megan... '

I clamp a hand over my mouth as my tears flow. And as I sob, my body giving in to the emotions I've been holding back, the words I never thought I'd hear myself say spill from my lips. 'She says Justin tried to rape her.'

There's a stunned silence on the line. I can hear Harriet's slow, soft breath, but for a moment she says nothing.

'Rape?'

'I know. I can't believe it,' I cry.

'How? When?' she gasps.

'She said it's all true about the fire, but she says Justin deliberately trapped her inside the shed after she'd rejected him and he'd tried to rape her.'

'When?'

'I don't know exactly. When they were teenagers, I guess.'

'Do you believe her?'

'I don't know what to think anymore,' I say.

'What does Justin have to say for himself?'

I hesitate for a second or two. 'I've not spoken to him yet. I was going to wait until he got home.'

'Do you need me to come over? I can be there with you if you'd like?'

'No,' I say. 'I think that would make matters worse.' Although the idea of having some moral support when I have what is going to be the most difficult conversation any wife can have with their husband is appealing.

'Well, if you change your mind, let me know. I'm here for you, Megan. You know that.'

'I do. Thank you.'

'So what are you going to do? Are you going to leave him?' she asks.

'Leave him?'

The thought hasn't even occurred to me. I've done everything to cling on to my marriage after the fire. I can't leave him. I don't even know if what Arabella is accusing him of is true.

'Sorry, I just assumed... '

'I know my husband. He's not a rapist,' I say with a conviction I don't entirely feel. 'It all happened a long time ago. I mean, if he really did what she said, why didn't she report it?'

'Because she was just a teenage girl? I don't know, Megan. Lots of rapes go unreported, but it doesn't mean it didn't happen.'

I shake my head vigorously, even though she can't see. 'No, he's not like that.'

'Okay, well, you know your husband best,' she says. But I don't like her tone, as if she thinks I'm protecting him.

'Yes,' I assert, 'I do. Don't you think I'd know if he was capable of something like that?'

'Sorry, I didn't mean to upset you.'

'And if it happened like she said, why on earth would *he* want to come back to Treloar? It doesn't make any sense,' I say.

'No,' Harriet agrees. 'That does seem odd.'

'You know I can believe all this stuff about a fire which got out of control and Arabella passing out. That sounds like bored teenagers getting up to mischief. But to accuse Justin of rape, that's unbelievable. I mean, he was the one who saved her when she nearly died!'

Harriet's breath is slow and regular in my ear. 'A hero,' she says, eventually, but I don't miss the note of sarcasm in her voice.

She thinks I'm blinkered and that I'm only saying these things to save my marriage.

Am I?

Am I being too sceptical and ignoring the evidence in front of my eyes?

What evidence? It's her word against his. For all I know, she's made this up after I told her about the death of my children. It might have been the only thing she could think of to justify evicting us.

'I hate to bring this back to practicalities, but do you want me to carry on looking for properties?' Harriet asks.

'What?'

'If Arabella's still insisting on evicting you, you'll need some other options.'

'Oh, right, yeah. Thanks.' I hadn't even thought about that. We're going to have to move, and the sooner the better. I can't stay here now. And I can't imagine why Justin would want to either.

'Don't worry, everything will work out. I promise.'

'I wish I shared your optimism.'

'What time's Justin due home?' Harriet asks.

'I don't know. Whenever his course finishes. He was going to let me know when he leaves.'

'Are you sure you don't want me to come over? I mean, how's he going to take it when you tell him what Arabella said?'

I bite my lip. He's going to be furious, I'm sure. It's one of the worst things you can be accused of as a man, isn't it?

'Thanks, but it would be better if I handled it on my own,' I say.

'Sure, you know best. But if things get, you know, out of hand, call me. I can be there in fifteen minutes.'

She hangs up and the line goes dead. I sit staring at the phone for a minute after she's gone.

What did she mean by that? If things get out of hand?

She doesn't really think I could be in any danger from Justin, does she?

Chapter 25

I'm on tenterhooks all afternoon waiting for Justin to let me know he's on his way home.

He has a long drive and is bound to be tired and grouchy when he gets back. These courses take so much out of him. I'm not sure he's going to be in the best frame of mind to answer all my questions, but it can't wait. All I can do is cook one of his favourite meals and have a bottle of wine opened and waiting for him.

It's almost four when I finally receive his text.

Just leaving now. Hopefully home after 7 x

Great, that means he'll be caught in all the rush hour traffic which is bound to sour his mood.

While I wait, I cook an arrabbiata pasta sauce with fresh tomatoes, heavy on the basil, garlic and chilli, and leave it simmering on low.

It's closer to eight when I finally hear his car pull up and he kicks open the front door, struggling with his suitcase. He calls out in surprisingly good humour.

'Hi honey, I'm home,' he says with a comedic Texan drawl. It's a thing we always used to do. It never failed to put a smile on my face, but not tonight.

I greet him in the hall, drying my hands on a tea towel.

'I missed you,' he says, showering me with kisses, lifting me up and twirling me around.

I do my best to reciprocate, concealing my stiffness, my desire to hold him at arm's length until I've got to the bottom of Arabella's accusations.

'I missed you too.'

He looks exhausted. His shirt is crumpled, his tie hanging loose, and he has dark bags under his eyes, but he's less tetchy than I feared. This is good news, at least. He doesn't seem to notice that I've brushed my hair and put on a little make-up.

'Dinner's almost ready,' I say. 'Just waiting for the pasta to cook. Wine?'

'Great, thanks. I'm starving.'

I pour him a generous glass of red which he takes with him when he runs upstairs to change.

In the kitchen, I serve up two generous bowls of pasta with a trembling hand. Why am I so nervous?

I've laid the table in the dining room and lit some candles. I wanted to set the right tone and besides, I don't want him distracted by the TV on in the corner tonight. What I have to talk to him about is too important.

'What's the occasion?' he asks, when he returns in a waft of aftershave. He's put on jeans and a soft, powder blue cashmere sweater.

'No occasion,' I say, with a tight-lipped smile. 'I just thought it would be nice to sit at the table for a change. Come on, eat.'

I let him fill his stomach with pasta and wine, biding my time, waiting for the best opportunity to tell him I've spoken to Arabella.

While he eats, he tells me about the drive home, the traffic, the people on the course, which restaurants they ate at, and how Nigel, whoever he is, drank too much on the first night and was sick in the back of a taxi.

I nod and smile through every one of his stories. He doesn't seem to notice that I'm quiet tonight, letting him do all the talking.

Eventually, he sits back and wipes his mouth on a napkin and scrunches it in a ball on the table.

'So, what have you been doing while I've been away?' he asks.

I should tell him about the leak in the bathroom, going for a run in the woods, sneaking a peek through the window of the big house, discovering Finn squatting there, and the unexpected return of the Carlyons.

But there's only one thing on my mind.

'I met Arabella today,' I say, refilling Justin's empty glass.

'Really? Where?' He frowns at me over the top of his wine. 'I thought she'd moved to London.'

'She came to visit her parents, but popped in to see me,' I explain, still juggling in my head how I'm going to put her accusations to him.

'That's nice.'

'She was quite aggressive.'

'Seriously?' His face clouds.

'Actually, she made a bit of a scene. She wants us out of the house.'

'What?'

'She's evicting us, Justin,' I say. 'She was more or less yelling at me to pack up our stuff and leave there and then.'

'That's crazy. What's got into the woman?' He shakes his head, as if he's disappointed but not surprised. He doesn't ask why.

'I had to call Harriet.'

'Good, we're paying enough every month. About time she earned her money. And did she sort it out?' Justin asks. He rests his forearms on the table, leaning closer to me.

'Not exactly. Arabella's absolutely adamant she doesn't want us here. I think we're going to have to look for somewhere else to live.

Sorry, I know how much you love it here, but she's made up her mind and there's nothing we can do about it.'

Justin's eyes narrow and a vein in his forehead throbs. 'That would suit you, wouldn't it?' he says with a growling menace that catches me by surprise.

'What? No, I don't want to leave. Of course I don't.'

'Come on, Megan. You've been set against living here from the moment we arrived. You haven't even given it a chance and now you've found the perfect excuse to bail out.' He bangs his fist on the table, making the plates jump.

'That's not true,' I protest, horrified he could think that. It might be true, but I've never given Justin any reason to think I wasn't one hundred per cent committed to living at Treloar. 'Maybe I was a little unsure to start with, but I'm settling in now. Anyway, it's irrelevant what I think. Arabella's made up her mind and she wants to evict us. It's her decision. She looks after all the properties on the estate now, according to Harriet.'

'I'll speak to her,' Justin grunts. The good mood he was in is evaporating as rapidly as mountain dew on a warm summer's morning. I need to tread carefully.

'I've already tried,' I say, lowering my gaze as I run my fingers up and down the stem of my glass. 'I went up to see her at the house when she'd calmed down. I thought if I told her about the fire and that we have nowhere else to go, she'd understand. I even tried telling her about Felix and Sebastian.'

'We don't need to justify ourselves. We have a rental agreement.'

'It doesn't make any difference. And I'm not sure I want to stay anyway if we're not welcome.'

'What do you mean, not welcome? Who said that?'

I take a deep breath in through my nose and let it out slowly. I've spent all afternoon pondering how I'm going to say this to Justin, but there's no easy way of telling your husband someone's accused him of rape.

My mouth's so dry, I can barely swallow and the pasta sits heavily in my stomach.

'Arabella made some allegations,' I say, eventually. 'About you.'

'Me?' He scowls.

'She said there were some things that happened here when you were younger.'

'What things?'

'You know, things that happened between you. She told me about the fire,' I say, my heart hammering against my ribcage.

Justin snorts dismissively. 'You know, you shouldn't believe anything that woman says. She's a fantasist. She's always had a wild imagination. A bit fucked in the head, if you ask me.'

'Right,' is all I can manage. 'It's just that she said you trapped her inside a burning shed and that as a result she collapsed, unconscious.'

I hold my breath.

Justin digs into the surface of the wooden table with his thumb nail, his face hard and unforgiving. 'Did she tell you I saved her life? Who d'you think pulled her out?'

'She also said you... ' I stammer, my words drying up.

'She said what?' Justin raises his voice with a rumble of simmering anger.

'She said... she said you tried to rape her.' The words that were stuck in my throat like hot, jagged lumps of tar are finally free. There, I've said it.

I glance up at Justin, waiting for him to respond. To see how he'll react. But of course he didn't do it. God, this is so stupid. Why did I even bring it up? He wouldn't have. It's not in his nature. It's just the wild fantasy of a confused teenage girl. She probably had a crush on him and came up with this spiteful lie when he turned her down.

Justin is silent for a second as the darkness of fury descends over him and his whole body tightens.

'She what?' he snarls.

'I know, it's ludicrous. I told her that.' Why did I say anything? I should have kept my big mouth shut. I can see from his reaction he didn't do it. He doesn't need to deny it.

'How dare she. I told you, the woman's deranged. Totally and utterly out of her mind. She always was a troubled teenager. I thought she'd have grown out of it by now.'

I laugh nervously. 'It's crazy, isn't it?' He's still not denied it though. 'I mean, it's not true, is it? It can't be?'

An ominous silence settles between us and I can't hold Justin's gaze. The way he's staring at me with a stranger's eyes makes my blood freeze. Maybe I should have asked Harriet to come over after all.

'Are you serious?' he asks.

'No, of course not. I'm being silly. Sorry, I shouldn't have said anything.'

This was such a big mistake. I wish I could turn back time and roll those words back into my mouth, but the genie's out and there's no turning back.

When he bangs the table with his fist again, it almost collapses. The plates jump and my wine glass wobbles perilously.

'Do you really think I'm capable of those things? Rape? Murder? You're out of your fucking mind!'

I wrap my arms around my body, trying to shrink into myself, pulling my neck into my shoulders, wishing the ground would open up and swallow me.

'I'm sorry,' I mumble. 'I shouldn't have said anything.'

For someone who loathes confrontation, I have a big mouth sometimes. I don't know what I was thinking.

'I don't believe this,' he screams. 'How long have we been married?'

'Justin, please. Don't.'

'How long?' he repeats.

'Twelve years.' My voice is little more than a whisper, a faint creak from the back of my throat.

'You know me better than anyone. So how could you doubt me?'

'I don't. Please, I'm sorry. Forget I said anything. I'm tired and I've not been thinking straight. You know after Felix and Sebastian died —'

'Don't you dare blame this on them!' he yells.

'I'm not. I'm just saying... '

I need to get out. I need some space. I stand unsteadily, pushing back my chair. I collect our plates and hurry into the kitchen with Justin marching after me. I hear his footsteps and feel his hot breath on the back of my neck.

'Don't you walk away from me while I'm talking to you.'

I drop the plates in the sink and grab the worktop to hold myself up, my legs jellying.

'Do I look like a rapist to you? Do I?' he shouts so loudly in my ear, I flinch.

Why couldn't I just keep my stupid mouth shut? He's had a long few days. He's exhausted from the drive home. And I've thrown two baseless accusations at him. No wonder he's so angry.

'I don't believe them.' I turn to face him, desperate to make things right between us again. I hate it when we argue.

I put a hand on his shoulder, a signal of reconciliation, but he swats it away.

And in that moment I see my mother standing in the hall berating my father on the night he left home and abandoned us. The sadness and disappointment in his eyes. The indignation in hers. Her bony finger jabbing his chest, pushing him to his limits. I hear the scraping of his suitcase being dragged out from under the bed. His heavy footsteps on the stairs. The front door slamming. My father disappearing, never to be seen again.

Have I become my mother?

Have I learned nothing from the way she drove my father away?

I've tried so hard not to be her. To be reasonable and supportive. Not to repeat her mistakes, and yet...

Justin's hand is suddenly on my throat, his thick fingers squeezing and pressing, forcing my chin up and my head back. He pulls me away from the sink and throws me against the wall on the other side of the room without letting go. He lifts me up until I'm struggling to keep my toes in contact with the floor. I can't breathe. A threading pressure builds in my head. Panic blooms in my chest. His face is up close to mine, so close I can smell garlic and alcohol on his breath.

I snatch his wrist, but it's locked on my throat, impossible to prise open.

He has me pinned and helpless, my lungs gasping for air.

'What else did Arabella have to say?' Hot spittle peppers my skin and his eyes blaze with venom.

I croak, but I can't get any words out. I'm suffocating.

'Tell me!' he screams.

He releases his grip a fraction.

'Nothing,' I gasp.

'Are you lying?'

'No.'

He stares into my eyes, scanning my face as if he's trying to read what's going on inside my head. I don't want to cry but I can't help the tears that well up and stream down my cheeks.

'If you don't trust me, why don't you just say it?' he says.

I've never seen him like this before. I should have asked Harriet to be here. Somehow she knew, even though I couldn't see it myself.

YOUR HUSBAND IS A DANGEROUS MAN.

'I do,' I wheeze, my head wheeling as the edge of my vision blurs. 'I do trust you.'

'Well, you've got a funny way of showing it.'

And then he lets me go. Just like that.

I collapse to the ground, coughing and spluttering, clutching my throat, relief flooding my body.

Justin steps back and looks down at me as if I'm nothing but a pile of dirt.

'I'm going to bed,' he mutters. 'We'll talk about this again in the morning.'

Chapter 26

After I've cleared up and made sure all the doors and windows are locked, I have no choice other than to crawl into bed with Justin, even after the way he treated me tonight. If he finds I've slept in one of the spare rooms, it will only make him angry again.

He's never raised a hand to me before. Or spoken to me like that. It was as though I'd woken a sleeping monster. But it was my fault. I should have known better than to question him, especially about something so obviously not true.

For most of the night, I can't sleep. I lie on my back with the duvet pulled up to my chin, replaying events over and over in my mind, while beside me Justin snores without a care in the world.

I've never thought he was dangerous. Those text messages just a provocation by someone with a grudge against him looking to drive us apart. But then I've never seen him act like that before. He was a man possessed. His eyes wild. His anger unbound. I never thought I'd be afraid of my own husband. I thought I could trust him implicitly.

Exhaustion eventually takes its toll and I must finally fall asleep, because I'm suddenly being woken by Justin nudging my shoulder.

'Megan? Are you awake?'

I crack open a sticky eye. Justin's propping himself up on one elbow, looking down at me as if everything that happened last night was nothing more than a bad dream.

'What time is it?' I ask, my throat as croaky as a ninety-a-day smoker, the pain of speaking a reminder of what he did to me.

'Half eight.'

Every muscle in my body is coiled tightly and I glance at him timidly, trying to read him. Is he still cross with me? Is he going to make me pay again for accusing him of those terrible things?

'Listen, I'm really sorry about last night,' he says, reaching a finger to touch my cheek.

I recoil, turning my face away, like his hand is a red-hot poker.

'The thing is, I was tired and I'd had a long drive home. I shouldn't have overreacted,' he says. 'You weren't to know you can't believe a word that comes out of Arabella's mouth.'

'It's fine,' I mumble.

'No, it's not. I was bang out of line and I'm really sorry. It'll never happen again.'

I shrug sulkily, but I should never have questioned him. I guess I was confused and angry. It's been an emotional year.

'Am I forgiven?' His lips stretch into a grin, his eyes filled with remorse.

I don't want to fight. 'I guess,' I say.

'I didn't mean to hurt you,' he says. 'You know that, right? But it was upsetting to be accused by my own wife of those awful things. You understand, don't you?'

'I know. I shouldn't have doubted you,' I say.

'That's right, because if you think I could do any of those things, you don't know me at all.'

We really did step perilously close to the edge last night. Couples have split up over less. I don't know what I'd do on my own. I'd be lost.

'I'm sorry. I do trust you. I love you,' I tell him.

'And I'm going to make it up to you for being such an arsehole.' His arm snakes under the sheet and coils over my stomach as his head collapses on the pillow.

'Let's forget it, shall we, and move on,' I say.

'Definitely. Water under the bridge.' He shuffles closer and nuzzles my neck with his scratchy morning stubble.

It tickles and I giggle. 'Stop it,' I say. 'I'd better get up.'

'Not yet,' he murmurs, his hand on my breast. 'You know I love you, don't you? You're the only woman in the world for me.'

'I love you too.' I kiss the top of his head and try to roll away, but he has me pinned. 'I should have a shower.'

But he pushes my knees apart with his elbow, hitching up my nightdress.

'Maybe tonight?' I suggest, trying to claw my nightie back down, but his kisses on my neck become more urgent.

It's been a while since we've made love. Only a handful of times since the fire, but I haven't been in the mood. Neither of us have. It still feels wrong. We're supposed to be grieving. Sex is the last thing on my mind these days.

He rolls on top of me, his kisses eager, trying to find my mouth, even as I turn my head away.

'Justin... ' I mumble into his bare shoulder. 'Not now.'

'Don't you love me?'

I'm not ready, but he's already pushing inside me. I wince with a burning pain and dig my fingernails into his back, biting my lip.

He pants and thrusts as I lay there rigid with shock, his body dampening with sweat from his efforts.

And in a few short seconds, he tosses back his head in ecstasy and screws his eyes shut. His powerful arms quiver and his hips buck. I hold him tightly as I feel him relax, relieved it's over.

He rolls off me, spent, and collapses on his own side of the bed with a sigh of contentment.

'That was good,' he whispers. 'You know, we really should do that more often.'

I tug my nightdress back down over my legs and lie staring at the ceiling.

What the hell was that all about?

Justin looks at me with sleepy satisfaction, his eyes half-shut. He strokes my cheek with the back of his finger. 'Let's go out for the day,' he says. 'There's somewhere I want to show you.'

'Okay,' I say meekly.

'It's a beach we used to go to. It'll be fun. I'll do us a picnic, but don't forget to pack a swimming costume,' he says, jumping out of bed and heading for the bathroom.

A swimming costume? It might be warm enough to get away with a T-shirt outside when the sun's out at this time of year, but I hope he isn't planning on a swim in the sea. It's going to be freezing. But he seems so excited, I don't want to burst his bubble, so I shut my mouth and say nothing.

An hour later, we're in his car. He has his hand on my knee and a big grin across his face. He seems to have forgiven me for what I said last night, so I hope we can move on.

We arrive twenty minutes later at a beautiful secluded cove that you'd never know existed from the cliffs above. To reach it, we clamber down a treacherous, dusty trail with loose stones that slip and slide under my feet as I struggle to keep my balance.

The sand is fine and white with a glistening blue sea rolling in on white-capped waves. It's about as picture-perfect as you could imagine.

Justin rolls out a tartan blanket and we tuck ourselves into the nook of a rock out of the wind with a weak sun warming our faces.

He lies on his side, propping his head up on his hand as he watches the breakers crashing in the distance. 'I used to come here all the time with Mum and Dad,' he says. 'We spent hours swimming in the sea.'

'It sounds lovely.' I pull my knees up to my chest with a rash of goosebumps puckering my exposed arms.

'It was amazing, although you have to watch for the currents. They can be dangerous because of the rocks. Did you bring your costume?'

'Under my clothes,' I say, but I have no intention of stripping off. It's surprisingly chilly down here by the water.

'Great, come on then.' Justin jumps up with the energy of a spring lamb. He throws off his T-shirt and shorts and stands staring at me expectantly with his hands on his hips. He's wearing a pair of long trunks that hang just above the knee.

He can't be serious. 'It's a bit cold for swimming, isn't it?'

He runs a hand through his chest hair. 'You'll be fine when you get in. It's invigorating. Good for your circulation.'

He holds out a hand to pull me up, but I'm really not sure. Apart from the danger of hypothermia, I've never been a fan of open water swimming, unless it's somewhere like Greece where the warm Mediterranean Sea is so clear you can see the bottom.

'Why don't you go in. I'll stay and watch,' I suggest.

'Megan, don't be difficult,' Justin snaps, his good humour evaporating. 'Cold water swimming is good for the heart. It would do you a power of good.'

He's clearly not going to take no for an answer. He's going to get me in the water whether I want to or not. And I don't want to get into another fight.

I might as well get this over with, so I grab his hand and let him pull me to my feet. Slowly, I slip out of my clothes and stand shivering in the thin material of my swimsuit as I watch the wind catch the foamy white peaks of the waves. Now I'm actually contemplating going into the water, it looks much rougher than before.

Justin drags me down the beach to where the wet sand is smooth and compacted.

'The trick is to dive straight in,' he says, beaming with excitement. 'You don't want to hesitate or think about it. No mucking about.'

'Right,' I say, but my teeth are already chattering. The sooner I get in, hopefully the sooner he'll let me out again and I can get warm.

He keeps a firm grip on my hand as he wades into the water surging noisily onto the beach in a white foam. Its cold chill nips at my toes and ankles, but Justin shows no hesitation, pulling me in deeper and deeper until I'm up to my knees and I can no longer feel my feet, which I've already scraped and knocked painfully on hidden rocks protruding from the sand.

'Amazing, isn't it?' he says.

How is he not feeling the cold?

'Sh- sure.' I fake a smile.

He keeps dragging me out further and further while I try to concentrate on anything other than how cold it is. The flock of seagulls circling and soaring in the blue sky above. The formation of the rocks and how long ago they must have been formed. The fishing boat hovering on the horizon.

But it doesn't work. My whole body screams at me that this is utter madness, but I know Justin won't let me go back to the beach until I've at least attempted to swim.

When the water reaches my waist and the swell rises to my chest, my breath snatches in my throat. It's so numbingly, ice-jarringly cold, I can almost feel my internal organs retreating into the deepest cavities of my body. And that's when I notice the powerful undercurrent, tugging at my legs and threatening to snatch my balance as I fight against the force of the surface waves. At moments, it feels like I'm being pushed and pulled in opposite directions.

'It's mind over matter,' Justin says. 'If you think about it being cold, you'll feel the cold. Just enjoy the moment. The freedom. The exhilaration.'

Exhilaration? There's nothing exhilarating about freezing to death in ice-cold choppy seas. This is total madness. How anyone could think this is fun is beyond me.

I look back at where we've left our belongings and realise with fear how far out we've come. I'm barely able to keep my toes on the bottom, bobbing up and down with the tidal surge. The urge to wade back and wrap myself up in a warm towel is overwhelming.

Suddenly my balance goes as a powerful wave I didn't see coming hits my back and an undertow kicks out my legs. The bottom slips from under my feet and my head dips under the surface.

And then I'm tumbling.

Head over heels.

Out of control.

Over and over and over.

No way of knowing which way is up. Which way is down.

Where the hell is the surface?

A muted rush of water in my ears. The sting of salt in my eyes. Utter confusion and panic. My lungs are bursting with the urge to breathe while fear spikes adrenaline around my veins.

White bubbles and sand and grit blur my vision. I thrash wildly, my arms and legs pumping in all directions, hunting for the surface, disorientated and buffeted by the current, until eventually I catch a glimpse of light. The sun climbing in the sky as clear as any sign pointing me in the direction I need to go.

I kick out, desperate for air.

But I can't move.

Pressure on top of my head is holding me down.

A hand?

What the fuck?

I kick again. Pull with my arms. I don't want to die. Not like this.

I edge closer to the surface but another wave rolls over the top of me and my body spirals through the water.

Finally my hand breaks the surface. Then my arm. My shoulder. My head and face.

I gasp for air, sucking it in hungrily, filling my lungs and spitting out water with salty brine on my lips and tongue.

A hand grabs me under the arm and lifts me up, holds me tight.

'It's okay, I've got you.' Justin's voice. He's here. He's saved me! Thank god.

I peel open my eyes. I'm in his arms. He's pulling me back to the shore. I'm safe.

For a moment, I thought I was being held under the water, but I must have imagined it, the force of the waves on the top of my head pushing me down. What other explanation could there be? There was no one else around other than Justin and there's no way he would have tried to drown me. He just wouldn't. I'm not letting the demons in my head take me down that road.

He's not dangerous. He's my husband, for pity's sake. He saved me.

Just like he saved Arabella from the fire in the shed all those years ago.

My feet find the bottom and I scramble, half carried, back to the beach where I collapse on the wet sand, my breath fast and hurried, my heart beating like I've sprinted a lap of an Olympic track.

Justin kneels at my side, holding my head, stroking my face.

'What happened?' he asks, his expression a picture of worry and concern.

'I don't know,' I splutter, coughing up water.

'One minute you were there and the next you were gone.'

'The currents,' I gasp.

'I'm so sorry, I should never have insisted on taking you in. I could have lost you. Let's get you warm.'

I stagger back to the rock where our clothes are in heaps on the blanket spread out across the soft sand. Justin picks up a towel and wraps it around my shoulders, rubbing the tops of my arms as I start to shiver uncontrollably.

'You gave me quite a fright,' he says. 'You could have drowned.'

'Yes,' I agree.

I could have died.

Chapter 27

Justin wants to stay on the beach but all I want to do is get back to the lodge and take a warm bath.

'Come on, Megs, don't spoil the day. I've made a picnic,' he says, as if nothing's happened.

I don't have any appetite and now the sun's vanished behind thick, grey cloud, the cold has penetrated my core. I can't seem to warm up, even with my T-shirt and jeans on and wrapped in two towels.

'Why don't you have some coffee at least. That'll make you feel better.' Justin pours from a silver flask into a plastic cup.

'I'd rather get back, if that's alright,' I say through chattering teeth.

I don't want to stay another minute here, staring at the sea, being reminded of how close I came to drowning.

'Home? Already? But we've only just got here,' Justin says like a petulant child. He glowers at me like it's all my fault the day's been ruined.

'We've been here a couple of hours.' My skin is covered in goose-bumps and frozen to the touch. I need to get home and warmed up.

'You've not even eaten your sandwiches.'

'I'll eat them later,' I say.

'Fine. Be like that. Spoil the day for everyone, why don't you?' His tone catches me off guard. He throws the plastic sandwich box and flask of coffee into a bag, hurls it over his shoulder and stomps off without me.

I'm momentarily stunned into inaction.

Is he joking? Is he going to turn back in a minute or two, laughing?

No, he's not. He's serious. He carries on walking, heading for the dirt trail back to the car. He doesn't even look back. He's pissed off with me because I'm cold and wet and I want to go home.

He took me into the sea where he knew there were dangerous currents, and yet somehow this is *my* fault?

I guess he *is* still angry with me about last night.

'Justin!' I yell after him, stumbling as I struggle to gather up the blanket.

I have to sprint to catch him as he's halfway along the trail.

I'm out of breath and my thighs are burning. 'Justin, slow down,' I plead.

But if anything, his pace quickens, until I'm virtually jogging to keep up. At least it's finally warmed me up a little and my teeth have stopped chattering.

He says nothing as we make it back to the car and dump our stuff in the boot. On the journey home, we sit in silence. Justin drives too fast, speeding recklessly around blind corners and accelerating aggressively when the road straightens out. At least he doesn't object when I turn up the heat.

The atmosphere is as sharp as a blade but I don't want it to be like this between us. We're supposed to be a team, united against the world. It's what we promised each other after the fire, but there's a chasm opening up, slowly and surely. I thought if we could survive the death of our children, we could survive anything. Looks as though I was wrong.

I know I shouldn't have ambushed him last night with those accusations, but he's not entirely blameless. He acted like a spoiled brat and what the hell was that all about, storming off at the beach? Something's happened to us this week. Is it the move to Cornwall? Treloar? The lodge? I wish Harriet was here right now.

When we pull up at the house, and Justin kills the engine, I brace myself. Are we going to spend the rest of the day in silence? Or is he going to continue to rant about how I've ruined his day by almost drowning myself?

To my surprise, his head drops sadly onto his chest. 'I'm sorry, Megs. I wanted today to be so perfect.'

'I know. And it was a lovely idea.'

'I just want you to be happy here, the way I was always happy when I came to Treloar,' he says.

After everything I've heard from Lady Grace, Colin, Finn and Arabella, I wonder how happy those times really were, and how much sentimentality has shaded his memories. The last time he was here, Arabella almost died. That's something that would leave a lasting impression on most people, but Justin never even mentioned it.

'I am happy.'

He swivels in his seat and takes my hand. 'God, your hands are like blocks of ice,' he says, frowning. 'You poor thing. Let's get you inside and warmed up. Don't worry about the car. I'll unpack everything later.'

He leads me inside with an arm around my shoulders as if I'm his eighty-year-old grandmother, but it's better than the cold, silent treatment. He lays me on the sofa, brings me a thick blanket from our bed and lights the fire. It's the first time we've lit it since we've been here and it immediately makes the room feel cosy. Then he rushes off to the kitchen and comes back with a steaming mug of hot chocolate.

I could get used to this.

This is the man I fell in love with. But after the fire things have inevitably been different. We've both lost so much and, like a berry withering on a branch, a bit of both of us shrivelled and died with the boys. Although we've tried so hard to hold it together, the trauma was always going to take its toll.

I'm sure he blames me for the fire, for Sebastian and Felix's deaths, although he's never said as much. I should have made more of an effort to get him to talk about his feelings. Instead I've allowed him to bottle them up and let them fester. Is that what last night was all about? Is that why he was so angry with me? Not just because I'd accused him, but because in his heart he's never really forgiven me for the fire?

He might need some therapy. A professional to tease out of him what he's really thinking and feeling, although I doubt he'd agree to it. He thinks all therapists are charlatans. And how do I go about suggesting he might need help without him flying off the handle again? He's so volatile at the moment.

When he's unpacked the car, Justin returns to check up on me. He kneels on the floor in front of the sofa and strokes my hair.

'It was stupid asking you to come swimming with me,' he says. 'I shouldn't have suggested it.'

'I'm a grown woman. I can make my own choices.' I say it to placate him, but we both know he gave me no choice. In the mood he was in, if I'd have refused, he'd have hit the roof.

'I should have known better. I knew there were strong currents. What if... ?'

His eyes bubble with tears. Strange, I've rarely seen Justin cry. Once when the doctor confirmed the boys were dead. And again at the funeral. Never before or since.

'But I didn't,' I say. 'I'm fine.'

He bows his head, chastened.

'I was a bit shaken, that's all,' I continue. 'Worse things happen at sea.' I chuckle at my joke, but there's nothing funny about it.

'Megan, don't. I keep thinking you could have died. And then what would I have done? I don't think I could survive without you. Promise you'll never leave me.'

His words should sound like a declaration of love, the way he used to talk to me. But his expression, eyes narrowed, lips tight, makes it feel like a threat. I shudder.

'Of course I'll never leave you.'

He finally smiles. 'We're meant to be together forever.' He squeezes my hand affectionately.

Are we?

I always thought that's what I wanted too. But last night, I saw a violent side to Justin I didn't like. And then there were all the things Arabella said. And, of course, those phone messages I'd been so quick to dismiss.

What if he is dangerous?

What if he really did hold my head under the water as a warning that he holds my life in his hands, and if he wanted to take it, he could. Easily.

Megan, stop it. You're being a fool.

'There is something we need to talk about, whether you like it or not,' I say.

His brow furrows.

'This house. I know you love it here, but we're going to have to look at other places. Maybe we could get somewhere with a sea view? Harriet's already said she'll trawl through her books to see if the agency has anything suitable.'

'Harriet?' he hisses, withdrawing his hand from mine like he's been stung. 'I might have known this was something you'd been cooking up with her.' His face darkens and the hoods fall over his eyes, menacingly.

'It's not like that. Arabella's adamant we can't stay and Harriet said she'd help us find somewhere else so we don't end up homeless.'

'She can't just turf us out, you know. We have rights.'

'But she owns the house,' I say. 'Ultimately, if Arabella wants us to leave, we don't have a leg to stand on.'

'Well, I'm not going anywhere.'

I shake my head. He can be so stubborn. 'Justin, she's evicting us. At some point, we're going to have to move.'

'I'll talk to her. I'll make her change her mind.'

I sigh. 'I've tried that already. She won't listen.'

'You don't know her like I do. She'll listen to me.'

'Fine. Go ahead. I suppose it can't do any harm,' I say. 'But I think she's only here for a few days. You'd better try to catch her soon.'

Justin stands up with a determined look. 'I'll go now. What's the point in waiting? Will you be okay here on your own?'

He seems to have forgotten I've been here all week on my own. 'I'll be fine.'

He gives me a peck on the cheek and marches out of the room. I listen to him pulling on his shoes and then, when the door slams shut, I let out a long sigh of relief.

What a morning. What a week.

It's at times like these you need good friends. What would Harriet say? Would she think I was wrong tackling Justin about Arabella last night? I need to call her while Justin's out.

I toss the blanket off my legs and go to look for my phone. It was in the bag we took to the beach, with the coffee and the sandwiches. Where's Justin put it?

It's not in the hall on the shelf where we keep the keys. Or on the dining room table. I wander into the kitchen where Justin's left the sandwich box and flask drying by the sink.

There it is, on the worktop by the kettle.

I snatch it up and find Harriet's number.

I wait for the ring in my ear, but when all I get is silence, I check the screen.

No SIM card.

That's odd.

Maybe the phone got knocked about while it was in the bag.

I use the prong of a fork to spring open the slot where the SIM card usually sits, assuming it's a simple fix. But when it slides open, there is no SIM card. It's gone.

Which means I have no way of calling Harriet. Or anyone else.

Justin must have removed it. But why? Who does he think I'm going to call?

This is strange.

I'll send a message via the wifi instead and see if Harriet's free to pop around for a natter. It would be good to have some moral support, and if Justin gets funny about it, I'll tell him I was asking her to speak to Arabella about the tenancy.

I compose a brief message and hit send.

But instead of flying off into the ether, a red exclamation mark appears under it with the words 'Not delivered.'

And then I notice the wifi symbol is missing from the cracked screen. This is feeling more than a coincidence.

I dive into the cupboard under the stairs where the router's kept, expecting to see its lights flashing with some kind of error message. But there are no lights on it at all. And when I follow the electrical lead that should be plugged into the wall, it's not only been unplugged, but the plug removed, leaving two copper wires poking out.

What is Justin playing at?

It has to be him. He's trying to cut me off, but why?

Panic builds in my chest and my heartbeat drums frantically.

DON'T IGNORE THIS MESSAGE. YOUR HUSBAND IS A DANGEROUS MAN.

I shake the words out of my head.

No, this can't be happening.

Is he punishing me? Is this all because of what happened last night? Because I accused him of rape? Of attempted murder?

What if it's all true? What if everything Arabella told me is exactly how it happened. Of course Justin would be angry. He doesn't want me to know what he's really like. What he's capable of. Because he knows I'd leave him. Our marriage would be in tatters.

My hand drifts to my throat, still painful from where he grabbed me last night. I thought I was going to die. And in the sea earlier, when I thought I was being held under. It *was* Justin. Showing me how easily he could end my life, if he chose to do it.

Just like with Arabella. He showed her how easily he could have killed her if he wanted to.

For the first time since we met sixteen years ago, I'm afraid of my husband and what he's capable of, what's going through his head and what he's planning to do next.

Have I been deluding myself all these years?

All those friends I cast adrift because of him. All the times he told me what to wear and how to do my hair. All the times he said I wasn't ready to go back to work. He wasn't protecting me or looking out for my best interests.

He was isolating and controlling me.

Whoever hid that phone in this house trying to warn me about him was right. Justin *is* a dangerous man. And I need to get away before he kills me.

'Megan? What are you doing?'

Fuck. I didn't hear the door. And now he's back.

That was quick.

I poke my head out of the cupboard and smooth down my hair, conscious my chest and face are flushing.

'Nothing. I was looking for my trainers. Did you speak to Arabella?'

His scowl tells me everything.

'It was a complete waste of time,' he growls.

I close the cupboard and compose myself, trying to control my trembling hands and voice. I need time to think.

'She won't even consider changing her mind,' he continues. 'She's given us until the end of the month.'

'I'm sorry,' I say, but frankly another day in this house with Justin would be too long.

'Who the hell does she think she is? I'm not having that bitch dictate where I can and can't live.' He pirouettes and smashes a fist into the wall, sending chunks of plaster and paint flying.

'Justin!' I gasp, my hand flying to my mouth. I've never seen him like this before. At least, not until last night.

He doesn't seem to notice the blood pouring from his knuckles. He runs his hands through his hair and stares at the ground, shaking his head.

'I'm sorry, Meg. I've fucked up. I should never have brought you here.'

'It's okay. It's not your fault.' I try to sound like I still care, while watching him hawkishly, keeping my distance until I can work out what I'm going to do. 'Why don't you call Harriet and see if she can help. Maybe, as a neutral, she can talk Arabella around.'

Harriet is my one hope. If I can't get a message to her, perhaps I can trick Justin into inviting her to the house instead.

'I thought she'd already tried,' he says.

'Yes, but there's no harm in seeing if she'd try again, is there?'

'You're right. What would I do without you, Meg?' The old charming Justin surfaces from the darkness. The way his moods and behaviour change in a flash is chilling. 'I'll call her.'

'Why don't you ask her over and we can come up with a game plan?' I suggest.

'Good idea.'

He pulls his phone from his pocket and makes the call.

I hold my breath, waiting for Harriet to answer, praying she'll come.

Never mind her sorting out the tenancy, she might be the only person I can rely on to save me from my husband.

Chapter 28

Harriet agrees to come over that afternoon, even though it's a weekend.

'She says she'll be here as soon as she's finished a viewing in Falmouth,' Justin says, slipping his phone in his pocket.

'That's good,' I say, smiling. I don't want to risk another confrontation with him so I don't mention my missing SIM card or that the wifi's been disabled. 'I'm still feeling cold, so I think I'll have another lie down.'

I curl up on the sofa under the blanket in front of the fire and close my eyes, pretending to sleep. Justin acts concerned and brings me a pillow from the bedroom, but I can't drift off, not with him in the house. He could be planning anything.

Fortunately, he leaves me in peace. I hear his footsteps on the stairs and the creak of the floorboards in one of the spare rooms where there's a desk. I guess he's catching up with work on his laptop. At least it gives me some space while we wait.

The next hour feels like a lifetime, but eventually a car pulls up outside and a sharp tap at the door signals Harriet's arrival.

Justin bounds down the stairs and is at the door before I can get up, inviting her in, thanking her for coming.

I toss my blanket over the back of the sofa and run my fingers through my hair, hoping to give it a bit of volume. It's still caked in brine. I should have had a shower, but I've had other things on my mind.

'Hey, Harriet,' I say, wandering into the hall, trying to look casual.

Harriet looks achingly gorgeous, but today I don't care. All I care about is letting her know I need her help.

Justin shows her into the dining room. She takes a place at the head of the table while he sits at the opposite end, facing her, like two political leaders about to discuss world peace. I pull up a chair between them.

Harriet reaches into her bag for a notebook and pen, and when she catches my gaze, I open my eyes wide, trying to signal that something's wrong without Justin catching on to what I'm up to. That I desperately need her help.

But she just smiles back, clicks her pen and folds open her notebook to a clean page.

'We've got a big problem,' Justin says, clasping his hands on the table, all businesslike. 'The Carlyons want to evict us and I want to know what you are doing about it.'

He's taking that tone with her again, like she's one of his minions here at his beck and call. How dare he speak to her like that when she dropped everything to come over. Is it because she's a woman? Or is he just so arrogant, he speaks to everyone like that? I haven't noticed it before, but maybe I haven't been paying attention.

Harriet appears unfazed, mirroring his body language, her hands resting on the table like his, watching him with an equally serious expression, head cocked slightly to one side.

'I'm not sure there's much I can — ' she begins with a disarming smile, but Justin's having none of it.

He shouts her down before she can finish. 'No, don't give me that. You're the rental agent.' He jabs a finger at her. 'We signed the tenancy with you. We're not in breach of that contract, so as far as I'm concerned, Arabella doesn't have a leg to stand on.'

If Harriet's flustered by Justin shouting and ranting, she doesn't show it, maintaining a supremely calm show of professionalism.

'Yes, that might be the case,' she says, 'but as the legal owners of the house, the Carlyons retain the right to evict you with two months' notice. I believe that's what Arabella has now agreed. I'm afraid you don't really have any further recourse.'

'Then talk to her and make her change her mind. You're the agent. Start earning your fees.'

'Of course I can try — '

'Do more than try,' Justin says, thumping the table. 'She's taking liberties. This is our home now. Where else are we supposed to go?'

'Yes, I understand.' A slight flush rising from Harriet's throat is the only outward sign that Justin's getting under her skin, but she's handling him well.

'Do you?' He skewers her with a wide-eyed stare of anger.

This is getting out of hand.

'Why don't we all calm down a bit,' I say. 'Justin, why don't you put the kettle on and make some coffee? There's no need to fall out, is there?' I rub his leg under the table, hoping he'll think I'm being affectionate. If I can get him out of the room for just a minute, I can speak to Harriet alone.

'Don't interrupt while I'm talking, Megan,' he snarls at me, the ferocity of his tone making me startle.

'I just thought we could — '

'Why don't *you* make it?' He throws his arms in the air. 'Can't you see I'm trying to save our home here?'

'Yes. Sorry.' I lower my gaze, embarrassed to have been spoken to by him like that, as if I'm a naughty child trying his patience.

I risk another glance at Harriet. Our eyes meet in solidarity. Now she can see what he's really like. I want to scream at her, wave my arms in her face, yell, 'Look, he *is* dangerous. I need your help. Save me.'

She wets her lips with a quick dart of her tongue and looks back at Justin. She doesn't know the half of it. That he half-throttled me to death last night, nearly drowned me at the beach this morning and disabled my phone and the wifi, cutting me off from the world. Unless I can find a way of telling her, she's not going to do anything.

I scrape my chair back and stand. Harriet smiles sympathetically. But it's not her sympathy I need.

'Coffee would be lovely, thank you, Megan,' she says.

'And bring some biscuits while you're at it,' Justin demands, without even looking at me.

I slope off to the kitchen, dejected. This isn't going at all to plan. I should have given it some more thought. I thought the biggest problem was going to be getting Harriet to the house. It never occurred to me how difficult it would be once she was here to raise the alarm without alerting Justin. But he's making it virtually impossible.

Come on, think, Megan. There has to be a way.

Maybe I could spill coffee over Justin, and while he's distracted somehow communicate to Harriet that I need her help.

But would that really work? This isn't a soap opera or a Hollywood movie. This is real life. What if I ended up scalding Justin? Despite everything, I couldn't do that to him. I couldn't risk the confrontation I know it would provoke. And it might not even work anyway.

I need something sure fire.

Morse code tapped out on the table leg?

A secret note slipped into Harriet's bag when Justin's distracted?

'Help me!' scratched into the back of a chocolate digestive?

They're all stupid ideas.

In the dining room, I can still hear them talking. Justin still shouting. Harriet implacable. I admire her. She's refusing to be bullied and it's winding him up into a proper state.

I'll just have to hope Justin leaves us alone briefly. Put my faith in fate. What else can I do? I can't risk anything that puts my life, or Harriet's, at further risk.

I return to the dining room with three mugs of coffee and a plate of digestives on a tray. It rattles as I place it on the table with trembling hands.

'Yes, I'll have another word with her,' Harriet is saying, her voice calm and reassuring, 'and of course I'll explain about the fire and the awful time you've both been through, but all I'm saying is — '

'You *have* to get her to listen,' Justin barks.

Harriet takes a calming breath and repeats herself. 'I'll have another word with her.'

She leans across the table and helps herself to one of the mugs of coffee.

In the corner of my eye, I can see Justin's still steaming. His face is red and his hands are balled into fists.

'In the meantime,' Harriet continues, 'I've started looking to see if we can find you something else, in case Arabella is absolutely set on her decision.'

She's only trying to let Justin know she's on the case and isn't going to leave us homeless, but she might as well have lobbed a hand grenade into the room. Justin looks like he might well combust.

'Have you not heard a word I've been saying?' he rages. 'We're not moving.'

Harriet barely blinks. 'Totally, but I just wanted to let you know I'm on your side and we're going to get this sorted one way or the other.'

'Then prove it and get Arabella to change her mind.'

Harriet sips her coffee and murmurs in appreciation. 'Lovely coffee, Megan. Do you grind your own?'

'What? Oh, no, it's just a supermarket own brand. Nothing special.' I giggle nervously.

'Well, it's delicious. Must be the way you make it.'

I glance briefly at Justin, who's staring open-mouthed at me, as if he can't believe the banal turn the conversation's taken.

'Two heaped spoonfuls in the cafetière and some hot water. That's all,' I say sheepishly, aware of Justin shuffling uneasily in his chair.

'So listen,' Harriet sets down her mug and angles her body towards me, offering Justin her shoulder, to make matters worse, 'when can you fit me in for my first training session? I really enjoyed the assessment.'

My blood runs cold. What is she doing? She knows how Justin feels about me going back to work. She must think I've squared it with him, but I've not had the chance. That's been the last thing on my mind.

'Training session?' Justin asks with an edge to his voice that almost stops my heart.

'It's nothing,' I blurt out. 'Harriet popped around while you were away and wanted some fitness advice, that's all.'

Harriet frowns. 'Come on, Megan, don't be shy. You can tell him. I don't mind.' My stomach tightens and I think I'm going to be sick. 'Megan's going to take me on as her first client here in Cornwall,' she says, looking straight at Justin with a grin. 'Isn't that great? And I know loads of women around here who'll be queuing up to sign up too.'

Oh god. What is she playing at? She's dropped me right in it. He's going to go berserk. He made it absolutely clear I wasn't ready and now he'll think I've deliberately gone against him. In the mood he's in, this isn't going to go well.

I can't look at him, but I feel his brooding presence at the end of the table, like a bubbling volcano ready to erupt.

'It's too soon for Megan to go back to work,' he growls. 'She knows that. I made it quite clear. So whatever's been going on behind my back needs to stop. There will be no training sessions.'

Harriet's immaculately trimmed eyebrows shoot up. 'Are you serious?'

'I think I know what's best for my wife.' He thumps the table again, like some boneheaded caveman staking his claim on me.

'Do you?' she asks, peering at him over the top of her mug.

Oh, god. I want to be anywhere but in this room, right now. Or even in the house. I want to be as far from Justin as it's physically possible to be, because when Harriet's gone, I'm going to bear the full brunt of his anger. And the scary thing is, I no longer know what he's capable of doing. He's already assaulted me and tried to drown me. Next time, he might just finish the job...

'I think I know my wife. And in case you've forgotten, she's been through an enormous trauma. She's lost two children. It's not the sort of thing you get over easily,' he says, with a chilling menace.

'I'm well aware of that but — '

'It's too early for her to return to work. Maybe, in due course, when she's had time to process what she did, we can talk about it.'

They're talking about me as if I'm not in the room, like I'm a child in a custody battle with no mind of my own. I appreciate Harriet's fighting my corner, but I really wish she'd shut up. This isn't helping.

'I'm sorry you feel that way,' Harriet says, putting her mug on the table, slowly and deliberately. 'But personally I think it would be good for her while she's stuck here alone and you're off gallivanting here, there and everywhere with your job.'

'Gallivanting?' Justin spits.

'I'm sorry, Justin, but I consider Megan to be a friend, and I have to say, I think you're being a bit overprotective.'

'I know my wife best,' Justin repeats slowly.

'Yes, so you said.'

'That's enough. I think it's time you left.'

No, no, no. She can't leave. Not yet.

Harriet checks her watch and huffs. 'Yes, you're right. I need to be getting back to the office.' She stands, tosses her notebook and pen in her bag and hooks it over her arm. 'I'm sorry if I caused any offence, Justin. It's only that I'm fond of Megan and I can see she's feeling a little adrift.'

'She's fine,' he says.

'Right. Well, thanks for the coffee, Megan. I'll see you soon.'

My eyes open wide in panic, begging her to read the signs. To see my fear. Surely she can tell something's wrong? I mean, how much more obvious can it be? Once she's gone, I'm going to be left here alone with Justin, cut off, totally isolated and utterly at his mercy. The moment she walks out of the door, my opportunity's lost.

'Harriet... ' I begin, the words drying up in my mouth.

'Yes?'

I glance at Justin, who's shooting me looks like daggers.

'Nothing. It's nothing at all.' The breath escapes from my lungs like air from a punctured balloon. There's no way I can stop her from leaving and no way to signal for help without looking suspicious.

'Okay, well, call me soon,' Harriet says, making the universal telephone hand gesture.

I can't. Justin's stolen my SIM card and cut off the wifi. I have no way of contacting anyone and I'm terrified of being left alone in the house with him when you're gone.

My lips tighten into a thin smile. 'Sure,' I croak.

'I'll let you know how I get on with Arabella,' she says to Justin.

He's still sitting at the end of the table, smouldering.

Maybe there is a small window of opportunity after all.

I jump up. 'I'll show you out,' I say, grabbing her elbow and steering her towards the hall.

Just a few seconds is all I need. The chance to whisper in her ear.

'No, no, I'll do it.' Justin stands up so quickly, he knocks his chair flying. 'You clear away the coffee.'

He nudges past me and places his hand on the small of Harriet's back, directing her out.

Harriet blows me a kiss. And then she's gone.

Justin glares at me as he follows her out, as if with the unspoken promise that he's not done with me yet.

I stand frozen, my legs paralysed, as the front door opens and slams closed.

I hold my breath as I hear the growl of Harriet's car and the crunch of its tyres.

I'm alone again in the house with Justin and with no one in the world to help me.

He appears in the doorway, his eyes dark and hooded, hands by his side, his shoulders squared, and he glares at me.

'I think it's about time we had a little chat,' he says.

Chapter 29

This is it. He's going to kill me.

I grab the back of a chair, my legs like jelly.

'Justin... ' I beg. 'Please.'

'And when exactly did you plan on telling me you'd starting working again?'

'It's not... I didn't... It was only that — '

'I thought I made it perfectly clear that you're not ready, Megan. Look at you. You're a mess. And yet, what did you do the second my back was turned?' he screams, striding forwards, looming over me.

I buckle under the onslaught, dropping to my knees and covering my head with my hands.

'So did that feel good, embarrassing me like that? Making me look like an idiot in front of that woman?'

'No!' I sob.

'You know, I've only ever had your best interests at heart. I've gone out of my way to look out for you. To protect you from yourself. How many other men do you think would have stuck around after what you did? He spits the words like poison. He grabs my wrist and pulls me to my feet. 'Look at me!' he yells, spittle flying into my face.

'I'm sorry. I'm really, really sorry.'

'You killed my boys, Megan. You killed them with your carelessness, but all I've ever done is show you forgiveness. I never even thought about walking away, when I probably should have done. And this is how you treat me. You should be ashamed of yourself.'

'Harriet begged me,' I cry. 'I thought it would help me settle in.'

'That woman is nothing but trouble. I want you to keep away from her.'

'But she's my friend. She's my *only* friend.'

'I've told you before, you don't need friends like her. People like that are poisonous. You see how she's driving us apart, talking you into doing something I've made clear you're not ready for?'

'It's not like that.'

He has hold of both of my wrists, gripping them so tightly my hands throb.

'Where does this end, Megan? Last night you were accusing me of being a rapist and of trying to kill Arabella. And now this. Do you really hate me that much after everything I've done for you?'

'I don't hate you.' Tears stream down my cheeks. 'I love you.'

'You have a funny way of showing it.'

'I'll make it up to you. I promise.' At this moment, I'm ready to promise him the world. Anything to make him let go of me.

'You make me sick, you know that?' He finally releases my wrists, shoving me at the same time.

I crash into the legs of a chair and cry out in pain, but he doesn't seem to care that I'm hurt. There's venom in his eyes I've never seen before. Do I really know this man at all?

He glowers at me with contempt, as if I'm worthless. Dirt on his shoe. How have we come to this?

If I had any doubts before, they've been well and truly confirmed. Justin *is* a dangerous man and I need to get away from him before he kills me.

'Get this coffee cleared up. I'm going back upstairs to work. And I want no more trouble from you today.'

I bow my head, just grateful it's over. For now.

As Justin's footsteps disappear up the stairs, I brush my hair out of my eyes and dry my cheeks. I never thought I'd be that wife who was scared of her husband. But then I never thought Justin would be the kind of man who could behave so aggressively.

I gather up the mugs and what's left of the biscuits and stagger into the kitchen.

What am I going to do?

I can't stay here in the house with him. But where would I go? I'd pinned all my hopes on Harriet being able to help me, but I was being a fool. She can't help. The only person who can help is me. I have to do this by myself.

As I put the mugs in the dishwasher and rinse out the cafetière, a thought forms in my mind. I'm not totally alone here at Treloar, even though it feels like it. The Sir Roger and Lady Grace are home now. Plus, there's Arabella and Colin. If I can reach the house and explain the danger I'm in, surely they'll be able to help me.

I dry my hands on a tea towel and step into the hall. The house has fallen silent. No, not quite. When I listen carefully, I can hear the tap-tap-tap of a keyboard. Justin working on his laptop. I only need a few minutes head start and I can be at the house before he can stop me.

I tip-toe to the cupboard under the stairs and pull on my running shoes, freezing every time I hear the creak of a floorboard or joist in this dusty old house.

The rubber soles of my shoes squeak annoyingly loudly as I creep to the front door. Wincing, I try the handle, hoping I can sneak out without Justin hearing. By the time he's worked out I've gone, I should be safely away. Perhaps I can even persuade Arabella to drive me into Falmouth.

I tug at the heavy oak door, but it won't budge.

It's locked! And the key is missing.

I try with both hands, but I can't get out. I'm trapped in the house with a monster.

'Looking for these?'

I spin around, frantic.

Justin's meandering down the stairs with a self-satisfied grin on his face and the front door keys dangling off his finger.

'You locked me in,' I gasp.

'For your own safety, Megs. What other choice did I have?'

'So you're keeping me prisoner now?'

He frowns. 'Don't be silly. You're not a prisoner, but I have a duty to look after you. Like I've always done. You're upset. I can't have you running off and doing something silly, can I now?'

'Open this door,' I demand, although my voice sounds reedy and desperate.

Justin closes his fist around the keys 'No, it's best if you stay indoors today.'

I launch across the hall, sprinting for the back door, snatching at the handle.

But it's also locked.

I run into the lounge and try the patio doors, but I can already see the key is gone. Sure enough, the doors refuse to open.

'You bastard,' I scream. 'Let me out!'

'Not until you've calmed down. I want you to prove to me I can trust you again.'

'Prove *you* can trust *me*?'

He nods.

Oh god, the man's deranged.

But what choice do I have? I can either fight him or...

There is only one other way. If he doesn't think he can trust me, then I need to win back his trust. At least until I can find a way of escaping from him.

I take a big breath, deep into my lungs, centring myself. Calming myself. Transforming myself into the character he wants me to be.

'I'm sorry,' I say. 'I've been a real bitch, haven't I?'

'I forgive you,' he says, like he's a priest or something.

'I didn't mean to go behind your back. I can see how that must have made you feel,' I say, softening my tone. Becoming the old Megan again.

'And accusing me of those horrible things?'

I shake my head. 'I'm such an idiot. I don't know why I believed Arabella. Of course you're not capable of any of it. You're a good man. A kind man.' I force myself to close the distance between us and put a hand to his cheek. 'And I love you. I don't know what I'd do without you.'

'I don't know what you'd do without me either.' That smug grin makes me want to punch him in the balls, but instead I concentrate on not recoiling when he kisses me. I even wrap my arms around him and pretend I'm yielding to his embrace.

'Let's not talk anymore about it,' he says. 'For now.'

He pushes the door key into his jeans pocket. It's going to take a bit more than an empty apology and some faked affection before he trusts me to let me out again. I just need to be patient. It's the only way.

'Why don't you finish your work? I'll cook us something nice tonight,' I say, running my hand down his chest. 'I'll make it all up to you.'

'That sounds good.'

He plants one last kiss on my lips and, with an affectionate pat on my backside, trots back upstairs to his laptop and I let out a sigh of relief.

All I need is for him to believe that he can trust me not to run away. As he said himself, I know him better than anyone, so how hard can it be?

Chapter 30

That evening, after we've eaten, Justin is totally charming. He clears up after the meal, massages my feet as we watch TV and even fetches me a peppermint tea before bed. And I play the part of the adoring, dutiful wife, laughing at all his jokes, listening attentively when he rants about work and not flinching every time he touches me.

But in my head, all I can think about is his hands around my neck, the panic as he held me underwater and the malevolent look in his eye when Harriet told him I was taking her on as a personal trainer. This isn't the man I fell in love with.

This man is dangerous and the sooner I can get away from him, the better.

The following morning, he insists we go out for the day. It begins with a trip to a gorgeous little café in a working boatyard on the river where a dozen or more yachts are out of the water on stilts. The wooden-clad building at the water's edge is nothing more than a glorified cabin but inside it's warm and cosy, with a wood-burning stove pumping out heat, the white painted walls adorned with black and white photos from the area and the air thick with the stomach-rumbling smell of coffee and freshly baked pastries.

He orders us lattes and eggs on toast for breakfast before we head off in the car to explore further. We drive past countless secluded coves and pretty coastal villages, along clifftop passes and through meandering green lanes as if Justin's trying to convince me of Cornwall's undisputed beauty and that if he can just open my eyes, I'll be able to see what a wonderful life we could have here. But I don't need convincing. It's the perfect place for holidays and adventures, but I don't want to live here. Specifically, I don't want to live here with Justin. I don't want to live anywhere with him. I don't want any part of his life anymore. I'm better off without him.

The idea of being on my own and starting over would have terrified me even a few days ago. Justin was all I had and, I thought, all I needed. But I was deluded. He's suffocating me and if I don't leave, he could end up killing me. But for now, I have to continue playing the part I've spent the best part of twenty years auditioning for. I just need to keep it together long enough for the opportunity of escape to come my way.

For lunch, we head to a trendy restaurant owned by a celebrity chef. It overlooks a white sandy beach and has picturesque views to die for across the cove. Typically, he orders for us both, not even bothering to let me look at the menu, and afterwards, with stomachs full, we walk along the beach with the wind whipping our hair.

It's funny, he thinks this has clinched the deal. That one decent meal in a fancy restaurant has changed my mind about him and Cornwall. And of course, I let him believe it, all the while with one eye on the exit of this toxic marriage.

'Isn't it wonderful here?' he says, clutching my hand tightly as our feet sink into the soft sand.

We must look like some kind of loved-up couple in the first throes of a new romance and not just a man holding tightly onto his frantic wife to prevent her making her escape.

'It's amazing,' I coo, grabbing his arm in what I hope he takes as a sign of affection. 'We're so lucky to have this on the doorstep.'

'You see, I knew that once you'd given it a chance, you'd learn to be happy here.' The smile that creeps across his face gives me an unexpected thrill of delight. Who thought it would be so easy to deceive him?

It's late afternoon when we return to the lodge. Justin shepherds me inside, locks the door behind us and pockets the key. So much for winning him around. It's clearly going to take a little more time and effort. But how long? I can't keep up this pretence forever. It's exhausting.

'Nice cup of tea?' Justin asks as I kick off my shoes and head for the lounge.

'That would be lovely. Do you want me to do it?'

'No, no, I'm fine. You put your feet up,' he says.

I slump on the sofa and instinctively pull out my phone, momentarily forgetting it's next to useless. Maybe I can at least get him to reinstate the internet. If he's going to be working from home, he's going to need it.

'I noticed the wifi's not working,' I say, innocently as Justin appears with two mugs of steaming tea.

'We don't need it.'

I arch my eyebrows. 'Don't you need it for work?'

'I can use the data on my phone,' he says.

Shit. I hadn't thought of that.

'It's just I was going to check the weather for the next couple of days,' I lie. 'I wanted to see if it was going to be dry enough to go out for a run.'

Justin settles on the sofa next to me and crosses his legs. 'Megan, we're surrounded by the most glorious countryside and we have each other. We don't need wifi or the internet. If you want to check the weather, watch the news,' he says, with a hint of irritation.

I don't want to rile him, but it might be too late as he sets off on another rant.

'The whole world's become far too reliant on the internet,' he says. 'What did everyone do before it was even a thing? It'll do us both good to unplug for a while.'

'You're absolutely right,' I agree, reaching for his hand and squeezing it with a smile, the mere touch of his skin making my flesh crawl.

'I'm glad you agree.'

'And my phone? Is that why you took my SIM card?'

'The removal of temptation, that's all,' he says.

'I understand.'

'I knew you would. I'm protecting you, that's all.' He pats my hand like I'm an aged aunt and I have the sudden urge to throw my tea over him.

But I mustn't.

I have to wait.

When we turn in for the night, I sense another opportunity. I didn't dare to attempt anything last night, but this evening when we're in bed and Justin starts snoring, I roll back the duvet and slide my legs out to investigate.

He's locked us in again, but the keys must be here somewhere. I didn't see where he put them, but the chances are they're still in his trouser pockets.

The floorboard wheezes under my weight and I wince. Justin grunts and rolls over. I count to ten, my heart pounding, then tip-toe across the room.

His jeans are in a heap by the wardrobe. He never bothers hanging them up, which usually makes me cross, but tonight I'm grateful.

I stoop down and feel around in both pockets. I find his wallet and a scrunched-up tissue, but no keys.

'Megan? What are you doing?'

I jump up with a squeal of terror. Justin flicks on his bedside lamp and I have to squint to protect my eyes.

'Nothing. I was just going to use the bathroom,' I say, scurrying towards the door.

'I've hidden the keys,' he says, his voice thick with sleep. 'So don't even think about trying to get out.'

'I wasn't,' I protest.

He sits up and scratches his nose. 'I'm watching you, Meg. Even when I'm asleep, I'm watching you.'

A shudder runs from the back of my head all the way down my spine. Even though we both know that's impossible, I don't doubt him for a second.

When I get back, and climb into bed, Justin's asleep again with the light off, air whistling softly through his nose.

I need to take more care. If he catches me trying to escape again, he'll never trust me. At least I have the run of the house at the moment, but if he thinks I'm actively plotting something there's no telling what he'll do. Lock me in the spare room? In the cupboard under the stairs? Or worse?

I sleep fitfully for the rest of the night, running through plots and plans. If I can make it to the main house and raise the alarm, I'm sure I'll be fine. But how am I going to slip away without Justin noticing?

I could overpower him, attack him with a knife or a hammer, but I'm not sure I have it in me to hurt him, even after everything he's done. And if I don't do it right, it could all go badly wrong very quickly.

I could drug his tea and wait for him to pass out. But with what? I think I have a few old sleeping pills in my toiletry bag, but I've not touched them since the fire. It was taking them with alcohol that left me sleeping through while my boys perished. Maybe I could mix them in his wine. But how many would I need? I don't want to kill him. No, it's too risky.

Maybe I could steal his phone while he's in the shower or distracted cooking? Surely it wouldn't be that difficult and I know for a fact he has Harriet's number. But what's his passcode? I have no idea. It's another stupid idea.

Eventually, the darkness of the night is chased away by the hazy light of morning and Justin's alarm makes me jump. I've hardly slept a wink.

'Morning, gorgeous,' he says, rolling over and wrapping an arm over me. 'How did you sleep.'

'Good. Must have been all that sea air yesterday.'

'Me too.' He sits up suddenly and stretches. 'Right, I'd better jump in the shower.'

'You're getting up already?' I ask, confused.

'It's Monday. I have to be in the office this morning,' he says, leaning over and kissing my forehead.

My heart cartwheels. 'You're going into work?'

Of course, he was always due back today, but with everything that's been going on, I'd completely forgotten.

'Will you be okay here on your own? I shouldn't be back late.'

'Of course,' I gasp, trying to conceal my excitement. If he's not here, there's no way he can stop me leaving. 'I'll be fine.'

He slides out of bed, pads across the room and disappears into the bathroom. I listen to the toilet flush and the clank of pipes and rush of water as he turns on the shower.

Meanwhile, my mind goes into overdrive, planning my day. Who knew he was going to make it this easy for me. Playing the compliant wife all day yesterday is going to pay dividends.

As soon as he's gone, I'll head up to the Carlyons' house and ask to use their phone. I'll call Harriet and tell her everything. I'm sure she won't mind coming to pick me up. Hopefully, she can drop me off in Falmouth and I can withdraw some cash. And then I can jump on a train. I don't know where I'll go yet. Anywhere. It doesn't matter. Just far away from here.

'What are you going to do today?' Justin asks, stepping back into the bedroom with wet hair and a towel wrapped around his waist.

'Oh, um, I don't know,' I say. 'Maybe some chores around the house. There's a heap of washing that needs sorting and I thought I might clean the kitchen floor.'

He nods thoughtfully, like I've passed some kind of test. Then I watch as he gets dressed, pulling on a blue shirt and a pair of suit trousers. Is this the last time I'll ever watch my husband dressing for work? Oh god, I hope so.

The rush of adrenaline makes my whole body tremble with anticipation and fear. This is finally my chance.

'I'll grab some breakfast on the way,' he says, coming around to my side of the bed and planting a lingering kiss on my lips. One last kiss. It's as much as I can do to stop myself shoving him away. 'I should get going. I'll see you tonight.'

And then he's gone. As if there's nothing untoward going on between us. Like he's not kept me locked in the house for the last two days. Or tried to strangle me. Or drown me.

I hold my breath as I listen to him bound down the stairs, only letting it go when I hear the front door open and slam shut.

At last, I'm alone. And so nearly free.

But another sound reignites all my fears.

The sound of the key turning in the lock.

No! Please, god, no.

I hurl off the duvet and sprint for the stairs, almost tripping down them in my haste. Wouldn't that be an irony if he came home and found me lying in the hall with a broken neck.

I stub my toe on the tiles but the pain doesn't register as I throw myself at the door and try the handle, confirming my worst nightmare.

The bastard's locked me in.

I should have known he wouldn't make it that easy for me.

Everything I'd been planning and hoping drifts out of my hand like a breath of smoke.

I hammer on the door with my fist as Justin's car growls into life and pulls away.

'Justin!' I scream. 'Let me out.'

But he's gone. And I'm left trapped in the house. A prisoner in my own home.

Chapter 31

Time slows down to a crawl as I stand at the door, weighing up my options. I can't believe he's locked all the doors and left me trapped in the house. What if there's a fire?

Then I'd have to climb out of a window...

Bloody hell, the windows. Why didn't I think of that before? I bet he's not even thought about them. As far as I'm aware, none of them are fitted with locks. I race into the dining room which has the biggest sash window on the ground floor and potentially offers the easiest way of getting out.

Sure enough, there's no lock on it. All I need to do is lift it and climb out.

With a renewed vigour, I run back up to the bedroom and throw on my jeans and the T-shirt I wore yesterday. Then I gather some underwear, some clean clothes and some toiletries and shove them all in a bag for life I find under the kitchen sink.

And then I'm ready. I take one last look around the house in case there's anything I've forgotten. I don't have the slightest pang of doubt or regret. It's not a home. I'm not going to miss living here in the slightest.

The dining room window jerks open with a bit of effort, dislodging old cobwebs and dust which cascade onto the carpet. It's clearly not been opened in years. I throw my bag of clothes out first and then squeeze my body through the narrow gap, my hips protesting, a reminder I'm not as fit or as flexible as I used to be. Still, that's all going to change soon when I get my life back again.

I fall inelegantly into the garden and scoop up my bag.

It's only a short walk up the drive to the main house, but it feels too risky to walk brazenly out in the open. Justin's probably halfway to Plymouth by now, but even so, I take the safer option along one of my running trails through the woods. Better to use the cover of the trees, just in case.

Just in case of what?

What's happened to me?

When did I turn into this haunted woman, afraid of her own shadow?

It's going to be hours until Justin's home, but I start to jog, careful not to trip on the roots and brambles that lie in ambush along the twisting path. It would be just my luck to turn an ankle as I'm almost free.

When Treloar House comes into view through the leaves, my heart soars. I'm so close.

I slow down to catch my breath and peer out from behind the trunk of a crooked horse chestnut tree, looking for Justin's car. I know I'm being paranoid, but I wouldn't put it past the bastard to have second-guessed my plan and to come looking for me.

But there's no sign of him or his car.

I scurry out of the woods and across the lawn, running like a crazy woman with my grocery bag swinging at my side. I vault onto the patio in front of the house and keep running, aiming for the main entrance.

But what if no one's in?

Of course there will be. A maid answered the door last time. There's bound to be someone who can let me in to use the phone.

But before I reach the door, I spot another figure skulking in the shadows. A man. Tall and angular.

My heart misses a couple of beats.

'Finn?'

He freezes when he sees me, fear in his eyes.

'What are you doing here?' I ask.

He looks shiftily over his shoulder and runs a hand over his straggly beard. 'Nothing.'

'Are you back living with your parents?'

'Not exactly.' He edges away, back in the direction he's come.

'Wait.' I hold up a hand to stop him. 'Please. I need to ask you something.'

He stops and frowns quizzically, shoving his hands in his pockets. 'What?'

'Did you leave an old phone in the lodge for me to find?' I ask, stepping closer like I'm approaching a startled deer.

'Phone?'

'Was it you who's been sending me messages about Justin? Please, I just need to know the truth. It's been driving me crazy.'

'No,' he scoffs, as if I am actually crazy. 'I don't know what you're talking about.'

'Are you sure?'

He glances over his shoulder again and then grabs my arm, guiding me away from the house to a clearing behind a clump of rhododendron bushes, as if he's afraid of being spotted with me.

'Look, I don't know anything about a phone or any messages, okay?'

'Okay.' I'm not sure whether or not to believe him. 'But it was you who was squatting in the lodge, wasn't it?'

'Maybe.' He looks down at the ground and scuffs his foot across the earth, clearing a small patch of fallen leaves.

'And where are you staying now?'

He hesitates, then looks me up and down. 'With Colin for a bit, just while I get myself back on my feet.'

'You still haven't patched things up with your father then?' I ask.

He shrugs. 'None of your business. Anyway, what are you doing sneaking around up here again?'

'I wasn't sneaking.'

He raises a wild, wiry eyebrow. He has stains all down his T-shirt and his arm's purple with bruises. His hair doesn't look like it's seen a brush or a comb in decades.

'So what *were* you doing?'

I poke my tongue into my cheek. Is there any harm in telling him? He's hardly likely to bump into Justin any time soon. 'I'm leaving Justin,' I say. 'He's sabotaged my phone and cut off the internet. I was hoping to use the phone in the house.'

'You're leaving him because he cut off the internet?' Finn frowns.

'No.' I swallow a hard lump in my throat. 'I'm leaving him because he tried to kill me.'

'What?' Finn explodes.

'Someone left me a phone in the lodge and used it to send me messages warning me that Justin was dangerous. But I didn't believe it. Until now. I thought it might be you or your sister, because I know all about the fire, and I couldn't think who else it could be,' I say, the words tumbling out of my mouth.

Finn stares at me, scanning my face.

'It wasn't me. Sorry,' he says.

'Right.'

It's not really important who was trying to warn me. Still, for my sanity, I'd like to know.

'Do you think it might have been Arabella?' I ask.

'I don't know. I suppose it could have been.'

'In which case, I need to thank her.'

'Where will you go now?' Finn asks.

'I - I'm not actually sure,' I stammer. 'But away from here. Far, far away.'

'Well, good luck. I never trusted Justin, and I couldn't understand why he'd want to come back here.'

'I think because he had so many good times here and conveniently forgot the bad memories,' I say. The truth is, I have no idea. Whenever I've tried talking to Justin about what really happened at Treloar with Finn and Arabella, he's denied everything.

'You're better off without him.'

'Yes,' I say. 'I know.'

Finn turns to leave, heading for a trail that leads deep into the woods.

'Come with me to the house,' I say. 'I'll talk to your father and explain everything, that you weren't responsible for the fire. That it was all Justin. I'll tell him you weren't to blame.' I desperately want to fix what Justin broke between Finn and his family and this is the only way I know how.

Finn stops and looks back towards me with a tight smile. 'Thanks,' he says. 'But it's a bit late for that.'

'It doesn't have to be.'

'Too much water, Megan. Too many bridges.'

He sets off again, trudging along with his head down and his shoulders rounded. A man broken and defeated. And there's nothing I can do about it.

Chapter 32

The maid who answers the door isn't the same woman who let me in the last time I was here to talk to Arabella. She's older with flecks of grey in her jet black hair. Stern-looking with deep creases around her eyes.

'Yes?'

'I'm Megan.' My voice sounds weak. Pathetic. 'We're renting the lodge. I need to use your phone. It's urgent.'

The woman stares at me as if I've just asked her if I could pluck out her eyes and pickle them in a jar.

'Please, it's an emergency,' I add, sounding even more pathetic.

The woman is clearly torn. I don't suppose they're used to getting many visitors.

'Wait here,' she says, about to shut the door in my face.

But I stick out my arm and force it open. I'm not being fobbed off by her, or anyone. Not today. 'Please, tell Lady Grace it's Megan Pike and I need to use her phone as a matter of urgency.' What the hell. She might as well know the truth. I have nothing to hide. 'Look, my husband tried to keep me locked up in the house and I'm terrified that when he gets back home he's going to... he's going to hurt me.'

The woman blinks rapidly four or five times, assessing me, trying to work out what to make of this mad woman on the doorstep claiming her life's in danger.

'You'd better come in,' she says.

I glance down the drive, still half expecting Justin to come tearing along in his car to drag me back to the lodge, telling everyone I'm out of my mind and I don't know what I'm talking about. That I'm stressed. Overtired. Still grieving.

But he doesn't.

I'm safe.

For the moment, at least. He can't hurt me while I'm in the house.

My heart rate finally slows to something approaching normal as the door closes behind me and the maid leaves me standing in the hall.

'Wait here,' she instructs solemnly, before gliding away with perfect poise and posture.

I catch the smell of boiled cabbage, and maybe a hint of beeswax. It's not a pleasant odour. It reminds me of the care home where my grandmother lived for the last few years of her life. Not what I expected at all from such a grand house.

From where I'm left standing, the phone's within easy reach on a table less than six strides away. Tantalisingly close. It's one of those old-fashioned Bakelite phones that looks like a relic from the nineteen-twenties with a dial and a heavy handset on a long lead.

I could just go ahead and call Harriet without waiting for permission. But that would be rude and I can afford to wait a minute or two. I'm safe. Justin isn't here.

A few moments later, the sound of voices carries down the hall, followed by shuffling footsteps and Lady Grace appears in a waft of lavender, with the maid hovering a few feet behind.

'My dear Megan. Is everything alright?' she asks, the deep lines on her face concertinaed into a look of concern.

She glances at my jeans. I follow her gaze and notice with embarrassment they're covered in mud and grass stains from where I dropped out of the window at the lodge. I try to brush them off, my cheeks flushing hot.

'I'm sorry to impose but I was hoping I could use your phone,' I say. 'It's a bit of an emergency.'

'Of course. Help yourself,' she says, waving towards the phone on the table. 'I trust everything is okay?'

'He tried to kill me and has been keeping me locked in the house.' The words are out of my mouth before I can stop them.

Lady Grace's face folds in horror. 'Who?'

'My husband. Justin.' My eyes unexpectedly water with tears. 'I have to get away from him but he's disabled my phone.' I hold up my mobile as if that somehow explains everything.

'Do you need to call the police?'

'What? No, it's fine. I just need to get away. My friend will come and pick me up, I'm sure.'

I snatch up the receiver and put it to my ear, find Harriet's number in my phone and start to dial. I had no idea how long it took to call someone using one of these old phones with its rotary dial, waiting for it to circle back to its starting position before dialling each number. It seems to take an age with Lady Grace and the maid watching over me.

Eventually, the line clicks and rings.

I shoot Lady Grace a grim smile as I wait for Harriet to pick up, my foot tapping on the floor impatiently.

Whenever I've called from my mobile, Harriet's picked up straight-away. I guess she doesn't recognise this number. She has no idea it's me.

I'm losing hope that she'll answer at all when finally the call connects.

'Harriet Quinlivan,' she says brightly.

'Harriet. It's me. Megan,' I gasp with relief.

'Megan?'

'I'm calling from Treloar House. Justin's taken the SIM card out of my phone and cut off the wifi so I couldn't call you from my mobile,' I tell her.

'Woah, slow down. What's going on?'

'It's Justin,' I sob. 'I'm leaving him. Please, would you be able to pick me up? I'm so sorry, I didn't have anyone else to call.'

'Leaving him? Why?'

'I'll tell you everything later, but right now I really need to get away from here. Will you come? Please? I can pay you for petrol.'

'Don't be silly. Of course I'll come. I'm just with a client on a viewing, but as soon as I'm done here, I'll be there,' she says.

'Thank you.'

'Are you okay? You sound upset.'

'I'm fine,' I sniff. 'I had to climb out of a window to get out. I was trying to tell you when you came over the other day, but... it doesn't matter. Please, hurry.'

'Bloody hell, Megan. I'm so sorry. I'll be there as soon as I can. Sit tight.'

'I will.' I glance at Lady Grace and smile again. 'They're being very kind to me here. Come up to the main house when you're ready. I'll be waiting.'

'I'll be there in an hour.'

An hour? I thought she'd be able to get here quicker. 'Sure,' I say weakly. 'I'll be here. Thanks.'

'Okay, I've got to go. I'll see you soon.'

And then she hangs up.

There's nothing I can do but wait and hope Justin doesn't decide to make an unexpected return to check up on me.

'Is she coming?' Lady Grace asks.

'Yes,' I say. 'She's on her way. She'll be here in an hour. I'll wait outside.'

'Don't be so silly. You can wait here.'

'Are you sure? I don't want to cause any trouble'

'You're not any trouble. Come and make yourself comfortable.' She leads me into a room at the front of the house where two large sofas are positioned facing each other either side of a grand fireplace. Hundreds of leather-bound books fill floor-to-ceiling shelves around two of the walls and in the corner, there's a writing desk covered in paperwork. 'Julieta, could you bring some tea,' she says to the maid, who retires with a gracious bow.

'I don't want to impose,' I say, wringing my hands, conscious that I look as though I've slept in a field.

'You're not imposing,' Lady Grace says, patting my hand. Her skin is cold but I appreciate the gesture.

'Mother? What's going on? I heard voices.' Arabella breezes into the room but pulls up sharply when she sees me. 'Oh, what are you doing here?'

'Megan's had a frightful shock, darling. She's waiting here for her friend to pick her up,' Lady Grace says.

Arabella cups her hands in front of her chest and looks me up and down with disgust, her pretty nose wrinkling. 'What sort of shock?'

'It's Justin.' I bow my head. 'You were right. He's not the man I thought he was.'

'Why? What's he done now?' she asks, her tone clipped.

I chew my lip and stare at my feet. 'He tried to kill me,' I croak.

'Oh, really?'

When I look up, she's frowning while still managing to somehow look repulsed that I'm here, in their family home.

'When I told him what you'd said, about the fire and how he'd attacked you, he strangled me. And then he took me swimming in the sea and he held my head under the water. I don't know whether he was just trying to scare me or kill me, but I've realised I can't stay with him, especially as he's had me locked in the house for the last two days.'

Finally, her face softens and she exchanges a look I can't read with her mother.

'I'm sorry,' Arabella says. 'I tried to warn you.'

'I know. I should have listened.'

'Come on, sit,' she says, pointing to one of the sofas.

'I'll leave you girls to chat,' Lady Grace says, withdrawing from the room as the maid returns with tea. 'Let me know if there's anything else I can do.'

I perch on the edge of one of the sofas with Arabella sitting opposite and watch the maid pour from a pot into two floral bone china cups.

'I am a bit confused. You said you didn't know Justin had taken the tenancy for the lodge, so how did you know to leave me that phone?' I ask.

Arabella scowls. 'What phone?'

'The old phone I found in the attic.'

She shakes her head, her expression blank. 'I don't know what you're talking about.'

'Come on, the messages you sent me about Justin being dangerous. You must have sent them. You just said you tried to warn me.'

'I'm sorry, Megan. But I don't know anything about a phone or any messages,' she says.

'Well someone was trying to warn me. And if not you, then who?'

She shrugs. 'I only found out about Justin being back when Finn called.'

'I see.' I'm as confused as ever. The phone didn't mysteriously materialise in the house on its own. Someone must have put it there and someone must have been sending those messages. But if not Arabella, who?

'What are you going to do?' she asks.

'I don't know, but I need to get away from here. From Justin.'

'Do you have any money?'

'I have some savings hidden away. I'm sure I'll be fine.' I wipe a tear from my eye. 'The thing is, we've been married for more than ten years and I had no idea of the monster I was living with.'

Arabella grimaces. 'He can be charming. I wouldn't beat yourself up about it.'

'But he stood by me after the fire and after Felix and Sebastian died. If it hadn't been for Justin, I'm not sure I'd have survived,' I say, trying to piece together how everything between us has fallen apart so quickly. Has he always been like this and I've not been able to see it?

'Well, you're doing the right thing now and that's the main thing.'

'Tell me what he was like,' I say, 'when you knew him as a teenager. You used to be friends, didn't you?'

'For a little while. But I was always suspicious of him.'

'Why?'

'I don't know. He was arrogant. A bully, I suppose. He liked to put people down,' she says, staring into the cup she's balancing on her knee. 'And then you know about how he attacked me and the fire.'

'Yes, you told me, but I still don't really understand what happened. You said he tried to rape you?'

Her dark, dusk-shaded eyes moisten and she swallows hard. I don't want to rake up bad memories, but I have to know. I need to understand.

'Yes,' she says. 'He did. He thought it was all a game but he wouldn't take no for an answer.'

'A game?' I frown. How could Justin think rape was a game?

'It all started the first year he came to Treloar,' she says. 'I can't even remember whose idea it was, but we called it the *Game of Dares.* It started innocently enough. One of those silly things to pass the time during the summer holidays, but it quickly escalated into something much more dangerous.'

I remember now Colin mentioning something about the children challenging each other to increasingly dangerous stunts. How he'd caught Justin driving his car blindfolded through the grounds and Finn almost jumping from an upstairs window.

'The thing is, Justin always had to take it too far,' Arabella continues. 'And that's how he almost ended up killing me. It wasn't an accident. He knew what he was doing and he blamed Finn. And that's why I'll never forgive him.'

Chapter 33

August 9, 1995

Justin casually produced the cigarettes like they were nothing more noxious than a packet of sweets. A cool red and white box that he placed on the ground between them. On top of it, he laid a plastic lighter, then leant back with his head supported in his hands.

They were hanging out by the hollow tree stump in the woods, bored as usual, the long summer holidays dragging on for an eternity with nothing to do but look for mischief.

'Where did you get them?' Finn asked, wide-eyed with wonder.

There were kids at the boarding school who smoked around the back of the science block, thinking they were cool, but Arabella had never seen the appeal. They looked like idiots, hunched over and grey, hands cupped to their mouths like desperate addicts puffing away.

'Go on, I dare you. Smoke one,' Justin said, fixing Finn with a challenging stare.

God knows where he'd got them. Justin looked old for his age but he was still only fifteen.

'I don't know,' Finn said, glancing at his sister and back again at the little red and white box. He licked his lips and wriggled his fingers like he was seriously contemplating doing it.

'Are you scared?' Justin sat up, flipped open the pack and ripped off a foil wrapper. Then he tapped the box from the bottom until a few of the cigarettes popped up and took one out. Slipped it between his lips and held the pack towards Finn. 'Go on, take one.'

It was obvious he was going to do it. So weak-willed. Pathetic really.

Finn reached tentatively for the packet, pulled a cigarette out and held it between his fingers, trying to look like he knew what he was doing. But like those boys behind the science block, he looked like an idiot. And more fool him if he was actually contemplating smoking it.

'What about you?' Justin offered the packet to Arabella.

'Gross,' she said, shaking her head so rigorously, her hair flew into her face. 'I'm not doing that.'

'Chicken.' Justin kept the packet in his hands as he picked up the lighter, sparked a flame and lit his cigarette, squinting as the smoke hit his eyes, looking like a seasoned smoker.

Then he offered the flame to Finn, cupping his hand around it to protect it from the non-existent wind while Finn leant in and sucked on the end of his own cigarette, like he was pulling on a straw.

What a loser.

Finn coughed and choked, his eyes watering and, for a moment, Arabella thought he was going to puke. He'd gone a funny shade of green and his eyes were bulging.

She laughed, while Justin leant back on his elbow, smirking.

'You'll get used to it,' he said, blowing out a stream of grey smoke.

Disgusting.

Undeterred, Finn tried again. He inhaled once more but with the same effect, coughing and spluttering only slightly less violently than the first time.

'Last chance,' Justin said, raising a bushy eyebrow in Arabella's direction. 'Otherwise you'll have to do a forfeit.'

She tossed a long plait of hair over her shoulder and stared at the packet Justin was wafting under her nose. He blew smoke at her and she waved it away with a yelp.

She couldn't remember who'd first come up with the idea of the dares last summer. It might even have been her suggestion when she was thinking of how to impress the mysterious older boy who'd appeared at the lodge with his parents for a few weeks during the summer.

The first dare was certainly her idea. It was easy, really. All you had to do was sprinkle some salt on your arm and see how long you could hold an ice cube against it. It was a lot more painful than it sounded, the mixture of ice and salt causing frostbites that left them screaming in agony. But it was a laugh and they wore their sores like tattoos of allegiance.

Finn won that game, but also endured the worst injury. The raw, angry welt that appeared on his forearm took weeks to heal and even now you could see where he'd been injured.

Justin said afterwards that it wasn't much of a dare and that the stakes were too low. So on a trip in to Falmouth on the bus, he challenged Finn and Arabella to steal some sweets from a corner shop. Arabella won that one, producing four chocolate bars and a sherbet fountain she'd hidden down her top, while Finn had totally bottled it and run out empty-handed.

As a forfeit, Justin instructed Finn to steal a bottle of booze from their father's drinks cabinet. And when Finn returned triumphantly with a nearly full bottle of vodka, Justin dared them to a drinking game Arabella couldn't remember much about. It was as much as she could do to stand, let alone walk afterwards. Finn told her later he'd had to drag her back to the house after she'd spewed her guts up everywhere, and that they'd been caught by Colin who yelled at them for being so irresponsible.

But thankfully he never told their parents. They wouldn't have been impressed.

'Fine,' Arabella huffed. One cigarette. How bad could it be? Better than the forfeit Justin was bound to come up with. 'Give me one then.'

She put it between her lips and snatched the lighter from Justin, glaring at him through her fringe.

'You don't have to smoke the whole thing, Sis,' Finn said, holding his cigarette awkwardly at arm's length as it smouldered between his fingers. Just because he was older than her, he always thought he had to look out for her, like she was still a baby.

She lit it, staring at him defiantly, determined not to make as much fuss as he had.

She sucked a tiny amount of smoke into her mouth and immediately blew it out again through pursed lips. It was just as disgusting as she feared. A horrible bitter taste filled her mouth and it gave her an instant headache.

'Of course she has to smoke the whole thing,' Justin said, observing her. 'That's the whole point. Otherwise it's a forfeit.'

Fine. She wasn't going to be shown up by Justin, who she suspected wanted her to fail. So she sat and smoked the whole bloody thing, drawing smoke into her mouth and blowing it straight out, until it had burned almost down to the filter.

Never again. It was totally gross. She couldn't understand why anyone would want to do that willingly.

As Justin stubbed his cigarette out in the earth, crushing it under his thumb and flicking it away into a patch of brambles, Finn looked up with a spark of excitement in his eyes.

'I have a dare for us all,' he said.

Arabella subtly stubbed out what was left of her cigarette and buried it in the soil while the other two were distracted.

'And it's way better than smoking cigarettes,' Finn continued.

Justin glowered at him. 'This had better be good.'

'I dare you to drink your own piss.'

Justin sat up like he'd been stung in the arse.

'Ugh, that's rank,' Arabella said, screwing up her nose. How had he even come up with that idea? Such a boy thing to suggest. She definitely wasn't going to do that.

'Come on, what's wrong with you?' Finn grinned. 'It's not like you have to drink someone else's.'

'I don't think that makes it any better.' Justin rolled onto his stomach, plucked a blade of grass out of the ground and rolled it between his fingers.

'I don't mind going first. I'll grab some cups from the house,' Finn said, totally undeterred by Justin and Arabella's lack of enthusiasm.

'I'm not doing that. No way,' Arabella said.

'Nor me,' said Justin, to Arabella's relief.

If the dares didn't get Justin's approval, they usually didn't happen. As the oldest, Justin tended to get his way. And if he didn't want to drink his own piss, they weren't going to drink piss.

'It's supposed to be rank. It's a dare, remember?' Finn said, exasperated.

'Can't you come up with anything better than that?' Arabella rolled her eyes and leant back on her hands, savouring the warmth of the dappled sunlight fingering through the trees as it fell across her face.

'Why don't you suggest one then,' Finn spat back. Now they'd gone and upset him and he was being all sulky. God, boys could be such a pain.

Actually, she did have an idea. Something she'd been thinking about for a few weeks, but wasn't sure if she was brave enough to pull it off. Only one way to find out.

'Alright then. I've got one,' she said, sitting up and brushing the dirt from her hands. 'I dare you to go swimming in the lake,' she said.

'Duh! Easy!' Finn said, pulling a face. 'That's not much of a dare. We go swimming there most summers.'

'Naked,' Arabella added.

'Skinny dipping?' Justin asked, sitting up and pulling his knees to his chest. That had certainly got his attention.

'Yup, if you're not scared of getting caught.'

'Which lake?' he asked.

'Bowman's Lake.' She pointed through the trees towards a private lake at the bottom of the valley. 'Hardly anyone knows it's there. It's usually deserted.'

'Apart from the anglers.' Finn grinned.

'So?' she said, looking directly at Justin. 'Are you up for it? Or are you chicken?'

He gave her a sly smile which gave her an unpleasant flutter in her stomach. 'I am. Are you?'

'Sure. Why not. What about you, Finn?'

'Yeah, whatever you want,' he said, tossing a handful of dirt into the air. He was clearly still cross that they'd dismissed his piss-drinking dare. But this was going to be so much better. Arabella was going to enjoy this one.

It was only a short walk through the woods to the lake where the sun was glistening off the water and the sound of birdsong echoed off the rocks. As they reached the water's edge, Justin wasted no time in stripping off his T-shirt.

Arabella dragged her eyes away, a flush of heat rising to her cheeks, as he revealed a muscular torso and bulging biceps. Even though there was only a couple of years between them, Finn was still a little boy in comparison, with puny arms and a hairless, sunken chest. Justin looked more like a grown man. Her heart skittered.

When she dared to look up again, he was still staring at her, his eyes never leaving her face as he peeled off one trainer and then the other, tucking his socks inside them and tossing them to the ground. And then he unfastened his belt.

He was so brazen about it. He didn't try to hide from her gaze or protect his modesty. Not like Finn, who'd scampered off behind a tree.

'What about you?' Justin asked, eyes wide with hope and expectation as he tucked his thumbs into the waistband of his jeans. 'It was your dare. Aren't you coming in?'

He winked at her and when his fingers travelled to his crotch, she spun around, turning her back on him, horrified.

'I'm not stripping off in front of you,' she called out. She heard the rustle of clothing, the brush of cotton against skin.

'That's not fair.'

'You go in first and I'll join you,' she said coyly.

'Fine,' Justin huffed. 'Finn? What are you playing at? Where are you? Get your lily-arse out here and into the water while your sister gets undressed.'

Finn crept out from behind the tree, his hands over his crotch, shoulders rounded and looking sheepish. He tiptoed through a carpet of pine needles and she heard the splash of water.

Justin laughing.

Finn swearing about the cold.

More splashing.

When she was sure they were both in the water, she finally turned around.

She was surprised to see they had already swum out at least twenty metres, their heads bobbing up and down, their shoulders catching the rays of the sun.

'What are you waiting for?' Justin shouted. 'The water's lovely.' He kicked off and lazily began to backstroke, his arms stretching straight and tall out of the water.

'It's a bit cold,' Finn warned her.

'It's a bit cold,' Justin mimicked in a silly, high-pitched voice. 'Don't be such a wuss.'

'Fuck off, Justin.'

'So are you coming in or not?' Justin hollered as his shoulders sank back beneath the surface and he started treading water.

Arabella grinned and grabbed the hem of her T-shirt. She lifted it a fraction, just enough to give him a flash of her taut stomach, letting him think she was stripping off.

Then with a laugh of delight, she let her T-shirt go and ran around gathering up the boys' clothes in big heaps in her arms. She thought about taking their trainers too, but decided that would be too cruel, especially as they were going to have to walk back to Treloar through the wood.

'Hey, what are you doing?' Justin screamed, waving his arm in the air to get her attention.

She looked up and laughed. Justin's face was an absolute picture. She wished she'd thought to bring her camera. It would have been a great memento to remind him of the day she pranked him and he totally fell for it.

'See you boys later,' she shouted. 'You have fun together.'

And without another look back, she trotted off into the woods, giggling to herself while discarding items of clothing as she went.

Chapter 34

July 31, 1996

Finn took a step back, and then with a steely look of concentration and his tongue jammed firmly into his cheek, he launched into an explosive sprint. His arms and legs pumped hard and his feet slapped against the stony ground, kicking up puffs of dust and grit. At the edge, where the rock disappeared into a sheer drop, he leapt like a long jumper, propelling himself off on one leg, his arms wheeling and the sinews on his neck standing out under the early morning sun.

Ahead of him, dangling in the air from the crooked bough of a tree clinging to the top of the cliff, was a gnarled length of wood tied to a short, knotted nylon rope. He stretched for it. Hands spread. Tendons straining.

His body hung in the air, caught in stasis between jumping and falling, until his fingers wrapped around the wooden handle worn smooth by many hands. He grasped it tightly, arresting his fall, taking the strain in his forearms and shoulders. His body swung, slicing through air under the momentum of his jump, and he whooped with delight, his scream reverberating off the towering sheer rock that enclosed the lake at the foot of the old quarry.

And then he let go.

He pulled his knees up to his chest and a second later hit the surface of the water with a satisfying splash and disappeared under a tumult of bubbles and foam.

When his head bobbed up and he shook his hair out of his eyes, he had a broad grin stretching from ear to ear.

Arabella, watching from above, applauded his effort, her claps echoing off the stone.

'Not bad,' she shouted.

'You next,' he yelled back.

Arabella gathered her hair into a loose ponytail over her shoulder, took a step back and steadied herself, fixing her sights on the rope swing that looked perilously far from the edge. Further than she imagined she could jump, even if it wasn't hanging over a twenty-metre drop. But a dare was a dare and she wasn't going to chicken out with Justin watching. She had a point to prove.

She adjusted her bikini top, wriggling it lower down her chest. She didn't want it coming loose when she hit the water, not with Justin and her brother watching. That would be beyond embarrassing. She wasn't a child anymore. She was fourteen and blossoming into womanhood.

'What are you waiting for?' Finn floated on his back with his arms spread wide.

Arabella glanced at Justin. He was hunched over in his swimming trunks, arms wrapped around his body, chewing his fingernails.

It was the first time she'd ever seen him scared. He'd always launched into all of their challenges with a bullish zeal, happy to lead the way and show the others how it should be done.

Seeing him now, like this, pale and nervous, gave her a rush of pleasure. Justin could be such an arrogant know-it-all sometimes. It was good to see his confidence take a knock.

It was Finn's challenge. He called it the *Leap of Faith,* although it was nothing new to them. Arabella and Finn had been coming here for years. The trick was to close your mind to the height of the drop and concentrate on nailing the jump. If you hesitated, you wouldn't get a decent launch and then there was no way you'd reach the swing.

Arabella skipped into her sprint, sharp stones digging into her feet, and threw herself off the cliff, aiming to carry her momentum by swinging her arms forwards. But as soon as she'd leapt, she knew she'd made a mistake. She wouldn't make it. The rope handle slipped past her fingertips and she was falling, the powerful tug of gravity snatching her ankles, pulling her down.

Air rushed in her ears and she hit the water with a hard slap and disappeared under the surface.

The cold shocked her lungs, but she resisted the desperate urge to inhale until she kicked upwards and her head resurfaced.

'That's cold,' she said, shivering, a stinging pain down one side of her body where she'd hit the water out of control and at an angle.

'Two out of ten for style,' Finn laughed.

'At least I did it.' She breast-stroked over to her brother, clearing the water for Justin.

'Your turn,' Finn yelled up to him.

Justin peered over the edge, silhouetted by the rising sun.

He stood there for ages, just looking down, craning his neck as if he was afraid of getting too close to the drop.

'Get on with it, will you? It's easy. Arabella's done it and she's a girl,' Finn taunted.

'Oi, don't be so sexist.' She punched her brother on the arm.

'Are you scared?' Finn shouted unhelpfully. 'You know there's a forfeit if you don't jump?'

Arabella shaded her eyes as she gazed upwards, but Justin didn't move.

'I don't think he can do it,' she whispered. 'Looks like he's afraid of heights.'

'Bloody hell. I'll go up and talk to him.'

Finn swam to the water's edge, clambered up onto a rocky ledge and, like a mountain goat, shimmied up the side of the cliff, picking out foot and hand holds that were invisible to Arabella. Rather him than her.

She stayed in the water, her body finally adjusting to the cold, drifting up and down on her back.

She couldn't hear what Finn was saying to Justin, but he was gesticulating wildly with his hands. It was obvious he wasn't going to jump. A smile crept across her face. It was the first dare he'd failed to complete, but more than that, he'd shown himself as vulnerable and he would hate that. Justin the invincible, scared of heights. That was hilarious. Not so arrogant now.

'He's not going to do it,' Finn yelled down to her, making a cut-throat gesture with his thumb. 'You might as well get out and we'll have a think about a forfeit.'

They weren't really supposed to be in the old quarry now it was run as an outdoor adventurous pursuits centre, with rope bridges and zip wires drilled into the rock. For families, school groups and businesses looking for that ultimate adrenaline high, the marketing billboards screamed at the entrance in gaudy colours and large fonts. It was somewhere you could come and climb and abseil, as well as canoe and kayak on the water. But Finn had discovered that if you turned up early enough, you could just walk in and have the place to yourself.

'We'd better get out of here,' he said, checking his prized Casio waterproof watch he'd been given last Christmas as he and Justin joined Arabella at the water's edge after scrambling down from the cliff.

She'd pulled on a pair of cut-off denim shorts and was towelling her hair dry. Her skin was still puckered from the early morning swim and her teeth chattered from the cold.

'What about Justin's forfeit?' she asked, shivering.

Finn sucked in the corner of his lower lip. 'I'm not sure yet, but we'll think of something.'

Justin was unusually quiet as they trudged back to where they'd abandoned their bicycles, near the brightly coloured shipping containers where the centre's equipment was stored. Not so full of bravado and banter this morning. He was obviously painfully embarrassed.

'You alright?' she asked.

Justin nodded, his mouth pressed tightly shut, as he scuffed along a few feet behind them.

Up ahead, a catering van chugged and spluttered onto the site through a narrow entrance cut between the jagged rocks. It parked by the containers, near their bikes, and a balding man in a white T-shirt and red stripy apron hopped out. He dropped open a serving hatch on the side of the vehicle and busied himself getting everything ready for the first customers of the day.

Perfect. A drink, something hot and sweet, was just what Arabella needed to shake off the penetrating cold that had seeped into her bones.

'Anyone for a hot chocolate?' she asked, fishing for her purse in the bottom of her rucksack.

'Sure,' Justin said, sulkily kicking up a cloud of dust.

'Yeah, I'll have one.' A bright sparkle shone in Finn's eyes. 'But it's also given me an idea,' he said, jumping on Justin's back like a little kid. 'For your forfeit, you have to let the tyres down on that van without that bloke catching you.'

Justin looked up, his gaze following Finn's arm towards the catering van. 'Right,' he said, sounding unconvinced.

'All four tyres and you can't get caught or the forfeit's void,' Finn elaborated.

'And how am I supposed to do that with the bloke standing there?'

'I'll distract him,' Arabella said. There was no other way he'd get away with it. A fizz of excitement bloomed in her stomach. It was a good forfeit. Better than anything she could think of.

'What do you think?' Finn asked, pogoing on the spot.

Justin threw his head back and stared at the sky. 'Fine,' he said at last. 'If that's what it takes to shut you up.'

Great. This was going to be fun.

Arabella boldly led the way and approached the man in the van with a coquettish smile while the boys kept close behind her.

'Yes, love?' The man popped his head up from inside and placed his hands wide on the lowered hatch that doubled up as serving counter. He hadn't shaved and there were sweat patches all over his T-shirt.

Arabella fought the urge to make a face, especially when she caught a whiff of stale body odour.

'Three hot chocolates with cream and marshmallows, please,' she said.

'No problem.'

Justin didn't waste a second. As soon as the man turned his back, he dived onto the ground, scrambling for the front tyre. Arabella watched from the corner of her eye as he fiddled with the dust cap, and a few seconds later she heard the unmistakable hiss of air.

It was surprisingly loud, especially in the early morning quiet, broken only by the occasional caw-caw of crows.

'I think it's going to be a lovely day,' Arabella said loudly, hoping her voice would mask the sound.

'Supposed to be sunny till midday but they're forecasting rain later,' the man said, glancing over his shoulder as he fixed their drinks, pouring milk into a silver jug and frothing it at a machine at the back of the van. The loud hissing it made was perfect cover for the mischief Justin was getting up to below his feet.

'Oh,' Arabella said, 'that is disappointing. I thought it was going to be sunny all week.'

She had no idea. She wasn't the least bit interested in the weather forecast.

Justin scurried past her knees, hidden under the lowered hatch, and launched himself at one of the rear tyres. Another hiss of escaping air.

Two down. Two to go.

But he'd better hurry. The man had almost finished their hot chocolates and Arabella wasn't sure what else she could do to distract him.

'Are you always here during the summer?' she asked.

'I'm 'ere most days.'

Justin crawled on his belly, commando-style, under the vehicle.

Another hiss of air. A third tyre deflated. He was actually going to do it. If only Arabella could keep the guy talking.

He placed three polystyrene cups piled high with cream, a scattering of marshmallows and a dusting of cocoa powder on the counter and pushed them towards her.

Justin still had one more tyre to go. She heard him shuffling and grunting and had to suppress a giggle. She couldn't believe they were actually going to get away with it.

'Do you have any sugar, please?' Arabella asked.

Just a few more seconds, that's all Justin needed.

Finn reached across Arabella and took one of the cups, sipping from it and giving himself a silly cream moustache.

The man in the van opened his mouth to answer, but froze when they all heard the unmistakable sound of air escaping. The wheezing gasp of a tyre being deflated.

The man's face darkened and folded in puzzlement. Arabella smiled sweetly, trying to look innocent. She should say something. Try to distract him again. But she couldn't think of anything to say.

The guy leant out of the hatch, peering down at the ground.

Unfortunately, at that precise moment, Justin climbed out from under the van, grinning with triumph and brushing the mud and dust off his knees and shorts.

He froze when he saw the man staring at him in disbelief, and then yelled, 'Run!'

The man glanced at Arabella, who smiled again apologetically. She threw some coins across the counter, turned and ran, forgetting their drinks. Finn dropped his cup in his haste. It splattered with a sloppy thump as it hit the ground.

'Oi! Stop! Come back here, you little shits!' the man yelled after them.

He couldn't have known what Justin had done. Not yet anyway. But running away was a bit of giveaway they were up to no good.

Arabella ran hard, her rucksack flapping, struggling to keep up with the boys. Her legs and lungs burned but she didn't dare to stop. Or look back. In her imagination, the man had jumped out of the van and was chasing after them. And being the slowest, she'd be the one he caught first.

'Wait for me,' she gasped as Justin made it back to their bikes ahead of Finn.

By the time Arabella made it back and threw her leg over the saddle, the other two were already cycling off into the distance.

In her haste, and with her feet frantically hunting for the pedals, she almost went straight over the handlebars.

But then she was away. Flying free.

She finally risked a look over her shoulder. The man was nowhere to be seen. They'd done it and got away with it. She whooped for joy.

They didn't stop until they reached the main road, where they regrouped, out of breath and grinning like hyenas.

'That was close,' Finn said, feet planted on the ground as he straddled his bike, gulping in big lungfuls of air.

'What if he calls the police?' Arabella asked. It hadn't even occurred to her at the time that they might be breaking the law. Her parents would go spare if they got into trouble with the police, especially with their father's job as an MP.

'Don't be stupid,' Justin laughed. 'He's not going to call the police.'

'You don't know that,' she snapped back.

'Oh, don't be pathetic.'

'I'm not being — '

'Come on, you two. Stop arguing,' Finn said, cutting her off as he wiped sweat from his brow. 'Let's get back. We don't want to be caught hanging around here.'

Justin stretched out in their favourite spot in the woods, by the hollowed-out tree, with his hands behind his head, legs crossed and a look of contentment on his face.

The scared Justin who had stood, terrified, at the top of the cliff had long since vanished. The old Justin, cocksure and arrogant, was back.

Arabella didn't know what to make of him when he was like this. In part, she found his unwavering confidence appealing. It was flattering an older boy like him wanted to spend time with her. He was so much more mature than any other boy she knew her age. Not that she knew many. The boarding school was girls only which limited the opportunities for fraternising with the opposite sex.

He was tall and muscular, had a totally disarming smile and the way he looked at her sometimes made her stomach flip. And yet, he was always trying to prove himself by putting her down and showing off. Whatever they did, he always had to be the best. Was it because he was just ultra-competitive? Or did he secretly have a chip on his shoulder because he attended an inner city state school while she and Finn were both privately educated? It didn't make a blind bit of difference to her. There were some dim kids in her class, as well as the bright ones. It's just they all had rich parents who could afford to send them away.

'I can't believe you wouldn't jump,' Finn said, leaning on his elbows as he sprawled stomach-down on the hard ground.

Justin prickled. That was the beauty of today's dare. They'd finally found his weakness. Justin Pike was afraid of heights and despite all his bravado, he couldn't overcome it or keep it hidden from them.

'It wasn't a big deal,' Arabella said, 'but my grandma could have made that jump.' Finn threw his head back and laughed. It was a rare chink in Justin's armour and she wasn't going to let this go easily.

'What were you afraid of anyway?' Finn persisted, ignoring Justin's obvious discomfort, as he lay tense, eyes narrowed and his jaw clamped shut.

'I know,' Arabella shouted eagerly, like she'd just worked out a maths problem in class. 'It's because chickens can't fly.'

Finn fell about with laughter. It wasn't often she made her big brother laugh. She grinned with a self-satisfied swell of satisfaction.

'I'm not chicken,' Justin growled.

'So why didn't you jump?' Finn asked.

'I did the forfeit, didn't I?'

'It wasn't much of a challenge though, was it?' Finn absentmindedly drilled a hole in the mud with his finger.

'And you nearly got caught,' Arabella reminded them both.

'I'd like to have seen you do it.' Justin sat up, nostrils flaring. *'But what if he calls the police?'* He put on a whiny voice, mocking Arabella's words.

'It's alright for you, but Daddy would kill us if we got into trouble with the police. If it went in the papers, he'd never forgive us,' she said, recalling the lecture he'd given them at the start of the summer. How they had extra responsibilities to behave because the press was always looking for a scandal about politicians.

'Oh, please.' Justin rolled his eyes theatrically. 'Anyway, it was a stupid dare.'

'Why can't you just admit you were scared?' Finn pressed.

'Because I wasn't.'

'So why didn't you jump?' If only she could get him to admit he had a problem with heights. To confess he had a weakness and that resolute self-confidence was just a front. It would make him so much more likeable. Not everything they did had to be a competition.

'I have a better challenge,' he said. He pulled open his rucksack and produced some rolling tobacco, a packet of cigarette papers and a lighter.

'You want us to try smoking again?' Finn said with disappointment. 'We did that last year.'

Justin dived back into his bag and retrieved a small, brown lump of something wrapped tightly in cling film. He held it up to the light between his thumb and forefinger.

'What's that?' Arabella asked, squinting at Justin's hand.

'An eighth of hash.'

Finn's eyes opened wide with wonder. 'Cannabis?' he gasped.

'Yup. Who wants to try some?'

Arabella shook her head. 'I don't do drugs. They're for losers.'

'Worried what Mummy and Daddy will say?' he whined. 'Are you scared the papers will find out?'

'Of course not.' Arabella prickled at the suggestion. It was just everyone knew you shouldn't touch drugs. It might only be cannabis today, but it was a slippery slope to ending up unconscious in a grubby flat with a needle sticking out of your arm. Like in that film, *Trainspotting*, everyone was talking about.

'Right, well then I dare you both to smoke a joint with me,' Justin said, unfurling a cigarette paper on his knee and loading it with a thin line of tobacco. 'Let's see who's the real chicken.'

Chapter 35

July 31, 1996

Arabella watched with fascination as Justin set light to a corner of the lump of cannabis and crumbled it into the cigarette paper with the tobacco. Then, as he expertly rolled it between his fingers, sealed it with a lick of his tongue and twisted one end into a taper.

'You don't have to smoke any,' he said, holding up the joint for them to admire. 'I mean, if you're too scared.'

'I'll try some.' Finn's eyes grew wide.

Justin jammed the joint between his lips and lit it, his body deflating as he inhaled. His shoulders sagged and his eyes rolled up into his head.

'Just take small drags until you get used to it,' he instructed as he passed it to Finn.

Finn closed his eyes as he inhaled. The end of the joint flared and glowed as his cheeks hollowed and his chest rose.

Arabella had caught Finn smoking a few times last year after Justin had introduced him to his first cigarette, but it was remarkable how at ease he now looked with a joint in his hand.

He held the smoke in for a few seconds and then coughed, his lungs hacking.

Justin laughed and took the joint back.

'What about you?' He waved it under Arabella's nose. 'Are you chicken or not?'

Her pulse thrummed through her veins. You could always spot the girls at school who did drugs. The dropouts and the weirdos with jet-black dyed hair, dark lipstick and heavy eyeliner who looked like they'd escaped from a freak show. Two of them had been expelled after a teacher found cannabis in their rooms. All that money and privilege, wasted.

Arabella wasn't one of those girls. She was far too sensible. She had better things to do with her life. And no way was she taking a step onto that slippery slope. No thanks. If Finn wanted to throw his life and his future away on drugs, just to prove himself to Justin, that was his look out. She was having nothing to do with it.

'Drugs are for losers,' she sneered, throwing back her head.

Justin and Finn shared a knowing look and giggled.

'I told you, she's scared,' Justin said, winking at her brother. 'I knew she wouldn't do it.'

'Go on, Bella. Try it,' Finn urged. 'You can't be a square all your life.'

'I'm not a square,' she hissed. 'I just don't want to ruin my life with drugs.'

'You're so boring.' Justin affected a yawn. 'It's only a bit of weed. It won't kill you. You need to learn how to let your hair down.'

'At least I'm not scared of heights,' she spat back at him.

A dark veil fell over Justin's face. He stared at her with ill-concealed contempt, chewing his cheek. 'Are you going to take the dare or not?' He watched her through narrow, watery eyes as he took a long, slow drag from the smouldering joint.

'If you're too scared you can take the forfeit instead,' Finn offered, eyes bloodshot and flat.

'What kind of forfeit?' she asked.

Justin smirked. 'I have something in mind but you won't like it.'

'What is it?'

He tapped the side of his nose with his finger, causing a crumb of ash to fall onto his arm. 'You'll see.'

He had a cruel, barbaric look in his eye, like an executioner sharpening his axe. Whatever he had in mind was going to be far worse than smoking a joint, she was sure. Was it worth the risk for one tiny smoke?

'Just one drag?' she said.

'One toke, that's it.'

What harm could it do? She was hardly going to develop an addiction after one small puff, was she? And it would show Justin once and for all that she wasn't boring. How could he even think that? She'd thrown herself into the *Game of Dares* as readily as either of the boys. And he'd not even been able to make the jump off the cliff at the quarry.

'Alright, give it to me,' she said.

Justin took one more drag and handed over what was left. It had burned down to half its original length and the end was disgustingly wet with the boys' saliva. Arabella grimaced as she put it to her mouth, trying to look nonchalant. She didn't want to make a fool of herself with them both watching so intently. It couldn't be any worse than that awful cigarette Justin had made her smoke last year, could it?

As she inhaled, hot smoke stinging her eyes, the burning cannabis crackled. Her lungs tightened. Her stomach rolled.

'Hold it in,' Justin said, rising onto his knees.

She tried but her body had other ideas. She spewed out a mouthful of smoke as her lungs protested with an irritated cough. Tears rolled down her cheeks and the inside of her head pitched and wheeled like it was a helium balloon snatched away on an autumnal breeze.

She wheezed uncomfortably and a flush of nausea rose from her stomach. For a moment, she thought she was going to be sick. She put a hand on the ground to steady herself and felt the brush of Justin's warm skin as he took the joint back from her.

'Not so bad, was it?' he said, snickering.

'If you're into that kind of thing.' She craned her neck back and breathed in the clean air, trying to purge her lungs.

'Why do you always have to make such a fuss?' Finn scowled. So typical of her brother, always trying to impress Justin. What an idiot.

Justin finished the joint and crushed it into the earth. He collapsed on his back with his hands on his chest, eyes closed. Finn, meanwhile, was scrutinising a sycamore leaf, holding it up to the light, marvelling at its beauty and all the tiny veins that ran through its core.

'It's such a beautiful texture. Such incredible colours,' he murmured.

As if Arabella needed any more evidence that drugs turned your brain to mush.

'I have an idea for a dare,' she said.

'This should be good.' Justin pushed himself up into a half-sitting position, a loose curl of hair hanging over his brow.

'Finn? Are you listening?'

'What?' He looked up with a faraway glaze over his eyes.

'Put that leaf down. It's my turn to choose a dare,' she said, snatching the leaf and angrily tossing it over her shoulder where it drifted slowly to the ground. This was definitely going to test them both. She was going to enjoy seeing how Justin would try to squirm out of this one. 'I dare you to kiss Finn.'

'Are you out of your mind? I'm not kissing him,' Justin said, his body stiffening. 'I'm not gay.'

'I don't mind kissing you,' Finn said. 'It's only a game. It doesn't mean anything.'

'The forfeit is much, much worse, I promise,' Arabella said, enjoying Justin's discomfort maybe a touch too much, although she had no idea what to suggest for a forfeit. But surely his pride wouldn't let him fail another dare today.

'I'm not doing it.' Justin hooked his legs up to his chest. 'I'll take the forfeit. It's got to be better than kissing him.' He jabbed his thumb towards Finn and screwed up his nose in disgust.

'Oh, you really can be such a square sometimes,' Arabella said, putting on the same whiny voice Justin had used when he'd mocked her earlier. She smiled slyly. She was enjoying this.

'Shut up,' Justin growled.

'One little kiss. That's all.'

Justin looked like he'd swallowed a lemon.

'Just so we're clear,' Finn said, frowning, 'what are the rules? A quick peck on the lips? Is that what you're saying?'

Arabella shook her head. 'Uh-uh. A full ten-second snog. I'll be timing it.'

'Alright,' Finn nodded. 'I'll do it.' He really had no shame.

'Justin?' Arabella raised an eyebrow and ran her fingers through her hair, still damp from the morning's swim.

If he went through with it, she'd never let him live it down. It's something she'd always have to goad him with, especially when he was acting like an arse.

Remember that day you snogged my brother in the woods?

It brought a joyous grin to her face. This was fantastic. And from Justin's softening expression, it looked like he was about to agree to do it. For the second time that day, she wished she'd brought her camera.

'Ten seconds and that's it?' he said.

'Ten seconds,' she confirmed.

A breeze that had been rustling the leaves in the trees all around them eased off and a heavy silence fell, as if the whole wood was holding its breath, waiting for Justin to decide.

'Fine,' he huffed. 'I'll do it. Let's get it over with.'

Arabella's heart soared. She couldn't believe it. She'd actually persuaded Justin Pike to snog her brother. He was going to regret this for a long time.

Finn pulled him to his feet and the two boys stood awkwardly facing each other, Justin's unease radiating off him in waves, unable to look Finn in the eye.

'Finn, let me borrow your watch,' Arabella said.

Finn slipped it off his wrist and tossed it to her. She caught it in one hand and squinted at the numbers ticking by.

'Are you ready?'

Finn put his hand on Justin's shoulder. 'Fuck off,' he snarled, brushing it away.

Arabella could have wet herself. This was so funny.

'This stays between us, right?' Justin added, waving a finger of warning at Arabella and Finn.

'Why are you so uptight?' she giggled. She couldn't help it. It was Justin's face. All scrunched up with disgust like someone had made him eat a cow pat. 'It's only a little kiss. Right, on your marks. Set. Go.'

Finn grabbed the back of Justin's head and planted a kiss on his lips. Justin's arms flailed wildly at his sides.

'One. Two. Three... ' Arabella counted, deliberately slowly, drawing out the seconds. Justin's embarrassment was delicious. She didn't want this to end.

'... eight. Nine. And... ten. Okay, you can stop now,' she said, rolling on the floor in a fit of laughter.

Justin shoved Finn away and wiped his mouth aggressively with the back of his hand. He spat out a globule of saliva and winced. 'Gross,' he muttered under his breath.

Finn's reaction was the polar opposite. He couldn't have looked any more pleased with himself. And seeing Arabella rolling around on the floor, he started laughing too, until he could barely stand.

'The look on your face,' he said, pointing at Justin. 'Priceless.'

'Is that it? Are we done?' Justin asked.

'Yes, you passed the challenge. It was a beautiful moment and I hope the two of you will be very happy together,' Arabella spluttered through laughter. It was so easy to wind him up.

'Shut up.'

'What about you?' Finn said, his laughter drying up as he looked at his sister. 'It's your turn. I dare you to kiss Justin.'

Panic rose in Arabella's chest, drumming against her ribcage. 'Don't be stupid,' she gasped.

'Come on, it's not fair otherwise. You have to take the dare too.'

Justin folded his arms. The look of embarrassment and disgust that had been plastered all over his face a second before had been replaced by a look of interested amusement.

She hadn't thought this through. Of course Finn was going to demand this of her. She could hardly kiss her own brother. That would be equally gross.

'Do the dare, otherwise you'll have to take a forfeit,' Finn grinned.

Arabella had never kissed a boy before. Not that she hadn't thought about it. A lot. She'd even caught herself imagining what it might be like to kiss Justin. To feel his firm, muscular body pressed against hers. But not here, like this, in front of her brother.

And he was so much older than her. Probably a lot more experienced. And besides, he was an arrogant prick. She didn't want to give him any ideas that she liked him or anything. He might be good-looking and have a sexy swagger, but she hated the way he always made her feel worthless. Not good enough. Like when he'd called her square and boring earlier.

Justin held out his hand, inviting her to come to him. 'Come on, what do you say? It can't be any worse than me having to kiss Finn.'

'I - I don't know... ' Arabella stammered.

'Ten seconds. That's all.'

Her heart thumped loudly in her chest and she lost all feeling in the tips of her fingers and toes. Heat rose to her cheeks and her legs trembled.

And then Justin was leading her away by the hand and she was following him, unable to stop herself.

'Hey, where are you going?' Finn hollered after them.

'I'm not kissing your sister with you watching, you freak,' Justin said.

With a warm, moist hand, he led her behind a knobbly oak tree with low-hanging branches that spread out like a canopy. He pressed her back up against the hard trunk and her breath caught in her throat.

'Alone at last,' he whispered, leaning closer, his breath tinged with tobacco smoke.

Oh god, was this really happening?

He placed a hand on her hip and smoothed a loose hair away from her face. Heat radiated off his body. She was paralysed. Not sure what to do.

Did she want this?

In her dreams, she'd thought she had. But now she wasn't so sure. It didn't feel right. This wasn't supposed to be happening. But she couldn't think straight. Her head was swimming and all she could think about was how close his face was to hers. How their noses were almost touching.

'Justin, I... '

But he shushed her quiet with a finger on her lips.

She tried to swallow but her mouth and throat were arid dry. Her knees buckled and she had an unexpected compulsion to cry.

And then it was happening.

The roughness of his youthful stubble scratching her chin. His mouth pressing urgently against hers. His tongue on her lips. In her mouth.

At first she kissed him back. But it was too much. Too overwhelming. He was too insistent. Animalistic. She didn't want it to be like this.

She wanted him to stop. But he had her pinned against the tree. She couldn't move. Couldn't get away.

And then his hands were everywhere. On her breasts. Pawing at her stomach. Tracing a line along the tenderest part of her inner thigh.

She froze.

No, she definitely didn't want this.

'What's wrong?' he gasped in her ear, his voice rich with lust and longing. 'Don't you want it too?'

No!

She wanted to scream at him. Tell him that no, she didn't want this. She was only fourteen, for fuck's sake.

'Justin... ' His name slipped from her mouth. She tried to tell him no, but she couldn't speak. Couldn't do anything.

She tried to push him away, her hands on his broad chest. But she couldn't move him. And his hands kept roaming, going places she didn't want them to go.

'You're so beautiful,' he murmured.

One hand under her T-shirt now, pushing up her bikini top.

Stop. No. Don't.

But she couldn't form the words. They screamed silently in her head while her body was paralysed with fear and shock.

Firm fingers unbuttoned her shorts, popping them open. His hand slid inside and she squeezed her thighs together, but it didn't stop him. She didn't want to be touched there. She didn't want to be touched anywhere, but he was being so rough. So insistent and she didn't know how to make him stop.

'Are you still a virgin?' he breathed in her ear, grabbing her by the neck and forcing her head back so she couldn't breathe properly.

With a free hand, he unzipped his own shorts.

Tears of anger and frustration welled in Arabella's eyes.

What the hell was happening to her? She looked down on herself from above, the girl pinned beneath his heaving body unrecognisable.

This was all wrong.

She didn't want this.

She wouldn't let this happen to her.

'No!' she screamed in his face, the force of her outburst taking him by surprise.

She shoved him in the chest with all her strength. He stumbled back, frowning.

'What?' he said, as if he had no idea what he'd done wrong. But he knew alright.

'I don't want to do this,' she yelled.

She slipped out of his grasp, ducking away from him, around the trunk of the tree. But he snatched her wrist and stopped her from running.

'Where are you going?'

'Leave me alone,' she shouted, her voice finally coming back to her after deserting her when she'd needed it most.

She pulled her wrist and stumbled free.

'Don't be such a tease,' he sneered. The look in his eye made her shudder with fear.

She adjusted her T-shirt, pulling it down over her stomach, and buttoned up her shorts as she staggered away.

'Bella?' Finn appeared through the trees. 'What's going on?'

She marched on, ignoring him. All she wanted was to get out of the wood and away from Justin.

'Arabella, come back,' Justin shouted after her.

'Leave me alone.'

'Bella! Don't go. I thought it's what you wanted.'

She stopped. Spun around. Faced him, with tears streaking her face. Anger bubbling through her veins. How dare he treat her like this.

'You're a fucking pig,' she screamed. 'How fucking dare you.'

'I'm sorry,' he said, holding his hands up in innocence. 'I thought it's what you wanted.'

'No,' Arabella screamed. 'It's not what I wanted. And I never want to see you again.'

Chapter 36

August 3, 1997

She'd had a long time to think about what happened in the woods last summer. What might have happened if she'd not found her voice. And now Arabella was determined to make Justin pay.

For a long while, she wondered whether she'd been to blame. Whether she'd given him the wrong signals, going off with him behind that tree when Finn proposed the kissing dare. She never actually told him no. So how was he to know?

But that was bullshit. Justin knew exactly what he was doing. He knew she was only fourteen. That it wasn't something she wanted. It was so typical of his arrogance and overconfidence that he thought if he wanted something he could just take it.

Well, it was time to take him down a few pegs. And Arabella knew exactly how to do it. She was going to give him the fright of his life and leave him so humiliated, he'd probably never forgive her. But so what? It would be worth it.

'I know, we should go to the beach for the day,' she suggested, as if the idea had only just occurred to her as she lay back under the canopy of trees near the old hollowed-out oak with the warmth of the summer sun on her face.

She'd had to swallow her pride and pretend everything was still cool between them when he'd turned up at Treloar again that summer. Neither of them mentioned what had happened the previous year and he certainly hadn't offered an apology, which made her even more determined to go through with her plan.

Justin peeled off his baseball cap and let his hair fall loose. He'd let it grow long, which Arabella didn't think suited him at all. It made him look unkempt and seedy. Or maybe that was just the way she looked at him now.

'I don't know,' he said. 'I thought we could hang out here for a bit.'

'Boring.' Arabella mocked him with a loud fake yawn.

'Yeah, come on, it'll be fun,' Finn said, nodding in agreement. 'The weather's supposed to be good all day.'

She'd had to confide in her brother to get him on side with her plans, although when she'd first told him that Justin had tried to rape her, he completely overreacted, threatening to break every bone in his body. It was sweet that he cared, but it wasn't the way, even if Finn had been a physical match for the older boy.

No, she had a better way, but she needed Finn's help.

'And do what exactly?' Justin slipped his hat back on and adjusted it so it shaded his eyes.

'I don't know, but it beats sitting around here getting bored all day,' Arabella said.

'I've got some beer stashed in my room,' Finn said with a cheeky smirk. 'We could grab a few cans and take a picnic.'

'A picnic?' Justin sneered. 'What are you, thirty or something? We're not taking a picnic, but you can grab those beers.'

'So you'll come?' Arabella jumped up, flushing as her skirt rose up her legs and she caught Justin's eyes roving hungrily over her body.

'I suppose so,' he said sulkily.

'Great. I know the perfect place.' She thought he might put up more resistance. Half the battle was getting him to agree to go to the beach in the first place, but she had to hand it to Finn, the offer of free beer had clinched it.

After Finn had run back to the house to pick up the cans, they caught a bus to a secret cove Arabella had scouted out a few weeks earlier as her plan had come together.

The bus dropped them off on the busy road near the top of the cliffs and Arabella led the way down a dusty trail to the beach, through the nettles and the brambles that stung and scratched their bare legs, slipping occasionally on loose stones. It had been almost a year since Justin had attacked her and a few scratches weren't going to put her off getting her revenge.

The beach had been a rare find, far from the busy tourist haunts where the crowds flocked during the summer like ants around a dribble of honey. It wasn't a big beach, but it had soft white sand snared between two fingers of ragged brown rocks that extended into the sea. And because of its size, its inaccessibility and its distance from the tourist shops and bars, they had it virtually to themselves.

They set up camp in a sheltered spot with their backs against the rocks and cracked open the warm beer, sharing stories from their last year in school, and in Justin's case, tales of some bad dates and drunken scrapes.

Arabella listened to his stories with a fixed smile, laughing in all the right places, never once letting her mask slip. Never letting him see how much she now loathed being with him.

'Have you thought of any good challenges for this year's *Game of Dares*?' she asked casually when he'd finished a particularly unsavoury story about a near riot that had broken out on one of the school buses.

It sounded horrific and about as far removed as she could imagine from her experience of school where all her friends had names like Camilla and Hermione and they all played hockey and had to wear smart pleated skirts and long socks.

'I've had a few ideas,' Justin said, with a sneer.

Arabella's stomach flipped and she had to take another sip of beer to steady her nerves.

'Well, I've got a really good one this year,' she said, grabbing her rucksack and jumping to her feet 'Come on, follow me.'

Justin groaned.

'Not chicken, are you?' Arabella stood over him with her hands on her hips.

He glowered at her, finished his beer and pulled himself up as Finn gathered all the empty cans in his bag and threw it over his shoulders.

'What is it?' he asked suspiciously.

'You'll see. Come on.'

She took them back up the narrow dirt trail, puffing and panting with the effort of the climb that made her legs burn and her skin flush with perspiration.

'Where are we going?' Justin moaned behind her.

'Just a bit further.' She brushed aside a thorny bramble and stepped over a clump of nettles that had grown across the path, not caring about the stings and scratches. Her mind focused on the challenge ahead, already thinking about the look on Justin's face when he saw what she was going to propose.

At the top of the trail, she picked out a second path which meandered along the top of the cliffs. Below, the sea shimmered an iridescent blue and Arabella was forced to squint as the rays from the sun bounced brightly off the waves.

'How much further?' Justin whinged. 'I'm knackered.'

Arabella grinned. 'Not far now,' she called cheerily.

Eventually, they came to a rocky outcrop that jutted dramatically out from the cliff edge and hung precariously over the water like a shelf. Below it, nothing but sharp, ragged rocks and the sea crashing against the shore.

'What the fuck's this?' Justin demanded as Arabella threw down her rucksack and breathed in the salty sea air.

The alarm in his voice and the tension in his body was delightful and more than made up for the long hike up from the beach. She knew this would challenge his bravado. Last summer he'd been a gibbering wreck at the old quarry and he couldn't even attempt the rope swing jump. This challenge was ten times scarier.

'Oh, sorry,' she said, her hand flying to her mouth. 'I forgot you were afraid of heights. Are you okay with this?'

Arabella jumped onto the outcrop and stood at the edge, peering down at the drop. It must have been at least forty or fifty metres straight down to the sea. Enough to make even Arabella's legs wobble.

'What's the dare, Bella?' Finn asked, hopping up and down on the spot, as excitable as a puppy, even though he knew exactly what the challenge involved.

They'd been through it carefully together, refining it to ensure maximum discomfort for Justin. If they were going to make him pay for what he did to Arabella, it had to be good.

'It's really simple,' she said with a grin. 'All you have to do is walk along the edge.' She said it like it was nothing more taxing or scary than a stroll in the park.

'That's a piece of piss,' Finn said. He hopped onto the outcrop and paced it out, holding his arms out at shoulder height for balance. 'It's only six steps wide.'

'Except you have to wear this.' Arabella pulled one of her father's hideous patterned ties from her bag and held it aloft. 'Over your eyes as a blindfold. And you have to walk right along the edge.'

'Screw that,' Justin hissed. His face was pale and he was sweating heavily, large dark patches growing unpleasantly under his armpits.

He still hadn't overcome his fear of heights then? Excellent.

'I'll go first and show you how it's done,' Arabella said. 'Tie it around my head.'

She handed the tie to Finn who secured it over her eyes and tied it off behind her skull. Then he helped her step up onto the outcrop and guided her to the edge where it fell away dramatically into the sea.

One wrong step and she'd plunge to her death. It was that simple.

Except, she and Finn had been practising, without the blindfold, of course. They both knew every inch of the rock. Where to place each foot. All the bumps and rises, notches and grooves, until they were confident they could do it with their eyes closed. Which eventually they did.

She'd never have been foolish enough to have tried it blindfolded if she didn't know what she was doing. But Justin didn't know that. As far as he was aware, it was the first time any of them had been here.

'This is so exhilarating,' Arabella said, as Finn set her in place with the outside of her foot less than an inch from the edge.

She lifted her arms and deliberately swayed at the waist as if she was trying to catch her balance.

A light breeze lifted her hair off her shoulders and ruffled her skirt. She took a steadying breath and felt a familiar lump under the ball of her right foot. A furrow under the heel of her left. She knew exactly where she was and the path she needed to take to stay safe. Not that Justin had the faintest clue.

The only drawback with wearing a blindfold was that she couldn't see his face. She'd have loved to have watched the sheer fear in his eyes, knowing he was expected to do the same terrifying walk in the next few minutes.

The rush of adrenaline was a total buzz. It came not just from the possibility she could fall, but because she knew how Justin would be feeling.

She took a tentative step forwards, feeling with her toe, concentrating on maintaining her balance. As long as she stayed upright and kept her head, she knew she'd be fine.

'How am I doing?' she asked.

'Yup, all good. Put your foot down now,' Finn instructed.

Her foot found a firm grip and she stepped forwards, transferring her weight. She felt another depression in the rock. She was bang on the right path, maybe a fraction to the left, but it was nothing to worry about.

Slowly, she took another step. Another familiar marker under the sole of her trainer. And another. Until a few short steps later it was done. She was safe.

Finn grabbed her arm and pulled her back to the safety of the footpath.

'I did it,' she screamed, whipping off the blindfold, elated. 'Did you see?' she asked Justin, who was down on his haunches looking like he was about to vomit.

'My turn.' Finn snatched their father's tie and pressed it over his eyes.

Arabella tied it around his head and led her brother onto the rock.

Justin had gone deathly quiet. It wasn't like him not to have an opinion on a dare or to offer his wisdom about where the other two were going wrong. But not today. He was as quiet as the wind before a storm. He could barely even look at Finn as he lined up along the rocky edge, his body swaying as found his balance.

'Take your time and be careful,' Arabella warned him, before stepping out of the way so Justin would have an unobstructed view.

Like Arabella before him, Finn took one tentative step at a time, throwing in some dramatic wobbles and twitches for effect, feeling ahead with his toes, ensuring there was rock beneath his foot before committing to a step.

And then he, too, was across.

Arabella snatched his wrist and pulled him away from the edge as Finn whooped with delight and yanked off the blindfold.

'I think that's the scariest thing I've ever done in my life,' he said, clutching his chest and breathing as heavily as if he'd just sprinted up from the beach.

'Well done, Finn.' Arabella patted her brother on his back, before turning to Justin.

Was he actually shaking? Not so tough now.

'Right, two down. One to go,' she said, smirking. 'Up you get, Justin. Your turn.'

He stood slowly, his eyes fixed on the rock jutting out over the sea. He wiped his hands on his thighs and his Adam's apple rose and fell as he swallowed. Arabella couldn't remember seeing anyone as scared as Justin was in that moment. And she was loving every single second of it.

She offered him the blindfold, but he just kept staring ahead, his body shivering with fear.

'Come on, Justin, you've got this.' Finn pumped his fists in Justin's face, trying to fire up his courage, but Justin swatted him away, irritated.

'Fuck off,' he growled.

'Not chicken, are you?' Arabella teased. 'It's really easy. It's only six steps, but if you're too scared, you don't have to. Nobody's making you.'

'Of course I'm not scared,' Justin said through gritted teeth.

'Come on then. What are you waiting for?'

Justin snatched the blindfold from Arabella and wrapped it around his head and eyes. Finn glanced at his sister and shot her a wicked grin. He was enjoying this almost as much as she was.

'Let's get this over with,' Justin grumbled, holding out an arm to be led onto the rock.

The way he shuffled up the edge was pathetic. What a baby.

Arabella lined him up with his foot an inch away from the drop into the sea and rotated his shoulders so he was pointing in the right direction.

'Okay, you're all set. All you have to do is take six small steps and you've done it,' she said. 'Just don't think about the edge or falling and you'll be fine,' she added for good measure.

And then she left him standing there. Alone and helpless, his knees knocking and his arms wavering at his side.

Arabella joined her brother on the path to watch the show, confident Justin was paralysed with terror and wasn't going anywhere. She only planned on leaving him there for a few seconds, to make a point.

After all, she didn't want him to die. Not really. And as long as he didn't move, he'd be fine.

But as the seconds ticked by, she had no desire to rescue him or pull him back from the brink. She wanted this moment to last forever, for his fear to stay with him.

'Get on with it,' Finn shouted.

'Shut up,' Justin barked back, wobbling dangerously and lifting one foot off the rock to catch his balance.

Arabella snatched a breath. For a moment, he looked as if he might actually fall. She hadn't really considered that was a possibility before now.

Finn lurched forwards, as if to grab Justin, but Arabella snatched his elbow and held him back. 'Just a little longer,' she hissed.

Finn stared at her. 'Come on, Bella. He's had enough.'

'A few more seconds,' she begged.

He glared at her and looked back at Justin, whose body was now twisting away from the path and towards the drop. If he took a step forwards, he'd surely fall.

Finn shrugged off his sister's hand and grabbed Justin by the arm. 'That's enough. Come on, mate. Let's get you away from there.'

Justin didn't put up any resistance, letting Finn guide him back to safety. He pulled off the blindfold and threw it angrily onto the ground.

'Not so brave now.' Arabella couldn't help herself. 'Thought you were a tough man.'

'Screw you,' he yelled at her. He snatched up his rucksack, flung it over his shoulder and marched off.

But they weren't ready to let him off the hook that easily.

Finn raced after him. 'Hey, Justin, you failed the dare,' he yelled. 'You know what that means, right?'

Justin kept walking and didn't look back.

'You failed the challenge, mate. That means you need to do a forfeit.'

Chapter 37

August 3, 1997

When they finally caught up with him, Justin was sitting on the kerb at the bus stop with his knees pulled up to his chest, drawing circles in the dirt. Finn danced around him, flapping his arms and clucking like a chicken.

'Oh, take a jump,' Justin hissed. He picked up a handful of grit and threw it angrily into the road. At least some of the colour had returned to his cheeks.

'Don't be like that.' Arabella stood with her hands on her hips at Justin's side, enjoying every moment of his torment. 'It's just a game.'

'A bit of fun...' Finn added, beaming with delight, 'with consequences, of course. You failed the challenge, you need to do a forfeit. You know the rules.'

Justin grabbed another handful of dirt and for a moment Arabella thought he was going to hurl it in Finn's face. Instead, he turned his hand over and let the dust trickle out of his fist like sand flowing through an egg timer.

'What forfeit?'

Finn glanced at Arabella, but she'd been so focused on the dare at the cliff edge, ensuring it would maximise Justin's humiliation, that she'd not given any thought to the inevitable forfeit that would follow.

It was a missed opportunity. She was still angry with him and here was the chance to compound his discomfort. To cut him down. To shame him.

'What about — ' she began, her mind working furiously to think of something as she glanced around, hoping for inspiration.

'You're a chicken, right?' Finn said, cutting her off and pointing his finger in the air as if he'd been struck by a Newtonian-sized idea. 'So your forfeit should be an actual game of chicken.'

'Yes!' Arabella clapped her hands with glee. 'That's perfect.' Although she didn't know what Finn had in mind, it sounded like the kind of thing that would pile the pressure on Justin.

Justin stared at them sullenly from under the peak of his cap. 'Go on.'

'When the next lorry comes along, you have to make it stop,' Finn explained.

Justin's brow creased. 'That's it?'

'By lying down in the road. And you can't get up until it's come to a complete standstill or you fail,' Finn added.

Arabella glanced down the road. They were standing on a slight rise where the oncoming traffic was obscured by a long, winding curve in the carriageway. It would be difficult for a driver to spot anyone in the road, let alone if they were lying down, especially as it was a fast section and traffic whizzed past at speed.

The same thought obviously occurred to Justin. 'No way,' he said. 'That's insane.'

'I'll go down the hill a bit and when there's a lorry coming, I'll wave,' Finn continued. 'All you need to do is lie down in the road and wait.'

Arabella frowned. There was risky, and there was downright idiotic. They'd planned the cliff edge challenge meticulously and would never have let Justin fall. They'd have grabbed him the moment he looked in trouble. But this was different. The danger was completely out of their control.

He could actually die.

And as much as she hated what he'd done, she didn't wish that on him. Especially as she and Finn would be held responsible.

'Are you too chicken?' Finn grinned, clucking and flapping his arms again.

'Fine.' Justin jumped up indignantly. 'If that's the best you can come up with, I'll do it.'

'That's the spirit.' Finn smirked with triumph and marched off beyond the crest of the rise until Arabella could only see his head and one arm waving at them.

'Are you ready?' he yelled.

'Get on with it,' Justin grumbled. He licked his dry lips and dusted off his hands.

So, it was really happening. Justin was so desperate to prove himself, he was actually willing to put his life on the line. It was madness. Arabella should put a stop to it, but she couldn't, and like driving past a motorway pile-up, she couldn't tear her eyes away either.

They waited for what felt like an eternity. Plenty of cars came tearing past, roaring over the brow of the hill and accelerating away. Two panel vans passed in the opposite direction, their drivers regarding Justin and Arabella with suspicion. But no lorries.

Justin tapped his foot impatiently, the neck of his T-shirt damp with sweat.

Finally, Finn started waving frantically. 'There's one coming,' he yelled. 'Hurry.'

Justin took a deep breath and ran into the road. He briefly caught Arabella's gaze, fear glinting in his eye, before getting down on the ground and lying flat with his head pointing towards the oncoming vehicle, his body parallel to the white lines that marked the centre of the carriageway.

Arabella's hand flew to her mouth. She chewed on a finger as a lorry appeared over the crest of the rise. It was enormous. One of those articulated trucks with a long trailer and canvas sides.

Its engine grunted and altered pitch as the driver changed gear. Maybe a sign he was slowing down. Perhaps he'd spotted Justin in the road already.

But he was still approaching fast.

Too fast.

Even if the driver did see Justin, Arabella wasn't sure he'd be able to stop.

Time slowed down. Justin remained motionless with his arms pressed to his sides even as the growl of the lorry became louder. Over the crest now and picking up speed. Not slowing down at all. If anything, it was speeding up.

Arabella watched the driver in horror through the smeary windscreen, not convinced his attention was entirely on the road. He kept glancing down as if he was distracted by something inside his cab.

Please, look up and see him.

Please, stop.

She intoned the words over and over in her head. Praying and hoping. She definitely didn't want to see Justin die. What he'd done to her had left her ashamed and grubby, and she wanted to make him pay so badly. But not like this.

The lorry kept coming. No sign of slowing. The driver hadn't seen him.

She had to do something.

Without thinking, she shot into the road, waving her hands above her head. 'Stop!' she yelled, the lorry bearing down on her.

The driver's jaw fell open in a silent scream, his eyes growing as wide as dinner plates. All the sinews on his neck stood out, his arms and shoulders locked, gripping the steering wheel tightly as he jumped on the brakes.

Tyres squealed. Air brakes hissed. The trailer rattled and groaned.

But it kept coming. Sliding and slewing down the tarmac towards her and Justin.

It wasn't going to stop.

She jumped out of the way, diving into the verge and squeezing her eyes tightly shut.

She didn't want to see or hear. Her stomach tightened.

And then after all the ear-splitting commotion, there was silence.

A horrible, gut-wrenching, soul-destroying silence.

Justin was dead. He couldn't have survived. And it was all her fault.

Slowly, she pulled herself up out of the dirt and forced herself to look. The lorry had come to a halt precisely over the spot where Justin had been lying.

Oh god.

'Justin?' her voice faltered.

He couldn't have survived. Not being run over by a lorry.

She stared at it in muted shock. What the hell had they done?

A hand emerged from under the front wheel. Followed by an arm. And a shoulder. Finally, Justin's head and upper body appeared as he dragged himself out from under the vehicle with stupid grin all over his face.

He stood shakily, brushed himself down and slapped the side of the cab with the palm of his hand, as if it had all been planned for maximum effect. He sauntered towards Arabella as if nothing had happened.

'I thought you were dead,' she screamed, running to him and thumping his chest in anger and relief, tears bubbling in her eyes.

'Sorry to disappoint you.' He fended off her blows, laughing.

'What the hell are you playing at, you bloody idiots.' The lorry driver had climbed down from his cab and was marching towards them with his fists clenched.

'Quick, run!' Justin grabbed Arabella's hand and they sprinted away, jumping through a prickly hedge back onto the dusty trail that headed towards the beach.

Behind them, Finn shouted for them to wait.

Their legs pumped fast, their bodies fuelled by adrenaline, not daring to look back.

Until eventually Justin slowed up and skidded to a halt on the loose scree as Finn caught them up.

'It's okay, he's gone,' Justin panted, doubling over with his hands on his knees.

Arabella collapsed into the undergrowth, a painful stitch like a dagger in her side.

'I thought it had hit you,' Finn said, clutching his sides and shaking his head like he couldn't believe what he'd just seen.

'You didn't even flinch,' Arabella added. He was either brave or incredibly stupid. Who in their right mind would stay lying in the road with ten tonnes of metal and rubber bearing down on them at speed?

Justin shrugged nonchalantly. 'That makes us even, right?'

Finn glanced at his sister. 'I guess so,' he said.

Arabella looked away, still breathing hard. She couldn't deny he'd successfully completed his forfeit, but that didn't mean she was ready to forgive him yet.

Justin pushed his cap up off his eyes. 'And so I guess that means it's my turn to name the next dare.'

Arabella's heart sank. 'I don't know,' she said. 'Don't you think we're getting a bit old for games?'

'No, you don't,' Justin hissed. 'You're not getting out of this that easily. I did your forfeit. Now you can both do my dare.'

'What is it?' Arabella mumbled, not sure if she wanted to know. After what she and Finn had put him through, he was bound to raise the stakes. But how could he top what they'd made him do?

'You'll see,' he said with a malevolent sneer. 'But we need to get back to Treloar for what I have in mind.'

Chapter 38

August 3, 1997

'We're going to need some newspaper, leaves and some matches.' Justin emerged from a storeroom attached to one of the estate's disused stable blocks dusting off his hands.

He'd wasted no time after they'd returned scouting out various sheds, stables and outbuildings, sticking his head through doors and poking around shelves and in boxes. But he still wouldn't tell them what he had planned.

'Matches?' Finn's eyebrows shot up.

'Not going all chicken on me, are you, Finn?' Justin asked, folding his arms across his chest.

'Of course not. Whatever it is, bring it on, that's what I say.'

Arabella had skulked around behind the two boys, curious but anxious. She should walk away and tell them what they could do with their stupid dares. That would be the sensible thing to do. But her head needed a serious word with her pride. One more dare to show them what she was made of, and that would be it. No more. They'd be even and she could walk away with her head held high and never have to have anything more to do with Justin ever again.

'Are you going to tell us what this dare is then, or what?' Arabella asked haughtily. Why the hell did Justin need matches?

'Collect the stuff and I'll tell you,' he said.

That stupid smirk was back on his face again, like he was some kind of god just because he was an idiot who happily lay in the path of an oncoming lorry and didn't flinch. As if she was impressed by that.

'And what are *you* going to do?'

'I'm going to get things ready here.' He disappeared back inside the storeroom.

Arabella and Finn poked their heads around the door and watched him empty some old animal feed out of a metal bin into a plastic sack, and place the bin in the centre of the room.

'Come on, hurry,' he said, when he noticed they were still standing there.

'I'll get the newspaper and matches,' Finn announced, sprinting off towards the house.

'I suppose that means I'll be getting the leaves,' Arabella muttered to herself, grabbing a black bucket and heading into the woods.

Finn and Justin were waiting for her when she returned, bucket brimming with vegetation she'd plucked from the trees and bushes.

Justin took the bucket from her and placed it alongside the bin in the shed. Then he produced a box of matches from his pocket and held it aloft as if it was the Olympic flame.

'Are you ready for your next challenge?' he asked with excitement gleaming in his eyes.

Arabella groaned inwardly.

'This one is called the Smoke Shed Challenge,' Justin explained. 'It's a timed dare. We'll each take it in turns to see how long we can last in this shed when it fills with smoke. Whoever lasts the longest wins. The other two have to take a forfeit.'

'Awesome,' Finn grinned.

Was he serious? Surely he wasn't really going to start a fire in the shed. It was completely irresponsible. If Arabella's father found out, he'd skin them alive.

'Arabella?' Justin stared at her with narrowing eyes. She shuddered. 'Are you game?'

'Yeah, of course,' she said, lifting her chin and hoping her tone gave off an air of indifference.

If she didn't do this and prove to Justin she wasn't daunted, all their earlier efforts to bring him down to size on the cliff would be for nothing. She'd do this one last dare, show them just how fearless she was and then she'd be done with it all.

'There's no shame if you want to back out,' Justin said, trying to get under her skin. She knew what he was playing at. 'It's a test of mind over matter, but not everyone has the mental fortitude. It's what the SAS use to assess who has the kind of self-control not to panic when they're put in uncomfortable situations.'

'Bring it on,' Arabella said, with more conviction than she felt.

Justin grinned and she had a bad feeling she'd played right into his hands. 'Okay, why don't you go first and set the benchmark?'

'Fine. If you're too scared to go first, I'm happy to show you how it's done.'

'I'll get the fire going.' Justin stepped into the shed with the matches.

A few moments later, he re-emerged in a cloud of thick, billowing smoke, coughing, his eyes red and streaming tears.

He pulled the door shut and held it closed, gripping the handle tightly.

This was a terrible idea, but Arabella couldn't back out now. It didn't matter how long she survived in the shed, she just needed to go in and show them she wasn't scared.

'Give it a few minutes for the smoke to build up and then you can go in,' Justin said, fixing Arabella with a challenging stare, like he didn't think she could do it. 'Finn, do you have your stopwatch ready?'

Finn gave him the thumbs up.

Justin grinned at Arabella. 'Really think you can do this, Bella?'

Acrid fumes crept out from the gaps around the door, spiralling up into the warm summer sky. Her heart drummed with a frenzy inside her chest and her tongue felt swollen in her mouth.

'I know I can do it,' she said. 'But can you?'

'Well, let's see how long you can last. Remember, it's just mind over matter. And if you can't last very long, it just means you have a weak mind.'

She was going to show him who had a weak mind.

'Let me in,' she said, pushing him out of the way and shouldering open the door.

The wall of smoke hit her square in the face. It was so thick she could barely see.

Justin shoved her in the back and she stumbled inside. He pulled the door closed behind her, plunging her into semi-darkness. The only illumination came from a faint glow in the metal bin, but that was the least of her concerns. The hot, noxious smoke burned her lungs, filling them in a couple of desperate gasps until she was coughing and spluttering and her eyes stinging so painfully, she couldn't keep them open.

It was far worse than anything she'd imagined and it took all of her willpower not to turn around and run straight back out.

But she couldn't. There was no way she was giving Justin that satisfaction.

If only she could last a minute, sixty seconds, that would be something. He'd have to give her credit for that.

She sunk to her haunches and pulled the bottom of her T-shirt over her nose and mouth. And in her head, she tried to count the passing seconds, but it was so hard to concentrate while her lungs felt like they were going to explode.

The metal bin crackled with the heat.

She tried to hold her breath. She could easily swim the length of a pool underwater, so it shouldn't be difficult. But this was different. The smoke had already irritated the lining of her lungs and all she wanted to do was cough.

Panic bloomed in her chest. She tried to fight it. To find a place of peace and calm in her head. But this was awful. She was suffocating. Her lungs about to burst. She doubled over as the involuntary compulsion to cough and splutter wracked her body.

What was she doing? This was stupid. Why was she putting herself through this just for the sake of a dare? For the sake of saving face? A dare wasn't worth dying for.

Screw what Justin thought.

She had to get out.

She hauled herself to her feet, disorientated and light-headed, coughing violently with spittle flying from her mouth.

She felt her way along the wall with her hands until she came to the smooth painted surface of the door. Found the handle. Gripped it with both hands and yanked it.

But the handle wouldn't move.

It was stuck. And no matter how hard she pulled on it, it wouldn't budge.

What the hell?

She tried again until her arms ached and her muscles burned.

Oh god, she was trapped. And she couldn't breathe.

She was going to die.

Fear flooded her body and desperation gave her renewed energy. But no matter how hard she tried, she couldn't open the door.

How was it even possible? There was no lock and surely the heat couldn't have warped the frame.

Unless...

Oh god, unless one of the boys outside was holding it closed.

She banged on the door. 'Help! Let me out,' she screeched, the back of her throat scorched and raw.

Her legs gave way and she collapsed to her knees.

She banged again. And again.

The door remained closed.

It had to be Justin. She'd humiliated him and this was his payback.

But why wasn't Finn stopping him?

'Open the... door... Justin... Finn. I can't breathe.'

The edge of her world folded in and dizzying thoughts of death spiralled around her head. She had no strength left. She couldn't breathe. Couldn't even cough as she sank to the floor, the fight evaporating from her soul.

And then a sudden calmness and peace.

In the background the fire crackled. Her world went black.

And that's the last thing she could remember.

Chapter 39

I sit motionless, completely transfixed by Arabella's awful story. It's a wonder she sleeps at night. I still have nightmares about the fire that took Felix and Sebastian. You don't go through something like that without it leaving scars.

'I don't remember much after I passed out,' she says. 'Finn told me later that Justin had been holding the handle from the outside. He begged him to open it, but he wouldn't listen, until it was almost too late.'

'I'm so sorry,' I whisper.

Arabella folds her hands in her lap and picks at the fabric of her dress. 'So you can understand why I could never forgive him.'

Like a house of cards caught by an unexpected gust of wind, everything I thought I knew about my husband has come crashing down.

'I never thought I'd see him again,' she says, dabbing a tear with the corner of a tissue. 'And after a lot of time and therapy, I thought I'd finally moved on. I couldn't believe he'd dare to come back to Treloar.'

'He never mentioned any of this, otherwise I'd never have agreed to come. I just had no idea,' I say.

'One of the worst things was that Justin had the gall to blame Finn, even though he had nothing to do with it. And my father has never forgiven him,' she says.

'Justin, at least, dragged you out of the building though?' I say. 'That's true?'

She snorts derisively. 'Finn couldn't open the door because I'd collapsed in front of it, and that's when Justin panicked, apparently. It took two of them to get inside, then Justin pushed Finn out of the way to reach me. It was nothing more than guilt,' she says. 'Finn ran off to call for an ambulance and alerted Daddy, who was furious. Of course, he wanted to know what had happened and Justin brazenly lied to him and told him the fire had been all Finn's idea. Then he tried to claim he'd saved my life. Can you believe it?'

'Did you try talking to your father?' I ask. 'And explain what had really happened?'

'Of course, but he'd already made up his mind. Justin and his parents never came back though, so I assume he had a word with them and told them Justin wasn't welcome.' Arabella sniffs and straightens her back, composing herself. 'So, what will you do now? Will you divorce him?'

Divorce? I haven't really thought that far ahead. It seems so... final. But I suppose I'll need to look into it. There's no coming back from how Justin's treated me, especially as I now know the truth about what happened here at Treloar. I probably should have spotted the signs earlier, but I've been so desperate to cling onto my marriage, I've been blinkered all this time.

'I guess, yes, that's probably the next step,' I say. 'But what's important now is finding some space to sort my life out without him in it.'

'You'll be fine,' Arabella says, glancing out of the window. 'That looks like it might be your friend now.'

The low rumble of a car engine grows louder.

Thank god.

Will Justin try to come after me though? Persuade me I've made a big mistake? I can't imagine he'll accept I'm leaving without a fight, but I'll have to deal with that later. Although, if he can't find me, he can't harass me, can he? I will need to talk to him, of course. If nothing else, there are the finances to unpick and my share of the house to fight for.

God, there's so much to think about.

I jump up with an embarrassed glance at Arabella. With my dirty jeans and carrying everything I own in a supermarket bag, heaven knows what she must think of me. 'Thank you for letting me wait and for telling me the truth.'

'Good luck, Megan.'

I race into the hall and throw open the front door as Harriet appears at the bottom of the steps.

'Oh, Megan,' she cries, trotting up the stairs with some difficulty in a tight pencil skirt. She wraps me in a warm embrace.

Relief radiates from every pore of my body.

'Please, can we go?' I ask. I don't want to stay here a second longer. Every minute I remain at Treloar is another minute when Justin could be back and I don't have the energy to face him.

'Of course. Let's get you out of here.'

'I don't know what I'd do without you,' I say, struggling to hold back tears of relief.

It never occurred to me before that Justin sabotaging all of my friendships in Plymouth was a deliberate attempt to isolate me. Thank god for Harriet.

She hurries me towards her car that she's skidded to a halt behind the Carlyon's black Range Rover.

'I think it's safer if you ride in the boot,' she says with an anguished look.

I frown. Is she serious? 'The boot?'

Harriet nods and presses a button on a key fob which releases the boot catch. 'You'll be fine. There's a blanket in there you can use as a pillow.'

'I'm not sure that's really necessary, is it?' I can't get in the boot, trapped in a tiny space like that. It's ridiculous.

'Megan, I don't have time to argue.' She raises her voice. I suppose she's just as stressed as I am and doesn't want to run foul of Justin. 'You don't want him seeing you if he comes back, do you?'

'No, I suppose not.' I hadn't thought of that, although the chances of Justin suddenly returning to the estate seem extremely slim.

'And it's only a short journey. You won't be in there for long.'

'You'll be able to drop me off in Falmouth?' I ask, eyeing up the cramped compartment behind the front seats, wondering how on earth I'm going to fit. Maybe if I lie on my side and pull my knees up to my chest like a sleeping baby it could work. And it's only about a twenty-minute drive into Falmouth. It's not the end of the world.

'Yes, of course. Wherever you want to go.' Harriet wafts a dismissive hand in the air. 'But come on, we need to hurry.'

'I can get some cash out in the town and catch a train up north somewhere.'

'Yes, yes. Come on. We don't have all day.'

Her kindness makes me want to burst into tears again. How wonderful to have someone like Harriet who's prepared to drop everything to help me. Today has been such an emotional rollercoaster.

I toss my bag of clothes into the boot and contemplate how I can climb in elegantly, before concluding there's no way to do it with any semblance of grace.

'And you'd better give me your phone too.'

'My phone?'

'You don't want him tracking you, do you?' she snaps, holding out her hand.

'It's not working. He took the SIM card,' I explain.

'It doesn't matter. We'll get you a new one. For all you know he's installed tracking software on it. Best not to take any risks.'

'Yes, sure. You're right.' I slide my mobile out of my back pocket and hand it over to Harriet.

'Right, get in,' she demands.

I take one last look around at the house and the estate. It's a stunning location which under any other circumstances would be a wonderful place to live, but not after what's happened. Not now I know the truth. With a sigh, I hoick my leg up and roll my body into the car, squeezing myself uncomfortably into the tiny boot that smells faintly of petrol.

'Hold tight. We'll be there shortly,' Harriet says, standing over me with one hand on the boot lid.

'Thank you,' I croak.

And then the boot closes with a clunk and I'm totally enveloped in darkness.

Chapter 40

As the car jolts down the drive, it's clear this isn't going to be the most comfortable journey of my life. The back of my head keeps banging against a wheel arch and my hips ache from the unnatural foetal position I've had to curl into. My discomfort only gets worse as Harriet drives off the estate and speeds up along the narrow and winding country lanes.

My knees clatter against exposed metalwork, a searing pain jags through my cramped shoulders and my neck feels as if it's being painfully twisted and bent out of shape. I'm going to be covered in bruises for weeks.

But worse is the nausea which swells in my stomach as my body is thrown one way and then another in the darkness. The smell of petrol doesn't help and it takes all my concentration not to vomit.

Why did I agree to this? It's completely unnecessary, but I guess Harriet's only trying to do the right thing. And I can hardly complain when she dropped everything to come and rescue me. I should be grateful I'm not still locked in the lodge.

I don't know what I'll do next. Where I'll go. How I'll survive. But I'll make it work. I have family in the north west I could try. A cousin in Cumbria I've not seen for years. I'm sure if I explained, she'd happily take me in, at least until I'm able to get back on my feet.

Justin and I have been together for so long, the thought of being on my own again is terrifying. I can't remember what it's like to be single. To think only about myself. To get up when I want. To wear what I want to wear. To go where I want to go. For too long, Justin controlled my life. It's going to be a big adjustment, but I have no choice. I've made my decision. This is the real new start I needed all along.

Harriet brakes sharply and my spine slams into the front seats. I squeal in pain and squeeze my eyes shut. How much further? I can't bear much more of this.

She's certainly not hanging around. It feels as if she's taking the corners like she's in a race car, engine growling, foot down hard. It's probably my lack of perspective shut away in the back in the dark. In reality, she's probably pootling along like an old lady.

When the car finally slows and comes to a halt, my head and stomach continue to roll, but at least the journey's over. I don't think I could have lasted much longer.

Harriet ratchets on the handbrake and kills the engine.

My ears hiss in the absence of the road noises. Are we in Falmouth already? I expected to hear the sounds of a busy town. Traffic and people. Seagulls. But there's only silence.

Of course, she'll have pulled up in a quiet backstreet somewhere. She could hardly park outside the station and casually let me out of the boot with everyone watching. It makes sense she'd find somewhere quiet and out of the way.

A car door opens and closes, rocking the vehicle on its suspension. I stretch my neck and press my feet into the bodywork, trying to elongate my legs, waiting with anticipation for the first restorative breath of fresh air when Harriet lets me out.

Her footsteps trip-trap away into the distance.

'Harriet?' I murmur.

I strain to hear what's going on outside. Nothing, other than the faint sound of birdsong.

Where the hell has she gone?

A minute passes. And then another.

My panic rises.

'Harriet!' I yell. 'Let me out!'

Still nothing.

I hammer on the bodywork with my fist. It makes a dull, hollow thudding noise. 'Harriet!'

What is she doing?

Why's she left me in here?

The air is thick and suffocating. My chest tight. I can't breathe.

'Harriet!'

The boot lid pops open and light streams in, so bright it pains my eyes. I squint at the shadow of the figure that appears above me.

'Megan, I'm so sorry,' Harriet says. 'I thought I saw Justin's car and had to make sure he hadn't followed me.'

She grabs my hand and helps me to clamber stiffly out. All my joints have seized up and the muscles in my arms, legs, neck and back protest painfully.

But the air is cool and sweet, and I drink it in like nectar, stretching and rubbing my neck and lower back.

As my eyes become accustomed to the light, I stare around at the surroundings. At the trees and flowers, bushes and long grass. The rolling hills in the distance.

I glower at Harriet. 'Where are we?' She's clearly not taken me to Falmouth like she promised.

'I couldn't just drop you off at the station and let you head off on your own,' she says. 'I want you to stay with me for a few days. Just until you get yourself straight. I have plenty of room, so there's no point arguing.'

She points to a house at the end of a dirt track where she's parked the car. It's a quaint cottage with a pretty garden, surrounded by verdant rolling hills. Like the Treloar estate, it appears to be in the middle of nowhere.

'I don't know what to say. Are you sure?'

'And don't worry. Justin will never find you here.'

My plan had been to get as far away from Justin as possible but the idea of staying with Harriet is appealing. Or am I making a mistake? We can't be more than ten or fifteen miles from Treloar. And if Justin works out that Harriet's helped me to escape, he could easily find out where she lives, guess that she's taken me in and come after me.

'I was going to look up a cousin in Cumbria — '

Harriet holds up a hand and shakes her head. 'No, no, I won't hear of it. You're in no state to be left on your own. I have a lovely spare room you can use and if, in a few days, you still want to go, then I'll run you into Falmouth and I won't stand in your way.'

'Really? You're serious?'

What have I done to deserve a friend like this?

She reaches into the boot and grabs my carrier bag of belongings. 'Come on, I'll show you around.'

'I don't know what to say. This is the kindest thing anyone's ever done for me.'

'After everything you've been through in the last year, it's the least I can do.' Her smile gives me a warm glow.

The tour of the house doesn't take long. It has a small kitchen, a dining room and lounge, plus two bedrooms and two bathrooms which is going to be handy if we're going to be living together.

'Make yourself at home,' Harriet says. 'Treat it as your own.'

It's like a show home. Everything's in immaculate condition. There's no mess or clutter anywhere, not even a pile of unopened post on the table by the front door. All the walls have been painted in fashionably muted greys and whites and many of the rooms have exposed oak beams and quirky roof spaces.

'It's perfect,' I say. 'I don't know how I'm ever going to repay you.'

'Having you here is reward enough. It'll just be nice to have some company around the house for a change. Let me show you your room.'

The guestroom at the back of the house has everything I could want. A big double bed, already made up with a colourful duvet cover, a wardrobe, a chest of drawers and a shelf on the wall filled with paperbacks. There's even a writing desk under the window, which oddly has been covered up behind a wooden panel nailed to the frame, allowing only the narrowest slivers of light in.

'I'm afraid the window pane's cracked, so I've had to board it up until I can get a glazier out to fix it,' Harriet says with an apologetic grimace. 'Do you mind?'

'Of course I don't mind,' I gush. I can hardly be fussy about it when she's offering me a room in her house out of the goodness of her heart. And besides, it makes the room feel secure. I won't have to worry about anyone breaking in while I'm sleeping. Not that Justin would stoop that low, would he?

I doubt Justin's going to take it lightly when he discovers I've gone. Of course, he'll have no idea what's happened. Should I have left a note? It was the last thing on my mind when I escaped this morning, but what's he going to think when he gets back to an empty house? I don't want him calling the police and creating a fuss, thinking I've been abducted or something. I'll have to call him and tell him, although the thought of speaking to him and explaining fills me with dread.

'I meant what I said,' Harriet says. 'You can stay here as long as you like. But do you have any longer-term plans?'

'Not really,' I shrug. 'I never thought I'd leave Justin in a million years. After the fire and losing the boys, I was determined it wouldn't destroy our marriage, because we'd lost everything else. But it turns out, I was clinging on to something I should have let go a long time ago.'

'It's good you've made a clean break. I know a good divorce solicitor who can help. If you want, I can put you in touch with her.'

'Thanks.' I look down at my hands where I've been inadvertently picking my fingernails and now they're bleeding. Everything seems to be moving so quickly. I only left Justin this morning. 'I'll think about it.'

'Okay, you don't have to rush anything. Take your time.'

'It's just too early to think about the future. I don't know what I want yet.'

'Of course,' Harriet says, with a sympathetic pat on my arm.

I can't believe I've fallen on my feet again. Someone must be looking down on me.

That evening, Harriet suggests a takeaway. We settle on Chinese and while she pops out to collect it, leaving me with a bottle of Pinot Grigio, I take the opportunity to have a proper look around the house.

I still don't know much about Harriet. All she's really told me is that she'd recently come out of a long-term relationship and that she's a sucker for taking in rescued cats and dogs.

That's it. That's the thing that's been bugging me at the back of my mind since the moment I arrived. Where are the animals? She told me she had a house full of cats. At least six, I'm sure she said. So where are they? I've not seen any evidence of a cat or a dog since I arrived. No food bowls or beds. There's not even so much as a cat hair to be seen on the sofa. And what happened to the puppy she brought me as a housewarming gift I couldn't keep? I thought she was going to take him in? Maybe she returned him to the kennels. That still doesn't explain the lack of cats.

Unless she lied to me.

But why would you lie about something like that?

And what about this long-term partner, Ollie, she said she recently split from?

I can't see any evidence that someone else has been living in the house. Surely, she didn't lie about him too?

I should have paid more attention when she was telling me about him. Instead I was too wrapped up in my own problems.

I don't like to snoop, especially as Harriet has been so kind to me, but after a glass of wine on an empty stomach, my curiosity gets the better of me and I begin to prowl around the house.

The pictures on the walls are mostly originals. Watercolours and the odd oil from local artists depicting tempestuous seas and dramatic Cornish sunsets. Floor-to-ceiling shelves in the lounge are full of an eclectic mix of fiction and non-fiction tomes. Classic heavy works by Joyce and Tolstoy. Plus historical, political and philosophical hardbacks by authors I've never heard of. And she's still clinging onto a collection of old CDs, I see. Some jazz. A few late nineties pop bands. A bit of classical, mostly Mahler, Vivaldi, Barber. Nothing edgy.

I poke around in the kitchen, checking the contents of her fridge (disappointingly sparse) and her cupboards (full of tins and packets of pasta), but stop myself at her bedroom door. That's going beyond nosy and crossing a line.

On a shelf in the dining room, I finally find answers to some of my questions. There are a collection of photos in frames, most of them featuring Harriet, smiling at the camera, in the company of another woman. She has short, dark hair cut into a severe bob. Cool, piercing eyes. She's kind of beautiful in a classic way with a pixie nose and freckles, and a hard, determined look that makes me think she has a skin of armour. Impenetrable. Standoffish, until you get to know her.

There's something about the closeness of their bodies in one of the images, Harriet's arm slipped around the other woman's waist, that rearranges the pieces in my head. Ollie? I've had it wrong all this time. Harriet's long-term partner wasn't a man at all. Funny, the presumptions we make.

I take one photo off the shelf and run my thumb over the glass, tracing the line first of Harriet's face and then that of this other woman. Harriet said it was a recent break-up. I wonder how it ended.

Somewhere outside I hear the faint crackle of tyres on the stony dirt track.

My heart rate spikes. My body freezes. My ears straining.

Someone's coming.

Harriet?

Or someone else?

Please god, not Justin. Not while I'm in the house on my own. Surely he can't have found me already.

I hurriedly place the framed photo back on the shelf and dive into my room, flicking off the lights and turning the key in the lock.

I steal into the darkness and with the blood surging through my veins, cower behind the wardrobe.

And wait.

Chapter 41

'Megan? I'm home.'

The sound of Harriet's voice floods my body with relief.

I stand, feeling faintly foolish, and emerge from my hiding place behind the wardrobe. Justin's made me so jumpy.

Sheepishly, I slip out of my room and meet Harriet in the hall as she's kicking off her shoes, a white plastic bag groaning with food in one hand.

'I heard a car. I thought it might have been Justin.'

'I told you, he's not going to bother you here, okay?' she reassures me.

'I know. I'm being silly. Sorry.'

'No need to apologise. Come on, let's eat before it gets cold.'

We eat on our laps in front of the TV in the lounge but I don't have much appetite. Reluctantly, I spoon some rice, beef and noodles onto my plate and nibble on the corner of a prawn cracker, but I can't really face eating. My stomach's still queasy and I'm worried about Justin.

He must have discovered I've escaped by now. I should have left a note to explain I was leaving him and why. But I was in such a hurry. All I could think about was getting away. I hope he doesn't alert the police. That would be awkward.

'Do you think I should call Justin?' I ask. 'I ought to let him know I'm safe.'

Harriet's fork stops halfway to her mouth. 'Do you want to call him?'

'Not really.'

'Then let him stew,' she says. 'He's brought this on himself.'

'But what if he's worried about me?'

'Phone him then,' she snaps.

'I can't. You took my phone.'

Harriet continues eating and doesn't give my phone back or offer me hers.

'Can I ask you a question?' I push a slice of beef across my plate. 'You told me you had cats. Where are they?'

Harriet finishes what she's chewing, clears her throat and puts her plate down on the coffee table. 'I do,' she says. 'But I don't let them in the house.'

'Why not?'

She wrinkles her nose. 'So unhygienic. All that hair everywhere and bringing in dead mice and birds all the time. I can't be doing with it.'

That's weird. I'm sure she told me the house was in constant chaos because of her cats. 'So where do you keep them?'

Harriet huffs. 'They're quite happy outside. They get fed and watered and they're safe from the foxes.'

'What, like in a cage?' The way she'd described it before made it sound like the cats had the run of the house. Being caged in the garden doesn't sound so caring.

She laughs. 'They're animals, Megan. They're supposed to be outside.'

'And the puppy you brought for me? Does he live outside with the cats?' I ask, incredulous. So much for the devoted animal lover she made herself out to be.

'He's in a kennel,' she says, 'but to be honest, he's too energetic. I don't have the time for it. I'll probably take him back.'

'Oh,' I say. 'I see.' What's the point of having pets if you keep them caged up outside? It strikes me as odd, but obviously Harriet doesn't think it's strange in the slightest.

'More wine?' she asks.

She tops up my glass almost to the brim. Not that I care. The alcohol's numbing my anxiety and hopefully it will take my mind off Justin, at least for the rest of the night. 'I was looking at your pictures while you were out.'

Harriet glances at me and raises an eyebrow. 'Which ones?'

'The ones in the dining room. Is that your ex?' I ask, emboldened by the wine.

She lowers her gaze. 'Yeah. That's Ollie,' she says.

'Were you together for a long time?'

'Seven years.' Harriet stares sullenly into her glass.

'What happened? Sorry, do you mind me asking?'

She shrugs. 'She went back to her husband.'

'Oh,' I say, trying to conceal my shock. 'I hadn't realised... ' The heat rises from my chest and up my neck.

'She thought she knew what she wanted and I thought we were happy,' Harriet says, the heavy weight of sadness descending over her like a thick blanket. 'But sometimes these things aren't meant to be.'

'I'm really sorry.'

'It's okay. Life goes on. I'll find someone new. That's how it works, isn't it?'

I feel bad now. I shouldn't have mentioned it. Is that what this obsession with animals is all about? Is she just looking for someone or something to love? And to be loved in return?

'I guess that makes us the same. Two fucked-up singletons.' I tip my glass to her.

She smiles and tips her glass back at me. 'Do you think you'll find someone new?'

'Oh, I don't know.' It's only been a matter of hours since I left Justin. I don't even know where I'm going to live or what I'm going to do for money without thinking about jumping back into the frying pan of a relationship. And who the hell is going to look twice at me? A mother who couldn't even keep her own kids alive? 'Maybe in time. When I'm ready.'

'How many times have you been in love?' she asks, catching me by surprise with the question. 'I mean, properly head over heels in love?'

'Truthfully? I guess Justin's the only man I've ever really loved. At least I thought I loved him.'

Harriet's eyes grow wide with amazement. 'You can't be serious? How old were you when you met?'

'Twenty-three.'

'And you'd never been in love before?' She pulls her legs under her thighs so she's sitting cross-legged on the floor, her mouth hanging open in surprise.

'I mean, Justin wasn't my first love, obviously.' I don't want her thinking I'm some kind of weirdo. 'But none of the others were ever serious.'

Harriet slaps a hand to her forehead. 'You married the first man you fell in love with?'

I bristle at the insinuation I've somehow acted naively. 'I thought he was the one. What about you? How many times have you been in love?'

'Too many times to remember.' She laughs, tossing her head back and running her fingers through her long, blonde hair.

'Have you ever been married?'

'Never.' She says it like she's proud of it, that she'd never been foolish enough to commit to one person.

'How long have you known you were... ?'

'What? Queer?' She cocks her head to one side, studying me. 'I've always known.'

'I'm sorry, I had no idea.'

Her eyes narrow and for a moment I fear I've said something wrong. 'Why are you apologising?'

'Oh, no, not because of that,' I say, horrified she's misunderstood. 'I just meant that you've been such a good friend when I really needed somebody and I realise now I hardly know anything about you.' I hang my head, ashamed that I've been so selfishly introspective.

Harriet puts her glass down, crawls across the floor and kneels in front of me. I tense at her touch as she lifts my chin with her fingers, even though I'm trying really hard to be cool with such an intimate gesture. 'Don't feel bad,' she whispers. 'You've been through hell. You're allowed to be a little self-centred.'

I laugh nervously and take another sip of wine, casually attempting to put some distance between us. I don't want to give her misleading signals. She's a good friend, that's all.

'Seriously though, thank you for today. If you hadn't come to pick me up and offered me somewhere to stay, I don't know what I'd have done.' I want her to understand how grateful I am and that I appreciate she's put herself out for me, when she doesn't really know me at all.

'It's nothing.' She waves her hand in the air like she's a princess dismissing a servant.

'No, it's not. It's incredibly generous and I'll never forget your kindness.'

'Awww, that's sweet.' She stands unsteadily and flops down on the sofa next to me, knocking my arm. Wine splashes across my jeans.

'And at some point I'll definitely repay the favour.'

Harriet wraps an arm around me and snuggles her head onto my shoulder. I'm not entirely comfortable with this sudden display of familiarity, but what can I say?

'You can stay here as long as you want,' she murmurs, pressing herself even closer to me.

'Well, maybe just for a few days until I can work out a plan.' I take a large gulp of wine, emptying my glass. I'm not sure what to do with my arm that's hovering over her head. It doesn't feel appropriate to put it around her. That would be weird.

She lifts her face to look at me and smiles. 'Please, don't go rushing off.' She presses her palm to my cheek tenderly.

Oh god. This is awkward. What do I do? Every muscle in my body is rigid. I can't push her away without making a big thing about it, and after everything she's done, I don't want to upset her.

'I won't,' I giggle nervously. 'Is there any more wine?'

I try to lean towards the bottle, hoping she'll take the hint and move away.

But she doesn't.

She has me pinned in the corner of the sofa, staring at me so intently I can't even look at her.

'Megan?' she says.

'Yes?'

'I want you to stay.'

And suddenly her mouth is on mine. Kissing me. Pressing tenderly. Her lips soft and warm.

I'm frozen with shock.

I can't move. I can't breathe.

Her fingers curl around the back of my neck, her nails scraping through my hair, raking across my skin.

No, I don't want this. This isn't right. I can't let this happen.

'Harriet, no!' I yell, pushing her away and springing out of my seat. 'It's not... That's not... '

She rolls back on the sofa, eyes growing wide with shock, staring up at me as if somehow *I've* done something wrong.

'What is it?' she gasps.

I resist the urge to wipe my mouth with the back of my hand. 'I - I'm not like you,' I say, running a palm over my forehead. God, that didn't come out right at all. 'I mean, I've just split up with my husband, Harriet. I can't... I don't want... '

What was she thinking? Now she's gone and ruined everything. How can I stay here now?

'Okay, I'm sorry,' she says, putting her hands up in surrender. 'I misread the signs. I apologise. Come on, have some more wine.' She grabs the bottle and offers it to me.

'No, thank you. I've had enough.' I can't even look her in the eye. 'It's been a long day. I think I'll turn in.'

'Megan... '

I turn and stumble out of the room, unsteady on my feet, my head pounding. I've definitely drunk too much.

I fall into my room and push the door closed, welcoming the veil of darkness. I think about locking the door, but that's ridiculous. Harriet's made a pass at me, that's all. She's hardly going to come sneaking into my room in the middle of the night.

I collapse on the bed with my heart thudding and my mouth dry.

How can I stay here now, after this? Is that why she invited me here, to make a move on me? Why she was so keen to come and pick me up when I called? We were supposed to be friends, but this has changed everything. It's going to be too awkward to stay. We'd be forever tiptoeing around each other and I don't think I could ever feel comfortable in the house with her now.

It's unfortunate, but tomorrow I'll tell her I've changed my mind, that I'm going to stick to my original plan and head north. I'm sure she'll understand. I'll ask her to drop me at the station and we can both move on. It's probably for the best. Staying here in Cornwall was always a risk with Justin so close.

Maybe it's a blessing in disguise.

Chapter 42

The memory of last night's awkward kiss with Harriet hits me like a lorryload of bricks a moment after I wake with a fuzzy head and a nauseous stomach. I sit up and rub my eyes, my brain foggy and dull. I've not slept well in the strange bed, particularly as my mind has been in overdrive all night, thinking everything through. And besides, I never sleep soundly when I've been drinking.

Nonetheless, my determination to move on and get out of Cornwall, far from Justin and Treloar, remains resolute. I just need to break it to Harriet without offending her, and then she can drop me into Falmouth where I can hopefully lay my hands on some cash before Justin freezes me out of the account, and hop on a train north.

I can hear Harriet's already up. The kettle clicks on and begins to hiss and burble. I might as well get it over with and face up to her. No point putting it off, especially if she's working today. I don't know what time she leaves, but maybe she can drop me off on her way in. No hard feelings.

I slip out of bed, pull on my jeans and T-shirt and run my fingers through my hair. It could do with a wash, but it might have to wait if Harriet's leaving soon.

I pad across the floor, grab the door handle and tug. It creaks and groans, but when I try to pull the door open, it won't budge.

That's funny. I thought about locking it last night but remember making a conscious decision against it. Unless I did lock it and don't remember.

In the darkness, I feel around the handle with my fingertips, hunting for the key.

But it's not there.

There's only the empty keyhole.

Strange. Did I lock the door and remove the key? I don't think so. In fact, I'm sure of it. But what other explanation is there? Unless Harriet locked me in from the outside...

No. That's crazy. Why would she do that?

I flick on the harsh overhead light that hangs from the ceiling. There's definitely no key in the lock.

I hurry back to the bed and hunt all around in the bedclothes, the bedside cabinet and the floor. Where else would it be? It's not in any of my jeans pockets. Or on the top of the chest of drawers. Or in any of the drawers. Or the wardrobe.

Now I'm panicking.

I rush back to the door and hammer on it with the flat of my hand.

'Harriet! Are you there? I can't open the door. It's locked.'

I press my ear against it. She must have heard me, surely?

'Harriet!' I scream. I thump the door with both hands, making the kind of racket that would wake the dead.

But still nothing.

I can't believe this.

An image of Arabella trapped inside that burning outbuilding flashes through my mind. Justin on the other side of the door, holding it shut. It must have been the most terrifying experience of her life. I'm beginning to understand how she must have felt.

'Harriet! Harriet! Help me!'

Footsteps.

She's outside the door. I can hear her breathing.

Why isn't she saying anything?

'Harriet? Are you there?' I say, more softly.

'Stop making such a terrible din. Some of us have hangovers, you know.' Her voice is dull and distant.

'I can't open the door,' I cry. 'It's locked and I can't find the key.'

'It's for your own good.'

What?

'Harriet? What do you mean? Have you locked me in?'

'Stand back, please. I've brought you breakfast,' she says, so calmly I wonder if she's completely lost her mind.

'You locked me in the room?' I gasp. 'But why?'

My foggy head spins, trying to make sense of it all. Why did I have so much to drink last night?

'Stand back, please, Megan. It's for your own safety.'

'Okay,' I whisper. If it means she'll open the door, I'm willing to do whatever she asks. I take a few tentative backwards steps until I'm standing by the bed.

'Wait by the window,' she says.

I take a few more steps across to the boarded-up glass where weak rays of light are filtering into the room.

'Okay. I'm by the window,' I shout.

A key scratches in the lock.

It turns and clicks open.

Through the gloom, I see the handle being slowly depressed. The door swinging open. And Harriet standing there, silhouetted in the frame, carrying a tray in one hand and what looks suspiciously like a kitchen knife in the other.

'Harriet? What's going on?'

She kicks a black plastic bucket into the room. It tumbles over and rolls across the carpet on its side.

'In case you need the bathroom,' she says.

She wants me to pee in a bucket? Has she completely taken leave of her senses?

'Why did you lock me in?' I demand. 'Was it because of last night? The kiss? I'm sorry if— '

'Shut up,' she snaps.

I jolt, the aggression in her tone catching me by surprise.

'I thought we were friends. And if I upset you last night, it's only because I wasn't expecting it.'

I remain by the window as she steps into the room, dressed impeccably as usual in a fawn trouser suit, her make-up perfectly applied. She places the tray on the bed. There's a mug of what looks like it could be tea and two slices of buttered toast. My stomach rumbles. I've hardly eaten anything in the last twenty-four hours, but I can't think about food right now.

'I was worried about you. I didn't want you disappearing off in the middle of the night, running back to that worthless husband of yours,' Harriet explains.

'But I wouldn't... I couldn't... '

This is madness.

'And so, yes, I'm sorry but I locked the door before I went to bed. I'm just looking out for your best interests, Megan. It's what friends do, isn't it?'

'Oh, Harriet, I have absolutely no intention of running back to Justin.' I move towards her but her arm jolts up, aiming the knife at me and I back off.

'I don't believe you.'

'Okay, but just put the knife down, will you? There's no need for that.' My heart's racing like a greyhound after a rabbit.

'I'm going to work now,' Harriet says, still holding the knife at arm's length. 'We'll talk later.'

She backs out of the room, her gaze fixed on me, the knife unwavering.

'You're not going to keep me locked in here all day, are you?' I ask, as the realisation hits me.

'I'll be back at teatime. Try not to get into any mischief while I'm gone.'

She snatches the door and slams it closed. I rush at it in a panic, grabbing the handle. But I'm too slow. The lock grinds and clicks. And I'm trapped in the room again with no way out.

'Harriet!' I yell, attacking the door with my fists and feet, fury and panic bubbling up into a cocktail of violence. 'Let me out of here! You can't keep me locked up. I'm not an animal.'

But it's pointless. She's not going to let me out. I know it deep in my heart as truly as I now know the woman is insane.

And as if I needed any further proof, I hear the front door open and click shut as Harriet leaves for work. A few moments later, her car starts and I listen, slumped on the floor, as it slowly pulls off and the low rumble of its tyres fades away.

Chapter 43

With nothing else to fill my time, I spend the rest of the day plotting my escape. First, I check the boarded-up window but without a wrench or a screwdriver, it's impossible to remove the chipboard panel that's blocking out the light. And there's nothing in the room I can use as a tool either. There aren't even any coat hangers in the wardrobe.

Then I turn my attention to the door. I initially hoped the lock might give if I threw myself at it, until I remember it opens inwards, which immediately put paid to that idea. I wouldn't even know where to begin picking a lock. Even if I still had my phone and access to the internet for guidance, it's obvious I'd need some sort of tool.

It's hopeless. There's nothing I can do but sit and wait for Harriet to return. Maybe when she's back and has had the day to think about what she's done, she'll change her mind and release me. She must know she can't keep me a prisoner here indefinitely.

I lie on the bed and stare at the ceiling, listening to birdsong outside. Why does my life seem to constantly spiral from bad to worse? What have I done to deserve this? Is it some kind of cosmic payback for the fire I started? For the death of my boys? I never meant to kill them. Haven't I suffered enough?

I don't even really understand what Harriet wants from me. She says she's trying to protect me, to stop me running back to Justin. But why would she think I'd want to do that? I've told her what he's done and that I'm leaving him to sort out my life. I don't need to be locked in a room with a bucket to pee in.

The woman is totally out of her mind. Maybe she even planned this. I mean, it's all very convenient that the window was already boarded up when I arrived. But I never questioned it. Maybe I'm too trusting.

If she has planned this, she must have acted quickly. I've only known the woman for a little over a week. I don't even know what she's hoping to achieve? What does it matter to her if I'm with Justin or not?

Unless she's fallen in love with me?

No, that's ridiculous. She hardly knows me. I shouldn't flatter myself. She might be getting over a broken heart, but that doesn't mean she's going to throw herself at me.

Although, she has been overly attentive, at my beck and call whenever I've needed her. And she brought me that puppy, which I thought at the time was a bit much. What was it she said?

They know I'm a sucker for all the waifs and strays and this little one badly needed a new home.

Oh god, is that what this is? Does she think I need someone to take care of me? That I'm weak and vulnerable because I'd lost my house and my children?

I sit bolt upright on the bed with the blood rushing in my ears and a sudden clarity of thought.

It was Harriet who planted the phone in the house. She sent me those messages warning me I was in danger from Justin. To get me questioning our relationship and to drive us apart.

And I've walked straight into her trap. I'm such a fool.

If I can't physically force my way out of this room, then the only other way is to talk my way out. I need to persuade Harriet she's doing the wrong thing. That I can be trusted. As much as it's going to pain me, I'm going to have to be compliant. Whatever she wants, I'll do it. At least until I get my chance to escape.

It's the only plan I have.

Harriet doesn't get home until gone six that evening. I listen to her car pulling up. Her footsteps up the garden path. The front door swinging open. And I prepare myself mentally, plastering a smile on my face to convince her I'm happy to see her home. I don't bang on the door demanding to be let out or scream and shout her name like a demented banshee.

'Megan? Are you alright?' she calls out with a catch of concern in her voice.

'Harriet? Is that you?' I call back pathetically. 'Have you had a good day?'

I figure if I act like a dutiful wife, we might get somewhere.

'Stand away from the door. I'm coming in.'

I jump off the bed and wait by the window, with my back in the corner, as far from the door as I can, trying to look non-threatening. 'I'm ready.'

The lock clicks back and the door swings open.

'Hey,' I say, my forced smile making my cheeks ache. 'I missed you.'

It's a shame she's had to bring the knife again, but it's down by her side and I pretend not to notice.

'I missed you too,' she says. 'But I have good news.'

'You do?' I don't suppose it's that she's come to her senses and is going to let me go, but I cock my head to indicate that I'm listening.

'I've spoken to Justin.'

'Oh.' I wasn't expecting that. 'What did he say?'

'I told him you want a divorce. I know a wonderful lawyer who can get the paperwork done quickly,' she says.

She's done what? I'm not sure I even want a divorce. At least not until I have had time to think it through.

Our marriage has been under enormous strain because of the fire and losing the boys, but it's only since we moved to Treloar that it's started to fall apart. And how much of that's because of the poison Harriet's been dripping in my ear? Making me question Justin. Our whole relationship.

So he lost his temper and grabbed me around the neck in anger that one time. But only because I'd provoked him. And did he really try to drown me in the sea? I was confused and disorientated. What if I made a mistake? And as for everything Arabella told me, it was all a long time ago.

'That's great. Thank you,' I whimper, doing my best to sound convincing.

'My pleasure. Soon you'll be rid of him for good.'

'I don't know how to thank you, Harriet. You've been amazing,' I say, edging forwards with my fake smile still firmly in place.

'You can thank me by not causing any trouble,' she says, raising the knife as a warning. 'Now back off.'

'I won't be any trouble, I promise.' I hold up my hands and retreat. 'And really, you don't need to keep me locked in my room. I'm not going anywhere.'

Harriet stares at me through narrow slits for eyes. She doesn't believe me. Yet. This is going to take time. I have to be patient.

'Please, Harriet,' I beg. 'Don't lock me up again.'

'I'll bring your dinner shortly.' She snatches the tray she left this morning and backs out of the room, slamming the door behind her.

My heart sinks at the sound of the lock turning.

This isn't going to be as easy as I thought. But how long's it going to take? A day? A week? A month? I'll go crazy locked in this room for all that time. No one knows I'm here. Thanks to Harriet, all Justin knows is that I've left him. And as for Arabella and Lady Grace, they think I'm on a train heading to Cumbria to disappear.

There's no one to raise the alarm and I have no way of calling for help.

I'm on my own.

If I'm going to escape, I have to do this by myself. I have no other choice.

Harriet returns an hour later with a bowl of pasta and a plastic mug of water. 'Here,' she says, thrusting the tray at me.

I momentarily forget about the knife and rush towards her. I'm famished and my throat is dry. She could have at least left me something to drink when she went out this morning.

'Easy,' she warns, as I snatch the tray out of her hands.

The pasta smells delicious. She's cooked it in a rich, tomato sauce with herbs and olives, and although she's only given me a small plastic spoon to eat with, the food's piping hot with steam rising and spiralling into the air.

It gives me another idea.

'This looks divine,' I say, glancing at Harriet as she stands in the doorway watching me. She's only a couple of metres away.

As she grins with pleasure at the compliment, I flip the tray and hurl it at her. She howls with surprise, ducking and fending off the bowl of pasta with her elbow. It crashes into the door and smashes on the floor, spewing pasta shapes and tomato sauce all over the carpet.

I dip a shoulder and charge, screaming at the top of my lungs.

But before I can knock her out of the way, Harriet has the tip of her knife at my throat.

I back off with my hands up.

'Don't make me hurt you,' she hisses, anger flaming in her eyes.

It was a stupid thing to do. Now I've riled her and wasted any chance I had of getting her to trust me.

'I'm so sorry, Harriet,' I sob. 'I didn't mean to hurt you.'

'Clear that mess up,' she orders, 'and if you think I'm cooking anything else, you're wrong. If you're hungry, you'll eat it.' She waves the knife at the tubes of sticky pasta on the carpet.

She's serious. But then, I'm so hungry, I can't afford to waste food.

'Hurry up,' she yells.

I drop to my knees and crawl across the floor, picking up pasta shapes with my fingers, popping them in my mouth, trying to ignore the grit that crunches in my teeth. It's totally degrading.

Harriet watches me the whole time.

I lick my fingers clean when I'm done and pick out a fibrous strand from under my tongue. I rock back on my haunches and look up at Harriet with wide eyes, trying to elicit some sympathy. She must be able to see how demeaning this is for me.

'Now pick up the pieces of that broken bowl and put it on the tray.'

I do as I'm told, careful not to cut my fingers on the sharp shards.

'May I have some more water?' I ask, picking up the empty plastic mug and holding it up to her in both hands.

She stares at me with cold, hard eyes, as if she's weighing up whether I deserve any.

I'm so thirsty, I should have drunk the water when I had a chance, but I wasn't thinking straight.

'Put it on the tray with the bowl,' she hisses.

I do as she asks and slink away back into the shadows like a street urchin.

She bends at the knees, scoops up the tray and edges out of the room.

'I'm sorry, Harriet,' I cry as she pulls the door closed. 'I wasn't trying to hurt you. I was just scared.'

The lock snaps shut and Harriet's footsteps drift away.

Chapter 44

I spend an awful night alone in the room, tossing and turning on the bed. All I can think about is an ice-cold glass of water, condensation dripping down its sides. Lifting it to my parched lips, a balm washing away a burning thirst with a crisp and refreshing relief.

Harriet never came back last night. She left me in my room to suffer. A punishment for my insubordination. Lesson learned. She can be crueller than she looks.

Why was I so quick to trust her? Probably because I had no one else. Justin had effectively isolated me and Harriet was the first and only friendly face I'd encountered since we'd moved to Treloar. Another lesson learned. It pays to choose your friends carefully.

I snatch pockets of sleep through the night with my thirst raging and my mind turning in and around on itself. When I finally give up trying to sleep, it's still hideously early. I attempt to read a cheap thriller from the shelf of paperbacks, but my head's groggy and I can't concentrate on the plot. My mind keeps wandering and I can't make any sense of the story.

Is it just a lack of sleep and dehydration?

Or has Harriet drugged me?

Oh god, I didn't even think about that last night when she brought me that bowl of pasta. If she'd wanted to keep me subdued, she could have easily slipped a sedative into the sauce and I'd have had no idea.

It's probably what I would have done in her shoes. If she has, there's not much I can do about it now.

It's no good. I can't read. So I toss the book to one side and lie on my back, thinking about my boys. It would have been Sebastian's birthday next month. He'd have been six years old. I'd have made him a cake in the shape of a football. Perhaps we'd have all gone bowling. And taken them for pizza for a treat. Organised a party at ours for all his friends with balloons and streamers and pass the parcel and musical chairs. All the games I used to play when I was a kid.

He'd have loved that, being the centre of attention for a change and not playing second fiddle to his brother.

Tears blur my eyes. I miss them so much. I'd give my life to turn back the clock. Do things differently. For a start, I'd dump that faulty heater the moment it started playing up. And I'd make sure I made the most of every single second with those boys. I'd never raise my voice to them. Or snap at them when I was trying to enjoy some quiet time. Or fob them off with a lame excuse about why we couldn't go to the park. I'd have done so many things differently, but it's no good dwelling on it. I can't turn back time. And here I am paying for my negligence in the most horrific way.

When I hear Harriet eventually rise, the water gurgling through the pipes as she takes a shower, the toilet flushing, doors creaking open, I lie still and don't move. I picture her moving around the house. Getting dressed. Applying her make-up. Brushing her hair. Putting on the professional mask of someone respectable and trustworthy.

It doesn't fool me.

Finally, she approaches my door after what seems like an age.

She knocks politely as if she's a hotel maid checking I'm decent before letting herself in.

'Megan, are you awake?'

I lick my dry lips and lift my head, but my throat's so parched my words come out as a hoarse croak. 'Yes, you can come in.'

'Are you standing away from the door?'

'I'm still in bed.'

After a brief hesitation, when I fear she's walked away, the lock clicks open. Light pours in from the hall and Harriet pokes her head in.

'How did you sleep?' she asks lightly.

'Yes, good,' I lie. 'Is there any chance of a glass of water, do you think, please?'

'Yes, of course,' she says, all traces of last night's irritation and anger gone. 'I'll bring you some. Won't be a moment.'

She pulls the door shut and locks it again. When she returns a few minutes later, she's carrying another plastic mug brimming with water.

She sets it on top of the chest of drawers while keeping a wary eye on me as she withdraws back to the door. She still has that knife, I see.

I jump out of bed and guzzle the water down without drawing breath. In my haste to drink, it dribbles out of the side of my mouth and down my chin. It's the best thing I've ever tasted.

I slump on the bed, panting, and wipe my mouth with the back of my hand.

'Someone was thirsty,' Harriet observes, like she's talking to a child.

'Are you working today?' I ask. 'I thought I could do some housework for you while you're out. It's the least I can do to repay your kindness.'

She shoots me a sly smile. Oh well, it was worth a try.

'Actually,' she says. 'I need to move you this morning. I'm worried after speaking to your soon-to-be ex-husband that he might suspect where to find you. I don't want him turning up and harassing you. You've been through so much already.'

'Moving me? Where?' Blood runs chill through my veins.

'Don't worry, it's nothing to be concerned about. I'm doing it for your own safety, Megan. Now are you hungry? Would you like some breakfast?'

I nod enthusiastically.

Ten minutes later she's back with the tray. She's brought me another two slices of buttered toast and a mug of warm tea which I gratefully pounce on and consume while she watches with amusement.

'The phone I found in the loft at the lodge,' I mumble with my mouth full of toast. 'That was you, wasn't it?'

She shrugs nonchalantly.

'And the messages?'

'I love you, Megan. I've loved you from the first time we met, but I could see how desperately unhappy you were,' she says.

I stop chewing and stare at her. Love me? I was right. She's infatuated with me.

'I'd lost my children,' I explain, but she waves a finely manicured hand dismissively.

'No, no, I don't mean that. I mean I could see how unhappy you were with *him*.'

She can't even bring herself to say Justin's name.

I'm about to protest and tell her she's wrong, that Justin had been my rock, my everything, but arguing with her isn't going to get me out of this house.

'So you thought you'd rescue me?' I say. 'Like I was an abandoned kitten?' I can't keep the vitriol out of my voice. What she's done is madness. The woman's a psychopath.

'I could see he wasn't right for you, Megan. He was dragging you down. And I was right, wasn't I? He attacked you, remember? And took away your phone. And the way he spoke to you, I could see he was controlling you. You needed me.'

'So you thought if you split us up, I'd come running to you?'

'I can offer you so much more than he did,' she continues, like she genuinely believes there's a chance of something between us. 'We can be happy together.'

I want to scream at her. I want to tell her she has it all wrong and that she's confused because she's on the rebound after having her heart broken.

But what good would it do?

She's not going to let me go if I don't play along with her stupid, self-deluded game.

'Where are you taking me?' I ask, pushing the tray across the bed. I've lost my appetite.

'Get yourself ready. When I come back, we'll be leaving.'

'Just tell me where we're going,' I beg.

'Not far, but somewhere your husband won't be able to find you.'

I suppose I'll find out soon enough. Maybe it'll be somewhere that's easier to escape from. Or somewhere where there might be an opportunity to raise the alarm. I have to live in hope.

I might as well get myself ready, like she asked. I don't have anything else to do. I throw my meagre belongings back in the supermarket carrier bag, slip on my shoes and sit on the end of the bed to wait.

Maybe I'll get the chance to escape while she's moving me, which means staying alert, even if my head is foggy and slow.

Twenty minutes pass before Harriet returns. I retreat back to the window and she lets herself into the room, still clutching the kitchen knife.

She points it at my face and tells me to step forward slowly.

When I'm within her reach, her free hand snaps up, and she snatches a handful of my hair. I cry out in pain as she twists my head and pushes it down so I have to bend over, my eyes facing the floor.

'Don't give me any trouble,' she hisses in my ear as she drags me out of the room.

At least she's not tied me up.

We scuffle awkwardly across the hall and she throws open the front door. A fresh breeze hits my skin but I don't have time to appreciate it. She forces me down the garden path and I stumble on a loose flagstone. Harriet yanks my head up aggressively and I squeal in agony. If she carries on the way she's going, she's going to rip my hair out of my skull.

'Walk properly,' she screams at me, waving the knife under my nose. 'I don't want to hurt you.'

She's already hurting me, but, of course, I don't say it.

I thought we'd be going in her car and I'd mentally prepared myself for another nausea-inducing trip in the boot.

But I was wrong. She's taking me into the garden. Across a long lawn, framed by wild hedgerows. Away from the house. Down a slope. Across a rough patch of ground. Stones dig into the soles of my feet. And I hear an eerie wailing sound.

It sounds like... cats.

I twist my head to see the bottom of a large wooden-framed cage encased in chicken wire.

Inside, there are at least three cats. No, four. There's another perched high on a shelf in the corner. Grey and white with long hair and a startled-looking face.

So that's where she keeps her rescue cats. In a pokey little cage out the back.

Another cat, so black its orange eyes look like they're popping out of its head, brushes up against the wire mesh and mewls pitifully.

'Oscar, shut up,' Harriet yells, kicking the wire mesh.

It jumps away indignantly and trots off haughtily, stopping momentarily to wash it's back leg.

'Where are we going?' I struggle to keep my balance on the uneven ground as Harriet marches me on.

'Here,' she says, pulling me up with another tug on my hair. 'Where no one will find you.'

When she releases the pressure on my head, I look up to see a rickety old shed.

'This?' I gasp with shock. Surely she's not going to put me inside that.

It's only about half the size of the room she'd been holding me in. It has no windows and a flat, felt-lined roof.

Harriet fumbles with a padlock. The door creaks open revealing a dank and dark interior.

'Get in,' she demands, finally letting go of my hair and shoving me inside.

It's awful. It's dark, dusty and full of cobwebs. I can even see a huge, black spider hanging from one of the beams overhead, its beady eyes watching me, its long, hairy legs ready to scuttle across the ceiling at the slightest disturbance. I shudder.

'Please, Harriet, don't leave me in here.'

'It's for your own good,' she says, closing the door. 'You'll be safe from him in here.'

I thought Justin and I were finished, but I've never wanted to see him more in my life. He's the only person in the world who can save me now. But he thinks I've left him. I wish I hadn't. It was a huge mistake.

Oh god, what a mess.

Harriet secures the padlock and I'm left in the darkness with only a few rays of light spearing through some cracks in the walls.

Is she seriously going to keep me imprisoned in a shed in the garden? My arms are already puckered with goosebumps. What's it going to be like when the sun goes down and the temperature drops?

I hunt in my carrier bag for a sweater and pull it on, flicking my greasy hair over my shoulders. I could try banging on the door and shouting to be let out. But what good is it going to do? Harriet's not going to let me go just because I make a fuss. And I don't want to give her any excuse to gag me or tie me up. That's the only thing that could make this situation any worse.

As my eyes adjust to the gloom, I notice she's left a pile of blankets in one corner. A bed?

I want to die. I have nothing to live for. No hope. No future. I'm totally at Harriet's mercy, no better off than the cats in their cage. Actually, that's not true. They at least have a wire mesh and can watch what's going on outside. I don't even have a window.

Something brushes the back of my neck and I jump, squealing.

I can't stay in here. I really can't. It'll drive me insane.

Outside, a car door clicks open and slams shut. An engine fires up. The car slowly pulls away. Tyres rumble down the dirt track. Harriet setting off to work as if nothing has happened.

She'll be heading into the office, all white teeth and smiles, floating around in a cloud of expensive perfume, pretending to the world to be something she's not.

And to think I thought of her as a friend. My only friend. Someone I could trust.

My self-pity morphs into anger.

I could kill her. How dare she treat me like this. Like I'm an animal.

But for now there's nothing I can do.

The shed's empty, apart from the blankets and the cobwebs. If there was anything I could have used to escape, she's cleared it out.

And so I have no choice but to sit and wait for her to return. There's no other way I'm getting out, unless she removes that padlock and opens the door.

I collapse onto my makeshift blanket bed with my knees tucked up to my chest, drop my head in my hands, and sob silently.

Chapter 45

The constant yowling of the cats reminds me I'm not totally alone, although it seems strange they're making so much noise. Are they frustrated, like me, at being caged up? Or is it something else? Are they hungry? In pain? They looked healthy enough from what I could see, but I wouldn't put it past Harriet to have neglected them.

At least it's some company, even if I can't see them, and I draw comfort from knowing they're there as I curl up on my blankets, miserable and dejected.

I don't expect to see Harriet again until she's finished work. Late afternoon at the earliest. So I'm surprised when I hear the distant sound of a car rolling up the track towards the house. It's not even midday. Maybe she's had second thoughts. Her conscience pricked by the thought of keeping me locked in a cold and dirty old shed all day.

I scrabble along the floor on my hands and knees to a small hole in one of the wooden panelled walls. It's the slimmest sliver of a gap. Just large enough to peer through if I press my eye against it.

With my breath in ragged gasps, I watch and listen. A car pulls up and its engine falls silent. A door opens and feet crunch along the stony track, but I can't see who it is. Maybe it's not Harriet. A postman, perhaps. A delivery driver? Whoever it is, they're walking slowly, as if they're looking around, not marching towards the house with purpose.

A shadow flits tantalisingly behind a bushy hedge. Is that Harriet? It's hard to tell.

The figure approaches the house, which I can just see in the distance at the top of a lawned bank. I blink to clear my vision and put my eye to the hole again. One of the cats lets out a long, low howl of despair.

No, it's not Harriet.

It's a man.

Not any man. It's Justin.

I gasp, hardly believing my luck.

Oh god, he's come to rescue me. Why else would he be here?

I jump up and bang on the door, hammering until my fists are sore.

'Justin! I'm in here!' I scream. 'In the shed! Help! Let me out!'

I sink back to my knees to peer through the hole again. Surely he must have heard me.

But he's gone. At least, he's not come running and I can't see him anymore.

I didn't imagine that I saw him, I'm sure.

No, there he is!

He's backing away from the front door now, his hands planted in his trouser pockets. I'm too far away to see his expression, but he obviously hasn't heard me.

I bang on the walls again, putting every ounce of energy I have into it.

'Justin! Help me! I'm in here! Help!'

I scream until I'm hoarse. Please god, let him have heard that.

Panting for breath, I slink down to the eyehole. Justin's wandering around the building, cupping his hands against the windows, staring inside. Harriet was right. He's not given up on me. He's trying to find me. And whatever she said to him, he's guessed she must have taken me in because I have nowhere else to go.

He vanishes around the rear of the cottage and I wait with bated breath for him to reappear. There must be something more I can do to attract his attention, but the shed is so far away that unless he explores the large garden, he won't find me.

This is unbearable. I can see my husband. He's here, hunting for me. But I have no way of signalling to him.

He takes one last lingering look at the cottage and seems to give up.

No, no, no. He can't go.

'Justin! Help! Please help me!' My hands are bloody and bruised, my voice a rasping yelp, but I keep banging and shouting.

This could be my only chance of getting out of here alive.

Once he's gone, that's it. No one else is going to come looking. No one's going to report me missing. Harriet could leave me to rot in this hellhole and nobody would ever know.

I fall silent and strain my ears. Justin's footsteps are drifting away, growing quieter.

Another quick peek confirms he's gone. He must have given up. Walked away.

No! This isn't fair. He's so close.

A car engine growls into life, the rumble as it pulls away the final confirmation that Justin's given up on finding me here.

More out of frustration than any hope he'll hear me, I throw myself at the door, pounding it with my grazed knuckles, kicking it with my feet and knees, until I can't kick and punch anymore, and I collapse to the floor with tears of despair flooding down my face.

My one chance of escape and it's slipped from my grasp.

I might as well give up. I'm now totally at Harriet's mercy.

I fall back on my blankets and curl into a ball under a dark cloud of despondency.

How does she think this is going to end? That if she keeps me here long enough, I'm going to fall in love with her and forget Justin? That I'll succumb to some kind of weird Stockholm syndrome fantasy of hers and conveniently overlook how she's treated me?

If that's what she thinks, it might still be my way out. Back to Plan A. Be nice. Be compliant. And hope she'll learn to trust me. I have no other option.

But how long's that going to take? How long am I going to be trapped in this shed with only the spiders and feline caterwauling for company?

I squeeze my eyes tightly shut, trying to push all the bad thoughts out of my mind and find some peace. I think about the house at Treloar. Justin's face on the first day we moved in. How he was as excited as a little boy. And then I think about my own little boys. Felix and Sebastian.

They appear to me as clearly as if they were standing before me, their cherub-like faces full of love and joy. My heart swells.

'Mummy, what are you doing?' Felix holds his hand out towards me.

My whole body effervesces with a mother's love.

In the darkness, I reach out as if I could touch them. Hold them. Pull them to me.

'Come on, Mummy, don't give up,' Sebastian says, with the slight lisp he's had since his front baby tooth fell out.

'I love you,' I whisper.

'We love you too,' they say, laughing in unison.

And in that moment, I know what I have to do.

I can't just sit here and do nothing, waiting for Harriet to trust me enough to let me back into the house and give me my freedom. That could take weeks or months, if at all. I have to do something positive. Proactive. And piece by piece, a plan forms in my mind.

By the time Harriet finally returns home later that afternoon, I know what I need to do.

I watch through the peephole as she trots up the garden path to the front door and lets herself into the house. I wait patiently.

Ten minutes later, she comes to check on me, carrying a plastic bottle of water in one hand and a kitchen knife in the other.

'Megan, are you alright?' she calls through the door.

'Harriet?' Every cell in my body wants to scream at her to let me out, but I have to play the game. Not do anything to antagonise her.

'Yes, it's me. Stand back, please. I've brought you some water.'

The light that pours in when she removes the padlock and opens the door is so bright I have to turn my head away and shade my eyes.

'I hope you weren't too bored in here on your own,' she says. 'I should have thought to have given you some books or something to read.'

What a joke. There's not enough light in the shed to read, even during the middle of the day. But I don't say that, of course. Instead, I smile sweetly and say, 'Oh, I was fine, thank you. How was work?'

I have no interest in small talk with her. In fact, all I want to do is stand up and punch her in the mouth, tear that stupid smile off her face and get as far the hell away as I can from here. But she needs to think I'm being compliant. Trustworthy.

'Oh, you know, the usual dramas,' she says, rolling her eyes. 'Are you hungry?'

'Starving.' I've had so little to eat and drink in the last few days, I'm feeling quite weak.

'What have you done to your hands?' She stares in horror at my bloodied knuckles.

I hurriedly hide them under my thighs. 'Nothing. They're fine.'

'You want to be careful you don't get an infection with all this dirt in here.'

Yeah, well, you're the one insisting on keeping me locked up in here and sleeping on a blanket on the floor.

'Is that water for me?' I ask, nodding at the bottle in her hand.

'Oh, yes, I almost forgot.'

She rolls the bottle across the floor and I stop it with my foot.

'Thanks.' I snatch it up, twist off the cap, and down it in four long gulps.

'Right, well, I'll warm up some soup for you,' Harriet says, her nose wrinkling as she watches me drink.

Soup? Is that all I'm getting?

'Great, thank you,' I force myself to say through gritted teeth.

While she heads back to the cottage, I get myself ready, planning what I need to do. If this is going to work, it needs to be seamless. Unfortunately, it means sacrificing my only half-decent meal of the day, but it's worth it.

I watch the house impatiently through my spyhole, wondering why she's taking so long, but eventually Harriet reappears carrying a bowl on a tray. She walks carefully, watching her feet as I urge her silently to hurry.

As she draws closer, I stand and flex my neck and shoulders, concentrating on keeping my heart rate from racing too fast.

'Stand away from the door, please, Megan,' she calls cheerily. God knows why she's in such a good mood this evening.

The padlock rattles and bangs as she unlocks it and the old rusty hinges on the door squeak as she peels it open.

The smell of tomato soup wafts in and makes my stomach tighten. God, it smells good...

But I can't think about that.

Harriet steps inside with the tray balanced on one hand while gripping the kitchen knife with the other. She's still not taking any chances with me.

'Take it,' she says, nodding at the bowl and a plastic spoon on the tray.

I glance up at her face, trying to read her expression. Does she have any empathy for what she's putting me through? Is there an ounce of guilt at what she's done?

I think about those pictures in frames in the dining room. Harriet with her arms around Ollie, the woman who broke her heart. They looked so happy. So ordinary. You'd never think by looking at Harriet that she'd be capable of this.

Is it why they broke up? Did Ollie discover something about Harriet that sent her running in fear back to her husband?

An awful, hideous thought occurs to me. Almost too horrific to contemplate.

What if Ollie didn't leave? What if Harriet killed her?

No, there's no reason to suspect that. Just because she's holding me hostage, locked in the shed, doesn't make her a killer. I'm letting my imagination run amok. I need to focus. Concentrate.

'Thank you. Mmmm, tomato, my favourite.' I reach for the bowl with one hand and the spoon with the other.

But as I step back, away from Harriet, I let the bowl slip through my fingers.

It crashes to the floor, soup flying everywhere. There's a loud crack. Harriet jumps back with a shriek, and I watch the bowl shatter into pieces.

'Oh god, I'm so sorry,' I gasp, contorting my face into an expression of horror. She has to think it was an accident.

'You stupid cow,' she hisses. 'You've got it all over my shoes.'

I drop to my knees, frantically trying to gather up all the broken shards.

'I'm such a butter-fingers.' The soup's already seeping into the wooden boards that form the floor, soaking into all the cracks and holes.

'That's two dishes in two days.'

While Harriet's staring down at her legs, trying to wipe specks of soup from her trousers, I quickly evaluate the damage I've done. I was concerned the bowl might not break on the wooden floor, but I didn't have to worry. It's smashed into five large pieces and countless smaller chips and slivers.

One piece in particular catches my eye. It's elongated, with a sharp point at one end. I place a hand over it and secretly palm it away, hiding it under my pile of blankets.

Then I focus on gathering up all the smaller pieces, scooping them up, careful not to cut myself. I offer them to Harriet, who holds out the tray.

'I think that's all of it,' I say, running my hands over the floor, searching for any other fragments I might have missed.

'You're going to have to go hungry again,' she huffs. 'I'm not wasting my time bringing you anything else. Perhaps you'll learn to be more careful in future.'

Her words echo in my head. It's the sort of thing I could hear myself saying to Felix and Sebastian when they'd been clumsy.

'I'm really sorry,' I mumble. 'I didn't mean to. I hope your shoes aren't ruined.' I suppress a grin. It's a small but unintended victory and it's wiped that stupid smile off her face for now, which is a bonus.

Harriet storms out of the shed and slams the door shut behind her. For a split second, I think in her fury she's forgotten to lock the padlock.

But then I hear the now familiar rattle and clunk as she fixes it in place.

I watch her storm back to the house with a grin on my face and when I'm sure she's gone, I retrieve my prize from under my blankets.

What would they call it in prison? A shank?

I run my thumb along its jagged edges and test the sharp point. As a makeshift dagger, it's not bad. It's not perfect, but it should be fine for what I have in mind.

Now I just need to wait for Harriet to return.

Chapter 46

My opportunity comes sooner than I expected. The sun is setting and the gloom inside the shed is now a treacly thick darkness. The cold has penetrated my core and I've had to pull on all the clothes in my carrier bag to keep warm. It looks like it's going to be a long, chilly and miserable night alone in the shed. Even the cats have gone quiet and the only sound is the occasional screech of a hunting bird and my internal voice as my thoughts race around my head.

Even if I can overpower Harriet, how do I get away? Who do I turn to for help? Do I call the police? Justin? What if my plan doesn't work? What if she tries to kill me? What if I'm injured?

I'm so preoccupied that I don't hear Harriet until she's right outside the door.

'Megan, are you awake?' The sound of her voice startles me. What does she want now?

I jump up, throwing the blankets to the ground. I scramble for my makeshift dagger that I hid in my toiletry bag in my supermarket carrier.

'Yes,' I say. 'I'm awake.'

'I felt bad that you might be hungry,' she says. 'I've brought you some cheese. And some crackers.'

Cheese and crackers? Honestly, what is she thinking? I've not eaten a proper meal in two days and she brings me a snack. If I had any doubts about her sanity, they've just been confirmed.

'Oh, thank you,' I reply meekly. 'That's kind of you.'

I pull out the shard of porcelain carefully and close my fist around it with its sharp tip pointing downwards. Then I brace myself.

'Are you standing away from the door?'

Shit. I'm not in position. If this is going to work, I need to surprise her. I need to be where she doesn't expect me to be.

'Yes. I'm just moving into the corner now, by the blankets.'

I wince as I shuffle across the floor towards the door as the padlock clunks open. I press my back against the side of the shed, behind the door, and snatch my breath, holding it in my lungs.

The door cracks open an inch.

'Megan?'

My eyes grow wide and all my senses go on high alert. I should have the advantage that my vision is accustomed to the dark while it will take Harriet's eyes a moment to adjust to the low light.

'Where are you?' she asks, a note of caution in her tone.

The door opens wider. I can smell Harriet's expensive perfume. Sweet and potent. It's a reminder of how badly I must smell after two days in the same clothes without a shower.

She steps inside. I'm so close I could reach out and touch her.

Come on, one more step.

She's carrying something. The tray, I presume. But I can't see her hands. I doubt she would have come without the knife though. She's not stupid.

'I'm sorry,' she says. 'I didn't mean to snap earlier. I know it was an accident.'

She takes another small step forwards.

With a scream, I launch myself at her, aiming the tip of my porcelain dagger at her neck.

She half turns to face me, her features tightening with horror as she sees that I'm behind her.

She drops the tray, trying to raise the knife.

But it's too late. I bury the tip of the shard deep into her flesh in the soft tissue between her neck and her shoulder.

She howls in agony and surprise, twisting and falling, sticky, wet blood pumping from the wound.

It's on my hand and my arm.

I let go of my weapon and shove her in the back as she's stumbling to her knees.

In the confines of the dark shed, everything becomes confused. We're all arms and legs tangled together and as I rush for the door, she snatches my leg. I don't want to hurt Harriet. All I want is to get out. To be free. But she's brought this on herself.

Instinctively, I kick out. I strike something soft and fleshy. Harriet yelps in pain and lets go.

And suddenly I'm outside. In the fresh air. Free.

I don't stop to look back. I don't hesitate. I don't wait. I just put my head down and run.

My plan is straightforward. To grab Harriet's keys and to steal one of her cars. I don't know where I'll go. I've not thought that far ahead. My priority is simply getting away.

Halfway across the lawn, heading for the house, I slow down. My limbs are unusually heavy and my breathing hard. A lack of food has left me lightheaded and sluggish, and I'm not thinking straight. I should have taken the opportunity to lock her in the shed. The last thing I need is her chasing after me.

But it's too late now. I'm not going back. I have to get out of here.

I glance over my shoulder and peer through the gloom. The shed door is swinging open on its hinges, but there's no sign of Harriet. God, I hope I haven't killed her.

As soon as I'm away from here and safe, I'll find somewhere to raise the alarm and get them to send an ambulance. It was only a flesh wound. She should be fine. Although there was a lot of blood...

I can't worry about that right now. I pick up the pace and jog to the cottage, adrenaline and desperation fuelling me onwards.

Thankfully, she's left the door on the latch and a set of car keys for her sporty two-seater in a bowl on a table in the hall. I grab them, but something forces me to hesitate on the way back out. Harriet's handbag is on the floor. Has my luck finally changed? It's too tempting not to check, sitting there gaping open, just begging for me to peer inside. It'll only take a second.

I'm glad I follow my hunch. Among the packets of tissues, a hairbrush, her purse and an assortment of blushers and lipsticks, I find her phone.

Bingo.

But my jubilation is short-lived. It's locked, of course, and I have no idea of her passcode. I try the obvious, 0-0-0-0 and 1-2-3-4, but that would be too easy.

Of course, I could call the police without needing to unlock the phone. I *should* call the police. But I really want to hear Justin's voice right now. I need to tell him I've made a terrible mistake. That I should never have left him. And I want him to come and rescue me.

I'm torn. I need Harriet to unlock the phone, but that means returning to the shed and facing her again. I don't know if I can.

But what if she's lying there, bleeding to death? As much as I hate her, I don't want another death on my conscience. Or to face a murder charge. Can you be convicted of murder if it was self-defence? I'm not even sure if it *was* self-defence. It's not as if Harriet attacked me. A clever lawyer, I'm sure, could make it sound like I acted unreasonably.

I stamp my foot on the ground in frustration.

Get in the car, Megan. Drive away.

But how can I, knowing Harriet could be dying? I have to check on her and get her to unlock this phone.

Shit.

I storm out of the house and tramp back down the garden path, across the lawn and past the big cage where Harriet's cats live. Two pairs of eyes watch me curiously. Alongside the cage, there's another small wooden structure enclosed by a six-foot chain-link fence. Behind the fence, I recognise the sad eyes of the puppy Harriet tried to gift me. She wasn't kidding when she said she'd put him outside.

As I tiptoe towards the shed, I wish I'd thought to pick up a weapon from the house. I don't know what kind of state Harriet is in, but if she's still alive, she's still armed.

'Harriet?' I call, edging closer.

I push the door fully open with my arm at full stretch.

'Harriet? Are you okay?'

It takes a moment for my eyes to adjust to the darkness inside the shed again, with my heart threatening to pound its way out of my chest.

I expect to find Harriet sprawled out on the floor in a pool of her own blood, writhing in agony.

But she's not here.

I stare in disbelief for a second or two, before whirling around with adrenaline burning through my veins. If she's not in the shed, where the hell is she?

I need to get out of here, and fast.

If she catches me, who knows what she'll do.

Every shadow in the garden is a potential threat. Every rustle of leaves, the harbinger of an attack. I can sense eyes watching me. Assessing my every move. The cats? Or Harriet?

I begin to shiver, fear permeating through my body. So much for unlocking Harriet's phone.

Call the police, Megan.

But she'll hear me and know exactly where I am. And how long will it take the police to get here? Too long. Far, far too long.

It's okay. I have her car keys. I just need to get to the car.

Slowly, I tiptoe back along the garden towards the house, scanning left and right, listening for any potential threat. Harriet's here somewhere. I know she is. I can sense her presence. But she knows the layout of the cottage and gardens better than anyone.

Finally, I spot the muddy track where her cars are parked. I tramp through a flowerbed and, throwing caution to the wind, break into a sprint, my legs pumping.

The cars are parked alongside each other. The white sports car slung low on its suspension, half-hidden behind the more utilitarian SUV. As I run, I dig the keys out of my pocket and press all the buttons until the doors of the sports car blip open, hazard lights flashing. If that hasn't given away where I am, nothing will.

I hope she's too badly injured to move anywhere fast.

And if I can only get into the car before she catches up with me. Now I really wish I hadn't let my fitness slip.

I skid to a halt as I reach the vehicle, my trembling hand stretching for the handle.

With one fearful glance over my shoulder, I yank it open and throw myself inside. Bright internal lights blaze on, illuminating the smart leather seats and hand-stitched steering wheel.

Harriet's still nowhere to be seen, but I don't kid myself. She's here somewhere and she's not going to let me get away easily.

As I pull the door shut behind me, the internal lights fade.

Habit forces me to pull on the seatbelt, but now I'm stuck with working out the ignition. Do I need to insert a key? Or is it one of those stop-start buttons? Frantically, I feel all around the steering column, panic tearing me apart.

And then I see it.

The big round button by the radio.

Start.

I press it with my thumb and the engine growls into life. Headlights flick on, casting a white glow into an adjacent hedge.

My eyes flick to the rear-view mirror.

Was that movement I saw?

Someone stalking around the rear of the vehicle?

I fumble with the keys, trying to find the fob. I press all the buttons all at once until the locks engage with a satisfying hollow thump.

It gives me a marginally greater sense of safety, but I know I won't be entirely safe until I get out of here.

I slam my foot on the clutch and ram the gear-stick into reverse, but something's poking awkwardly into my hip bone. Harriet's phone, for all the good it's going to do me now.

I fish it out and toss it onto the passenger seat, then with a heavy foot on the accelerator, back out onto the track and skid to a halt facing towards the road.

I almost expect Harriet to appear out of the dark and throw herself across the bonnet, clutching onto the wipers as I pull away, her face twisted in a horrifying rage.

But there's no one and nothing to get in my way.

I slam the car into gear and race away, bumping down the rutted track, with my head bouncing dangerously close to the roof.

And out onto the main road.

Another glance in the mirror.

Only darkness behind.

I'm free.

Chapter 47

I'm free, but I have absolutely no idea where I am or where I'm going. All I know is what Harriet told me, that her house is not far outside of Falmouth, but that's no use. I'm lost.

It doesn't help that the road is treacherously windy and the sun has long since dipped below the horizon, which means I'm having to navigate in the worst possible light, a hazy dusk which deceives my eyes on every tight corner. And none of the names on the signposts mean anything to me.

I still don't have a plan and I'm shaking too much to think of one. But there's plenty of fuel in the car and at some point, I'll pull over and gather my thoughts. Work out a way to contact Justin. But for now, I just want to put some distance between me and Harriet.

She had me totally fooled, letting me believe she was my friend, but worse than that, she had me convinced Justin was dangerous, even though there wasn't even any actual evidence against him. All couples have their difficulties, and we've had more than most, yet I was still ready to believe Justin was capable of doing me real harm. Perhaps that's the craziest thing about this whole mad situation.

I bang the steering wheel in frustration with tears bubbling in my eyes.

Why do all the bloody roads around here have to be so narrow and twisty? Twice, I've nearly ended up in the verge. I need to slow down.

Take my time. Wouldn't that be the final irony if I escape from Harriet but ended up dead after wrapping the car around a tree.

Finally, I spot a sign ahead which reveals I'm on the right road for Falmouth. I just need to keep going. There's a straighter section here, so I accelerate with the headlights illuminating overhanging trees and mossy stone walls alarmingly close to the edge of the road.

A sudden warble of an unfamiliar ringtone almost makes me veer off the carriageway.

Harriet's phone that I tossed onto the passenger seat is lit up with an incoming call. I glance down briefly.

Oh my god, it's Justin.

His name's come up on the caller ID. I can't believe it.

I snatch it up and press it against my ear with a sob of relief. 'Justin, it's me,' I cry, slowing down so I can steer one-handed.

'Megan?'

'Yes,' I gasp. 'You can't believe how relieved I am to hear your voice.'

Silence.

'Justin? Are you there?' I check the screen, panicking the call's cut out. Without Harriet's passcode, I'd have no way of calling him back.

'What are you doing answering Harriet's phone? She said you were filing for divorce.'

'No, it's all a big mistake. I'm sorry. I should never have left.' My words get choked up in my tears as emotion overwhelms me.

'Where are you? Are you driving?' he asks, sounding confused.

'It's Harriet. She convinced me you were dangerous and manipulated me into leaving. Oh god, it's all such a mess,' I gabble, my words spilling out.

'Slow down, Megan. What are you talking about?'

'She's kept me locked in the house and then in a shed in the garden for the last few days. I never thought I'd get out alive,' I explain.

'Who? Harriet? You're not making much sense. Are you still at the house now? I'll come over and meet you there,' he says determinedly.

'No, I've stolen Harriet's car — '

'You did what?'

Wait until I tell him I stabbed her in the neck. 'Listen, Justin, that's not important right now. I'm lost. I don't know where I am.'

I glance in the rear-view mirror and spot a pair of headlights behind. It's the first vehicle I've seen since escaping from Harriet's cottage. Would it make sense to pull over and try to flag them down?

'Okay,' he says, sounding perplexed. 'Where's Harriet?'

'I don't know. I left her at the house.'

'Right,' he mumbles. 'So you're safe?'

'I think so. For now. I just wish I knew where I was.'

'Okay,' he says, taking that tone he uses when he has a problem to solve, all serious and efficient. 'Are there any signs? Village names? Pubs?'

'I followed a sign towards Falmouth, but I could be anywhere. I just don't know,' I wail. I was holding it together reasonably well, but hearing Justin's voice, realising what I came so close to losing, has turned me into a wreck. And I really need to concentrate on the road.

I check the mirror again. The vehicle behind is closing fast now. It's travelling at some speed. Dangerously fast on these narrow roads.

'Right,' Justin says, like he's calculating what to do. But how's he going to help me when he doesn't have a clue where I am?

'Hang on,' I shout. 'There's a sign up ahead.'

'What does it say?'

I slow down as I approach a junction where the road intersects a more major carriageway.

'Right to Falmouth. Left to Helston,' I say, changing gear. 'Which should I take?'

The headlights in my mirror grow larger, dazzling my eyes, forcing me to squint.

'Take a left,' Justin says, clearly and decisively. It's exactly what I need. My head's not in the right place to make rational decisions. It hasn't been for a while. 'I'm going to jump in the car and find you. Whatever you do, don't stop for anything or anyone. Just keep driving and stay on the line.'

The lights behind are blindingly bright now, right up close behind me. But I don't have time to worry that some arsehole's right up my back. I don't know the roads. They'll have to be patient.

I indicate left and pull away aggressively fast, my wheels spinning.

Unfortunately, the car behind follows, heading in the same direction, and accelerates equally violently. In a few seconds, it's virtually hanging off my rear bumper. Far too close for comfort. If I were to touch my brakes, they'd go right into the back of me. If they're in that much of a rush, why don't they just overtake?

'Megan? Megan, are you still there?'

'Sorry, I zoned out for a moment. There's a car behind... '

Oh god. It hits me like an arrow between the eyes.

Harriet.

'What car?' Justin growls.

'I think it might be Harriet.'

'I thought you'd taken her car?'

I bite my lip as I glance back and forth between the road ahead and the rear-view mirror. What the hell do I do now? If I slow down, she's liable to force me off the road. If I speed up, I don't trust myself not to crash.

'I took the two-seater. She must be driving her company car,' I croak.

'Okay, don't panic. Just keep your eyes on the road.' But that's easy for him to say. He's not here with Harriet breathing down his neck on roads he doesn't know in the middle of who knows where.

'Justin, I'm scared.'

'I know,' he says quietly. 'But you're going to be fine. Keep your eyes on the road and don't stop.'

The road is wider, faster and straighter than the winding lane I'd been on, but it's still unfamiliar and in the darkening gloom it takes all my focus not to careen out of control. I don't know the twists and turns in the way Harriet must do, and every time I dab the brakes, it looks like she's going to come crashing through the back window.

I put the phone on speaker and lay it on the dashboard so I can use both hands to grip the steering wheel, my knuckles whitening. The interior of the car is completely illuminated now by Harriet's blazing lights.

'Justin? Are you still there? Talk to me, please,' I yell. 'I don't know what to do.'

'Just kee... eyes on the... forget I love you... hear me, Megan?' His voice breaks up and drops out.

'Justin!' I scream, glancing at the phone, but the bleeps tell me we've been disconnected.

Shit.

My clothes are damp with sweat and my arms ache from how tightly the muscles in my upper body are clenched. My eyes are stinging, my mouth dry and my heart rampaging. The last time I felt this kind of terror, I'd just woken up to find my house on fire.

What's Harriet playing at? Is she hoping I'll pull over? Or is she banking on me eventually running out of fuel? I need to listen to Justin's advice and keep driving. Keep my eyes on the road and concentrate on not spinning out.

Up ahead, the road curves away into what looks like a nasty, tightening bend. I tap the brakes tentatively, watching Harriet in my mirrors. She's so close, I can hear her engine over-revving above mine.

But the bend's not nearly so tight as I first thought. I've been over-cautious, slowed down too much, which gives Harriet the chance to pull out around me, as if she's going to overtake. But if I let her get ahead of me, she'll be able to make me slow down and stop. I can't allow that to happen. I have to keep driving until Justin finds me, so I hit the accelerator and change down a gear.

The car jolts forwards and the steering twitches.

Harriet drops back and slots in behind me.

My car judders in tandem with a loud thump as she rams me from behind.

What the hell?

I stare into the mirror in wide-eyed horror as Harriet drops back and accelerates towards me again.

I brace myself for the inevitable impact and scream when my back end starts to slide and I have to fight the steering wheel to bring the car back under control.

Where the hell is Justin when I need him?

And what is Harriet doing? Is she trying to kill me?

There aren't even any other cars on the road I can flag down. I'm on my own with a mad woman trying to kill me.

Once again, the lights behind me drift away as Harriet drops her speed, putting distance between us. And then accelerates.

I brace myself, but I'm still shocked by the ferocity of the collision. A crunching, wrenching sound rips through the vehicle and I'm shunted forwards, my head whiplashing towards the dashboard and back again.

My rear wheels slide out and this time there's nothing I can do to correct it. In panic, I jump on the brakes. My world starts to spin, trees and hedges passing in an indistinct blur.

Time slows down. I bounce in my seat. The phone flies off the dashboard. The seatbelt cuts into my shoulder.

Harriet's car flies past in a flash of lights and a growl of speed.

And as quickly as I lost control, the car comes to an abrupt halt, pitching my body forwards, and my head strikes the steering wheel.

Chapter 48

My world is all black and every bone in my body is screaming in agony.

Where the hell am I?

In a car.

Whose car?

Someone's yanking open the door, letting in a cool breeze.

I sort of remember now.

Driving too fast. Headlights in the mirrors. Being pursued by a lunatic. My car being rammed from behind. Losing control. Spinning. Crashing.

It's Justin. It has to be. He's found me.

I try peeling open my eyes but only one seems to be working. The other's completely closed up and my head is woolly. Is it Tuesday today? Nausea blooms in my stomach. Whose car *is* this?

An arm reaches across me, unbuckling my seatbelt.

'Justin?' I murmur.

Hands pull me roughly out of my seat, manhandling me into the cold.

With my one working eye, I notice the windscreen is cracked and fissured. The headlights are on, illuminating what appears to be the bottom of a ditch filled with winding, tangled brambles and straggly grass.

'Get out,' a voice growls in my ear.

That's not Justin.

I have to concentrate on the effort of turning my head, like it's being wound around by hand. The edges of my vision are cloudy and I have a thumping headache.

'Harriet?'

Everything comes flooding back to me in a dizzying flash.

Being imprisoned. Stabbing my so-called friend with a makeshift dagger. Stealing her car and being run off the road by her.

I don't have the strength to fight back. I let her drag me out of the vehicle and I collapse into a patch of damp grass.

'Where are we?' I rasp.

'We're going to get you home,' she says. There's a dark blood-stain around the neck and shoulder of her blouse, but it looks like she's pulled out the shard of broken bowl I stabbed her with.

Home to Justin?

No, that's not what she means.

'Come on, get up.' Harriet hauls me up under the arms, pulling me to my feet. She waves a knife in my face. 'I'll drive you back and we can get you cleaned up.'

Finally, I prise open my gummed-up eye. What is that? Blood? I wipe it with the side of my finger and inspect the scarlet smear. I must have cut my head when I banged it.

A little further on, just off the road, Harriet's car is parked on the verge. Red taillights glow in the dusky light. Orange hazards blink hypnotically.

I let her guide me towards it. I'm too scared, too beaten up, to resist.

But I have to.

Otherwise, all my efforts to escape will have been wasted and if I get in that car with her, it's over. She's not going to let me get away so easily next time.

I need to find some strength from somewhere.

Justin was on the phone. That's right, he called shortly after I drove away from the cottage. He's looking for me. He's on his way. I just need to hang on until he gets here. But Harriet has my arms in a tight grip, like she's never going to let go.

'I'm going to be sick,' I say, planting my feet and refusing to move.

I double over and pretend to retch, craning my neck towards Harriet's feet. There's no way she's going to risk getting vomit on her shoes, and predictably she lets me go.

With my hands resting on my knees, I draw deep breaths in and out, as if I'm battling with a serious bout of nausea. It gives me the opportunity to survey the surroundings and provides me with a moment to think.

The car I was driving, Harriet's little two-seater, is nose down, perpendicular to the road with its back wheels off the ground and the clawing smell of petrol heavy in the air. It'll need towing out.

Beyond it, and the ditch it's nose-planted into, a green field is lit up under a silvery grey moon hanging low in the charcoal sky. Beyond the field, nothing but dark and foreboding hills in the distance. On the other side of the road, there's just another field. There's nothing and nobody around for miles.

'This doesn't change anything,' Harriet says, looming over me with that knife she's still waving around. 'I love you, Megan, and I know you can learn to love me too.'

'You have a funny way of showing it,' I snap. 'You could have killed me.'

'I had to stop you before you did something stupid.'

'And if you think I could ever love you, you're even crazier than I thought,' I hiss. I'm done with trying to win her trust back. Look what good that did me. 'I love Justin. I made a mistake. I should never have left him. We're meant to be together.'

'After the way he treated you?' she snorts, jabbing the knife in my direction. 'After what he did to you?'

I'm not listening. She poisoned my mind before and I refuse to let her do it again.

'There will never be anything between us,' I shout. 'And if you think you can cage someone up to make them fall in love with you, you're delusional as well as crazy.'

She bows her head, looking contrite. 'You're right. I'm sorry, but I was desperate. I know it was wrong, but I'll make it up to you.'

'You made me think Justin was dangerous.'

'He is! You told me yourself he attacked you,' she says.

'Only because he was provoked, because I'd accused him of something horrible and he'd had a long day — '

'You're blind, Megan. Yes, I wanted you to leave him, but I've not made any of it up,' she says, as if she genuinely believes it.

I stare at her in disbelief. 'You didn't know the first thing about Justin when you hid that phone in the lodge and started sending those vile messages. You were only thinking about yourself and how you could drive us apart.'

It was pure guesswork. She made the allegations and let me fill in the blanks, convincing myself it was all true.

'If that's what you want to believe.'

'Those are the facts, Harriet. You can't argue with the truth.'

I throw up my hands in exasperation. Across the field, a light twinkles. What is that? A house? A farm? It's hard to tell from this distance, but it's almost certainly a building of some kind. Maybe if I could reach it, I could raise the alarm. But it's a long run, maybe a mile.

Possibly two. And I'm still hopelessly unfit. Looking around though, my options are severely limited. It's that or nothing.

'You're better off without him,' Harriet sneers. 'Whether or not you want to admit it. I'd never treat you the way he does.'

I suppress the urge to laugh. Can she even see herself right now? How *she's* treating me? But I'm not going to get into an argument about it with her.

'I took your phone,' I announce.

'What?'

'I stole it from your handbag when I took the car keys. If you want it back, it fell into the footwell when you drove me off the road.' I glance back at the car. 'I imagine you wouldn't want to be without it, although you must have another one. An anonymous number you used to send me those messages about Justin?'

I wait for her gaze to slide away from me to the car.

She opens her mouth to say something, but I have no intention of hanging around to hear it.

I turn and run.

I jump the ditch and stumble into the moonlit field, attempting to sprint hard to put some distance between us. I might be unfit, but I know Harriet is slower than me and I should be able to put my advantage to good effect if I can keep my footing.

Unfortunately, the ground is far more uneven than I anticipated, full of furrows and mounds that, in the last light of the day, make the going treacherous.

'Megan, stop!' Harriet yells.

I put my head down and run as hard as I can, stumbling and tripping, jarring my knees and ankles, praying I don't trip. I deserve some good luck for a change.

Soon, I'm out of breath and panting hard.

The light in the distance doesn't appear any closer.

Harriet shouts again, spurring me on. Urging me to run faster.

Tangles of long grass grasp at my feet, threatening to drag me down.

And then my left foot twists as it lands awkwardly on a mound I didn't see. I stumble, using my outstretched arms to catch my balance, and my right foot disappears into a deep divot, toe-first, snagging my heel. I scream as I fall, the tendons around my ankle stretched painfully to tearing point. A shooting pain travels up my leg and I collapse in agony.

Come on, Megan, get up.

I try standing and putting weight on the foot, but the pain is excruciating. If it's not broken, it's badly sprained. Either way, I'm not running anywhere on it.

The rustle of grass tells me Harriet is close behind. I roll onto my front in desperation and start to crawl, one hand in front of the other. Knee following knee. My ankle throbbing.

The rustling gets louder. Footsteps thunder across the verdant ground.

She's getting closer. And closer.

I can't move quickly enough.

Moisture seeps through the knees of my jeans. My hands become slick with mud.

And suddenly she's on me. She grabs a handful of my hair, yanking my head backwards. The cold steel of her knife pressed dangerously against my throat stills me into silence.

'And where do you think you're going?' Her breath is hot in my ear.

'My ankle,' I yelp. 'I think it's broken.'

'Stop being a baby.' She snatches my wrist and pulls me back towards the road, her car intermittently lit up by its flashing amber warning lights.

'No,' I wail. Why can't she just leave me alone?

I attempt to put up a fight, resisting as she pulls me, making myself a heavy, immovable lump.

There's no way I'm getting in that car with her.

'If you don't stop this, I'll gut you like a fish and leave you here to die.' Her face is contorted into an evil snarl as she aims the knife at me. 'How would you like that?'

I freeze with terror. There's something cold and hard in her eyes that tells me she'll do it if she doesn't get her own way. She'd rather I died here with a knife in my stomach than let me go free. And only a moment ago she was trying to convince me she's in love with me. But my life means nothing to her. I'm an object to be won or lost and disposed of if she chooses, that's all.

'Alright, I'm coming,' I wheeze, holding my hands up in surrender.

There's no way I can outrun her or overpower her while she's armed. I have no other choice than to do what she says.

I try standing again, but every time I put weight on my bad ankle, my whole body gives way. 'You'll have to help me.'

'For pity's sake, Megan. You should take more care. You can't be a personal trainer with a broken ankle, can you?' And just like that, the old Harriet is back. The Harriet I thought was my friend.

She helps me up and I wrap an arm around her shoulder, letting her take the weight off my leg.

'Slowly,' I beg as we limp back across the field, conscious she's still carrying a knife.

I look up to gauge the distance to the road, working out how long I have left before she inevitably bundles me into the boot of her car and has me captive again. Once more, I'm totally at her mercy.

Or maybe not...

Another vehicle is pulling up in front of Harriet's car. Its headlights washing over the road and the verge. It pulls to a stop. The driver's door opens. A man gets out.

And my heart skitters.

Chapter 49

Could it be?

It is.

It's Justin.

He's found me!

I could weep for joy.

He's looking directly this way. And now he's coming, jumping the ditch and striding across the field.

I don't think Harriet's noticed yet. She's looking down, watching where she puts her feet on the lumpy ground, being careful not to turn her ankle the same way I did. Even so, I need to create a diversion, to give Justin the chance to get close and surprise her. He doesn't know she has a knife, of course.

I scream in agony and collapse, clutching my ankle, slipping out of Harriet's grasp. She turns on me, snarling, her back to Justin.

'I just need a minute,' I gasp. 'I'm sorry, Harriet. It really hurts.'

'Get up,' she shouts. 'Don't test my patience.'

'Okay, okay. Just give me a moment.'

I pull up the leg of my jeans, pretending to inspect my ankle and calf. In the corner of my eye, I watch Justin jogging and hobbling towards us, making desperately slow progress.

'You have ten seconds to get up and then I start using the knife,' she threatens.

'Alright, I'm getting up. Give me a hand.' I wrap my palm around her outstretched wrist and pull myself gingerly to my feet.

I keep gripping her arm, stopping her from turning because Justin's so close now, she'll spot him the instant she turns around.

'You know, you can't just replace Ollie with me.' It's the first thing that pops into my head. 'That's not the way it works.'

'You need me, Megan, to save you from yourself.'

'What makes you think I need saving?'

'Come on, we've been through this. You're clearly not the best judge of character,' she says with a sly smile.

'Meaning?' I stiffen at the accusation.

'You and Justin. You still can't see how toxic your relationship with him was, can you?'

'Whose relationship are you calling toxic?'

Harriet spins around at the sound of Justin's voice, knife raised.

'Where the hell did you spring from?' she spits.

'Put the knife down, Harriet. We don't want anyone getting hurt,' he says, with a calm authority.

My pulse races out of control. I've never been so relieved to see anyone in my life. I was such a fool to walk away from him, to ever think he'd do anything to hurt me, but now I've put him in danger.

'I don't think you're in any position to be making demands, do you?' Harriet swipes the knife through the air, perilously close to Justin's face.

He steps backwards and sways out of her reach.

'The police are on the way,' he says.

'No, they're not.' There's a catch of uncertainty in her voice though. Is Justin bluffing? I hope not. This has gone far enough. I should have called them myself when I had the chance.

Justin catches my gaze and gives me a thin smile of reassurance. 'Are you okay, Megan?'

'My ankle. I tripped,' I say, swaying as I try to keep my balance on one leg.

'Why don't we go somewhere and talk this through?' Justin refocuses his attention on Harriet.

'What's there to talk about? I saved Megan from you. She told me all about what you've been up to behind closed doors. What you did to her.'

His eyes catch mine again. I glance at the ground. We do have some things to resolve, but not here. It has nothing to do with Harriet.

'You told me she wanted a divorce, but you didn't tell me you'd abducted her,' he says.

'I didn't abduct her. I rescued her. She called me asking me to pick her up from Treloar because she was afraid of you.'

'You made me get in the boot,' I say.

'And she says you kept her locked in a shed in the garden.' Justin's eyebrows arch skywards.

'For her own protection.' Harriet jabs the knife at him. 'You were the one trying to control her. Belittling her all the time. Knocking her confidence. Telling her she couldn't go back to work and deciding who she could and couldn't be friends with. It was you who tried to kill her.'

'What?' Justin screws his face up in disbelief.

'She told me how you tried to strangle her. Don't bother denying it.'

'That? It was a... misunderstanding. An argument that got out of hand. I'm her husband. I love her. She loves me.'

'Does she?'

'Of course she does.'

Harriet turns her head to me, glancing over her shoulder. 'Well? Do you?'

But I don't have the chance to answer.

Justin throws himself at her, grasping for the hand that's holding the knife.

Harriet tumbles into me, knocking me off my feet. I scream in fright, and then agony, as my ankle hits the ground and a bolt of pain shoots through my leg.

Alongside me, a tangle of their two bodies as they wrestle on the ground. Harriet shouldn't be any match for Justin, who's much bigger and stronger. But she kicks and flails and punches like a woman possessed. And it's far from a one-sided fight.

I roll out of the way, grasping my ankle, helpless.

I should do something, but what? It's best if I keep out of the way and let Justin get on with it. He should have the measure of her.

He's on top of her now, straddling her body, pinning her to the ground. But she still has the knife. In the thickening gloom, its silver blade glistens, catching the reflection of the rising moon.

They're both grappling for it in a flurry of hands and arms.

Harriet refuses to release it, her expression fierce. Her teeth bared. Her eyes flaming with aggression and determination. But Justin's bearing down on her. His hands are wrapped around hers, pushing the knife down, away from his chest. Trying to twist her wrist to force her to let it go.

Harriet takes one hand away and drives it into Justin's face, her palm connecting with his nose, a sickening crunch suggesting she may have broken it, while her fingers press into his eyes.

Justin howls in pain.

'Get off him!' I shriek, kicking out with my good foot, striking her on the shoulder, missing her head.

She bucks and jerks her body, trying to throw Justin off with surprising strength and energy, while Justin snatches at the hand on his face. Harriet's painted red nails dig into the soft bulges of his eyes and he battles to pull them away, while simultaneously fighting for the knife in her other hand.

He peels away one finger, bending it backwards against the joint, until Harriet screams in pain.

She bucks again, throwing up her hips, thrusting with her thighs, and as Justin spills forwards over her chest, losing his balance, he suddenly goes still.

Too still.

His eyes widen with shock and his mouth falls open, his tongue hanging loose.

'Justin!' I yell.

Harriet rolls out from under his motionless body and he flops to one side, the hilt of the knife protruding ominously out of his shoulder, his head back, gurgling.

'What have you done?' I gasp, staring at the spreading scarlet stain soaking through his shirt and the bloody mess that used to be his nose.

Harriet stands unsteadily, swaying like a drunk with a blood-soaked hand at her side, fingers splayed. Even in the low light, I can see the colour has drained from her face. She's as pale as a sheet.

She stares at the knife sticking out of Justin's shoulder, stumbling as she backs away, mumbling incoherently.

'What have you done?' I repeat. It wasn't supposed to end like this. I can't lose Justin now. Not after everything we've been through. How hard I've fought for him.

I crawl to him and cradle his head in my lap. His eyes slide sideways, catching mine. He looks so frightened. Shocked.

'It's going to be okay,' I tell him, smoothing his hair off his forehead. I don't know much about stab wounds, but I know you're not supposed to pull out an embedded object. We covered that at a first aid course I attended a few years ago and it's stuck with me. So I deliberately don't touch the knife. I'll leave that to the professionals. He needs an ambulance.

'Megan,' he gasps, his breath catching in his throat. 'I'm sorry.'

'Where's your phone?'

'Pocket,' he grunts.

I pat the outside of his leg and find his mobile tucked into the pocket of his trousers. I yank it out with my fingers and hold it up to his face to unlock it.

But there's no signal.

We're in the middle of bloody nowhere with no phone reception.

I raise it high above my head, hoping to catch even a single bar. Enough to make a call. Something. But it's hopeless.

Harriet's still standing there, watching, like she can't believe what she's done.

'Help me get him to the car,' I shout. 'We need to get him to hospital before he bleeds to death.'

Harriet looks up at me, her face blank.

'Harriet! Snap out of it,' I yell. 'Unless you fancy a thirty-year stretch for murder, I need your help. I can't carry him on my own.'

She shakes her head like she's shaking cobwebs out of her hair.

'I'm sorry, I didn't mean... ' she mumbles, but I don't have time for her insincere platitudes. We need to get Justin out of this field and into the care of paramedics.

'Help me lift him up,' I say, grunting as I stand, trying not to put weight on my swollen ankle.

Harriet snaps into action, swooping on Justin and helping him to sit.

'Can you stand?' I ask.

Justin grimaces and nods. 'I think so.'

Somehow, between us, Harriet and I raise him up and we begin a slow walk back to the cars.

We have to stop every few feet for Justin to catch his breath. But he's conscious and walking, sort of, which has to be a good sign. I'm not going to lose him. No way. Not going to happen.

It takes more than twenty minutes to cover the short distance back to the road and a concerted effort to help Justin over the ditch and up onto the verge.

He stands leaning against his car with his eyes screwed closed and his head thrown back, panting. His shirt is now almost completely drenched in blood, but we're over the worst. We just need to get him in the car.

'Where's the nearest hospital?' I bark at Harriet.

She blinks several times and stares at me blankly. I think the realisation of what she's done is hitting her hard.

'Harriet, listen to me.' I grab her shoulders and look into her eyes, our noses inches apart. 'I need to get Justin to hospital. Where do I take him?'

'Truro,' she mutters.

'Truro? God, how far away is that?'

I don't even know how to get to Falmouth from here, let alone Truro.

Harriet's eyes drift to the knife still embedded in Justin's body as I try the phone again. It would be so much easier if I could call an ambulance.

But there's still no signal.

'Right, we're going to have to drive,' I say. 'Help me get him into the car.'

Justin moans in pain.

Harriet backs away, shaking her head. 'No, I can't,' she says, her voice trembling.

'You caused this mess. Now you can help me clean it up.'

'I'm not going to jail. Not for you. Or him. Or anyone,' she says, with a wild, panicked look in her eye.

'I'll tell them it was an accident.'

She shakes her head.

And then she bolts.

But instead of going for her car, she runs around the front of Justin's and throws open the door. But rather than jumping in and driving off, she leans in and snatches the keys Justin's left in the ignition.

She dangles them in front of my nose like a prize.

'You won't get far without these,' she says, a cruel grin creeping across her face.

'Give them to me!' I try to snatch them back, but she's too quick. She palms them away, closing her fist around them.

Away to my right, I hear the rumble of another vehicle approaching. A pair of bright headlights pierce the gloom. And I'm torn.

It's the first vehicle I've seen passing since we've been here. Should I try to stop the driver and ask for help? Or bank on being able to get Justin's keys back from Harriet? It's a gamble. The driver might not stop. I might not be able to overpower Harriet.

'Good luck, Megan. You'll need it.' She barges past me, brushing me out of the way, heading for her own car.

I can't let her go. Not with Justin's keys. If she abandons us here, Justin will bleed to death. And I won't let that happen. I've seen too much death to last a lifetime.

As Harriet scurries past me, I snatch her wrist, pulling her back.

'Get off me!' she yells, but my grip holds firm. There's no way I'm letting her get away.

'Give me the keys.'

'No!'

We scuffle, pulling and pushing each other, while I struggle to keep balanced, avoiding putting weight on my injured ankle.

'I said give me the keys,' I bark, anger and indignation getting the better of me. I quite like this new, forthright me.

Harriet pulls away violently, but I use the momentum to spin her around, away from the driver's door of her car and into the road.

She stumbles, finally twisting out of my grip, tripping over her own feet at the precise moment the approaching car bears down on us, its headlights dazzling.

One moment, Harriet's in my grasp. The next, she's gone.

A horrible, sickening crunching thud is followed by the squeal of brakes and rubber skidding across tarmac.

The car comes to a jarring halt twenty metres down the road, its brake lights glowing red. Burning rubber scorching the air.

I stand frozen, staring in horror at the crumpled heap of Harriet's body folded up in the carriageway in a bloody mess. Her head's angled towards me, eyes open but gazing blankly, her arms and legs twisted and bent, her clothes ripped and blackened.

The driver of the car jumps out, stands in the road gazing backwards, holding his door to steady himself. Shaken. Caught up in something he has no idea about.

'What's happened?' Justin wheezes.

I take a deep breath, my legs trembling beneath me. 'It's Harriet. I think she's dead.'

Chapter 50

FOUR WEEKS LATER

The silence sits between us heavy and loaded, my foot tapping a hurried rhythm and Justin's shoulders tight and rounded. I almost didn't make it today. I woke in agony, my stomach cramping, but Justin wouldn't let me off the hook that easily. He brought me a hot towel and massaged my abdomen while talking me off a cliff. And now here we are, returning to the house I once proudly called a home, not sure what to expect or how I'm going to cope. I've shoved a wad of tissues in my bag, just in case, although I don't want to cry in front of the loss adjustor.

As we draw closer, my pulse runs faster, threading through my veins at a hundred miles an hour, while a thin sheen of sweat dampens my blouse. The streets are painfully familiar, even though we haven't been here for almost a year. The bright red postbox on the corner, the row of terrace houses with their matching picket fences, the traffic lights that always seem to be stuck on red. Everything looks the same. But different. Especially our old house.

The doors and windows have been boarded up and a sooty track extends from the window of the snug all the way up the outside wall. A grim reminder of how one stupid mistake can cost everything.

I snatch a breath as Justin pulls up outside, my throat constricting with tears and remorse. Our beautiful house, our home, once so full of love and life and happiness, is now nothing more than a burnt-out carcass.

Justin grips my hand. Squeezes it tightly.

'Are you okay?'

I was lucky I didn't lose him too. The knife in his shoulder came perilously close to his lungs. Another few centimetres and it would have been a different story. He might have survived. He might not. As it was, the damage was relatively minor, muscular mainly, and he's expected to make a full recovery, although he'll always have a nasty scar.

'Not really.' I give him a tight-lipped smile.

I didn't want to come but Justin thought it was important. We're expecting to find out whether we can go ahead with the rebuild. Not that either of us could ever envisage moving back here, but obviously we can't put it on the market in the state it's in.

We had a lot of time to talk while Justin was in hospital recovering. He's agreed we won't return to Cornwall and is amenable to my idea of buying an apartment here in Plymouth, maybe one of those new builds in the regenerated area down by the seafront with views across the estuary or the Sound.

The conversations about our relationship issues were tougher. I admitted I should never have confronted him with those horrible things Arabella accused him of, and while he didn't deny they'd happened, we both accept they belong in the past. That it isn't the man he is today.

He conceded he can be controlling, although he says it was only ever because he loved me and wanted to protect me. But he's going to work on it and even agreed he'd be open to seeing a therapist who can help us with our marriage. But we'll see.

I apologised for doubting him and letting Harriet's poison cloud my judgement, believing he was a danger to me when nothing could be further from the truth. After all, he was the one who saved me from Harriet. She was the real danger.

As for the day his temper got the better of him and he grabbed me around the neck, choking me, I've found that harder to forgive. And to his credit, Justin's not tried to excuse his behaviour. He conceded he has some anger management issues and has promised to work on it. I suggested some counselling. He's thinking about it.

As for the day he took me swimming in the sea and I was knocked under by the current, he's adamant he didn't hold me under. And I believe him. The more I think about it, the more I can see it was my imagination. The panic taking hold. My mind, already corrupted by Harriet's malice, playing tricks.

It would be wrong to say we've fixed our problems, but at least we're talking about them and trying to deal with them like adults. Any couple who've suffered the loss of children will know what an intolerable pressure it puts on a relationship, but I still want to be with Justin. He's my husband. I'm his wife. For better. For worse. I'm not giving up on the marriage and losing him after the year we've been through. I need him. He needs me. We're better together than we are apart.

Of course, the real problem wasn't us. It was Harriet. Although if Justin hadn't been so insistent on returning to Treloar, we'd never have met her. She would never have developed a fixation with me, although if not me, it would have been some other poor sod. And she'd probably still be alive.

I'm embarrassed by how easily I was taken in by her charm and her lies, but she was clever, sowing the seeds in my mind and allowing them to germinate and flourish.

The police confirmed she died from the catastrophic injuries she suffered when she was hit by that car. She was airlifted to hospital where they said they fought to save her life, but I think that's something they say to make the relatives feel better. I'm convinced she was already dead. I looked into her eyes as she lay on the cold tarmac. There was no life in them. As much as I hated her, I'm glad she didn't suffer an agonising death. When she was hit by that car, I'm pretty sure she knew nothing about it.

While I regret she had to die, and was never held to account for her actions, I don't feel a jot of guilt. It's not as if I pushed her. And if she hadn't taken Justin's keys, it wouldn't have happened. I don't want to say she only has herself to blame, but every action has a consequence. Like plugging in a faulty heater and causing a devastating fire...

The police questioned me at length. I told them everything about the phone and the messages, how Harriet had convinced me she was a trusted friend and how she plotted to ruin my marriage. I explained in floods of tears that when I rejected her, she held me against my will in her house and later in a shed in the garden. I told them how I escaped, that I'd stabbed Harriet with the shard from a broken bowl and stolen her car to get away. I wanted them to know the truth, the whole truth. I didn't want to hold on to any secrets. Secrets and lies are what ultimately destroy people.

The detective in charge of the investigation told me I wouldn't face any charges, although there would be an inquest into Harriet's death and I might be called to give evidence. I shuddered. The thought of relieving those days all over again in front of strangers fills me with dread. But I'll do what I have to do. At least it will bring some finality to the whole sorry story.

I climb out of the car, my legs jelly weak. The loss adjustor, a man called Barrett or Barnard or something, is waiting for us and greets us with handshakes and sympathetic smiles. He gives us hardhats and torches, much to my surprise. I didn't know we'd be going inside, and I'm not sure I'm ready for it.

He opens the door, secured with a board and heavy padlock, and takes us into what is left of the kitchen. It's filthy now, not fit to cook in, with every surface covered in black dust and dirt, the ceiling watermarked with ugly brown stains.

Justin strikes up a conversation with Barrett or Barnard, but I don't hear a word. All I hear is the roar of the fire. The crackle of timbers and furniture burning. The sound of my own screams, calling for help for my two beautiful boys.

I taste the soot in the air and feel the intensity of the heat. I smell the acridity of the choking black smoke that poured from the windows like inverted waterfalls and left charcoal trails in the corners of my eyes.

It all comes back to me in a terrifying, unbalancing rush, knocking the breath from my lungs and sending my head spiralling.

All those repressed memories. All those emotions. Fear. Panic. Horror. Helplessness.

A solitary tear rolls down my cheek, but I don't wipe it away. I'm not ashamed to cry for the loss of my boys. My beautiful, wonderful, innocent boys.

'Can I look around?' I ask, my voice barely a hoarse whisper. 'Is it safe?'

Barrett or Barnard is about to tell me no, but he catches Justin's eye, and seems to change his mind.

'Sure, but be careful,' he says.

I take one last look around the kitchen where I cooked for the boys that night. Two big pepperoni pizzas from the supermarket, shared between the three of us as a treat because Daddy was out. It's where I stupidly opened a bottle of wine and poured myself a large glass.

We ate in front of the TV watching some mindless Saturday evening light entertainment show, sharing the big four-seater sofa, laughing at all the jokes. And after I'd cleared away, I chased the boys upstairs to bed, growling like a monster.

'Remember to clean your teeth,' I yelled after them. Later, I would check their brushes were wet to confirm they'd done as I'd instructed.

Although it's the middle of the day, all the windows have been boarded up and the house is in darkness. I shine my torch up the stairs and take them slowly, one at a time, the sound of the boys' laughter ringing in my ears.

The stairwell has been particularly badly damaged by the fire. The walls blackened and charred. The carpet ruined. Even the painted wooden banister is scorched. A tarry stench like the damp remnants of a burnt-out bonfire sullies the air.

I hesitate on the landing, my head dizzy. If I close my eyes, I can recall that evening so clearly. The bathroom door left gaping open and the light still on. Discarded pants and socks and wet towels all over the floor. I used to complain all the time about how my life had become a merry-go-round of clearing up after the boys, cooking, cleaning, ferrying them around in the car. But if I could have them back, I'd never, ever moan about any of that again.

I poke my head around the bathroom door and instinctively pull the light cord, but nothing happens, forgetting the electrics have been switched off. Instead, I shine my torch across the top of the bath where our shampoo and shower gel bottles are still eerily lined up. Felix's plastic boats in a net bag hang from the taps. A yellow sponge has fallen into the tub and is lying on its side on the rubber non-slip mat. Four toothbrushes stand upright in a white cup on the basin. I swallow back more tears and turn away.

At the end of the hall are the two rooms I thought I wanted to revisit, but now I'm here I'm not sure I have the strength. I can vividly picture each as it was. The brightly coloured astronaut duvet on Felix's bed. The dinosaur cover in Sebastian's room. The Pokémon posters on their walls. The books shoved into their bookcases in a higgledy-piggledy mess. The toy cars and plastic building blocks littering the floor. School merit certificates tacked to their cupboard doors.

The memories come flooding into my head like a tsunami, washing everything else in my mind away. I can still hear Sebastian singing to himself while he's absorbed in a puzzle spread out across his bedroom floor. The thud-thud-thud of Felix kicking a football against the wall even after I've told him a million times not to kick balls in the house. The pair of them racing down the stairs demanding to know when their tea would be ready. The play fights on the sofa that always ended up with one of them in tears, usually Felix, even though he was older and bigger. Trying not to giggle while telling Sebastian off at the dinner table for poking two chips up under his top lip and pretending to be a sabre-toothed tiger.

The memories are there, vividly clear, but fading. Fleeting glimpses of the life we used to have. A snapshot of happier times.

And out of nowhere, another memory swoops in like a rampaging dragon, filling my brain with images of Felix and Sebastian lying in their beds, motionless, as thick black smoke swirls around their heads. Eyes shut. Limbs limp. Chests still.

Of course, it's a false memory. Something conjured up in my mind to fill in the blanks. I never saw the boys after I sent them to bed that night. It was the firefighters who pulled their bodies out of their beds, carried them out of the house and into the back of an ambulance. But it doesn't make the images any less real.

All around me, the walls and ceilings close in, oppressively close, boxing me in and threatening to crush me.

I have to get out of here.

I can't breathe.

My heart's fluttering like a startled butterfly trapped in my chest.

It's too much.

Too soon.

I should never have come.

My feet clatter down the stairs and I stumble into the hall where a stream of sunlight is fingering through the front door that's swinging lazily on its hinges.

I breathe in through my nose, filling my lungs, and wipe my cheeks dry. I should go back to the car and wait for Justin to finish. I wasn't ready to come back. I wish he hadn't talked me into it. I didn't want to see the house like this, tainting those precious memories I'd held so dearly. Now, when I think about it, I'm worried this is the image I'll recall. Not the happy days when we were a normal family.

But there's one more room I have to see. A room I *need* to see. A ghost from the past I need to confront.

I pad silently down the hall with a swelling dread in my stomach, careful not to brush against the sooty walls, and push open the door to the snug. The seat of the blaze, as the fire service described it in their investigation. Where I plugged in that faulty heater too close to the curtains and left it on when I went to bed. The cause of my sons' deaths.

Like a detective examining a crime scene, I stand in the doorway and study what's left, which isn't much. Fire has consumed almost everything in it and left nothing more than a blackened shell.

The carpet has completely disintegrated, the concrete floor covered in ash and the burnt remains of anything that was flammable. The

TV's melted into a strange plastic lump on the wall and in patches the plaster has blown, leaving sections of bare brick. The only recognisable pieces of furniture that have somehow survived are the big sofa in front of the TV and the tub chair by the window, although the fabric on each is charred and melted, leaving their frames and springs exposed like the rotting carcasses of whales washed up on the beach.

I close my eyes and take myself back to that night.

I'd let the boys stay up later than their usual bedtimes because Justin was out for the evening. But they'd become overtired and fractious and I was glad when they finally went to bed and I eventually had some time to myself.

I'd topped up my wine glass and finished a TV show I'd recorded. A documentary Justin wouldn't have been interested in. And then I decided I might as well get an early night. I'd not been sleeping well. So I foolishly finished what was left in the wine bottle and took a tablet the GP had prescribed for my insomnia. All that is clear in my memory. No doubts. No confusion.

But what I can't remember is going into the snug that night, nor plugging in the heater.

And that's something that's always troubled me.

Chapter 51

A hand on my shoulder makes me jump.

'Meg, come away from there. You shouldn't beat yourself up,' Justin says, standing behind me as I examine the devastation.

'You were the one who said I should come,' I remind him.

'I thought it would help you come to terms with the fire,' he says. 'Anyway, it's good news. They've given the go-ahead for the rebuild. With luck, it should get started within the next few weeks.'

'How long's it going to take?'

Justin shrugs. 'Six to eight months, all being well. Maybe longer, but with luck, this time next year, we can have it on the market and start looking for a new home.'

I should be pleased. We've moved around so many rented properties in the last year, it will be good to put down some new, permanent roots. But I can't get excited about it. This was our home. And without the boys, I can't imagine what it will be like trying to build a new life.

I shine my torch around the snug, desperately trying to remember why I came in here that night and why I plugged in that heater when we'd spent the evening in the lounge. It doesn't make any sense. Was I really that drunk? It was only a few glasses of wine.

Under the window, where the frame is so badly burnt it's buckled and twisted, my torchlight picks out a pile of broken glass. A heap of ragged opaque squares from the windowpane, shattered by the heat of the fire or maybe by the firefighters who smashed it to tackle the blaze.

Mostly, the fragments are all regular-sized and square, no bigger than peas. Apart from a couple of larger slivers of glass that catch my eye. There's a pattern on them. Something that looks familiar. What is that?

Curiously, I step across the floor, crunching over the incinerated debris. I should have worn boots rather than these silly flats.

'Megan? What are you doing?'

I stoop down, balancing on my haunches. My ankle twinges. The damage I'd done to it when I stumbled in that field running away from Harriet was only a sprain, but it took a while to heal and still gives me a bit of trouble.

I stare at the pile of glass, angling my torch at it, and instantly recognise the patterning on the large slivers. It's cut crystal. The only cut crystal we had in the house was a pair of whisky tumblers. A wedding present from friends, I think. We kept them in the kitchen, so how did one of them end up in the snug? It certainly wasn't me. I never drink whisky.

As I stand, turning the puzzle over in my head, I notice something else. A dark strip of fabric poking out from the cushion of the mangled tub chair.

I pull it free. My stomach flips and tightens, my head wheeling.

It's the bow tie Justin was wearing for his charity fundraising dinner on the night of the fire. I remember having to help him tie it. He could never manage on his own.

So why's it here, in the snug?

He told me he'd come straight to bed when he'd got in. Why would he lie to me?

The realisation hits me like a torrential landslide of mud and rock.

I spin around with the bow tie between my fingers, as if it's evidence of a sordid affair. Except this is worse. So much worse.

'It was you,' I gasp, staring at Justin in disbelief.

He made me believe it was all my fault. That *I* plugged the heater in. That *I* started the fire. That *I* killed Felix and Sebastian.

'What?' He acts as though he doesn't know what I'm talking about, but his eyes betray him. They dart uncomfortably, left and right. He shoves his hands in his pockets and licks his lips.

'*You* put the heater on and left it on all night,' I say, my voice trembling. 'The fire was *your* fault. Not mine.'

He chuckles nervously. But there's nothing funny about any of this.

Disbelief gives way to anger. How could he have let me go on believing I was responsible for the death of our boys when he knew the truth all along? All those days when I was inconsolable with grief, thinking it was me, when he stood by me and told me not to be so hard on myself, that it was an unfortunate accident. When all that time he knew. And he continued to let me believe I was to blame.

Never mind being dangerous. He's a monster.

'Megan, you don't know what you're saying.' He steps into the room and moves quickly towards me with a worried glance over his shoulder. I guess the loss adjustor's still somewhere in the house. He tries to put his hands on my shoulders but I furiously shrug them off.

'Don't touch me,' I hiss.

'Let me explain.' His tongue darts out between his lips like the snake he is.

'I don't need you to explain. You came home drunk, poured yourself a whisky and came in here to watch TV. Am I right so far? Except it was late. The heating had gone off hours before, so you plugged the heater in to take off the chill. What happened? Did you fall asleep? Forget?'

'I can't... I don't... ' he stammers.

'But you let me take the blame. Harriet was right all along. You *are* dangerous.'

'Megan, stop it.' He's composed himself now, looming over me. Using his height to try to intimidate me. But it won't work. Not this time.

'I was so desperate to make this marriage work, I've been totally blinkered to what you are.' I jab my finger in his chest.

'It's not what it seems,' he says. 'We can work through this.'

'How?' I ask, exasperated. 'You lied to me and let me think I killed Felix and Sebastian. How could you?'

'It's not like that. I don't remember plugging in the... '

'Stop lying,' I yell. Even now he's trying to twist the truth and wriggle out of it. He is unbelievable.

I've been such a fool, making excuses for his behaviour for all these years when I should have seen him for what he is.

'Please, Megan, don't make this into something it's not.'

'I should have followed my gut. I knew you couldn't be trusted the day I found out you'd slept with another woman in Amsterdam.'

'She was a prostitute. I told you,' he says, as if that somehow excuses it.

'And yet I still agreed to marry you. What was I thinking?'

'I love you, Megan.'

I shake my head as all those times he's tried to control me, isolate me, punish me, come cascading back into my mind. I thought he was being protective of me. That he had my best interests at heart. But that's what he wanted me to think and I was too weak-minded to see any different.

'You cut me off from my friends. You insisted on moving us to Cornwall where you thought I'd be isolated, and you've even tried to stop me going back to work,' I say.

'You weren't ready.'

'According to who? You? And what do you know about it? How can you live with yourself?'

'It was an accident, Meg. I didn't know the heater was going to go up in flames, did I?'

I put my hands to my face, rubbing my tired eyes. I can't believe this is happening. 'You didn't have to lie about it. You know, I seriously thought about ending it when they told us Felix and Sebastian were gone. I came this close.' I hold my finger and thumb up to his face. 'And all the time it was you. When I told you I couldn't remember going into the snug that night, you insisted it was my memory playing tricks. That I'd had too much to drink. That I shouldn't have been taking sleeping pills with alcohol. You made me feel worthless.'

'Stop it.' His face hardens and a coldness falls over his eyes.

'I should have called the police when I had the chance.'

He glowers at me. 'What do you mean?'

'When you attacked me at the lodge and strangled me because I'd had the nerve to ask you about the allegations Arabella made. I thought I was going to die that night, but I forgave you. I told myself it was a one-off. And then you tried to drown me the next day in the sea, or at least make me think I was going to die.'

'That's not true,' he gasps. He even has the gall to look affronted.

'Isn't it?'

'No, of course not. I'd never hurt you.'

I raise an eyebrow. Surely, he can see the irony? 'And when you thought I hadn't come to heel and you were worried about my friendship with Harriet, you locked me in the house, disabled my phone and switched off the wifi.'

'I never trusted her. I was protecting you from her.'

'Huh! Really?'

'She was the one who kept you locked in a shed, Megan. Not me.'

'I want a divorce.'

'What?' His face crumbles in a deep frown. 'Don't be ridiculous. Come on, we can work this out.'

He tries to put a hand on my arm, but I push him away, angry with him for everything he's done. Angry with myself for letting him get away with it. When he rocks back on his heels and comes at me again, I push him harder with both hands on his chest.

His demeanour immediately changes. A dark cloud settles over his expression and a fury glistens in his eyes. His hands fly to my throat and he grips my neck so tightly I struggle to breathe.

I clasp his wrists and try to pull his arms away, but he has a determined hold on me and isn't letting go. My eyes bulge and my lungs swell up like they're ready to burst as my vision begins to tunnel. He's crushing my windpipe, stopping me from calling for help. Barrett or Barnard is in the house somewhere. Where is he? I really need him right now. He's my only hope.

I can't die here, in this house where Justin killed my boys. I won't give him that satisfaction, but as I stare into my husband's dark, hateful eyes, a stranger's eyes, there's nothing I can do to stop him.

I try to swing my knee up, to catch him in the balls, but he blocks it with his leg, snarling in my face.

There's nothing in the room I can even use as a weapon. Everything we had has turned to ash.

My head throbs. He's strangling the life out of me. Last time, he let me go before I passed out. This time, I'm not so sure. There's something about the way he's looking at me with pure venom. I've called him out. Identified the liar and the cheat he really is and he doesn't like it. Anger consumes him but I can't stop him. My legs buckle, my strength draining away.

I'm going to die here.

But better that and be reunited with my boys than to face spending another day with this monster I called my husband.

'Is everything okay?'

Justin's grip releases instantly and I gasp in a desperate lungful of air, putting a hand to my throat as I clutch the wall to catch my balance.

'It's fine,' Justin growls at the loss adjustor, stepping away from me.

Barrett or Barnard, a small man with a bald head and suit trousers that hang above his ankles, fixes his gaze on me with a frown of concern. 'It's just that I thought I heard shouting... ' he says, hesitantly.

'He tried to kill me,' I croak.

'What?' He glances at Justin, uncertain.

'Ignore her. She's being melodramatic as usual.'

'He started the fire. He killed my children,' I sob.

'Don't be so ridiculous. She's hysterical,' Justin snaps.

'I... I... ' Barrett or Barnard stammers.

'Give me your car keys,' I demand.

'You're in no state to drive anywhere.' Justin folds his arms across his chest, challenging me with a scowl of warning.

'I said, give me the car keys,' I repeat, louder and slower, rising to my full height and jutting out my chin defiantly. He's not going to tell me what to do ever again.

I hold out my hand, my jaw rigid.

Justin looks at the loss adjustor and then, with a resigned sigh, digs into his pocket and pulls out the car key fob. He slaps it into my hand.

'Should I call the police?' the loss adjustor asks.

'I don't know. Justin, what do you think? Do you think the police would be interested in hearing about how you've been abusing me all these years? That you lied to the investigators about the cause of the fire? That twice you've tried to strangle me?'

'Bitch,' he hisses, his brows hooding over his eyes.

'Yeah, I thought so.'

Barrett or Barnard stands there looking between us with his phone in his hand, not sure what to do.

Maybe I'll phone them myself later. After I've let Justin stew for a while.

I brush myself down and straighten my blouse. 'Goodbye, Justin.'

With my shoulders pulled back and my head held high, I nudge past him as if he's invisible and, with a nod to the loss adjustor, walk out of the room. For the first time since we met, I can truly see that I'm better off without Justin.

Harriet might have been out of her mind, but she was right all along. Justin is dangerous and I'm better off without him. I was desperate and didn't want to repeat the mistakes my mother made, driving away a good man. But Justin wasn't a good man and my desperation was the blinker stopping me from seeing the truth.

Maybe I will try that cousin in Cumbria after all. There's no way I'm staying here in Plymouth or anywhere within a hundred miles of Justin. We're finished and if I never see him again, it will be too soon.

I don't have a plan, but I'll make it work.

Grief still hangs heavy on my shoulders. I'll never forget my two darling boys. But at least I've been unburdened of the guilt. Like a maggot in rotting flesh, it's been eating away at me for months. Undermining everything I did. Paralysing me. Tormenting me. Driving me slowly insane.

For almost a year, I had to live with the dark, burdensome belief that I'd killed Felix and Sebastian. Me, their own mother. But I had nothing to do with it. It was all Justin, but he never had the balls to confess it, preferring to heap the blame on me. And of all the terrible things he's done, that's the worst of them by far. It's psychological torture.

But he'll get what's coming to him.

Karma has a way of dealing with people like him.

'Megan, where are you going?' he cries after me as I step out of the house into the midday sun.

His voice makes me shudder, but I keep walking, head up, shoulders back.

'Get back here right now,' he screams.

Ha! As if I'm going to turn and run to him because he's throwing a tantrum. Has he learned nothing?

I blip open the doors of the car, climb in and buzz the windows down as I fire up the engine.

'It's over, Justin. I never want to see you again, so don't try to contact me. I'll never forgive you for what you did and frankly, I hope you rot in hell.'

'Don't leave. Let's talk about this,' he begs me.

'There's nothing to talk about.'

'Megan!' He slams his fist on the roof of the car.

I turn my head slowly and give him a look of disdain. Once, I'd have jumped, too afraid to stand up to him. After all, I thought I owed him everything. I thought he was the most wonderful, compassionate man in the world after forgiving me for the fire. But it was all lies and deceit. He stood by me because he was afraid the truth would be revealed and he'd be ruined. I gave him the power to control me.

He has no power left.

'Please, I'm begging you, Megan. Don't leave me.' It's so degrading.

I'm about to pull away when I remember the phone in my bag. Justin bought it for me to replace my old one, complete with a working SIM card. But I don't want him using it to trace me. I wouldn't put it past him to have installed some kind of tracking software on it.

I put the car into gear and, as I pull away, toss the phone out of the window.

As I accelerate off, I watch it bounce across the tarmac in the rear-view mirror while Justin stands looking forlorn on the pavement.

It feels good to be finally free.

Free of Justin.

Free of guilt.

Driving away to start a new life. A better life. A life on my own. A life I can lead being who I want to be with the memory of my two beautiful boys with me forever.

—

A word from the author

Being an independent author, responsible not only for writing the books but doing everything else, from marketing and advertising to sourcing covers and editing, can be a lonely business, but knowing I have such dedicated and supportive readers helps immeasurably.

If you'd like to keep up to date with all my writing news, please consider joining my weekly newsletter. I'll even send you a free e-book! You can find more details at bit.ly/hislostwifeor scan the QR code below.

Or follow me on Facebook - @AuthorAJWills, find me on my website ajwillsauthor.com or join me on Instagram at @ajwills_author.

I look forward to seeing you there.

Adrian

Also By AJ Wills

The Secrets We Keep

When a young girl vanishes on her way home from school, a suspicious media suspects her parents know more than they're letting on.

Nothing Left To Lose

A letter arrives in a plain white envelope. Inside is a single sheet of paper with a chilling message. Someone knows the secret Abi, and her husband, Henry, are hiding. And now they want them dead.

His Wife's Sister

Mara was only eleven when she went missing from a tent in her parents' garden nineteen years ago. Now she's been found wandering alone and confused in woodland.

She Knows

After Sky finds a lost diary on the beach, she becomes caught up in something far bigger than she could ever have imagined - and accused of a murder she has no memory of committing...

The Intruder

Jez thought he'd finally found happiness when he met Alice. But when Alice goes missing with her young daughter and the police accuse him of their murders, his life is shattered.

Printed in Great Britain
by Amazon

24083345R10229